WOODWIND INSTRUMENTS
a practical guide for technicians and repairers

WOODWIND INSTRUMENTS

a practical guide for technicians and repairers

Daniel Bangham

THE CROWOOD PRESS

Contents

Introduction — 7

PART 1: GETTING STARTED — 9

CHAPTER 1: Initial dismantle and reassemble of an instrument — 11
- Basic tools — 11
- All-purpose materials — 15
- A basic check-over and service of an instrument — 17
- Reassembling the instrument — 21

CHAPTER 2: Order of assembly — 23
- Clarinet — 23
- Flute — 24
- Saxophone — 25
- Oboe — 26
- Bassoon — 27

CHAPTER 3: Initial diagnosis – observations and tests — 31
- How woodwind instruments work — 31
- Initial observations and tests — 31

CHAPTER 4: Emergency fixes — 37
- Common problems — 38
- Clarinets — 40
- Flutes — 42
- Saxophones — 45
- Oboes — 47
- Bassoons — 49

CHAPTER 5: Care of instruments — 51
- How to store an instrument — 51
- How to prepare an instrument for playing — 51
- How to reduce the problem of water collecting in the tone holes — 51
- Aftercare — 51
- Lubrication — 52
- Oiling the bore — 52

PART 2: INSTRUMENT ANATOMY — 55

CHAPTER 6: The main sections of each instrument — 57
- Clarinet — 57
- Flute — 58
- Saxophone — 58
- Oboe — 58
- Bassoon — 59

CHAPTER 7: Bodywork components — 61
- Tenons and sockets — 61
- Tone holes — 62
- Bed plates and tone hole rims — 62
- Pillars — 63

CHAPTER 8: Keywork — 65
- Parts of a key — 65
- Keywork mechanisms — 72
- Replaceable parts — 75

PART 3: THE WORKSHOP AND REPAIR PROCESSES — 77

CHAPTER 9: The workshop — 79
- The workbench — 79
- General workshop tools — 81

CHAPTER 10: Checking and repairing bodywork — 87
- Bodywork faults — 87
- Tenon corks — 102

CHAPTER 11: Checking and repairing keywork — 111
- Unwanted movement in keywork — 111
- Waisted hinge screws — 123
- Improving pinned hinge rods — 126

		Damaged key corks and felts	126
		Faulty springs	129
		Other keywork checks	134
CHAPTER 12:		**Checking and replacing pads**	**137**
		Checking pads	138
		Replacing pads	140
CHAPTER 13:		**Overhauls**	**159**
CHAPTER 14:		**Regulation**	**161**
		Time of arrival	162
		Time of departure	163
		Special case regulation	164
		Setting the vent height	164
		Setting spring weights	165
CHAPTER 15:		**Re-assembly**	**167**
		Clarinet	168
		Flute	174
		Saxophone	178
		Oboe	184
		Bassoon	191
PART 4:		**SPECIALIST REPAIRS**	**199**
CHAPTER 16:		**Specialist repair tools and materials**	**201**
		Lathes	201
		Milling machines	203
		Measuring tools	203
		Tools for holding instruments	204
		Specialist repair materials	205
		Adhesives	206
		Abrasives and cleaning materials	207
CHAPTER 17:		**Specialist repairs**	**209**
		Spring work	209
		Improving the action of keys	211
		Removing a stuck hinge screw	212
		Tools needed to make a hinge screw	212
		Making a replacement hinge screw	213
		Tone hole replacement	214
		Tone hole replacement tools and materials	214
		Replacing a tone hole	215
		Repairing cracks	216
		Mending broken keys and joints	219
		Separating stuck tenon joints on wooden instruments	221
		Lining a socket	221
		Replacing a broken tenon	223
		Measuring tapered bores	224
		Bassoon repairs	229
		Alterations	230
PART 5:		**MATERIALS AND TOOL BUILDING**	**233**
CHAPTER 18:		**Materials used for the body and keywork of woodwind instruments**	**235**
		Metals	235
		Plastics	236
		Woods	236
		Composites	236
CHAPTER 19:		**Cleaning and polishing tools and materials**	**239**
		Polishing	239
CHAPTER 20:		**Making tools**	**243**
		Making a tenon scraper	243
		Making a rolling steady	243
		Making a sacrificial mandrel	245
		Threads of screws on woodwind instruments	246
		List of suppliers	247
		Acknowledgements	248
		Index	249

Introduction

Thank you for opening this book. I wonder if, like me, you are curious about how to make instruments more enjoyable to play.

This was my motivation when I started learning to repair instruments over forty years ago. Having spent my early teenage years struggling to learn how to play the flute, I happened to pick up a friend's Yamaha flute at orchestra practice and discovered a whole new world, one where it was no longer a struggle to get the notes out and it was actually fun playing the flute. I was immediately intrigued to know what the difference was between my 1960s Hsinghai flute and the Yamaha flute; they looked so similar yet behaved so differently.

I never did persuade my parents to get me a Yamaha, but they did find a technician to improve the Hsinghai; even then it wasn't really good enough. I now know why it never played very well and I hope by reading this book you too will understand why.

My curiosity was encouraged by Ron Morris, an inspirational craft teacher at our school, who later pointed me in the direction of Newark College of Music Technology, where I studied for two years. It was a few years later, when I returned to Newark as a visiting tutor, that I discovered my love of teaching.

Being invited to write this book has enabled me to continue my teaching and hopefully help new generations enjoy playing good-quality, well-maintained instruments.

The working title for this book was *The Woodwind Repairer*, but on reflection I felt the word 'repairer' rather underplays the role that a skilled woodwind technician has in musicians' lives. The work is not confined to just making an instrument work: it involves developing an understanding of what the musician is trying to achieve in order to enable improvements to be made and technical difficulties to be overcome. There is huge satisfaction to be had from hearing a performance on an instrument that you have had a part in improving and maintaining.

To accommodate the wide range of contexts in which this book may be used, the book offers low-cost or improvised solutions as well as those using expensive engineering tools. With lots of background information about how and why things are done in a particular way, it provides ideas on how to tackle new problems. Whatever equipment you have at your disposal, I hope you will discover where a minute turn of a screw or a subtle change to the shape of a cork can transform the experience and enjoyment of playing for the musician. As such, I hope that it becomes a companion reference book for woodwind technicians and players alike.

Even after forty years of looking after woodwind instruments, it is still a new journey every time a musician comes into the workshop with a problem. To be successful on that journey, we need to know where we want to end up. In our case, this is with an instrument playing to the musician's satisfaction. Note that this is subtly different to ending up with an instrument that is 'as good as new' or in perfect condition.

A good starting point for your journey is to handle lots of well-made instruments. It is knowing how they should look and feel that will enable you to spot the problems and damage when the musician comes to you for help. For the musician to have made their way to your workshop, they have reason to think something is wrong, so we need to listen to them. What are they experiencing? Why do they think something is wrong? What are the symptoms? Did a teacher advise them to come, and in which case, have they remembered the right message? Are they a professional struggling to perform a specific passage of music?

Then you start looking at their instrument; you can use the information the musician has given you and compare it to your own observations and comparisons to the good instruments you have handled in the past. You can then undertake the most appropriate processes to improve it.

The first part is as much about understanding people as it is understanding the

Fig. 0.1 Yamaha custom clarinet. Handling good instruments helps you learn what you are aiming for.

behaviour of an instrument. The repair itself is very much process-driven; if you follow a series of steps diligently you can expect a successful outcome.

An important aspect of this musician–instrument relationship is that it is different from your relationship with the instrument. When a beginner comes in with a problem, it may simply be that their technique or choice of reed is causing most of the problem, so you need to know what is being experienced by the musician, as you may not experience the same issues on the instrument yourself.

The same goes for us as technicians. We can use our experience and technical abilities to overcome the problems the musician is having, to fool or persuade ourselves that the instrument is okay and the adjustments we have made are 'good' or 'correct', when in fact they are not. It is so easy to say to yourself, 'I'm not sure what they are worried about – it plays fine for me' when you have larger and stronger hands than the musician and are pushing too hard on the keys. So don't be afraid to ask good musicians or repair colleagues to give a second opinion.

All skills require practice; musicians know this more than most, so treat instrument repair in the same way as practising an instrument. Practise and practise until you can do it well.

As well as offering you what I have learned over the years, I hope that this book will give you the confidence to challenge your skills and improve your own technique for yourself and your contemporaries. It takes hours of practice to become good at repairing and this book will launch and support you on your journey.

I hope you will read the book, enjoy your journey, and help to keep lots of instruments playing.

Author's note

The woodwind instruments covered in detail in this book are clarinet in B♭, flute, alto saxophone, oboe, and bassoon. For the less common woodwind instruments, such as cor anglais, bass clarinet and piccolo, the principles of repair and regulation are the same; some of the specific issues associated with these instruments are discussed in Chapter 17, Specialist Repair.

PART ONE

Getting Started

CHAPTER 1

Initial Dismantle and Reassemble of an Instrument

I am going to start by describing how you can start your repair journey through dismantling and re-assembling an instrument. At this stage you will be identifying problems as you go, but not necessarily fixing them.

Whatever instrument you want to focus on later, I suggest you start by working on clarinets. The skills needed for a clarinet are transferable to other instruments. For your very first attempt, I suggest you use a low-value clarinet, one you can afford to make mistakes on. As soon as you feel confident, use better instruments, ones that are already in good condition. That way you can get familiar with what an instrument should look and feel like, without getting distracted or side-tracked with problems. It is by handling good instruments that we learn what we are trying to achieve.

Basic tools

I remember when I first started my training, I felt overwhelmed by all the unfamiliar tools and equipment. But when it came to the first day of teaching, we started with the basics: a workbench, four hand tools and a few old instruments to take apart and put together. The idea was that we needed to get first-hand experience of dismantling the instruments before we could really understand the study material we were going to cover over the next few years. I am taking a similar approach. You don't really need to know all the names of the parts or the tools to be able to take it apart and put it together again. Just give it a go. (I will refer to parts of the instrument and processes you might not be familiar with at this stage; please look at the relevant chapters later in the book if you are unclear what I mean.)

Workbench

If you don't have a dedicated workbench already, create a temporary workbench from a sheet of plywood, with an apron

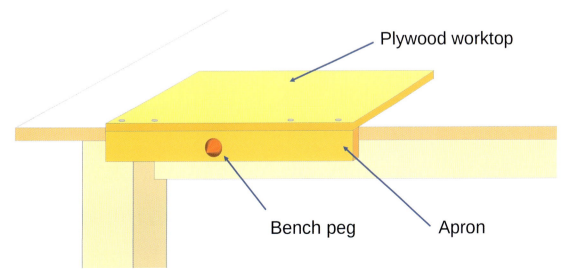

Fig. 1.1 Improvised workbench.

Fig. 1.2 Shaving brush.

Fig. 1.3 Screwdrivers in three sizes.

screwed on the front that can hook over the side of an existing table. Add a bench peg to this and you're all set!

A bench peg is traditionally a piece of hardwood turned on a lathe into a cone. Though this is the preferred shape, there is no reason not to make several pegs in a row, with dowelling of different diameters. They need to stick out about 15mm and be smaller than the bore diameter of the instruments you are working on.

Shaving brush

I have not found any other brush to give the instrument an initial brush down and clean that works better than a shaving brush. The density and stiffness of the bristles are perfect and there is no metallic collar that might scratch the instrument.

Fig. 1.4 A screwdriver with a long shaft allows you to get to screws deep in the keywork. Notice that I am steadying the tip of the blade with my thumb.

Screwdrivers

Your choice of screwdriver will be governed by what instruments you will be working on. Different instruments require different sized screwdrivers. The width of the blade needs to match the diameter of the screws you encounter. This is to ensure you do not damage the screw head or the surrounding pillar. The screwdriver blade should be just under the width of the screw head (maybe 0.1 or 0.5mm).

Useful blade widths are:

1.95mm for clarinets, oboes and flutes
3mm for saxophones
1.7mm for adjusting screws

The screwdrivers should have long shafts, which will give you better access to screws deep in the keywork. My best screwdrivers have a shaft 150mm long and the handle is another 90mm long (total 240mm) with a 1.95mm and 3mm blade width.

My screwdriver with a 1.7mm tip has a 50mm shaft and 90mm handle. The long shaft allows me to align the screwdriver on the same axis as the screw, even when the key is located well down the instrument's body.

Good screwdrivers of the right width for our industry can be hard to find. Until you have found or made your perfect screwdriver, I suggest you look at the tools used by the electronics industry, as they have screwdrivers with long shafts and 2mm wide blades. You will then need to use a diamond file, grindstone, or grind wheel to make the blade a tiny bit narrower. Figs 1.5 to 1.8 show how the width and shape of the blade affect how well the blade will engage with the slot in the screw as it goes inside the pillar.

I recommend that you have a shallow domed swivel end to the handle; this allows you to push hard against the screw

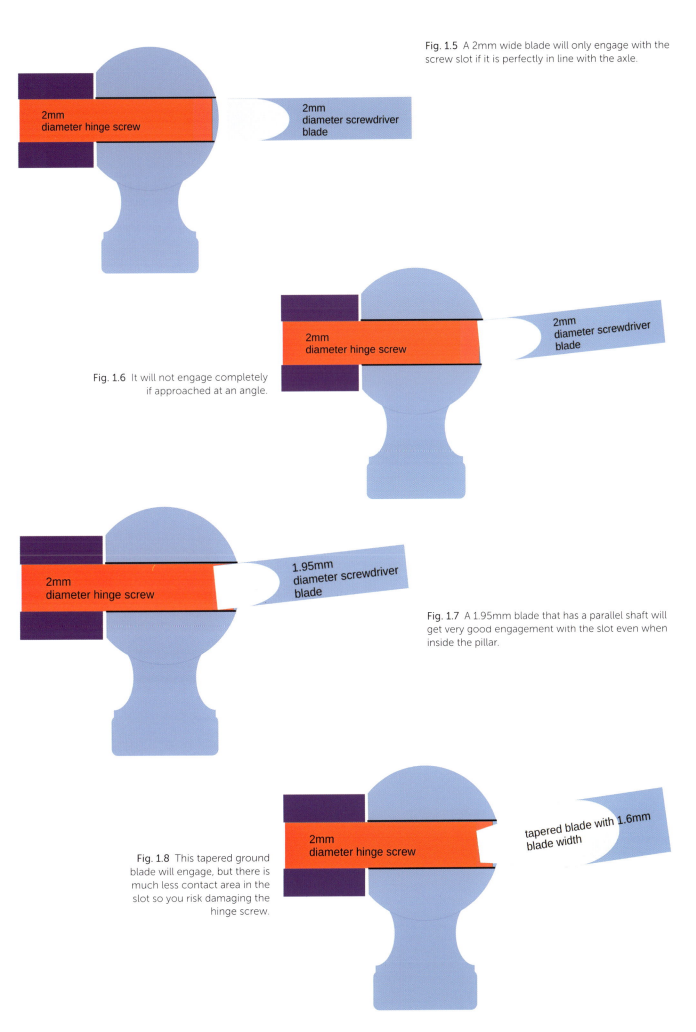

Fig. 1.5 A 2mm wide blade will only engage with the screw slot if it is perfectly in line with the axle.

Fig. 1.6 It will not engage completely if approached at an angle.

Fig. 1.7 A 1.95mm blade that has a parallel shaft will get very good engagement with the slot even when inside the pillar.

Fig. 1.8 This tapered ground blade will engage, but there is much less contact area in the slot so you risk damaging the hinge screw.

Initial Dismantle and Reassemble of an Instrument

Fig. 1.9 The tip of one of my favourite screwdrivers.

Fig. 1.10 My two favourite spring hooks: one made by Music Medic (top); the other I made myself.

head at the same time as rotating the blade easily. If you don't have a swivel handle, try to retrofit one.

Other factors that affect a screwdriver are the diameter of the handle (this changes the leverage you can apply and speed at which you can spin the screwdriver), the quality of steel used and the tempering it is given.

You can make your own screwdriver, from silver steel, or high-speed steel (HSS) drill stock.

Many screwdrivers offered for sale by specialist suppliers are susceptible to chipping on old and stuck screws. I have been very happy with the straight tapered wedge shape of the Kraus screwdrivers (Kraus tools are no longer available to purchase new, but it is worth seeking out second-hand Kraus tools as there are currently no manufacturers making specialist tools of this quality). The shaft of these screwdrivers is 4mm in diameter, and 5mm from the end, the diameter reduces to the blade width (Fig. 1.9). This gives the blade extra stiffness that significantly reduces the torsional and longitudinal flex.

Spring hooks

My two favourite spring hooks have a groove on the top end of the shaft; this makes it easier to manipulate the spring in difficult-to-access spaces.

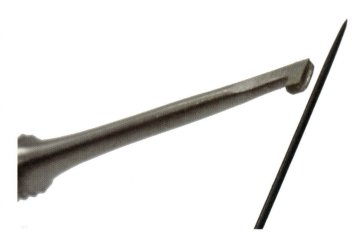

Fig. 1.11 At the end of the spring hook (left) is a groove that can engage with a spring (right). This allows you to push the spring through narrow gaps.

Fig. 1.12 I was sent this spring hook by Pearl Flutes many years ago. It is made from a large sewing needle with the eye heated, bent into a hook and the eye opened up to create the pushing slot. The needle is then held in a pin vice.

I recommend you make your own very narrow hook and pusher for working on clarinets and oboes. You need to be able to remove the hook from between the spring and the hinge tube when the gap is very narrow. The spring hook will need to be made from carbon steel, correctly hardened and tempered.

Pliers

Pliers are good for manipulating or bending keys when on the instrument. I have two or three sizes and styles of these, ranging from 30mm-long blades of 6mm width to 50mm long by 8mm wide. The blade thickness is very narrow, which is an important design feature.

The jaws on these pliers must be smooth; this prevents unnecessary damage to the surface you are holding. Parallel pliers should be the only pliers you use to grip hinge screws when

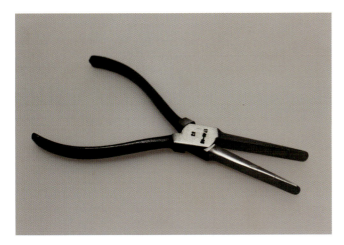

Fig. 1.13 Smooth jaw duckbill pliers.

Fig. 1.14 Maun parallel-action pliers.

Fig. 1.15 This is the Knipex parallel acting pliers; model 86 03 150, modified by Music Medic.

Fig. 1.16 This snipe-nosed variant of the parallel-action pliers (the smooth jaws narrow to a point) is excellent for holding key arms.

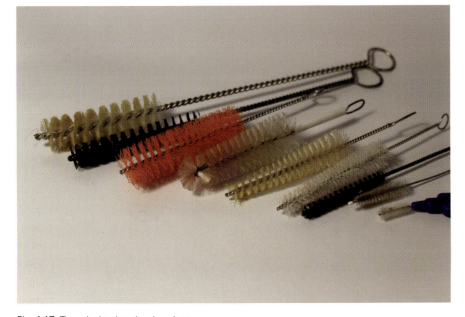

Fig. 1.17 Tone hole cleaning brushes.

removing keywork. They are useful for key bending and straightening. There are two types that I use: Maun Industries make the original and, in my opinion, best. I have two sizes: 140mm and 180mm (Fig. 1.14).

You can modify off-the-shelf pliers with a belt grinder.

Brushes

I have acquired a number of brushes over the years for cleaning out tone holes and small tubes.

All-purpose materials

Removable putty (Blu Tack)

This is a common material in the UK, but not so common in other countries. It is a soft putty that is designed to attach posters or pictures to walls and other hard surfaces. It acts as an adhesive but doesn't leave a residue when removed. I use it to temporarily seal tone holes when testing for leaks. I knead it for a while before pressing it over the hole. It leaves a clean surface.

Fig. 1.18 Blu Tack other brands are available, e.g. Poster Putty, Power Tack, Sticky Tack.

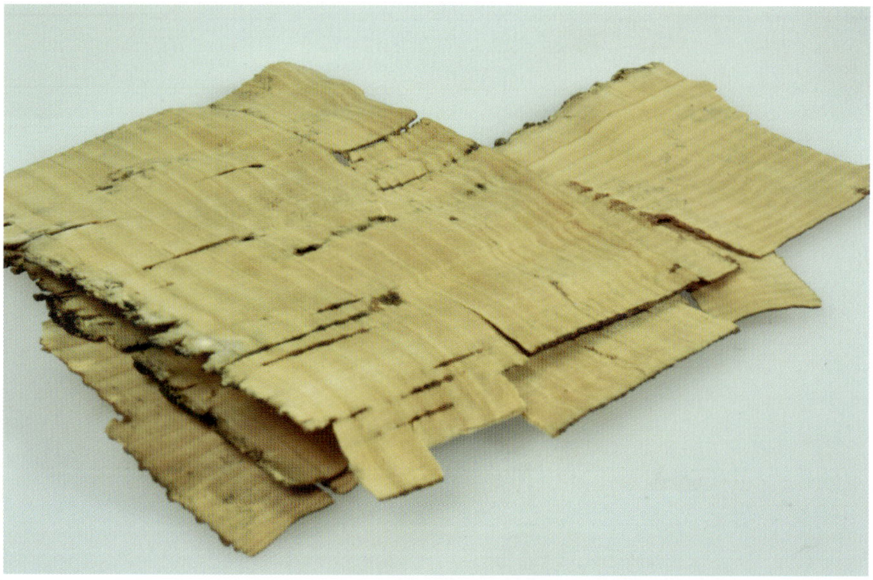

Fig. 1.20 Cork wafers. This wafer-thin cork is one form of cork that still works when old. It is used under adjusting screws to reduce metal to metal clicking noises.

Cork

The choice of dimension of cork to purchase depends on the instruments you are going to work on. In general, you will need wafer cork, and 1mm, 1.2mm, 1.4mm, 1.6mm sheet cork. The standard sheet size is 150 × 200mm. Bassoon repairers should try and get hold of the larger 12 × 4in size of sheet cork as you need the extra length to use on the bottom tenon joints.

Sometimes you may need thicker pieces of cork (for flute keys or E♭ key

Fig. 1.21 Keep your natural cork in an airtight container.

on a bassoon, for example), so why not use the cork from a freshly opened bottle of wine?

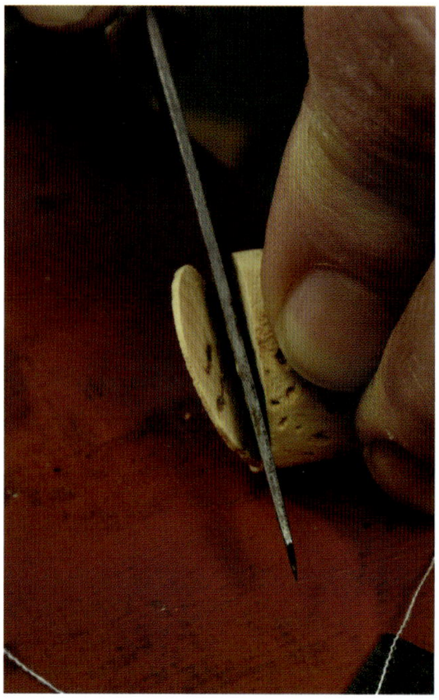

The two important qualities that cork should have are to be supple and flexible and to be free from knots and blemishes. I will reject cork from the supplier if it snaps when a sheet is bent to 90 degrees, or if there is little usable cork on a sheet. Set aside sheets that are blemish-free or extra supple for use on tenon corks. The other sheets can be used for heel corks. I try not to buy more than six months' supply at a time and I always keep the cork in a sealed plastic bag inside an airtight box (like a food storage box). This slows down the drying out process and keeps the cork in good condition.

Composite cork is a mixture of natural cork and rubber; it is firmer than natural cork and can be useful for regulation corks. The very thin (less than 0.8mm) sheet can be used under flute and oboe adjusting screws. It will not dent and deform like natural cork will.

Synthetic cork has no natural cork in it and I personally don't like the feel or texture of it; nor can I see any inherent or environmental benefit in it.

Fig. 1.19 Using a wine cork as a source of cork.

Fig. 1.22 Composite cork sheet.

Fig. 1.25 Ballistol oil, for long-term lubrication.

Fig. 1.23 A piece of thick felt like this can be cut to shape to make bumpers for saxophones.

Felt

Felt can be cut to shape to make bumpers for saxophones. The piano industry uses a lot of felt and can be a good source, as can old felt hats.

Key oil

Key oil is used on the point screws and hinge screws of an instrument to enable the player to perform fast passages with ease and with as little mechanical noise from the keywork as possible. The oil you choose also reduces friction between two rubbing surfaces and acts as a buffer between the metal parts to reduce the metal-to-metal noise made when a key is open or shut quickly. There is a balance to be made between these two functions: a thick or viscous oil will reduce the noise of keywork but can significantly slow down the action or speed of key operation; a very thin oil will lubricate well but the keywork will be noisy. To achieve the correct balance, invest in a selection of oils with different viscosities. The oils supplied by Yamaha are synthetic oils. They are chemically engineered to be uniform in viscosity and do not evaporate to leave a varnish or sludge that clogs the mechanism. Household and some car engine oils are made from a mixture of different oils with additives that might cause some problems after a period of time. The Yamaha oils I use are supplied as light oil for oboes and flutes, medium for clarinets and heavy for saxophones and bassoons.

Fig. 1.24 Yamaha key oil is available in light, medium or heavy grades.

Ballistol oil is an excellent penetrating oil to free stuck screws. It is a mixture of very volatile penetrating oils and some thicker fatty oils that get drawn into the mechanism and help long-term lubrication. The all-natural ingredients also work very well for cleaning and nourishing the body of instruments. I do not, however, use it as an oil for regular keywork.

A basic check-over and service of an instrument

Let's get to work by checking over and servicing an instrument. In our workshop, Wood, Wind & Reed, the word 'service' is used in the same way it is used for a car service – it is the routine checking of an instrument with no known faults other than general wear and tear. Servicing also applies to the checking of brand-new instruments.

Initial Dismantle and Reassemble of an Instrument **17**

We are going to dismantle, clean, oil, re-assemble and check the instrument. Anything that is found to be damaged will be recorded and dealt with separately. This is not a comprehensive or full overhaul; nor is it the repair of a broken instrument.

Fig. 1.27 Make yourself comfortable at the bench with everything at the right height.

How to remove the keys

I recommend brushing down the instrument with the shaving brush to remove dust and debris before taking the keys off to get a closer look. You need a suitable screwdriver (one that will fit in the screw slots of the instrument), spring hook and parallel-action pliers.

The order in which you take the keys off the instrument is not particularly important. As long as you don't have to apply force to remove a key, you are unlikely to do any irreversible damage. At this stage we are getting familiar with handling the tools and starting to learn where everything is situated and what function it has. If you're unsure whether you will remember the order, or might be interrupted during the process, photograph the instrument as you take it apart.

Taking the keys off involves unhooking the springs (Fig. 1.26) and removing the screws. There are two types of screws: pivot screws and hinge screws. They are not necessarily interchangeable, so return the screws into the pillars as they come out.

In the next chapter you will find photographs of the instruments with the keys numbered in the order in which you will re-assemble the instrument. You can use it as a template for the disassembly if you like. The instruments I have used as examples are made by Yamaha, and there may be differences in the mechanisms of other makes and models.

The first stage is to unhitch as many springs as you can, using your spring hook to push or pull the spring off the spring hitch. Don't worry if some are inaccessible.

Before starting to take the keys off, test how you are going to hold and support the instrument. When working on clarinets I like to support one end of the instrument on a bench peg: on other instruments you might use your lap, or an instrument holder. You will need to be able to hold the screwdriver with the end of the handle in the palm of your hand so you can apply pressure to the screw. The blade is fitted into the screw slot; steady the tip of the blade with a finger or thumb to provide accurate engagement. You will be unscrewing in an anticlockwise direction. Once the screw starts to move, ease off the pressure, but keep unscrewing until you hear or feel a slight clicking sound to indicate that the screw is fully released. The next task is to decide which screw to remove.

You will need to work out which pivot screw or hinge screw needs to be undone to release the key you want to remove. In most cases, it is fairly easy to work out which screw to undo, but on some clusters of keys it is not so obvious, for example, the two ring keys on the top joint of a clarinet (Fig. 1.28). The first ring key, C3 (see page 23), rotates on a hinge screw. The hinge screw has a point at the end that is one of a pair of pivots that holds the second ring key C4. To take the second ring key off, you unscrew the

Fig. 1.26 Here the spring hook is manipulating a spring under the F key (C18) on a clarinet.

Fig. 1.28 The top two ring keys of a clarinet.

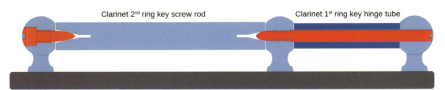

Fig. 1.29 Diagram of the top two ring keys, an example of a composite key axle.

Fig. 1.30 Use smooth jaw parallel-action pliers to remove the long screws.

Initial cleaning

Once all the keys are off, we can clean the instrument. Brush down the body of the instrument with a shaving brush and clean off old oil in the hinge tubes with pipe cleaners. A little, fresh, thin, oil on the pipe cleaner can help with this. There are special aggressive pipe cleaners with plastic or brass wire wound into the softer cotton for stubborn grease. I use cocktail sticks to clean out point screw holes.

Although the musician will usually swab the instrument after playing, the process can leave dust and dirt deposits to accumulate in the bottom of the tone holes. Clean the tone holes out with a small brush, such as a trumpet mouthpiece brush, or wet cotton bud. Pay attention to the undercut part of the tone hole. The photograph of the cross section of a clarinet shows fluff evenly lining the tone hole. The rough surface will change the way air vibrations will behave in the tube; this is called the impedance of the hole. The profile of the edges of the tone hole also affects the airway's impedance and is used by makers to subtly change the instrument's sound.

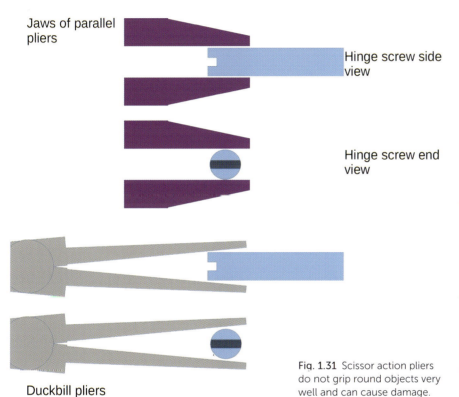

Fig. 1.31 Scissor action pliers do not grip round objects very well and can cause damage.

Many people like their instruments to look shiny and new after a repair. This is a time-consuming and therefore expensive process. Comprehensive polishing can only be done as part of a full overhaul. The appearance of keywork can be improved by rubbing with a cloth impregnated with silver polish, or by strapping with a strip of cloth and a small amount of polishing cream.

hinge screw on the right and the point screw on the left. To take the first ring key off you have to unscrew and remove the hinge screw on the right (the second ring key will become loose as well).

Sometimes a hinge screw will have a point on the end of it; this point is used as a pivot for the next key in the stack, as you can see in the diagram of a composite key axle (Fig. 1.29).

Once the screw has been unscrewed, you withdraw the screws with your fingers or smooth jaw parallel-acting pliers. They are the only sort of pliers you should use for this task as they grip the rod properly and without damaging the screw.

Store the screws in a safe place. I personally like to keep the pivot screws in the pillar they come out of and the hinge screws in the keys they belong to. Put the keys aside until later.

Fig. 1.32 This cross section of a clarinet shows dirty tone holes.

Initial Dismantle and Reassemble of an Instrument 19

Leak testing

Testing an instrument for unwanted air leaks is an important part of instrument repair. For clarinets, flutes, oboes and bassoons, you test the integrity using feeler gauges and a vacuum test. For saxophones you use feeler gauges and a leak light test. These processes are described below.

(If, at this early stage of learning to repair you find you cannot get the instrument airtight, I suggest you choose another instrument to work on, one that is in better condition. This first section of the book is to familiarize yourself with the parts of the instrument and to practise using the tools, not to find and repair faults.)

The vacuum test

The first step is to check that the body tube can be made airtight. Seal all the tone holes and finger holes with Blu Tack or similar, then block the bore at one end of the joint and draw a vacuum on the other end by sucking the air out of the tube. It should quickly become difficult to pull any more air out of the tube. At this point, stop pulling the vacuum and keep the end sealed with your tongue or lip and wait for the pressure inside to rise again and for the vacuum to collapse. If it is airtight, it will maintain the hard vacuum for some ten seconds or more. If the vacuum

Fig. 1.33 With all the keys off the instrument, seal each tone hole with Blu Tack.

Fig. 1.34 The air is being sucked out of the tube.

collapses within three seconds, you need to check your Blu Tack seals properly before trying again. If the Blu Tack is sealing correctly and the vacuum still collapses, the instrument may be leaking air from defects in the body itself; if this happens, I would strongly recommend you choose a different instrument to work with while you are still learning.

To complete the tests below, you need to have a joint that is airtight. For now, I will assume the body is airtight and you should leave the Blu Tack in place.

Test that each pad is sealing its tone hole

Starting with an airtight tube, and with Blu Tack still covering all the holes, remove the Blu Tack from one tone hole and add the key that closes that particular tone hole. Now perform the vacuum test again. The tube should be just as airtight as before. To get an accurate assessment, you will need to develop a gentle touch and only apply a very light pressure to the key when you press it; you can force a key to seal by pushing too hard on it. If the key passes the test, take the key off and re-block the tone hole with Blu Tack. Remove the Blu Tack from another hole, fit the appropriate key and test this one. Repeat for each key until they have all been tested.

When a key does not make the tube airtight, keep the faulty key off the instrument and block the tone hole up with Blu Tack and move on to the next key. How to replace a pad will be explained in Chapter 12. (If you need to get the instrument working straight away, *see* Chapter 4: Emergency Fixes.) If you have time, try to find out where the pad is leaking from; the fault might be that the pad is not touching all the way around the tone hole, there might be minute holes in the surface of the pad, or you may discover a chip or crack in the tone hole rim (the bed plate). Checking these details will help you develop a library of possible faults when checking instruments in the future.

Saxophone leak-light test to check pad sealing

There is no sensible way to check for leaks in a saxophone using air pressure, so you will need to assemble the instrument, bit by bit, testing each pad as they get put on. To help find significant leaks in saxophone padding, the best solution I have found is to use a leak-light. Putting a long, thin light down the body of a saxophone means you can see any light escaping around the pads when you close them.

Be warned, however: just because a pad passes the leak-light test does not necessarily mean the pad is sealing well. A leak-light only shows up serious leaks and can give false-positive results. A leak light will not detect all pad leaks because leather can be stretched over the edge of a tone hole rim without any support from the felt behind it. As soon as a vibration is set up within the instrument the unsupported leather starts to flap around and create a leak. I therefore suggest you always make a final check around the pad with a feeler gauge. This is described in detail in Chapter 12.

Fig. 1.35 The leak-light is the quickest way to check if a saxophone pad is sealing.

Fig. 1.36 A good spring hook makes putting springs in place easier.

Reassembling the instrument

With the body and keywork all cleaned and checked, you can now put everything back together. The next chapter covers the order of assembly for each instrument. Remember to put a drop of oil in the cone of each pivot screw and into the end of each hinge tube to keep the bearing surfaces well lubricated and quiet.

Some springs will need to be hitched on during the assembly process.

Checking the assembled instrument

You might have been working on a scrap instrument, in which case, you will have found lots of problems and the instrument still won't be working! But you will have learned more about the instrument, which is good.

If you have been working on an instrument that was in good condition when you started then the instrument should still be in good condition, if not better.

To check the condition of the assembled instrument, we need to test if it is well regulated. A well-regulated instrument is one that can play every note readily and clearly. In its simplest form, you play the instrument from top to bottom with every key combination, and if it plays readily and without interruption or hesitation, it is well regulated. If you are not a musician, or not a confident musician, then you can use a mechanical method of testing described in brief here.

Regulation is the word we use to describe the process of adjusting the relationship between the various connected keys and the body of an instrument. This includes making keys work in unison and setting the vent height of the keys. We will be covering regulation in depth later, but for now we will look to see that the pads are all the same height above the tone hole rim; they should all look about the same. Next, find the keys that are linked together (ones where when you push down one key, it also moves another key). If they are working correctly, the pads should arrive at their corresponding tone holes at the same time. See if you can confirm if they are, using a feeler gauge. Don't worry if the keys don't *start* moving simultaneously: there are some situations when it is important that they don't start moving together but only that they *arrive* together.

The instrument should now be working again and be in a better condition than when you started.

CHAPTER 2

Order of Assembly

The following chapter is a series of reference photographs of different woodwind instruments. I have numbered each key in the order that you will typically assemble the instrument. There will be exceptions to the order unless you are working on the specific model in the picture. In this book I will refer to keys by the number assigned in the pages below. I may also include the common key name as well where it is helpful to do so.

Clarinet: Yamaha YCL650

Top joint

C1: LH Eb/bb
C2: C#/g#
C3: F#/b
C4: D/a
C5: Throat A
C6: Throat G#

C7: Alternate B/throat A–B trill
C8: Alternate Bb/c–d trill
C9: Alternate F#
C10: RH Eb/bb
C11: Thumb F/c
C12: Thumb Bb/register key

Legend

- LH – left hand
- RH – right hand
- Capital letter note name indicates low register; lower case letter indicates upper register
- Sharp used in preference to flat except where common usage dictates otherwise
- 'Touch key' indicates where finger is in contact with a key
- 'Pad key' indicates a non-finger closure
- Pitch or letter name alone indicates a direct closure or hole

Fig. 2.1 Clarinet (YCL650) top joint assembly order. Key numbers are prefixed with C.

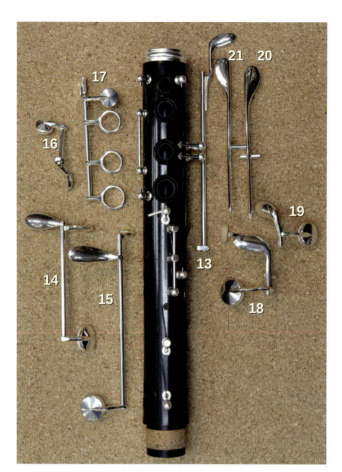

Fig. 2.2 Clarinet (YCL650) bottom joint assembly order. Key numbers are prefixed with C.

Bottom joint

C13: LH F/c
C14: RH F#/c#
C15: RH E/b
C16: Alternate B/f#
C17: Bb/f, also ring keys alternate fingering Eb/bb touch key
C18: RH F/c
C19: G#/d#
C20: LH F#/c#
C21: LH E/b

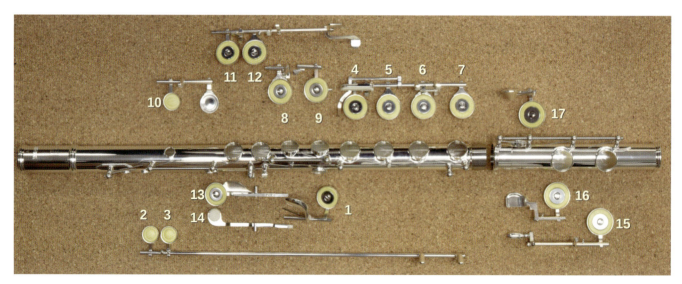

Fig. 2.3 Flute (YFL312) assembly order. Key numbers are prefixed by F.

Flute: Yamaha YFL312

F1: G#
F2: C–D trill middle register
F3: c–d trill upper register
F4: Correspondence F#
F5: F/alternate Bb
F6: E
F7: F# touch key
F8: G
F9: Correspondence (split) G
F10: C
F11: A
F12: Correspondence A and alternate Bb pad key
F13: Thumb B
F14: Thumb Bb
F15: Low C
F16: Low C#
F17: D#

Order of Assembly

Saxophone: Yamaha YAS480

S1: Correspondence F#
S2: F
S3: E
S4: D
S5: Low C# pad key
S6: Low C# touch key
S7: Low B
S8: Low Bb
S9: G# pad key
S10: G# touch key
S11: Side Bb
S12: Chromatic/fork F#
S13: Side C
S14: F# pad key
S15: Bis Bb (also known as 1 & 1 Bb linkage)
S16: Side C pad key
S17: Side Bb pad key
S18: Correspondence C pad key
S19: B
S20: A
S21: e
S22: f# pad key
S23: Automatic octave key mechanism
S24: f# pad key
S25: Eb/D#
S26: Low C
S27: Palm d
S28: Palm f
S29: Palm eb
S30: Thumb octave key
S31: Front/fork F (E)
S32: Crook octave key

Fig. 2.4 Saxophone (YAS480) assembly order. Key numbers are prefixed with S.

Order of Assembly

Oboe: Yamaha YOB241

O1: G#
O2: B–C# trill vent
O3: C–D trill vent
O4: RH G#
O5: G
O6: Correspondence Bb
O7: A
O8: Correspondence B
O9: C
O10: Conservatoire bar/link arm
O11: Thumb-plate/B
O12: Lower octave key vent
O13: Side/upper octave key
O14: Lower octave (also known as 'back octave') touch piece
O15: LH B–C# trill touch key
O16: C–D trill linkage arm
O17: RH F
O18: C–D trill touch key
O19: F#/conservatoire Bb & C touch key
O20: Correspondence E & fork F
O21: E
O22: D
O23: Low B
O24: Low C
O25: C#
O26: D#/Eb
O27: Fork F vent
O28: Fork F vent rocker arm
O29: D# vent key
O30: Low Bb linkage
O31: Feather keys, includes LH D#/Eb, low B touch key, low Bb touch key
O32: Low Bb pad key

Fig. 2.5 Oboe (YOB241) assembly order. Key numbers are prefixed with O.

Fig. 2.6 Oboe (YOB241) key 32, the bell key.

Bassoon: Yamaha YFG812

Wing joint back

B1: Crook key lock
B2: Link keys from c touch key and c# touch key, both to LH 3rd finger ring
B3: Vent key for c
B4: Crook touch key/F touch key
B5: Crook key/F touch key
B6: d touch key/flick key
B7: c touch key/flick key
B8: a touch key/flick key
B9: C# pad key
B10: Crook key linkage key

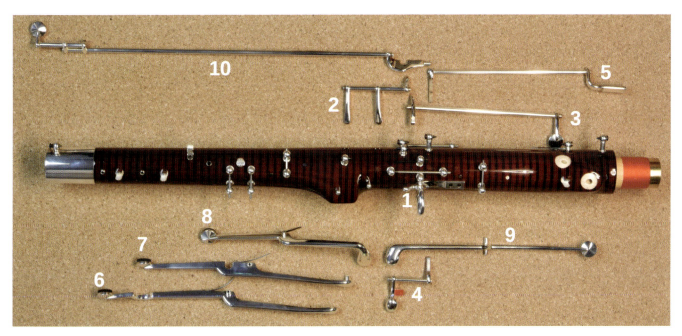

Fig. 2.7 Bassoon (YFG812) wing joint back assembly order. Key numbers are prefixed with B.

Order of Assembly

Wing joint front

B11: E–F# trill/eb
B12: D–Eb trill
B13: C ring touch key/3rd finger ring

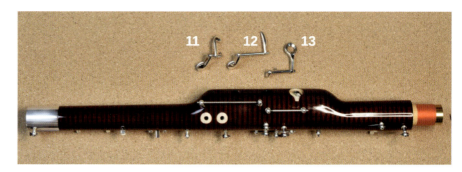

Fig. 2.8 Bassoon (YFG812) wing joint front assembly order.

Bassoon boot joint

B14: Low F touch key/g vent touch key
B15: F#
B16: G#
B17: RH alternate (front) Bb
B18: G touch key
B19: A ring/g vent
B20: Low F pad key
B21: C–C# trill

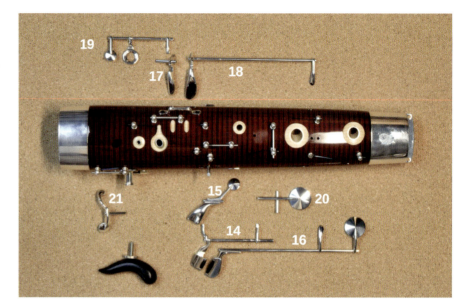

Fig. 2.9 Bassoon (YFG812) boot joint front assembly order.

Boot joint back

B21a: Alternate (front) Bb key connecting pin
B22: Bb pad key
B23: Bb touch key
B24: Thumb F# touch key
B25: F# linkage key rocker arm to close low F pad key
B25a: Thumb F# connecting pin to hold F key
B26: G# touch key
B27: G pad key
B27a: G touch key connecting pin to close G key
B28: G# key rocker arm to open G# pad key
B28a: G key connecting pin
B29: 'Pancake' low E

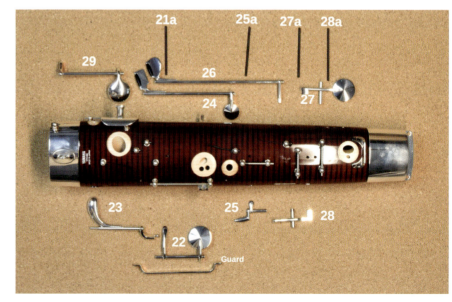

Fig. 2.10 Bassoon (YFG812) boot joint back assembly order.

Order of Assembly

Long joint

B30: Low C key
B31: Low D touch key
B32: Low D pad key
B33: Low C# touch key
B34: Low Eb
B35: Low C# pad key
B36: Low B touch key
B37: Low Bb touch key
B38: Low B pad key

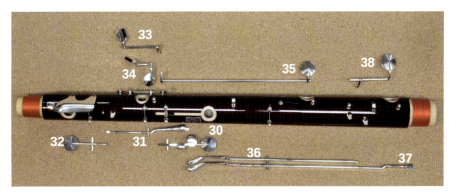

Fig. 2.11 Bassoon (YFG812) long joint assembly order.

Bassoon bell

B39: Low Bb pad key

Fig. 2.12 Bassoon (YFG812) bell joint assembly order.

CHAPTER 3

Initial Diagnosis – Observations and Tests

Before undertaking repairs, we need to know how to test an instrument and determine what, if anything, is wrong, or could be better. It may sound obvious, but you cannot fix something if you don't know what could be better, and likewise, you don't know if you have fixed it if you don't know how to test it.

You also can't see what might be wrong if you don't know how it is supposed to function in the first place. So we'll start by briefly looking at how woodwind instruments work and then how to discover why an instrument might not be working as it should.

How woodwind instruments work

Airflow

A woodwind instrument makes a good sound when the air column is resonating inside its tube.

The acoustic length of this resonating tube determines the pitch, or note, that the instrument sounds. By acoustic length we mean the distance between the mouthpiece at one end and the first open tone hole. A change in length is achieved by the use of fingers and keys to open and close the holes along the length of tube. For instance, as the holes are closed down the instrument, the acoustic length increases and the notes get lower.

If the instrument is working and the air column is resonating well, and we introduce a small hole in the tube somewhere along its length between the mouthpiece and the first open tone hole, it can either have an intended beneficial effect – for instance, when a speaker or octave hole is opened – or the hole can cause major disruption to the resonance of the tube and make it squeak, or not sound at all.

Keys

The keys on an instrument are a mechanical means of opening and closing tone holes. They allow the musician's fingers to cover more holes and over much larger diameters and distances than their fingers can reach unaided. It is therefore important that the keys operate smoothly and correctly at all times and are not bent or damaged. When a key gets damaged in some way, it can stop rotating or moving. This in turn will prevent a pad from sealing or opening a tone hole.

Pads

A pad is an airtight stopper that is attached to a key and closes over a tone hole to make an airtight seal. A pad can fail to seal a tone hole when a key is damaged, or when the pad itself is damaged. To work, the pad must have an airtight membrane that covers the tone hole and is touching the tone hole rim all the way around. If there is any tear damage to the surface of the pad or tone hole rim, it can allow air to pass though it and spoil the resonance of the tube.

In understanding the above, we can see that woodwind technicians are primarily concerned with leaks!

Initial observations and tests

It is possible to categorize two levels at which an instrument might need attention:

1. Emergency level: when there are problems that prevent an instrument from performing its basic functions.
2. Optimization level: when there are less distinctive problems where an instrument has become unreliable,

noisy or seems more difficult to play that it used to.

If it is not an emergency, we might be assessing the instrument to work out how much time is needed to complete the repair, or if it is a repair that we can do at all. In these situations, we want to use tests that can be done without taking the instrument apart. This might include a vacuum test, leak-light test, looking at how much cleaning is needed and checking if the corks and pads are in good condition. The instrument might be bent or damaged, in which case we must assess if it is economical to repair and just how much structural damage has been done.

It is only when we start taking the instrument apart that a full inspection, test, and diagnosis can take place.

Observations

Musician's observations

For a musician to have brought the instrument to you, they have reason to think something is wrong, so we need to listen to them. What are they experiencing? Why do they think something is wrong? What are the symptoms? Did a teacher advise them to come, and if so, have they remembered the right message? Are they a professional struggling to perform a specific passage of music? You can start by quizzing them on what has stopped working for them.

Comparing instruments

We can assume that something has changed on the instrument, but we don't know what it was like before they came to see us. This is why we need to gain experience from looking and handling good instruments. In that way we have an idea of what the instrument should be like, then match that to what we see on the broken instrument in front of us.

Repairer's observations

With the instrument in our hands, we can look for obvious damage such as missing, torn, or damaged pads, bent keywork or dents in the body. The aim of these observations is to identify what is preventing the pads from sealing a tone hole or to see if two connected keys are not operating in unison when they should.

- Inspect the surface of every pad for any that are missing, or any with holes, tears or missing membrane.
- Operate each key in sequence and feel if they are moving smoothly. Look out for: any key rubbing against another; any key that is slow to respond or fails to snap back into position; any bend in a key that is stopping it from closing on the tone hole; and any bent link arm that is spoiling the regulation between the keys.
- On a metal instrument you can look down the length of the instrument to see if a should-be-straight tube is curved. If it is bent, then it might explain the faults you might find in the next test.

Bends and twists will need to be repaired first. Very often reversing a bend will bring all the other elements of the instrument back to working condition without many other adjustments being necessary.

The pad might not be touching the tone hole rim all the way around or the surface of the pad might be torn or perforated. The needle spring in Fig. 3.1 is pointing to a hole in the pad that is big enough to impact the performance of the

Fig. 3.1 Damaged clarinet pad.

Fig. 3.2 This flute is so bent, it is probably not worth repairing.

instrument. Look at the pad membrane, the area of the pad that seals the tone hole, for any signs of abrasion, cracking or other damage. Any break in the surface will allow air to leak out of the tube.

The problem might be obvious, in which case you can go straight to the mechanical tests, but if it is not immediately clear, then it can often be helpful to ask the musician to demonstrate the problem.

Play testing

The art of play testing an instrument for repair purposes does not come naturally to an experienced musician. The natural tendency for musicians is to always get the best out of the instrument, whatever state it is in. They try to overcome any mechanical difficulties by pressing harder or blowing differently. The job of the repairer is to expose and highlight the mechanical problems that the musician may be overcoming in these ways.

To perform a useful play test, the musician (or repairer) needs to use a steady embouchure and gentle finger pressure on the keywork. Play a chromatic scale from bottom to top and back again over two registers. If a note does not sound, do not coax the note out by pushing harder or changing the embouchure; simply move onto the next note in the scale. If three or more consecutive notes fail to sound, the test can be abandoned.

While the instrument is being played, make a record of where the musician is having a problem. Is it with an alternate fingering for instance? Or is it only one note in a sequence that is not sounding nicely?

When performed well, the play test will reveal significant problems, and if undertaken sensitively, will often show up the pads that are not airtight, or the key combinations that are not working well. It is unlikely to pinpoint where the failure actually is. For instance, problems in playing low notes can often be caused by damage at the top of the instrument. It is impossible to cover playing techniques within the scope of this book, but it is something worth studying in order to become a good repairer.

Mechanical testing

Leak testing

Another test that most repairers will perform is to block all the holes in the instrument and gently blow air into, or suck air out of, the tube. If done sensitively it will show up if there is a leak somewhere in the tube. (This test cannot be performed on a saxophone.)

Vacuum test

Each repairer finds their own way of testing instruments for leaks. Most use a variation on this technique; All the holes are blocked and then a gentle air pressure or suction is applied to the end of the tube. You have to learn how to interpret the drift of air in or out of the instrument body. This technique can even detect if you have rough fingertips or fingerprints! I usually wet my fingertips before performing this test so that no air leaks from the finger holes.

Fig. 3.3 Vacuum testing a clarinet top joint.

Leak light test

When working on saxophones you can put a bright light inside the bore of an instrument and then close the pads and look carefully for any light escaping around the rim of the tone holes.

Fig. 3.4 Inserting an LED leak light into a saxophone.

Initial Diagnosis – Observations and Tests

Feeler gauge test

Often there is no significant mechanical wear or damage, and the pads pass the first visual inspection, so we now perform a 'feeler gauge' test (or a 'grip test'). In my view, the ability to accurately perform a grip test with a feeler gauge is one of the most valuable skills a good repairer can possess. All the repairers I have met around the world use a feeler gauge. It is a surprisingly difficult skill to acquire, and some of the students I have taught take a year or more to understand the feedback the test gives and develop the skills required to adjust the pad and seat it correctly.

For each key, lift the pad from the tone hole and position the tip of the feeler gauge in the middle of the tone hole. Now close the pad onto the feeler gauge, either under its own spring or with gentle finger pressure. Then slowly pull the feeler gauge out from under the pad, paying attention to how hard (or not) it is to withdraw it. The aim is to test each pad at four or more points around the circumference to see if the feeler is gripped equally at each position. If there is a point anywhere around the pad where there is less resistance or friction on the feeler gauge, this suggests the pad may allow air to escape or leak.

Regulation test

You can now test to see how the keys are interacting with each other. Check the operation of the keywork to find out if keys open and shut correctly and that connected keys open or close in the correct sequence. This is called the regulation of the instrument. In terms of emergency repairs, an example would be a cork coming off from under an adjustment screw and that will cause poor regulation and is a common reason for an instrument to suddenly stop playing. For more detail on regulation, *see* Chapter 14.

If an adjusting screw has rotated it may no longer be bringing the pads of two connected keys down at the same time; this might leave one pad open when it should be shut. For example, the adjusting screw shown on the left of Fig. 3.6 would only cause a problem if it was screwed in too far. The one on the right of Fig. 3.6 would cause a problem if it was screwed in too much or too little.

In this book I use the terms 'time of arrival' and 'time of departure'. Time of arrival is the most important type of regulation. It is the adjustment of the mechanism that brings two or more pads

Fig. 3.5 Using a feeler gauge to test the seating of a flute pad.

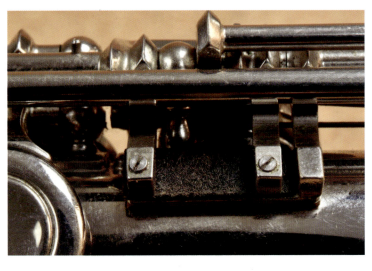

Fig. 3.6 Group of adjusting screws on a Yamaha flute.

in contact with their tone holes at the same time.

As a repairer you identify where to make a time of arrival adjustment by pushing down on the pad cups of the keys in question and looking for the link arms that should connect the two keys to each other. The gap between the link arms is where it needs adjusting.

Movement testing

With the keys on the instrument, check that the keys rotate smoothly on their pivot screw or hinge screw assemblies and test how much excess movement there is in the mechanism by holding each key in turn and trying to move it from side to side and front to back. While doing this, look to see if there is any movement of the key between the pillars parallel to the axis and look for any movement of the key at 90 degrees to the axis (which could also be described as across the key, perpendicular to the axis).

Test to see if any of the keys are sluggish to rotate, as this may indicate that old oil is gumming up the pivots or the key is bent.

Wherever an issue with the rotation of keywork is found, make a record of this, as you will need to solve this before doing any other repair work.

Conclusion

If after all these processes you still don't understand what the problem with the instrument is, go back to play testing the instrument to see if it may have something to do with the playing technique of the musician or the overall quality of design and materials used by the manufacturer.

Usually, however, the tests reveal the problems, and we can get on with fixing them.

Fig. 3.7 A loose screw in a pillar may cause a pad not to seat and therefore the instrument will stop playing below that note.

CHAPTER 4

Emergency Fixes

It is useful to know a number of quick and effective repairs that can be done in an emergency.

It is worth noting that often you will need these when musicians have performances, or exams coming up. In these situations they are using their instruments more and therefore the pads are getting wetter, and they are handling it

Emergency tool kit

- Blu Tack (adhesive putty, poster putty, mounting putty)
- Clingfilm (food wrap/cling wrap)
- Cocktail sticks (toothpicks)
- Contact adhesive (contact cement)
- Cork, wine cork (and flute head cork if appropriate)
- Cork grease
- Cotton buds
- Elastic bands (if possible, buy the brightly coloured silicone bands, as rubber bands will tarnish silver very quickly)
- Feeler gauges (such as cigarette paper or the tape from an audio cassette)
- Masking tape (low-tack tape)
- Matchsticks
- Pipe cleaners
- Powder paper (Yamaha)
- Rags (in strips)
- Sandpaper
- Scalpel or razor blades
- Spring hook (these can be purchased or home-made)
- Smooth jaw parallel-action pliers
- Screwdriver (size depending on the instrument you are working on – clarinets and flutes just less than 2mm wide, saxophone and bassoons 3mm wide; the blades need to be a close fit to the screw and a long shaft is very helpful)
- Thread
- Workshop roll (this is a strip of cloth-backed abrasive)

Fig. 4.1 My emergency tool kit.

more, while nervous, and are more likely to drop it or damage the instrument some other way.

Common problems

Here are some fixes that can be applied to many woodwind instruments.

A key has stopped springing back

The first step is to check that the spring has not been unhooked. If that is not the problem, then check that a key is not bent, a screw has not become loose, or that there is no other mechanical reason for it not to work. Solve those problems before resorting to using an elastic band. There is no easy way to explain how to use the elastic band to create the fix; you might have to be very inventive to find a way of creating a spring (Fig. 4.2).

Sticky sound coming from a pad

The exact cause of this problem is not, in my experience, fully explained. The emergency solution is to try and remove excess water and sticky substances using a pad cleaning cloth or powder paper. These are both products that are worth keeping with the instrument. Yamaha powder paper is a specially prepared paper, coated in a very fine inert powder. This powder attaches itself to the sticky areas of the pad and forms a barrier (Fig. 4.3).

The keywork is noisy

Oil the keywork. If the musician is about to be recorded, they might become worried about the amount of noise coming from the keywork. The correct way to make the instrument quiet is to follow all the instructions about taking up unwanted movement in the key mechanism. In an emergency, however, you might not have time, so you can reduce the noise by unscrewing the point screw or hinge screw of the offending keys and putting a drop of oil in the hole and screwing them back up again.

Fig. 4.2 Example of using an elastic band to replace a broken spring.

Fig. 4.3 Using Yamaha powder paper to cure a sticky pad problem on a flute.

Damaged pads

A torn or damaged pad can cause the instrument to squeak or not play lower notes. The quick fix is to create a new airtight surface to the pad using clingfilm, as shown.

Fig. 4.4 Insert a piece of clingfilm between the body of the instrument and the key. Keep the film flat where it passes under the pad.

Fig. 4.5 Tie the clingfilm securely onto the key. You might want to add a small piece of sticky tape to hold it in place.

Fig. 4.6 The pad cup and pad are wrapped in clingfilm and ready to be used. The pad will now work for many weeks until it can be repaired conventionally.

Missing pad

Replacing a pad with Blu Tack and clingfilm may not look pretty but it works!

Fig. 4.7 The pad is missing completely.

Fig. 4.8 Roll a small ball of Blu Tack and flatten it. Adjust the size to suit the missing pad. Put the disc of Blu Tack onto some clingfilm.

Fig. 4.10 Tie the Blu Tack pad in place with the clingfilm. Trim the ends of the clingfilm.

Fig. 4.9 Carefully position the Blu Tack pad beneath the pad cup.

Fig. 4.11 Once the pad is in place and the clingfilm is wrapped and tied around the pad cup, gently press the key down so the new pad can form round the tone hole bed plate. It is now ready to be used.

Emergency Fixes

Clarinets

Clarinets are quite robust instruments, so it is quite common for them to be left too long before being serviced. There are two types of emergency repair that may be required: those caused by neglect and those caused by the instrument being mishandled. I have listed them by the problems the musician may experience, and then the possible fix or fixes required plus more detail and images.

The joints wobble and it is impossible to get a good sound

This usually happens when a tenon cork is missing or damaged. There are four cork tenons on a clarinet, including one on the mouthpiece. Wrap a folded strip of clingfilm around the damaged tenon cork. Keep adding the film until you get a firm connection between the joints. I do not recommend the use of PTFE plumber's tape for this purpose.

The bottom note in each register won't sound

Fix by adjusting the crow's foot. When the bottom note in each register won't sound, especially when played only using the left-hand little finger to play C21, the problem is usually that the touch piece of C18 (F/c key) has been bent down towards the body of the instrument. Before bending anything back, check that the pivot screws holding C15 are secure.

In Figs 4.13 to 4.15, I have created a simple representation of the right-hand little finger keys (on the left of the diagram), as seen from the left-hand side of the clarinet. As a repairer you push down the pad cups to see where the regulation is needed and where it needs adjusting.

If you press the keys as a musician, the poor regulation shows up as the C18 pad being open.

You have two ways to adjust this in an emergency:

1. Put your right-hand thumb on the C18 pad cup and your left-hand thumb under the C18 crow's foot and bend the key upwards; check the time of arrival of each pad until they arrive at the same time.
2. The alternative method is to use cork or layers of masking tape on top of the crow's foot until the gap has gone and the two pads arrive at the same time.

All the notes on the bottom joint have stopped working

It is very common for the link arms between the top and bottom joint of a clarinet to be crashing into each other. They are keys C4 and C17. If you suspect this is the problem, then try twisting the top and bottom joint so the link arms are next to each other. The instrument will be awkward to play, but if it solves the problem, you have confirmed that you need to bend the link arms back to their correct positions.

Another reason the bottom joint notes might not be working (this is the most common problem when a clarinet is dropped) is that C10 (Eb side key) is bent under C9 (F# key). This stops C10 from closing, which in turn stops any note below that key from sounding. Try to bend the C10 key back out so it is clear of the other keys. Don't worry about getting it exactly as it was; this is an emergency repair, just make sure it is working.

Only one or two notes will play

If C6 (Ab key on top joint) is bent, then use your parallel-action pliers to bend it straight again.

Fig. 4.12 An emergency repair of a loose tenon can be made by wrapping the tenon in clingfilm.

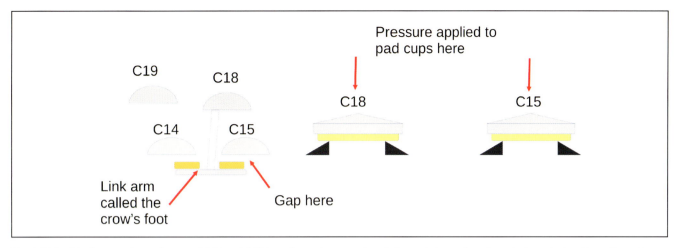

Fig. 4.13 In this diagram the pad cups of C15 and C18 have been depressed until the pads have closed on the tone holes. You will see there is a gap between the C18 link arm and the touch piece of C15.

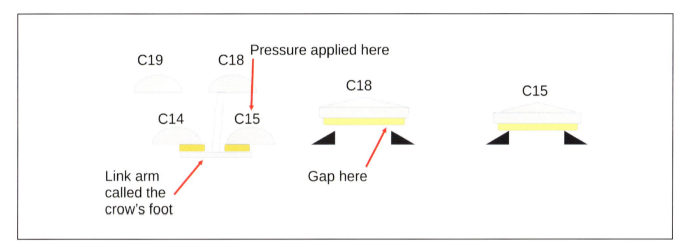

Fig. 4.14 This diagram shows the same problem as in the previous diagram, only this time I have drawn it with the touch piece of C15 pushed down until the C15 pad has touched the tone hole. This time you will see that the gap is now under the pad cup of C18.

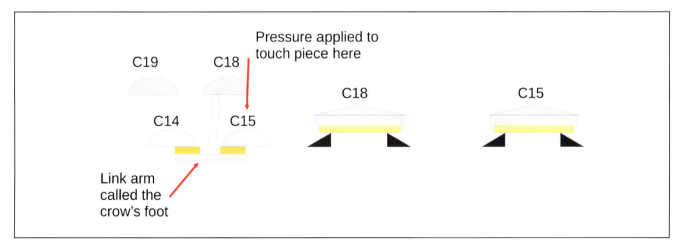

Fig. 4.15 Here we have the correct regulation.

Flutes

The flute will only play one note

Check if a spring has come unhitched; if it has, hook it back in place. The most common spring to come adrift is on the top trill key. Hook it back in place and all should be well.

Fig. 4.16 The trill key spring (F3) on this flute is unhitched. One end of it is in mid-air.

Fig. 4.17 Using a spring hook, manipulate the needle spring back onto the spring hitch.

Fig. 4.18 The needle spring is now safely behind the spring hitch, and it will keep the trill pad closed.

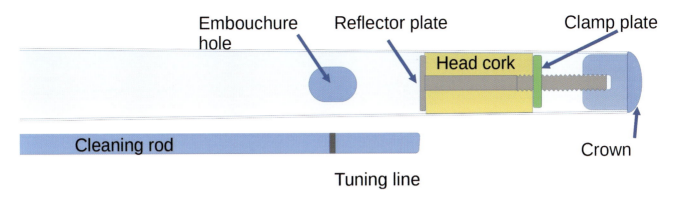

Fig. 4.19 The head cork assembly.

Fig. 4.20 Flute head joint showing where the line on the cleaning rod should be in relationship to the embouchure hole, when the reflector plate of the head cork assembly is touching the end of the rod.

The flute lacks power/focus or is out of tune

The only reason a flute will change its tuning is if the head cork position has moved. Adjust the head cork assembly position and/or seal it with clingfilm.

The head joint cork should be an airtight fit within the tube and the metal reflector plate should be 17mm from the centre of the embouchure hole. In Fig. 4.19, the line on the cleaning rod is marked at 17mm. (On premium-quality instruments, the reflector plate should be set to the manufacturer's specification; this will be the line on the original cleaning/tuning rod.)

To check the head cork is in the correct position, slide the cleaning rod (the end without a slot) up the bore of the head joint then look through the embouchure hole. You should see the tuning line that is marked on the rod in the centre of the hole (Fig. 4.20). If it is central, then the reflector plate is in the correct position. Next, block the open end of the head joint and try to draw a vacuum with your mouth through the embouchure hole. It should be perfectly airtight. If it is, and it is playing with power and focus, then there is nothing more to do. If it is not in tune or lacks power, then you will have to remove the head cork to find out what else is wrong and then improve the situation.

The tool in Fig. 10.83 is a useful head joint adjustment tool; it can be used to push the head cork assembly out of the head joint. It also has three rings cut into the surface. The ring in the middle is exactly 17mm from the end. The two rings on each side are spaced 5mm either side. These two side rings are to aid you in positioning the head cork. If you cannot find aluminium tubing the correct diameter (14–16mm), then you can make a rod out of hardwood or metal. Drill an 8mm diameter hole, 30mm deep in the end of the rod; the hole will fit over the screwed rod of the head assembly to make it easier to push the head cork out.

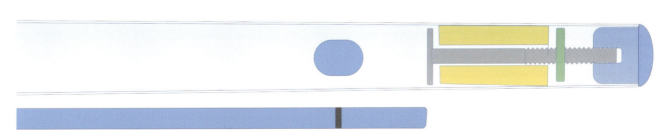

Fig. 4.21 This flute might play in tune, because the reflector plate is in the correct position, but it will lack power and focus. The cork has dried out and is not tight in the tube, there is a gap behind the reflector plate and around the spindle.

Emergency Fixes

Fig. 4.22 Flute head cork assembly out of the instrument.

Taking the flute head cork assembly out

Unscrew the crown. Push the head cork assembly out through the large end of the head joint using the flute head cork adjusting tool (or cleaning rod if that is all that is available)

As this is an emergency repair, you will not be replacing the cork, only making it airtight and positioning it correctly. Make sure the clamp plate is screwed tight against the cork.

If the cork is leaking, wrap clingfilm or thread around the cork. Insert the assembly back into the head joint from the large end and push it up to its correct position. Adjust the amount of thread or film, until it is a tight fit when in the correct position. Screw the crown back on.

One note on the flute does not sound, but the others below do sound

This is quite a common problem. For example, you might find that F does not work, but E and below do. Another example is that G does not sound very good, but E and below are great.

F does not work, but E and below do

There are two likely causes for this problem and two ways of confirming which it is. Use the relevant adjusting screw to fix the regulation.

1. Play testing: ask the musician to play the F (F5); while they are playing, use a finger to push down the F# pad cup (F4). Does the note improve? If it does, then you have found your problem. If it does not, then take your finger off the F# and push down the open G# pad cup (F11). Does that make a difference? Make the adjustments below as appropriate.
2. Mechanical testing: close the F key (F5) and look carefully to see if the F# (F4) pad is closing. Use a feeler gauge if needed. If it is not closing, then see below to fix it. If it is, then close the F# again and test the open G# pad (F11) for a gap.

In both cases you have a time of arrival problem. In the case of the F# key making the improvement, look for the adjusting screw or point of contact between the F key and the F# key. It can sometimes be hidden under other keywork. When you have found the adjusting point, tighten the screws or use layers of tape to close the gap and make the two pads arrive at the same time. If it is the G# pad cup that makes the improvement, then you adjust the time of arrival between the G key and the G# key.

Low C and below not working

Check that the low C# (F16) and C (F15) pad arrive at the same time; if not, then see if you can bend the C# touch piece up a little. It may also be that the Eb pad (F17) is open at the back. Bend the Eb touch piece upwards and test again.

Saxophones

Most saxophone emergencies are caused by a bent key or pillar that is out of alignment. The most common is a bent neck key.

The saxophone only wants to play in the second octave

This is most likely to be a neck key problem. Put the neck on the instrument, in its normal playing position. Focus your attention on the connection between the neck key (usually a loop key) and the pin on the octave mechanism that extends upwards from the body. The pin should be sitting underneath the neck key. There should be a gap between these two keys when at rest. If you are not sure if there is a gap, then slide a strip of paper between the loop and pin. If there is no gap, then bend the neck key away from the pin. Bend the key to create a gap.

Notes are coming out inconsistently

It may be that a key is not springing back into position as it should. Identify which key is not operating correctly. It might not be the key of the note you are trying to play.

If a spring is broken or missing, then we can use an elastic band hooked on the key and wrapped around the instrument in such a way as to replace the spring action. If the spring is unhitched, then hook it back on. Remember that careful observation of instruments when they are working well helps you spot when something changes.

The other cause for keys not returning properly is mechanical damage – a bent key or misaligned pillar, for instance, or old oil gumming up a hinge screw. You can try and undo the damage or overcome the problem with an elastic band to add strength to the spring.

Loss of playing performance, especially at the bottom of the saxophone

Look for a torn pad on the palm keys (S27, S28 and S29) or top trill keys (S21 and S22). If they look hard or damaged in any way, slide clingfilm under the pad and wrap it up and over the pad cup.

Sticking G# (S9)

Use Yamaha powder paper to clean the pad and tone hole rim.

Fig. 4.23 Using paper to test the gap between the neck key (S32) and the octave mechanism pin.

Fig. 4.24 This photo shows a problem with the regulation between the G♯ (S9) and F♯ (S1) keys, which are both closed in this photo. There should not be a gap visible between the adjusting screw in the centre of the photo and the pad cup below it.

Everything plays until the bottom C (S7), then it stops working

Diagnose the problem by playing low C (S7) and then get someone to push down the G# key (S9). If the C starts sounding, then the problem might be that the F key (S1) is not holding down the G# pad (S9). You will find that the adjusting screw that extends from the F# key over the top of the G# is not holding the G# pad down. Either adjust the screw or use layers of masking tape on top of the G# pad cup to fill the gap that you will see when the F# pad is closed.

The mouthpiece wobbles on the neck

This probably means the neck cork will be compressed, cracked or missing. The emergency repair is to wrap a strip of clingfilm round the cork or neck until a good fit to the mouthpiece is achieved.

The low notes are bubbling or burbling

S7 (low C) and S8 (B) are sensitive notes on a saxophone. It is helpful to know the following:

- That the acoustic design of a saxophone is optimized to have the mouthpiece pushed onto the neck two-thirds to three-quarters of the way onto the cork.
- The bore of a saxophone mouthpiece is parallel where it goes onto the neck cork.

With this information, the neck cork should be adjusted so that the mouthpiece could be pushed on fully. If it is too tight, then start by rolling the cork between a hard surface and a piece of wood, or the back of a hardback book, or similar. You aim to compress the cork evenly around the neck. Apply some cork grease and see if the mouthpiece will go on further. If not, you will need to sand down the cork until it fits.

With the mouthpiece in the correct position, ask the musician to play the bottom notes again. Hopefully, the notes will be much improved. If the player then complains that the instrument is now too sharp, you have the tricky task of persuading them that they are using an embouchure method that is too tight.

If that does not have the desired effect, you have to look at the seating of low Eb pad and for any pads that are not seating at the top of the instrument using your feeler gauge technique.

A (S20) hesitates before sounding

There is a group of keys quite high up the body of the saxophone that requires careful regulation. Keys S19 and S20 need to be able to close S18. S20 also needs to close S15 (known as the Bis key). It is S20 closing S15 that goes out of adjustment most often, partly because S20 is involved in two adjustments. To test, push down S20 and, using your feeler gauge, check that S15 is also sealing. If it is not, then either bend the S20 touch arm down or add some more felt or cork under the arm, and adjust until they arrive at the same time.

Oboes

The oboe is the most sensitive instrument regarding regulation, especially the time of arrival. It will be worth spending time reading the section detailing the regulation process in order to handle emergency oboe repairs well. You also might need to read the section on the subtleties of bending and screw adjustment.

Before making any adjustments to screws, make a note (photograph) of where the original position is and return it to this position if you find you have not improved it. In the meantime, if you want to start adjusting screws, do so by tiny increments at a time; if we take sixty minutes as one full rotation, then only change by five minutes at a time. Be prepared to reverse the adjustment you make, if it makes no difference, and try another screw.

Problems playing in the second octave

This will usually be due to water in the octave holes. Fixing this problem rather depends on how much time you have and on having an octave bush remover.

If neither time nor an octave bush remover are available, take the top joint, block the finger holes and the bottom of the joint with your fingers, and blow into the socket where the reed goes. Open each octave key in turn, blowing excess water out of the holes. The octave hole is tiny, 0.8mm diameter, so it won't feel like much air is escaping, but it will be, and it will be pushing out any water that has collected in the octave box. Use a pad cleaning cloth to remove any further water from under the pad.

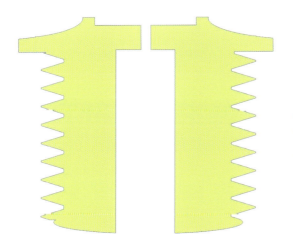

Fig. 4.25 Most student, and some intermediate, oboes have the octave bush screwed directly into the body of the instrument. This diagram shows the octave bush of a Yamaha YOB241. More expensive instruments there can have a more complex design.

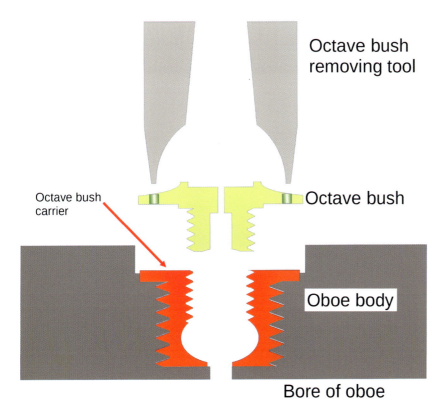

Fig. 4.26 Part of a typical octave bush assembly with removal tool.

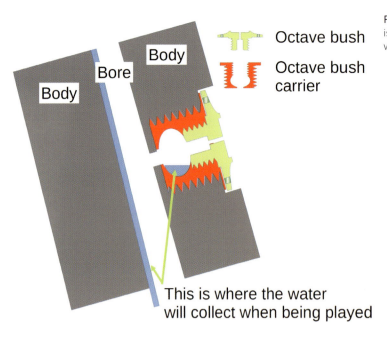

Fig. 4.27 When an oboe is played, the octave assembly is being held at about 20 degrees from the horizontal, so water collects in the chamber.

Fig. 4.28 This useful tool is used to remove octave bushes from oboes. (It is also needed for vintage flute repairs and some high-end clarinets that use retaining screws on their lower pads.) The distance between the two prongs can be adjusted with the brass collet.

Prop the octave keys open when not in use to allow the holes to dry. I also have long-term advice in Chapter 5: Care of Instruments.

To prevent this from happening as much in the future, suggest that the musician warms the instrument before playing, without blowing down the tube, and doesn't pull the swab from the bottom of the instrument upwards and out of the top! This squeezes the water out of the swab and into the octave holes.

If you have access to an octave bush removing tool, then you can use this to unscrew the bush. Clean out the water and screw it back in. Figs 4.25 to 4.27 show you what you will find when you unscrew the bush.

If you look at the diagram of an oboe when being played, you can see that condensed water will collect on the lower surface of the bore and in the reservoir made within the octave bush carrier. If you were to make the mistake of turning the instrument over on its front (when not playing), the water in the reservoir would fill the tiny octave hole.

The joints are wobbly or the tenon cork is damaged

If the parts of the oboe are not stable or not staying together, look to see if the tenon cork is cracked or missing. If there is damage, then wrap a strip of clingfilm around the tenon, adding or removing to obtain a firm fit.

The oboe can only play one note

Look carefully at the connections between the top and bottom joint. The most likely cause on high-end instruments will be that the second trill key link is bent and is keeping the second trill key open. If you feel confident in bending it back, do so; if not, use a screwdriver to remove the long key that links the second trill key to the bottom joint (O18); it's not often needed so you can leave the key off.

Various problems caused by the instrument being dropped

The most likely keys to get bent on an oboe are the feather keys (O31 right-hand little finger keys) and any long keys that extend below the tenon of the top joint. If the keys look bent, it is worth trying to bend them back, so they look like other similar instruments. On anything other than instruments of twenty years old, you are unlikely to break the keywork.

The bottom B♭ has stopped playing

It is most likely that the feather keys have been bent; you can find out if it is causing a problem by attempting to play low D (O22) and below. If they won't sound, the damaged feather keys are likely to be holding the low E♭ pad open (O29) and/or the regulation with O32 has gone out of adjustment. These issues can both be solved by bending the outer feather keys up and away from the body of the instrument.

Bassoons

The bassoon is a fairly robust instrument, as long as the musician knows how to put it together and take it apart comfortably. If a tenon joint gets stiff a musician can put excess strain on the keywork or tenons and cause damage. Keeping the tenon joints greased and adjusted helps. The pads on a bassoon tend to last a long time and the regulation is tolerant of small knocks and jolts. Where one can get into difficulty is with the body rotting and pads swelling over a long period of time, so it is a good idea for the instrument to be dried out after playing, especially if it has been used in a cold room or for many hours. However well it is looked after, the following problems may still occur.

The bocal is wobbly

Check for chipped or slipping cork. Wrap clingfilm around the cork and extend the wrapping, up the bocal, to provide anchorage.

The instrument seems less focused than usual

The bassoon will change shape (warp) if left for long periods without being played. You can wrap cotton thread over the top of the existing corks or thread; keep adding thread and cork grease until it fits together well.

The bottom notes are not reliable

Check that the push rods that go from one side of the bassoon boot joint are not getting stuck. There is not much you can do in an emergency other than to avoid using that fingering. This may not sound very helpful, but unless you have a toolbox with you, there is not much else you can do.

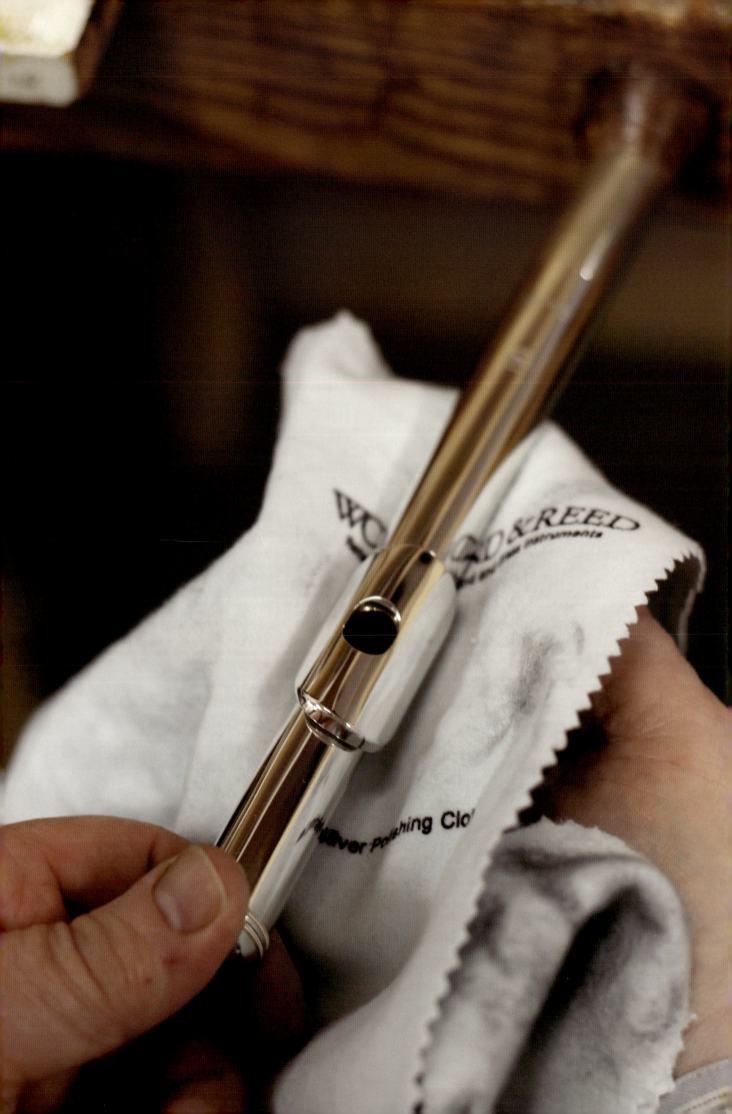

Chapter 5

Care of Instruments

To keep an instrument in good working condition it is useful to know what good practice is, and what should be avoided in terms of handling instruments.

How to store an instrument

Avoid letting any instrument go below 0°C and above 37°C. Sweltering humid conditions can cause metal to corrode and pads to swell. If it is too dry, pads can shrink, corks dry out and wood can crack. To complicate matters, a cold atmosphere is usually a dry atmosphere, so the worst place to keep an instrument in cold weather is next to a radiator. It is both dry and warm. The best place is somewhere cool with a stable climate. The boot of a car, for instance, is also not a good place for an instrument.

How to prepare an instrument for playing

When getting ready to play an instrument it is best if we can get the temperature of the upper part of the instrument as close to body temperature as we can. This has two benefits: firstly, instruments are designed to play in tune when the upper sections of the instrument are around body temperature and the surrounding temperature is about 20°C. Secondly, the warmed instrument is unlikely to suffer from condensation in the tube, where it can accumulate in tone holes and make pads wet.

It is common to see musicians warming their instruments by blowing down the bore. This is a mistake, as it pre-loads the instrument with water, which condenses on the cold instrument. A better way to bring it up to temperature is by tucking the top section under your arm or inside a warm coat for ten minutes or so prior to playing. Then, when not playing, keep your hands wrapped around the upper section to keep it warm. A warm instrument is also slightly easier to assemble, as the grease on the joins will be softer, enabling the parts to slide together smoothly.

How to reduce the problem of water collecting in the tone holes

It is not uncommon for musicians to complain about bubbling notes or water under the pads that stop the instrument from playing correctly. Problems with water condensation can be reduced by thinking about how the instrument is held when waiting to be played. Instruments are designed to have the tone holes go into the bore on the upper side of the tube, the side that is uppermost when being played. Any water that accumulates then drains down the lower side of the bore, away from the tone holes. Therefore, it is a mistake to turn the instrument over and have the side with tone holes facing downwards when not actually playing it. All that happens then is that the water flows into the tone holes, just where you don't want it to go.

Aftercare

After playing the instrument, it will be warm and wet inside, so it is good to disassemble, clean, and dry it. The section or joint that needs the most attention is the upper one, as it will have the most condensation in it. In all cases, do not pull the swab through the instrument quickly. The idea is to use the absorbent swab material to suck water out of the tone holes, so you need to give it time to do that. Pull the swab into the top joint and leave it there for a minute or two before pulling it back out again. If you pull the swab through the tube quickly, you will scrape the water into the tone holes and leave it there.

A good lint-free swab or pull-through is recommended (Wood, Wind & Reed developed the Dryer Swab for this purpose).

Oboes need particular care and attention since they have very narrow, tapered bores with tiny octave holes at the top of the instrument. If possible, use a very thin pull-through or swab, inserting the pull cord through the socket where the reed goes. When the cord reaches the other end, slowly pull the swab through the instrument, leaving it time to absorb water on its way. I believe it is a mistake to swab from the bottom upwards on an oboe because the swab will pick up water on its way up the tube, and at the same time the taper of the bore will start to compress the cloth and try to squeeze the water back out again. The easiest place for the water to go into will be into the tone holes and octave holes as it goes past – the very thing you are trying to avoid.

Keeping instruments assembled will cause the cork seals on the instrument to become permanently compressed and ineffective.

There are only a few pads that are spoiled on a saxophone by being kept wet: these are the palm key pads, G# pad and the closed standing Eb pad at the bottom of the instrument. Using a pad saver (fluffy stick) or pull-through has limited effect on keeping these holes dry; a better solution is to take the time to prop those keys open when not in use.

One common complaint from musicians is that they have a 'sticky pad'. This causes a clicking sound to be made when a pad is lifted from the tone hole. It is most common on pads that are normally left closed on the instrument (for instance, the G# pads on flutes or saxophones). The common explanation is that a sticky residue has accumulated between the pad surface and the bedplate tone hole rim. This can be treated with Yamaha powder paper or cleaning paper.

If the pad is damp, then capillary action of the water is acting like an adhesive; the solution therefore is to dry the pad. Some people have found that the skin or leather used on the pad is causing the problem, so changing the pad can solve it.

If you have a persistent problem with sticky pads on a saxophone, it is worth polishing the tone hole rims with a fine 3M 40-micron wet and dry paper. During the tone hole levelling or lacquering process, very small burrs can be created on the tone hole rim. These will not only retain contaminates, but also snag the pad surface, enough to stop it opening easily.

Lubrication

Cork grease is used on the cork seals between the instrument's sections or joints, and a fine oil is used to lubricate keywork mechanisms.

Oiling keywork will make it quieter and smoother. The repairer/technician is best placed to do this, as whoever undertakes this task should have a good understanding of the different oils available, their viscosity, and which is best for which instrument. Oiling should be done by removing the screw of each key and putting the small drop of oil in the pivot hole or rod and then reassembling.

It is not recommended to deliver the oil to the junctions between key and pillar as it is likely to run on the outside of the key and attract dust and grit, which will cause longer-term problems. Do not be tempted to use car engine oil or wood oil like linseed oil or domestic 'three in one oil'; these have additives in them that may become sticky over time. I do not recommend Vaseline or pure petroleum jelly on cork joints as it acts as a solvent on the contact adhesive.

Oiling the bore

Bore oil is the trade name for an oil we put on wooden instruments' bodies. The primary purpose of oiling is to prevent the cracking of the body, though there is some evidence that it can also change the tonal quality of the instrument too.

As a maker of boxwood clarinets, I know how important it is to stabilize the wood once the instrument is made. Woodwind instruments are constantly in contact with water when played, and then left for periods of time when they can dry out. The wood is therefore subjected to stresses and strains. To slow down the migration of water in and out of the wood, we try to block the end grain of the wood, which is where the migration takes place. End grain is found in every tone hole and at the ends of each joint of the instrument. I developed a method of sealing my instruments by vacuum impregnating the finished bodies with a drying oil (one that hardens) called tung oil (mixed with 20 per cent citrus oil).

Blackwood is a much denser and more resinous wood than boxwood, but it is still subject to some shrinking as it dries out, only more slowly than boxwood (and most other woods).

Unlike boxwood instruments, the risk of cracking a blackwood instrument is very low and the manufacturers take measures to stop them cracking by carefully seasoning and oiling the wood during manufacture.

As repairers we are concerned with the maintenance of the instrument, so we have to decide if and how we should maintain the wood. This topic has generated many discussions and debates over the years, mainly because there is no obvious way of actually testing the issue – we have to rely on anecdotal evidence. For example, repairer A will say that they have worked on instruments for forty years and never oiled an instrument and they only had a few cracks, whilst repairer B will say they always

Fig. 5.1 Bore oil.

oil with X brand of oil and have never had a cracked instrument. There is not much to be learned from those experiences. I have tried to make an instrument crack by blocking all the holes and filling the instrument with warm water, then standing it over a hot radiator for a week. It did not crack. So I am not sure what is to be learned from that either!

In summary, if you choose the right oil, it is unlikely to cause any harm, so it is probably worth oiling the bodies of wooden instruments occasionally, let's say every few years. If the wrong oil, for instance a drying oil, is used, or the oil is applied in the wrong way, by letting it touch the pads, it can cause harm. Here are my experiences of different oils:

- Linseed oil is often talked about, but in my opinion, it is not a good choice. It comes in two forms, raw and boiled. They are both drying oils which means they harden over time and form a varnish. Boiled linseed oil dries in days, and raw oil takes months. It is also a hydrophilic oil, which means it likes or absorbs water, which is not what I want.
- Proprietary bore oils are petroleum-based, non-drying oils with very low viscosity. They are hydrophobic and will repel water, and do not form a varnish. In my opinion, they will not do any harm and may help.
- Clove oil is non-drying oil with a distinct (pleasant) smell and is anti-microbial – a good choice.
- Balistol is a German product that can be used on metal and wood. It is food-safe and has both very volatile and heavy oils mixed in it. It is non-drying and good at penetrating. My favourite all-round choice.
- Almond oil is a hydrophilic oil; in other words, it will absorb water and mixes with water, so is not very effective as a bore oil. It is, however, non-drying, so it will not form a varnish layer on the bore.

When you apply any oil, make sure you take all the keys off and clean the tone holes, paying special attention to those keys with undercut tone holes. Apply the oil sparingly, both inside and out, and make sure the insides of the tone hole are coated, as it is the end grain in the tone holes that need to be sealed. Leave the instrument to absorb the oil for several hours or days and then wipe off the excess before putting the keys back on.

PART TWO

Instrument Anatomy

CHAPTER 6

The Main Sections of Each Instrument

This section offers some background information that we will build on during the rest of this book. You are probably familiar with the main parts of most woodwind instruments; however, since people refer to the parts in a variety of ways, I have named each part to avoid confusion. This chapter names the different instrument joints and the materials used to make them; Chapter 7 goes into more detail about the components of an instrument.

Woodwind instruments are tubes that comprise of two or more sections we call joints. The hole down the length of each joint is known as the bore. The tube wall has a series of holes in it called tone holes. The sections are connected with a tenon and socket joint that must be airtight.

Clarinet

The strengthening rings around the joints, and sometimes the bell, are usually made from metal, though chrome-plated plastic is now being used on some budget instruments, and carbon fibre on some premium instruments. Keywork is electroplated nickel silver or bronze alloy. The majority of blackwood instruments are also stained black to make the overall appearance uniform.

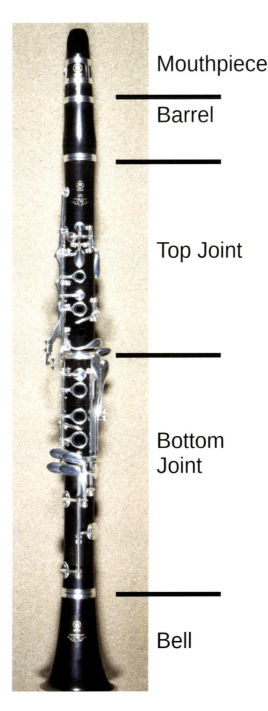

Fig. 6.1 Yamaha intermediate blackwood clarinet YCL650.
Mouthpiece: made from plastic or ebonite.
Barrel: usually made of the same material as the lower joints (barrels can also be purchased separately so may not always match the design, material or manufacture of the rest of the instrument).
Top joint, bottom joint and bell: student instruments are usually made from plastic, if not, it will be blackwood; a few are made with composite materials.

Flute

Apart from the few solid gold flutes that have been made, flutes are silver in colour. The majority are made from nickel silver with a thin layer of silver plating over the top. There are some which have a solid silver head joint, with the rest of the instrument being silver-plated nickel silver. A few are solid silver throughout.

It is worth knowing that on high-quality instruments there is sometimes a layer of rhodium plating over the silver. It is impossible to tell if an instrument has a rhodium coating unless it is in the manufacturer's specification. It is reasonable to assume that when a five-year-old instrument is untarnished, it might be rhodium plated. The keywork is nickel silver, brass or bronze and is electroplated. Very few instruments have solid silver keys.

Saxophone

Saxophones are usually lacquered – clear, gold-tinted or coloured. Black nickel plating was introduced in the 1980s and silver-plated instruments are favoured by military and brass bands. From the 1980s onwards, the lacquer has usually been acrylic or epoxy and is heat resistant. Earlier lacquers were cellulose-based and burn and discolour very quickly. It is worth knowing that from the 1990s, silver-plated instruments usually have a thin, clear lacquer coating to prevent tarnishing. It is best not to use silver polish on these instruments. Keilwerth makes a range of saxophones from nickel silver. The keywork is brass; the best manufacturers also include some keys with nickel silver pivot rods to increase strength and rigidity.

Oboe

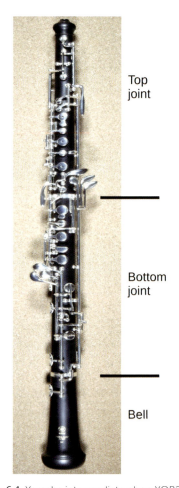

Fig. 6.4 Yamaha intermediate oboe YOB241. Top joint, bottom joint, bell: the vast majority are made from blackwood. A few are made with plastic, composite materials or rosewood.

Some student and intermediate instruments are made from plastic, but most oboes are made from African blackwood. Buffet in France used a resin-lined blackwood design for their student and intermediate instruments in the 1990s. Since 2020 some premium manufacturers have introduced resin, plastic or ebonite sections for the top joint of their instruments. Keywork is nickel silver, brass or bronze alloy that has been electroplated.

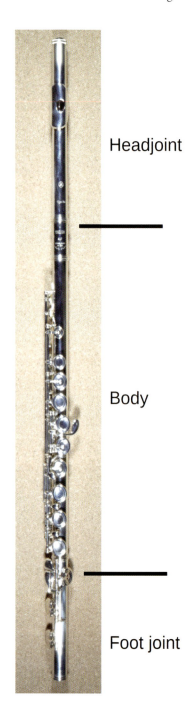

Fig. 6.2 Yamaha intermediate flute with solid silver head joint YFL312.
Head joint, body, foot joint: usually made from silver-plated metal; some are solid silver, and a few are gold or other precious metals

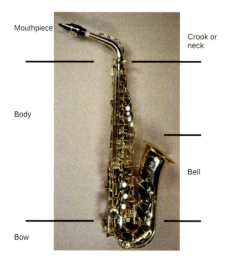

Fig. 6.3 Yamaha intermediate saxophone YAS480.
Mouthpiece: made from plastic, ebonite or metal.
Neck or crook and main body: the vast majority are made from brass; bronze is becoming more common, and silver is occasionally used.

58   The Main Sections of Each Instrument

Bassoon

The vast majority of bassoons are made from maple wood. Manufacturers in the US have made resin instruments; although they are very resonant and stable, they are also very heavy. You may still come across French system bassoons which are made of rosewood.

Wood, Wind & Reed commissioned a model of mini bassoon which, although it is made of plastic, it is light enough for children to handle.

The keywork is usually made from nickel silver. Some are made of a newer, high-performance bronze alloy as their long length requires strength and stiffness. The keys are electroplated.

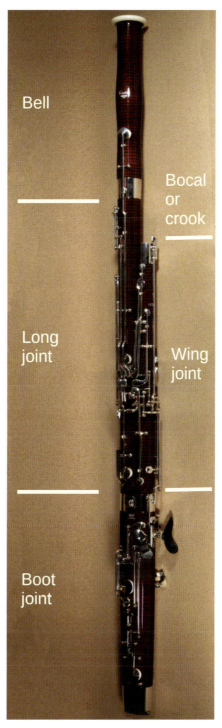

Fig. 6.5 Yamaha custom bassoon YFG81.
Crook or bocal: electroplated metal or solid silver.
Top or wing joint, boot joint, long joint, bell: maple wood.

The Main Sections of Each Instrument

CHAPTER 7

Bodywork Components

So far in the book, we have been working with bits of the instrument, without necessarily knowing much about them or even what they are called. In this section we find out what each part is and how they relate to the functioning of the instrument.

Tenons and sockets

The different joints of the instrument connect using a tenon and socket arrangement; the tenon fits inside the socket. On metal instruments the airtight seal is achieved by close contact of metal to metal. On wooden and plastic instruments, a cork seal is used.

Cork tenon and socket

This is typical for wooden or plastic instruments (Fig. 7.1). Over the years, manufacturers have experimented with subtle tapers in the shape of the socket and slightly different diameters on either side of the cork seal. The important thing is that the two joints are reliably held together with minimum opportunity to rock from side to side or allow air to escape.

Metal tenon and socket

Metal sockets can be found on flutes, piccolos and between the neck and the body of a saxophone (Fig. 7.2). The airtight seal relies on close metal-to-metal contact. (The lock screw on a saxophone neck socket is not to make it airtight but to stop the neck rotating whilst in use.)

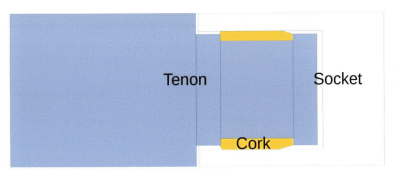

Fig. 7.1 Diagram of a tenon and socket with a cork seal.

Fig. 7.2 Cross section of a metal tenon and socket.

Tone holes

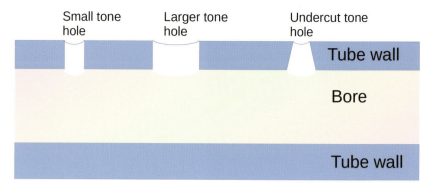

Fig. 7.3 Small, larger and tapered tone holes.

The name 'tone hole' is used because, when covered by a finger or key pad, the note the instrument sounds is altered. They start off as round parallel holes at very precise positions and diameters along the tube. The manufacturer can change the tuning of a note in the different registers by changing the position, the diameter and also the amount of taper the hole has. Tone holes of metal instruments can be soldered onto the body or drawn out of the metal tube.

Fig. 7.4 shows a clarinet tone hole with an undercut; like the undercut tone hole in the diagram, it is wider at the bore side than the outside.

Bed plates and tone hole rims

The cross section of a tone hole (Fig. 7.5) also shows the profile of the bed plate. On metal instruments there is no bed plate, only the tone hole rim. A tone hole that is closed by a pad will have a tone hole rim which is designed to make it easy for the pad to seal the hole. On wooden and plastic instruments, the area around the rim is called the bed plate and is to vent the air vibrations away from the instrument. The design of the tone hole rim should be specific to the pad material. A tone hole rim for a cork pad should be different from one designed for a leather pad. The rim of metal instruments can be rolled over to form a smooth top or may be left as a cut surface.

Fig. 7.4 The process of tapering a hole from the inside of the tube is called undercutting. This photo shows a clarinet top joint that has been cut lengthwise to show an undercut hole.

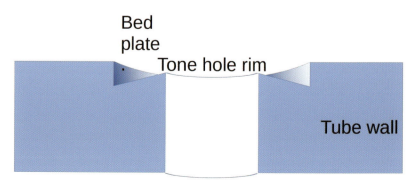

Fig. 7.5 A bed plate.

Pillars

These are the metal posts that support the keywork on the body (Fig. 7.6). Different body materials require different methods of attachment. On wooden instruments they can be screwed directly into the wood or onto a foot plate, having one or two wood screws on either side. Nearly all pillars will have a hole in the head that will be threaded or plain. The threads are delicate and are easily damaged if screws are incorrectly inserted (Fig. 7.7).

The manufacturer might use this design if the pillar is close to a fragile part of the instrument – for example, near the tenon or a tone hole, or if a spring is fitted that will try to unscrew a screwed pillar.

Plastic instruments use the same methods as above, plus the pillar can be 'press fitted' directly into the plastic or have brass inserts pressed into the body, into which the pillar is screwed.

Metal instruments have their pillars attached to a foot plate or a strap using silver solder. (A strap is a large foot plate with multiple pillars on it.) The strap or foot plate is then soft-soldered to the body. In general, the bigger the surface area of the foot plate, or when a strap is used, the more robust the instrument will be. Some high-end manufacturers use the strap or foot plate size as an acoustic influencer.

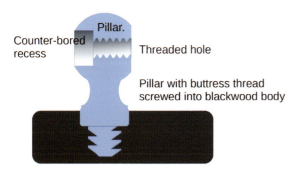

Fig. 7.6 The standard pillar for a wooden or plastic instrument. It has what is known as a buttress thread that screws into the body. The profile of the thread is designed for use into wood.

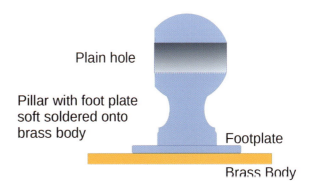

Fig. 7.8 This is the way that many saxophone pillars are attached. The pillar is silver soldered to a small plate; this plate is then soft soldered to the body of the saxophone.

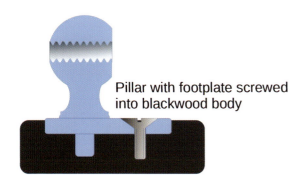

Fig. 7.7 Pillar with a screwed footplate.

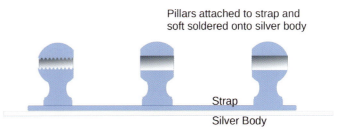

Fig. 7.9 Here we have a stack of flute pillars. Each pillar is silver soldered to a long strip of metal. This strip, or strap, is then soft soldered to the body of the flute.

CHAPTER 8

Keywork

By keywork I mean all the keys and the mechanisms and parts that connect them. We'll start with the keys themselves.

The keys of an instrument are the metal components that open and close the holes in the body tube. They come in different shapes and sizes with a variety of features. There are no common features between all keys. Any one key can have several of the features. For example, a pad key can also be a vent key. They don't all have a pad, or touch piece or tail. As you gain more experience you will become familiar with their uniqueness. I will describe the fixed components and the replaceable components.

Parts of a key

The instrument body is represented at the bottom of Fig. 8.1; a tone hole and bed plate are also represented. Above the tone hole is a yellow pad. This pad fits inside the rim of the pad cup on the key. The pad cup is attached to the pivot rod or hinge tube by the arm. On the opposite side of the axle is another type of arm called the tail. A tail usually has a cork or felt (often called a bumper) on its underside to regulate the height the key opens to, and to reduce the noise when the tail hits the body.

Touch pieces and touch keys

The area of a key which the finger or hand touches is called the touch piece. A key that has a touch piece is called a touch key (Fig. 8.2).

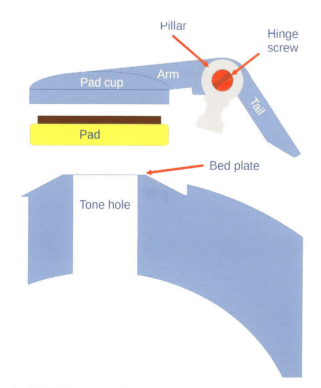

Fig. 8.1 This is an exploded diagram of a key.

Fig. 8.2 A touch piece: the first octave key on a Yamaha oboe.

Pad cups and pad keys

This is the part of the key that holds the pad. Some keys have pad cups and some don't. A key with a pad cup is called a pad key. The example shown has two special features: a small vent hole in the middle of the pad cup and a spatula key extension. The spatula is to allow the musician to keep the pad shut whilst opening up the vent hole.

Fig. 8.3 A pad cup on a key. Note the small vent hole in the middle of the pad cup and a spatula key extension on the left-hand side of the photo (lower side of the key when being played).

Tails

The tail of a key is used to limit the extent to which a pad can open. There is a regulation cork under each arm, called the bumper. The cork also makes the mechanism quieter than a metal-to-metal connection.

Fig. 8.4 Two tails on a Yamaha flute.

Link keys

A link key is a key that connects with another key. The part of a link key that touches another link key is called a link arm. This may have cork, felt, or an adjusting screw at the point of contact. The link key shown here has an adjusting cork.

Fig. 8.5 A link key. The two parts (link arms) are apart at the moment, but link (connect) together when needed.

Rocker keys

A rocker key has an axle across the body and transfers motion from one key to another. An example is the double rocker mechanism on some oboes, as seen in this photo.

Levers

A lever is a rocker key with a touch piece.

Adjusting screws

Adjusting screws are used to change the relationship of one key to another, or a key to the body of the instrument. As with so many things, small physical differences can make a big difference to the performance of an object. The adjusting screw is no exception.

On the left of Fig. 8.7 you have a traditional adjusting screw, with a head that is larger in diameter than the thread. There is plenty of material to make a strong screwdriver slot. It has a curved or domed bottom that will provide a progressive engagement with the silencing cork. The screw receiver is counter-bored to allow the domed screw head to fit inside. This not only reduces the sharp corners, it also makes it easier for the adjusting screw to be locked in place and it also looks great.

The middle diagram of Fig. 8.7 shows an adjusting screw that is cheaper to manufacture. It has a rolled thread which leaves the bottom end uneven, which in turn makes the adjustment and silencing more difficult. The screwdriver slot is much smaller and weaker and there is less stability in the unit.

The adjusting screw on the right of Fig. 8.7 is a Yamaha flute adjuster which is designed to be very compact and stable. The yellow insert is made of nylon and grips and stabilizes the screw. It has just the right amount of friction to avoid putting the screw head under undue stress and will not work loose.

It is important to understand which type of adjusting screw you are adjusting, as it is possible, for example, that you could be trying to screw in a traditional screw that won't go in any further because the head has locked up in the counter-bore.

There is one extra complication when it comes to adjusting screws and that is when the manufacturer does not shape the end of the screw appropriately. In Fig. 8.8 you can see that the nylon tip of the screw is cut at an angle. This will

Fig. 8.6 Two rocker keys on the bottom joint of a professional oboe.

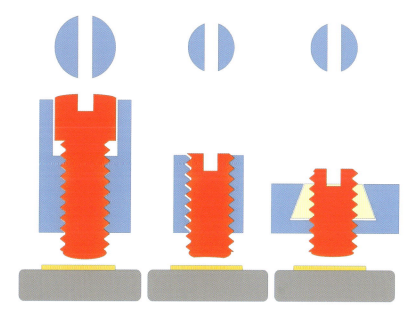

Fig. 8.7 Adjusting screws.

Fig. 8.8 Adjusting screw cut at an angle.

Keywork 67

make the adjustment very inconsistent, as in Fig. 8.9.

One way to solve this problem is to gently heat the end of the adjusting screw over a hot air gun or flame. Surface tension will make it into a dome shape (Fig. 8.10).

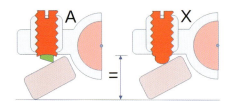
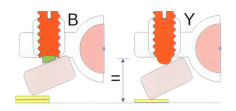
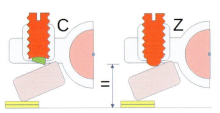

Fig. 8.10 Improved adjusting screw with a domed tip.

Fig. 8.9 Why an angled adjusting screw is a problem. The left-hand column has a screw with an angled tip, the right-hand column has a domed tip. On each row I have shown half a turn of the screw. Look at the amount of movement, represented by the yellow blocks. The domed tip has a progressive adjustment; the angled tip does not.

Feather keys

This configuration is unique to the oboe and cor-anglais and describes a group of keys considered to be in a fleur de lys shape.

Fig. 8.11 Oboe feather keys.

Spring hitches

One end of a needle spring is fixed, usually in a pillar; the other end pushes against the key to make it open or close as required. The point at which the spring contacts the key is called the spring hitch.

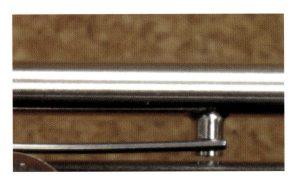

Fig. 8.12 A wire spring hitched in position on a YOB241 oboe.

Ring keys

Not all tone holes are covered by a pad. Some keys are closed by the finger alone and others by a combination of a finger and a ring key.

Fig. 8.13 A ring key.

Vent keys and vent holes

A vent hole is one that, when open, aids the venting of a key nearby. It is used in combination with another pad to achieve the correct pitch or tone.

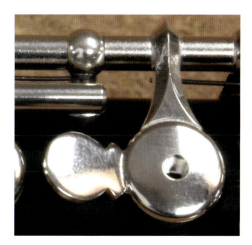

Fig. 8.14 Vent hole in the centre of a pad.

Key rollers

These are plastic rollers, often found on saxophones, that facilitate the smooth transition from one touch piece to another.

Key guards

Key guards are mostly found on saxophones and bassoons. Don't be shy about removing the guards to get better access to the tone holes or to get keys off. On student instruments the guards can be quite simple and not very strong, so check they are in the correct position as they can affect the vent height of certain keys.

Fig. 8.15 Key rollers.

Keywork

Key pearls

Key pearls are the plastic buttons that are placed on saxophone keys for the fingers. Older instruments will have natural mother-of-pearl buttons, but since the 1960s they moved to plastic. When heating the keywork to replace a pad, be careful not to melt the plastic pearls.

Pivot keys

Pivot keys are characterized by having pivot screws at each end and a pivot rod spanning the gap between them. So if you look at the key and it has short holes at each end, it is called a pivot key.

Pivot screws

A pivot key is held in place at each end with a small screw called a pivot screw. There are two types of pivot screw: one has a point at the end (point screw) and the other has a parallel end (barrel screw). There are different designs of point screw: the bullet point screw and the headless point screw.

Fig. 8.16 This is a close-up photo of a typical point screw to show its size.

Both designs of pivot screw are about 6mm long and 2mm in diameter.

The best design of pivot screw for a wooden instrument is the bullet point screw, as it can be adjusted to give a perfect action.

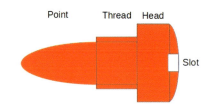

Fig. 8.17 Anatomy of a point screw. The large end on the right of the picture, is called the head, and the shoulder is where the head reduces in diameter to a threaded section. The head has a slot for a screwdriver blade. The point can be of various shapes and protrudes from a pillar to support the key. This one has a bullet style point.

Fig. 8.18 A high-quality Yamaha bullet point screw. This example has a curved point.

As the name suggests, the headless point screw does not have a head so it cannot lock against the pillar. This makes it very easy to over-tighten the screw. Most manufacturers use a Nyloc system to add friction to the screw and keep the screw in the correct position. If the original Nyloc stops working, then you can use a low shear threadlocking adhesive (Loctite 222). Be careful how much adhesive you use – I have been caught out when the liquid has crept down the screw and into the bearing, making it sticky.

Fig. 8.19 Headless point screw.

Fig. 8.20 This pivot screw is classified as a barrel or parallel screw. It is about 6mm long and the pin is 1.3mm in diameter. The parallel pin fits into a parallel hole in the pivot rod.

Barrel screws are the best design of pivot screw for a plastic or metal instrument; they are particularly suitable for plastic instruments as plastic expands and contracts a lot more than the metal keywork does. As a plastic instrument warms up, the distance between the pillars increases; the metal keys don't lengthen to the same degree. The parallel pivot is able to slide in and out of the parallel hole in the pivot rod without changing how much the key can move across the axis. This keeps the pad in the correct plane to keep the pad seated.

Point screw or barrel screw?

To confirm what type of pivot screw a key needs, look at the hole in the end of the pivot rod. If the hole is conical it uses a point screw, otherwise it will be a parallel or plain hole and requires a barrel screw.

Fig. 8.21 Though this screw has a point on the end, it is a barrel screw. The key has a parallel hole in the pivot rod. The point on the screw is to help the assembler to quickly locate the hole.

Pivot rods

The pivot rod is a solid rod with a hole at each end which fits between two pillars; the pivot screws fit into it.

Other pivot screw designs

Selmer spring-loaded point screw

In the 1980s Selmer Paris introduced a clever spring-loaded point screw that has proved very successful. This design has the advantages of both the barrel screw and the point screw.

Captive barrel screw design

I have also come across some alternative designs such as the brilliant captive barrel screw design by Pieter Wolf in Germany (www.guntramwolf.de), a great solution for bassoons and other large instruments.

Rudall Carte point screw

This is a very shallow pointed screw which is very slightly curved. It fits into shallow, straight-sided cones in keys. (I wonder if the idea for this came from the 1867 flute design that required the keywork to fit into tight spaces between pillars.)

Hinge screws

The other way a key is attached to the instrument is with a parallel metal rod called a hinge screw. The hinge screw goes through a pillar then right through a hinge tube (the key) and screws into a pillar at the far end. (Some early bassoons use a simple push fit pin.) Keys attached with a hinge screw are called hinge keys.

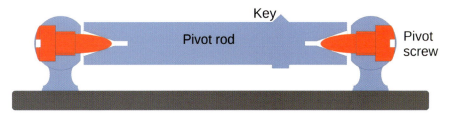

Fig. 8.22 Anatomy of pivot key. This diagram shows the pillars at each side attached to the black body and the pillars have red pivot screws in them. The pivot rod is the blue bar between the pillars.

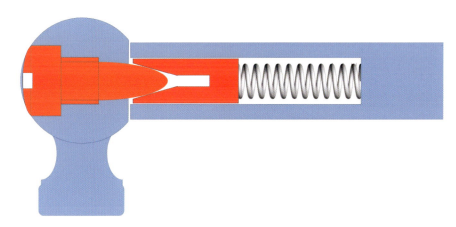

Fig. 8.23 Selmer's spring-loaded point screw mechanism.

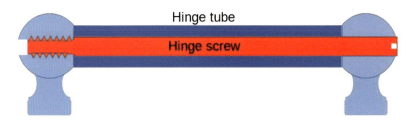

Fig. 8.24 When a key pivots around a long axle like the one in the diagram it is known as a hinge key. It is made from a hinge tube and a hinge screw.

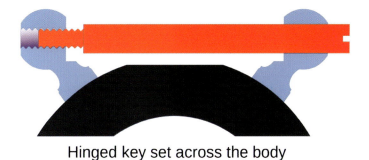

Fig. 8.25 Diagram of a hinge screw mounted across the body of a wooden instrument.

Keywork mechanisms

There are three types of key mechanism: pivot keys, hinge keys and combination keys. In this section you will be introduced to the parts that make up each type of mechanism. Methods for adjustment are covered in Chapter 11.

Stacks

A group of keys running on one hinge screw is called a stack. In many cases, a key on a stack will move another one in the stack, usually by a link arm between the adjacent keys.

Stack of pillars and keys. The hinge screw is most of the way through

Fig. 8.26 A stack is a row of keys are all supported on one hinge screw. In this diagram we have three keys set between four pillars.

Fig. 8.27 This stack is on the top joint of a Yamaha oboe.

Joins

A join is an area where friction can occur. For example, stacks are made up of several keys, all with hinge tubes, running on the hinge screw. The point at which each section of tube touches is what I am calling the join. This includes the ends of the keys where they meet their pillar.

Fig. 8.28 In this picture there are three joins on a stack with two keys. There is one join at each end where the hinge tube meets the pillars and there is one join just visible in the middle, just on the left of the central key arm. This Yamaha oboe is so well made that the join is almost invisible.

Hinge screws with pivot screws

The two ring keys shown in Fig. 8.29 are an example of keys held on with a hinge screw, which has a pivot point at the end to hold the second key.

Fig. 8.29 Two ring keys on a hinge screw with pivot point.

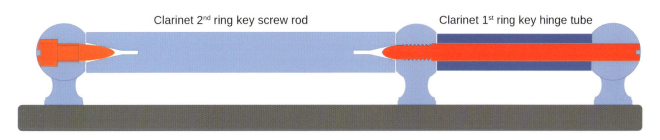

Fig. 8.30 Hinge screw with a point for another key at the end.

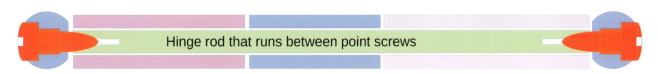

Fig. 8.31 This stack has a hinge rod, supported by point screws at each end.

Combination keys

A combination key has an axle called a hinge rod, which can rotate between the pivot screws. The hinge keys can rotate independently on the hinge rod.

Bridge keys

A bridge key connects two non-adjacent parts of the same key.

The advantages of bridge keys are that they are mechanically simple, easy to assemble and easy to maintain. The disadvantages are that they add weight to the mechanism and can be bulky. It is sometimes tricky to get complex mechanisms to fit in the space available.

Fig. 8.32 The bridge key in this photo is the bar that is curved at both ends, spanning most of the photo.

Keywork 73

Pinned hinge rods

Another way two non-adjacent parts of the same key can be connected (bridged) is with a pinned hinge rod, as shown in Fig. 8.33.

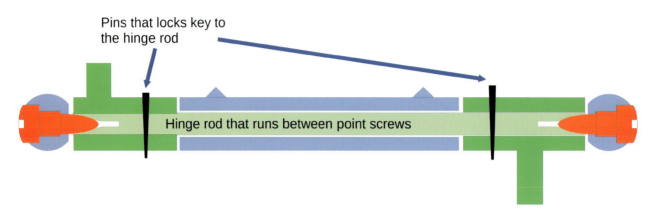

Fig. 8.33 A pinned bridge key. The diagram represents part of the right-hand stack of a flute (the pad cups are not shown). The light green parts are locked together with the pins to form one key.

Pinned hinge rods with clutch plates

All the keys that make up the stack have hinge tubes, but instead of a hinge screw there is a hinge rod that pivots on a pivot screw at each end. This assembled stack is then mounted between the pillars with pivot screws.

Other methods of locking the hinge rod to the keys include:

- Having a hinge rod with a splined end to the shaft, which pushes into the hinge tube.
- Having a very small grub screw that tightens up onto the hinge rod using an Allen key (Pearl flutes).
- Having very small screws rather than a pin that goes across the key and hinge rod (usually found on oboes).

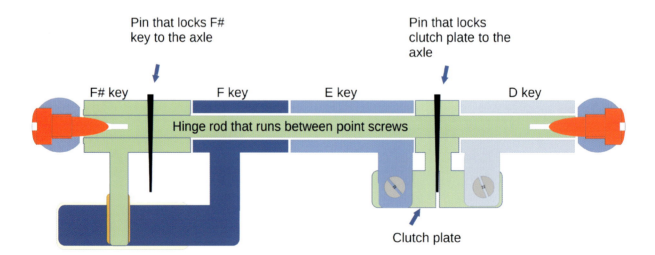

Fig. 8.34 This stack is a combination key with a pinned clutch plate. In this diagram, the F♯ key and the clutch plate are pinned to the hinge rod and are therefore fixed together to make one unit. The other keys are free to rotate independently.

Replaceable parts

There are a number of pieces on woodwind instruments that are expected to be replaced periodically.

Pads

The purpose of a pad is to make an airtight seal on the tone hole rim. The choice of pad material and construction has changed over the years. Over the last forty years there has been a move from soft pads to hard pads in flutes. On oboes there has been a move from softer leather or bladder pads to cork pads which are much harder.

Pads are circular in shape and the conventional construction is a cardboard disc with a layer of felt on top, then wrapped in an airtight membrane, which is glued onto the cardboard. The membrane is either highly processed animal membrane, synthetic membrane, or very thin leather. The leather used is tanned or cured in a special way and is called a pneumatic split. The leather is airtight but not waterproof, so the best leather pads have a thin layer of polythene between the leather and the felt.

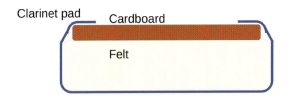

Fig. 8.35 Anatomy of a clarinet pad. This particular example has what is known as a French step. The cardboard is smaller in diameter than the felt. They sit better in the pad cup and can be manipulated more easily.

Fig. 8.36 Anatomy of an oboe or bassoon pad. On traditional oboe and bassoon pads the cardboard is much thinner and more flexible. The felt and cardboard are usually the same diameter. The flexible back is especially useful when seating bassoon pads as they are often very undulating. A bassoon pad is always covered in leather, not bladder.

Fig. 8.37 Anatomy of an open hole flute pad. The cardboard and felt discs are the same size. The cardboard is usually quite thin on pads for professional instruments; this allows small pieces of washer paper to be inserted behind the pad to profile the top surface to match the tone hole profile.

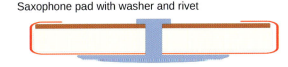

Fig. 8.38 Anatomy of a saxophone pad. The rivet is used to hold the large expanse of leather in place and reflect the sound out of the instrument.

Fig. 8.39 Anatomy of a cork oboe pad. The cork pad might need to be plain or have a hole in the centre.

Fig. 8.40 Anatomy of a synthetic pad. A good synthetic pad will have a rigid backing and softer seating material.

Cork

Cork is the bark of a cork oak. It has the unique property among natural materials of being able to be compressed and then return to its original shape without pushing outwards or pulling inwards the material that surrounds it. It will shrink and become brittle when allowed to dry out completely and cannot be re-hydrated.

Felts

There are many variations of two basic types of felt in woodwind instruments. The most common is simply called felt. Felt is made from animal, plant or synthetic fibres that are meshed together with the use of felting needles. The end product is a firm or springy fabric with no layers, grain, or weave. It can be cut in any direction, and it will stay together. If the felting process is applied to a woven fabric, it becomes a material called box cloth (used on top-quality snooker tables), so called because it was originally used to line boxes and chests. Box cloth was mainly used in the manufacture of flute pads. Felts come in a wide range of colours, thicknesses and as a raw material.

Fig. 8.41 This is a piece of thick felt that can be cut to make bumpers for saxophones. The piano industry uses a lot of felt and can be a good source.

Fig. 8.42 Box cloth.

Springs

Needle springs

These are traditionally blue steel springs and are used to keep a key open or shut as required. They are derived from the sewing needle manufacturing process and have a pointed end. It is now more common for manufacturers to use plain wire springs, which are not pointed (though we still refer to them as needle springs).

Needle springs come in sizes from No. 12 (0.35mm diameter) through to No. 000 (1.4mm diameter) in 0.15mm increments. The choice of spring diameter and material is chosen for you by the manufacturer and replacing like with like is important. These springs are held in place by the fishtail shape at the end that is pushed into the pillar.

Flat springs

Flat springs are found on the underside of keys and are used to keep keys open or shut as required. The exact curve of the spring can alter not only the weight of spring but also its feel.

Fig. 8.43 Selection of needle springs.

Fig. 8.44 Close-up of a flat spring attached to a key with a M1.2 screw onto a clarinet speaker key. The old imperial size would be 11 or 12 BA.

PART THREE

The Workshop and Repair Processes

CHAPTER 9

The Workshop

If you have got this far in the book, you are on your way to becoming a dedicated repairer. You might want to think about what sort of repair workshop you would like to run. You might decide to be a flute specialist, in which case you will need to invest in specialist equipment and practise on lots of different makes of flute. If you choose to be a competent generalist, you can set up a workshop with fairly modest equipment covering all woodwind. In this case, you need to be ready to turn away or pass on repairs such as crack-pinning, keywork repairs or those that require specialist tools and experience.

In all instances, it serves you and your clients to be professional and good at what you do. So the decision is not, 'How good am I going to be?' but rather, 'How specialized am I going to be?'

As with many professions, patience is helpful. Rushing things, cutting corners, and not checking what you have done only causes extra expense and embarrassment later.

It is possible to offer a professional and specialist service from a tiny workspace, such as a spare room or shed. It might be neat or chaotic; the way it looks will be part of your character. Those who have visited my workshops over the years will know that I always seem to fill the space I have. My actual workbench usually looks chaotic, but the workshop is organized and well set out. One of the big demands on space is the storage of instruments that are waiting to be repaired or collected.

The workbench

It is worth spending time making a bespoke workbench. Make it comfortable, efficient, and, if nothing else, getting the right height can prevent back pain in the future. For many operations, I like to work standing up, so I make part of my workbench high enough for that purpose.

Fig. 9.1 This is the workbench I have used for thirty years. It has been moved to different locations and re-sized several times. The things I like about it are:

- Its height
- The drawer under the main worktop
- The platform on the left (in white) for cutting cork
- The swan-neck LED light for close work
- Easy access to my pads
- Having all my tools within reach.

When creating my workbench, I started by choosing the stool and chair I liked the most. Then I tested out different heights of worktop with those seats. Since I also like a sliding drawer under my worktop, I had to make sure that my knees would clear the bottom of the drawer.

The drawer under the workbench gives me extra storage space and catches bits that fall.

Good lighting is essential. Overhead background lighting that does not create shadows is great and flat panel LED lights are perfect for this. A 600mm square panel over your bench is often enough. Like most repairers, I also have a 'task light' to focus on the work at hand. It does not have to be expensive. In my case, I have a magnification lens with combined LED lighting that is on an adjustable arm, and a swan-neck LED light.

Depending on your location, climate and type of work you are involved in, you might need to control the humidity in your workshop.

Fig. 9.3 Another view of my workbench. You can see that there are keys in a storage tray in the drawer, and I have the pliers I use most hung on the right side of my drawer. The new pads are easy to access, and my trusty wooden toolbox is on the right.

Fig. 9.4 Bench peg made from hardwood (one of two bench pegs I have on my desk). I found that the shape of the cone does matter: if it is too short, it requires too much pressure to keep the instrument in place; when it is too long there is a danger of splitting the instrument open.

Fig. 9.2 These flip-open storage boxes for pads sit to the right of my chair, in easy reach. I leave the container flipped open until I need another size of pad; that way I can easily find the right container if I need to return the pad.

Fig. 9.5 Bench block. This block of metal stores three grades of oil and a contact adhesive. Experiment with different diameters of dip stick to find the one that gives you exactly the amount of oil you want for each viscosity. By keeping the nozzle of the glue in a close-fitting hole it stays fresh and liquid.

Fig. 9.6 Here are two repair trays sitting in my bench drawer. I allocate each instrument to a separate tray during the repair process; that way all the parts are kept together. You can see green felt lining the tray to protect the instrument parts and make it easier to see pieces.

I like to have a high bench to do some repair jobs, so I spent time getting the right height for me. As a general rule, the top of your engineer's vice should be at the same height as your bent elbow when it is at your side.

General workshop tools

Vices and clamps

You might not be able to buy a vice with smooth jaws fitted so be prepared to hunt for smooth jaws or make some to fit to an existing vice. Many people simply cover the serrated jaws with a sheet of softer material like copper or aluminium. I personally think it is worth the effort to source smooth, hardened steel jaws. Check the quality of vice before buying; some I have seen are rather poor quality.

Fig. 9.7 Workbench at a comfortable standing height.

Fig. 9.9 Smooth jaw engineer's vice.

Fig. 9.10 This vice is great for holding dent rolling mandrels. It has both the 4-inch serrated jaws of an engineer's vice, and the V-shaped jaws of a pipe vice. I modified the vice by fitting a lock pin to stop it rotating when under extreme twisting load from the long saxophone mandrels.

Fig. 9.8 Having tools positioned at the correct height makes life more pleasant. This small drilling machine is raised up to a comfortable height on a wooden platform, with the tool bits stored below.

Fig. 9.11 Tool maker's clamps. These are remarkably versatile and can grip very tightly and precisely. I use them for spring removal, holding keywork, and for tool making. 50mm or 2in is a useful size.

The Workshop

Fig. 9.12 Pin vice.

Anvil

It is worth finding a good quality anvil or hardened steel block. It should be hard enough not to dent when hammering a fish tail on a blue needle spring.

Fig. 9.14 Hardened steel anvil.

Bench motor

The bench motor shown here, made in the UK by Peter Worrell, is designed specifically for the woodwind instrument trade. It has a hollow spindle to hold long rods. The small body allows you to rest your hand over the machine while using it, and this enables you to control your workpiece comfortably. The hand-wheel on the left end of the spindle can be used for handwork and slowing down the spindle. A foot pedal controls its variable-speed motor.

There are many easily available, high quality pin vices on the market. They can be used to hold needle springs, drills, cutting bits, punches, needle file handles, pinning wire and much more. If you have many pin vices you don't need to keep changing bits.

The simple clamp shown in Fig. 9.13 was made for me by my friend Rob Abineri. It's great for holding small parts when drilling.

Fig. 9.15 Bench motor.

Fig. 9.13 Universal clamp.

Hammers and mallets

Also called an engineer's hammer, a ball pein hammer has one end that is rounded. It is essential to have a good quality hammer, which won't dent when flattening needle springs.

A wooden mallet is a very useful tool for straightening keywork and gently moving pillars on saxophones. The beautiful example shown in Fig. 9.17 was made by a friend of mine, Pablo Pascual.

A 3-inch diameter rawhide mallet is the largest I have needed. They go down to 1 inch, which is also useful.

Fig. 9.16 Ball pein hammer.

Fig. 9.17 Wooden mallet.

Fig. 9.18 Rawhide mallet.

Fig. 9.19 Top: 8-inch Bahco Mill Saw file (model 4-138-08-1-0) gives a very smooth, flat finish.
Middle: 6-inch no. 4 cut pillar file.
Bottom: roach back or crossing file with an unequal oval section for curved surfaces.

Fig. 9.20 Swiss files. These are usually smaller than engineer's files and can come in many profiles (cross sections).

Fig. 9.21 File card.

Fig. 9.22 An antique jeweller's saw frame with a French design.

Files and saws

Try to keep different files for ferrous metals and non-ferrous metals. Don't let them bump against each other. A good file only used on brass or nickel silver will last for a few years.

I suggest starting with a ready-made kit and then adding extra files when you need them; for example, I find a barrette file is useful for filing undercuts.

A steel brush is used to remove material from between the teeth of a file. If the file card is not effective, then push a piece of brass along the line of the file teeth to clear the waste away.

Magnifying goggles

Fig. 9.23 Magnifying goggles.

Magnifying goggles are useful for the most intricate and fiddly aspects of instrument repair.

The Workshop

Tweezers and pliers

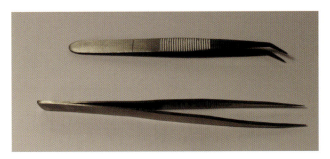

Fig. 9.24 The large round-nosed tweezers at the top are great for removing cork wedges from under the keys of new saxophones. The small tweezers at the front are used for positioning tiny pieces of silver solder and for placing adjusting papers on top-end flutes.

Fig. 9.25 High leverage pliers.

Cutters

Wad punches are sharp metal circular cutters for cutting felt and leather. High-performance shears for cutting sheet metal are also useful.

A sharps box is a safe place to keep your used razor blades before disposing of them appropriately.

Fig. 9.26 Wad punches.

Fig. 9.27 Metal cutting shears.

Fig. 9.28 Sharps box.

Health and safety

Whatever style of workshop you have, you need to keep health and safety in mind. It is not difficult or expensive – it just needs some thought. In the UK the rules now focus on risk assessment. Read up about any chemicals or materials you will use and follow their safety instructions and storage rules. If you are using a piece of machinery, get some education or read the manual and assess the risk to yourself and to others. A risk assessment helps you decide if the risk is low enough to be worth taking. Some repair procedures have to be undertaken without the safety guards, and this is a risk I have decided is worth taking. I have a risk assessment document that states that is the choice I have made. Here are some areas to consider:

- Trip hazards
- Dust
- Soldering fumes
- Damage from moving parts on lathes and drilling machines
- Chemicals
- Sharp blades and tools

In all cases, think about how to mitigate the risk. For example, don't wear loose clothing or jewellery and do wear closed-toe shoes, safety goggles, a mask, gloves, etc. as appropriate.

CHAPTER 10

Checking and Repairing Bodywork

The body of an instrument is the foundation for the keys and key mechanism. There are areas of the body that, if damaged, make it impossible for other parts of the instrument to work. In this section we will be checking the body for cracks, chips or breaks that would prevent it from creating a resonant air column. We will be checking and replacing tenon corks as part of this process.

Bodywork faults

A leak is an unwanted opportunity for air to escape. We commonly associate them with the pads on an instrument, but leaks can occur in the bodies of both wooden and metal instruments.

Wooden bodywork faults

It is not only cracks that can cause a leak in a wooden instrument; finger hole inserts and pillars can be the source of the problem too.

Cracks

Cracks in the wood can occur at any time during the instrument's history, but most often they will occur within the first year or so of significant use. Cracks don't happen very often, but feel traumatic when they do. In practice they are not such a big problem and repairing the crack is usually very effective. Cracks can directly affect the instrument's performance when the split passes across the tone hole or bed plate. On very rare occasions, it can be deep enough to allow air to pass from the inside to the outside of the instrument; these full-body splits usually happen in clarinet barrels. Most cracks are very shallow and can be filled and made invisible. Look for cracks before oiling the instrument, as oil will make the crack repair more difficult. If you suspect a crack – either because you can see visible signs, or the leak test shows a problem – start by looking at the tone hole bed plates and the finger bushes. Cracks are most common at the top of the instrument, running into or through the speaker key hole or between holes that are directly in line with each other, down the instrument (for instance, between the trill keys (O2 and O3) on an oboe or between the A tone hole (C5) and top ring keys (C3) of a clarinet). Cracks that go into tone holes will need special attention; please see the specialist repair section (Chapter 17).

Fig. 10.1 A crack going into a tone hole on the top joint of a clarinet.

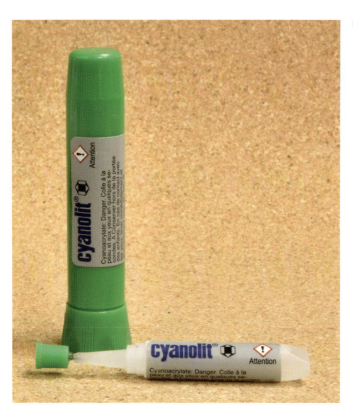

Fig. 10.2 Superglues.

The cyanoacrylate group of adhesives comes in a variety of viscosities. They work best with non-porous surfaces with a close fit. It is available in thin, medium, thick and gel. I use the thinnest variety, water thin, to fill cracks in wooden instruments; medium viscosity for chips in tone holes; and the gel for re-attaching tip rings and the like.

Each formulation and brand of superglue behaves differently, so please test and experiment with those available to you and read the technical specifications. Some don't like bonding rubber (ebonite), and some do. There is also an accelerator that helps to speed up the curing process. At the time of writing, I am using Hot Stuff, a formulation recommended by Ed Kraus, and Cyanolit suggested by Paul Van der Linden.

Repairing small surface cracks

To repair a shallow crack that does not look as if it will reach a tone hole you can simply fill it with very thin superglue. If the crack has been open for some time and looks like it might have grease or oil in it, swab the area with alcohol or degreasing agent.

Squeeze a small amount of superglue onto something non-absorbent, like metal or plastic, and using a needle spring, pick up one drop of glue, place the drop at the fine end of the crack and watch it be drawn into the crack. Add more glue until it's saturated. Move to the other end of the crack and repeat. Work your way slowly towards the middle of the crack. When the glue is set, file, sand, and polish away any excess glue. I suggest starting with a mill cut file, then move to fine wire wool or 3M fine Scotch-Brite. Finally, buff on a polishing mop.

Repairing larger cracks

If the crack goes into a tone hole or is very big you will need to refer to the pinning and tone hole replacement sections later in the book.

Loose finger bushes

Finger bushes are found mainly on clarinets and are the tone holes that fit within ring keys. If you look carefully, you will see the top of the chimney is raised above the surrounding body of the instrument; it is usually a separate piece of blackwood or plastic that is glued into the instrument's body during manufacture. The join where the insert is glued into a counter-bore can start to leak after several years, as shown by the white line on the right of Fig. 10.3. The solution is straightforward nowadays: you can apply a thin superglue to the area and it will soon find any gaps and seal them.

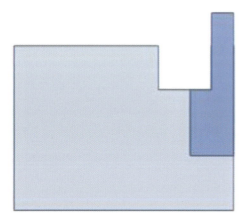
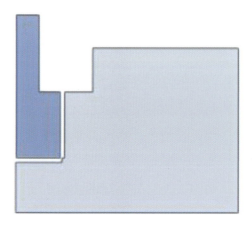

Fig. 10.3 Diagram showing the cross section of a finger bush which has been glued into the body of the instrument during manufacture.

Leaking pillars

I remember how surprised I was when I first came across an instrument that was leaking air from around a pillar, but it does happen. The bottom of the pillar hole can be quite close to the bore of the instrument and sometimes the pressure of trapped air or oil under the pillar when it is being screwed in can burst through into the bore. As usual, superglue comes to our rescue for this repair, but first you have to find the faulty pillar. I do this by packing Blu Tack around the base of each pillar in turn and testing the air tightness each time. In the past I have blown smoke into a sealed instrument and seen the smoke rise up around a pillar.

Loose or twisting pillars

Until the advent of modern adhesives, the only way to fix this problem was to pack out the pillar hole with pumice powder or paper washers. Now, however, we have epoxy and superglues that do a better job and faster. The great thing about these resin glues is that they are softened with heat, so if you need to change something later you can heat up the pillar and remove it. The only time an adhesive might not work well is when a needle spring is trying to force the pillar to unscrew all the time. This is most common on bassoons, but I have had problems with pillars on the bottom joints of older oboes.

Fig. 10.4 shows how Yamaha have very neatly screwed a pin next to the pillar; the spring takes the load and stops the pillar from unscrewing. You can create your own version of this if needed. An alternative is to lock the pillar itself. I have read about different methods for doing this which are quite complicated. My solution is very simple: drill a 0.8mm hole diagonally across the pillar and then push the blunt end of a needle spring down the hole to lock the pillar. It stops it from twisting and stabilizes it at the same time. Leave enough needle spring out of the pillar to be able to remove it in the future.

Chipped tone hole rims

Look for chips in the bed plates. The roughness on the surface of a tone hole

Fig. 10.4 The small screwed pin to the left of pillar that holds the needle spring will stop the pillar from rotating when the spring is under tension.

Fig. 10.5 Wood grain blemishes on tone hole rim.

Checking and Repairing Bodywork

can be caused by the tone hole cutting tool lifting the wood grain. These V-shaped nicks are quite fine but are enough to stop the pad from sealing correctly. The nicks in the upper left-hand side of the tone hole are larger than normal. On student and intermediate level instruments, fine blemishes can be removed using tone hole topping tools to flatten the rim. Take off as little material as possible, just enough for the nicks to have disappeared.

To deal with a larger chip and for professional-level instruments, you have to decide if a new tone hole is required or if you can repair the existing tone hole rim (replacement is covered in Chapter 17). To repair the tone hole, you can use a sharp needle spring to lightly roughen the wood in the area of the blemishes; this will give the glue a mechanical anchor and more surface area to adhere to. Using a needle spring, collect a small drop of medium or thick superglue and place it in the damaged tone hole. When hard, shape the glue to match the tone hole using a tone hole cutter if you have one, or you can use a file, scraper and abrasive film. Ensure that you do not leave the top of the tone hole with an uneven, undulating profile.

Removing thumb and speaker tubes

Speaker tubes and thumb hole bushes on clarinets can be held in position in a number of ways.

The most common is a push fit, often using hot shellac as a glue. These are pushed out by the curved handle of a small pair of pliers. Heat can be transferred to the end of, or inside, the tube with a hot rod of metal.

Others are screwed in; these will be indicated by a hexagonal top on the insert, or two holes at the top.

Thumb hole bushes can leak in the same way that finger holes can. It is desirable to orientate the internal curve (if it has one) to match the bore of the clarinet.

Metal bodywork repairs

The only place I remember finding a leak in the actual metal body of an instrument is on saxophone necks that have been bent and the side of the neck has split. Otherwise, it is always where one piece of metal joins another piece. This could be a fixed, soldered joint or a sliding joint, like you find on a flute head joint. We need to inspect and test these areas.

Flute bodywork faults

The most common problem is the head joint cork. The next most common problem is the sliding join between the main body and the foot joint. Very exceptionally will you come across a head joint socket that is no longer soldered to the main body.

Fig. 10.6 Removing a speaker tube using heat on the metal rod going into the speaker tube and using the handle of the pliers to lever out the speaker tube.

Flute bodywork repair tools and materials

Fig. 10.7 Flute tenon expander; this is used to expand the diameter of the flute body tube so it becomes a good fit into the corresponding socket.

Fig. 10.8 This is an adjustable hole burnishing tool. The blue section is a micro-adjusting mechanism that controls the diameter of the six rollers that can be seen just going into the flute bottom joint socket. I have recently started to use this tool to make flute sockets parallel, smooth, and round.

Fig. 10.9 You sometimes need to reduce the diameter of a flute tenon joint; there is very little option but to use a shrinking die. This is a hardened and polished steel collar with a slit down one side. this allows it to reduce in diameter under the pressure of the clamp. This reduction crushes, or 'swedges', the tube evenly into itself, making the diameter smaller.

Fig. 10.10 This mild steel tool is a low-cost version of the one above. It has one slit between the centre hole and an outer hole; each of the outer holes has a slit to the outside. This allows the tool to collapse inwards when the Allen key is tightened.

Fig. 10.11 Parallel flute mandrel, the correct size for the bore of a flute.

Fig. 10.12 A fine flute dent roller is useful when you need to work near a tone hole. This very clever design allows you to use both hands to apply even pressure on the roller. The polished rolling head is free at one end so it can be worked around the base of flute tone holes and in the narrow gaps between tone holes.

Fig. 10.13 This is a standard issue flute dent roller: a simple and effective design for the main body and head joint of flutes.

Fig. 10.14 Head joint mandrel: a tapered steel rod that fits inside the average flute head joint. This is held in a vice by the large end and is used to push the burnishing roller onto when removing dents or straightening a head joint.

Flute dents and bends

Fig. 10.15 Using a small roller next to a tone hole.

Most dents in flutes can be rolled out. The roller should be highly polished and very smooth, as marks on the roller will transfer themselves to the flute body. Support the instrument on a well-fitting mandrel held in a vice when rolling. If you need to get close to a tone hole, then the smaller roller pictured above works very well (Fig. 10.15).

If you have a flute where the main body has been folded or bent, it is sometimes best to use two mandrels, with one inserted at each end. That way you can get a good visual alignment and can then manipulate the tube as needed while keeping the rest of the body straight.

Flute tenon adjustment

A good flute tenon fit has a smooth sliding action that delivers an airtight seal and will not rotate while playing.

Check the socket is parallel

Before attempting to adjust the flute tenon, check that the inside of the socket is parallel (Fig. 10.16). Some low-cost flutes and even some more expensive instruments suffer from a tight entrance to the socket.

This is a manufacturing fault and is best addressed (if possible) before any other adjustment. Check for this constriction by measuring the internal diameter at various depths of the socket.

The constriction at the socket entrance is caused during manufacture when the end ring is soldered to the socket tube. The metal ring expands more than the socket as it heats up for soldering, and as it cools, it shrinks more so the thin metal tubing of the socket is crushed smaller. For many years, the only way I found to solve this problem was carefully scraping metal away from around the entrance, measuring frequently and then re-polishing the surface. If you choose this method, make the scraping as even as possible. During the polishing process, be very careful indeed and don't use anything other than 9-micron 3M film or 1200 grit wet and dry paper on the inside of the socket. Make sure you wipe and clear any debris after working; one tiny piece of grit can cause a problem later.

Once you have a parallel socket, use a roller burnishing tool, or another expanding tool, to increase the tenon's diameter slowly. I use various techniques: sometimes I will keep the instrument static while I tighten the expanding tool; on other occasions I will put a light grease on the surface of the tool and burnish the tube up and down on the expanding tool and slowly stretch the metal that way. My latest method is to use a roller burnishing tool (Fig. 10.8).

Keep testing the fit between socket and tenon.

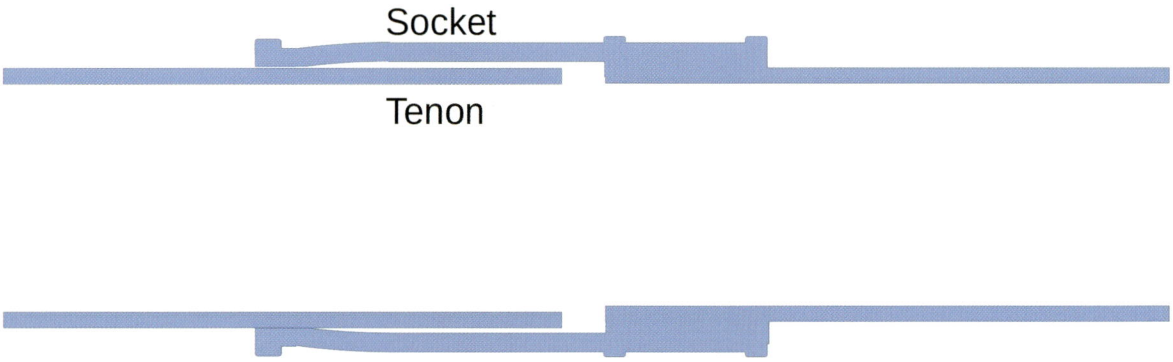

Fig. 10.16 Showing how the entrance to a flute socket can spoil the fit of the tenon.

Lightly grease the shrinking die before inserting the tenon into the tool. Tighten the die around the tenon and it will shrink or 'swedge' the metal into a smaller diameter. As with so many techniques, it is best to practise with scrap instruments first.

To finish the process, melt hard paraffin (candle) wax onto the tenon and wipe it off. My understanding is that a tiny amount of hard wax is left in the microscopic scratches and helps keep it smooth for a long time.

Gritty or stuck flute tenon

Unfortunately, we occasionally have a socket and tenon that gets stuck or very gritty and scratched. For many years I thought this was because the musician had not kept the two surfaces clean, and some grit had got lodged in the gap and caused the problem. I have since discovered that when two clean metal surfaces are rubbed together, the friction can sometimes momentarily weld the surfaces together in a process called 'galling' (no grit is involved).

My current method to improve this damage is to use an 8mm wide strip of 3M 40-micron finishing film and strap the tenon to remove all scratches. Then move to a finer grit (9-micron film) to polish the tenon. Next, I use a sharp, three-sided scraper to remove any high spots inside the socket and then either use micron paper to polish the inside, or use a roller burnisher to smooth and polish the socket. Then expand and adjust the tenon to fit.

Oval head joint tenon

You may find that some flutes will have a head joint tenon that is very slightly oval in section. This oval shape does not necessarily mean they are faulty if they slide together smoothly and effortlessly. Indeed, it is a design technique I have sometimes used to improve the resonance of a flute. The slight spring in the tube makes for good contact between the two tubes and enhances the vibrations in the metal.

Saxophone bodywork repairs

There are a few places where saxophones can develop leaks in the bodywork: the most common is where the neck fits into the body of the saxophone; another place is around the octave hole pip, when the insert is un-soldered. If you are very unlucky, you might have a vintage saxophone with soldered-on tone holes, which become partially un-soldered and cause leaks.

Saxophones' bodies do not only get dents – they also twist and bend. It is important to deal with any dents or bends on the body of a saxophone before attempting to assemble the keywork or padding. Even a dent the size of a thumbnail, if near a tone hole can cause the tone hole rim to be distorted and make padding very difficult.

If the body has received a knock or bend then the pillars can get out of alignment with each other, or a whole stack can be pushed to one side, preventing the pad cups from lining up with the tone holes correctly. Take as much time as you need to sort these problems out first, before attempting any other work on a saxophone.

Saxophone bodywork repair tools and materials

Fig. 10.17 Close-up of neck screw removal tool. The very sharp hard points of this tool dig into the end of a broken brass saxophone neck screw. You can then rotate the tool and the piece comes out.

Fig. 10.18 Saxophone neck expanding tool, made by Boehm in Germany. To work on saxophones, it is essential that you invest in a good-quality tenon expanding tool. The trailing arm design on this model keeps the rollers parallel and stretches the metal of the tenon evenly.

Fig. 10.19 Saxophone neck shrinking tool. This model comes with a selection of specific diameter collets to suit the different sizes of saxophone. The collets are hardened and tempered steel, polished on the inside, and have a split to allow them to collapse very slightly under the pressure of the long black lever on the right. The orange lever on the left controls the amount that the die can be closed up. You adjust it each time to get the specific diameter needed.

Fig. 10.20 Saxophone tone hole levelling tool with burnisher, also referred to as a tone hole lifting tool. The dark grey plate sits on top of a saxophone tone hole; the burnishing bar then hooks under the opposite side of the tone hole and is levered upwards to lift the tone hole out in that area. This can be repeated until the tone hole rim is level.

Fig. 10.21 Saxophone tone hole cutting kit by Ferree's Tools, also referred to as a tone hole topping tool – a great tool for making final adjustments to the top surface of saxophone tone holes (suitable for drawn tone holes, not rolled tone holes).

Fig. 10.22 Saxophone tone hole file. This is a fine Number 6 cut file which is especially wide to cover the entire tone hole to ensure a flat surface.

Fig. 10.23 Magnetic dent balls use a very powerful magnet on the outside of the instrument and a steel ball on the inside. As with most tools, it takes time to learn how to make the best use of them and what extra problems they can cause if not used correctly, such as scratching the lacquer or over-stretching the metal.

Fig. 10.24 Saxophone dent mandrels. The conical mandrels are worth the investment as an addition to the conventional round balls. You will need to remove the bell from the instrument to use these mandrels.

Fig. 10.25 Tapered dent roller.

Fig. 10.26 Special saxophone dent removal tool. This clever device was given to me by a retired repairer who had made one for alto and tenor saxophones. It is specifically to remove dents in the top of saxophone bodies, above the first speaker tube. The nylon wheel is attached to a bolt that moves the wedge-shaped sled on the left; this in turn pushes the brass slip on the top out. The brass slip is held in place by a flat spring attached to the body and the slip.

Fig. 10.27 Saxophone rim support. The green handle on this tool will need to be fixed firmly in an engineer's vice. The rim of the saxophone bell is cradled in the tool and supports the rim as you burnish dents out of the bell.

Fig. 10.28 Bow joint dent remover. Before using this tool, the U-shaped part of the tool is slid down the bell and lined up so that the round shaft can be screwed into position.

Fig. 10.29 This simple support tool is used to straighten the body of saxophones. You can make it yourself, but I purchased mine from Ferree's Tools many years ago.

Fig. 10.30 This tool is for straightening the main body of a baritone saxophone. It gets clamped around the collar at the top of the body and then you swing the instrument downwards and strike the tool on a bench. I have only ever needed to use this once and it was stressful!

Fig. 10.31 If you work on saxophones, you might collect a selection of different-shaped dent hammers.

Checking and Repairing Bodywork

Saxophone dents and twists

Removing dents from a saxophone is important when they might be distorting the shape or flatness of a tone hole. The skills required are similar to those of brass repairers, so get lessons from them if you can.

The process is made easier if you have a very solid clamp or vice to hold the tooling and make sure the tool is at the correct height for you. It might be necessary to have vices at two or three different heights. There will also be occasions when a second pair of hands will be needed.

Saxophone tone holes

Dents in the body of a saxophone, even if not very close to a tone hole, can cause a distortion in the tone hole rim.

It makes sense to remove as many dents as possible before attempting to replace any pads. Don't be tempted to level tone holes while you are padding the instrument; taking a bend out of one tone hole can easily distort one nearby. Even a tiny dent 10mm from a tone hole can pull down the metal around it and also distort the tone hole and make it uneven. This is why it is worth taking time to fix dents before starting to pad an instrument. Do them all together at the start of the process.

There are various ways that tone holes can be constructed. I have come across four types.

1. The most common is the straight drawn type. A machine flattens these in the factory. Unfortunately, sometimes the cutter finds it easier to cut the thinned metal on the side of the drawn tube than the thicker metal near the instrument's main body; this causes more metal to be removed on the front and back of the tone hole, making the tone hole uneven.
2. Rolled tone holes. This is a clever and expensive technique to perform and is very difficult to get right. The rolling process suffers from the same complication of thicker material near the body than the outer edges. So, again, the tone hole is often uneven. The advantage of a rolled tone hole is that it is acoustically better, mechanically stronger, and much kinder on the pad.
3. A great compromise, which is very expensive to manufacture and has only been done by Keilwerth in Germany, is to solder a ring of metal onto the top of the straight-drawn tone hole. This not only produces a truly level tone hole, but also makes it very strong and sturdy.
4. The final method of tone hole manufacture is the soldered tone hole. Here a sculpted tube is soldered onto the body. The Martin Saxophone company exemplify this technique. The long-term problem with this design is that the solder joints can break and leak.

Now I have described all the problems, let's see how we can deal with them.

If you are taking the instrument apart completely, you can use a mandrel and dent balls to take all the dents out (Figs 10.23 and 10.24). If you have well-fitting conical mandrels that fit under the distorted tone hole, you can place a flat disc of metal over the tone hole and tap down on it to force the tone hole rim flat.

When you are having to adjust individual tone holes, use a tone-hole lifting tool (Fig. 10.20).

If you cannot get the tone hole level with the lifting tool, as a last resort you can use the tone hole topping tool, or a file, to make the final adjustments (Figs 10.21 and 10.22).

First decide if the uneven tone hole results from a manufacturing fault or more recent damage.

Make sure you apply unbiased pressure to the disc (Fig. 10.35), otherwise you might create more problems. Some tone holes might only be accessible with a large, flat, fine file.

Fig. 10.32 A dent in the bow has distorted the tone hole rim.

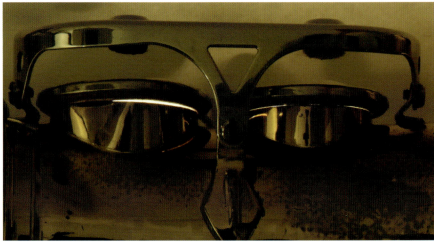

Fig. 10.33 Bent tone holes making it difficult to seat the pads.

Fig. 10.34 The lifting tool in action.

Fig. 10.35 Tone hole topping tool.

Low notes are not sounding – check for a twisted bell

If the bottom two notes don't play on an alto or tenor saxophone, first check to see if the bell is twisted in relation to the body. It is a common problem; when the instrument is lifted out of the case, the musician usually pulls it up by the rim of the bell. Pulling the instrument out puts strain on the bell/bow-to-body join and can twist the joint. So check the pad seating on the bottom two pads. You will usually find that the pads are open at the front. Holding the instrument between your knees and with the bell facing away from you, push or thump the bell rim to the left, and check the pads again. Check the pad seating at the front and back again, and repeat the process until the pads are seating correctly.

If you are dealing with dents in the instrument, you may well want to take the bell bow off. It is not worth getting hung up about un-soldering or removing the bell from the instrument, as it makes the rest of the repair so much easier. I would just get on and do it.

Fig. 10.36 Straightening a saxophone bell will often sort out the seating of the bottom two pads.

Checking and Repairing Bodywork

> ## Saxophone joints
>
> There are several ways a saxophone body can be held together. Older instruments are usually soft-soldered together. From 1950 onwards they are typically held together with a U-shaped band that is tightened by two screws. When reassembling, I usually put a silicone sealant in the joint. Yamaha started simply gluing the bell on their student instruments in the 1990s.

When you have good access to the bore of the saxophone, burnish the dents out with dent balls on a long rod. If a dent is particularly stubborn, I will position the dent ball under the dent or crease and then get a colleague to strike the rod that the dent ball is attached to with a mallet. I also have a complete set of conical steel mandrels that match the different cone sizes of saxophones. I use these for flattening tone holes as well as removing dents.

Using magnetic dent balls

Some dents can be removed using a set of magnetic dent removal balls. The tool works by having the steel dent balls inside the instrument and the very powerful magnet on the outside, with the brass body trapped between them. Dent balls only work in areas of the body that are clear of obstacles. They won't work close to tone holes or sling hooks.

- Choose the largest steel ball that will fit in the bore where the dent is and put to one side.
- Place a scratch-free cloth over the dent.
- Place the magnet on the cloth, centring it on the dent.
- Roll the steel ball into the bell towards the dent.
- At some point the ball will come within the magnetic field and the ball will snap onto the magnet.
- With luck, most of the dent removal will take place during that snapping process; if not, then slide the magnet back and forth over the dent and it should slowly come out, just like you were using a traditional dent ball.
- Listen to the movement of the ball and how easily the magnet moves to judge how well the dent has come out.

Using dent balls and tapered mandrels

You will need to remove the U-bend of the saxophone to use tapered mandrels, but it is worth taking the time to do that.

Hold the shaft in a vice and push the tapered mandrel up the body until it is under the dent. Use a rawhide mallet to tap out the dent, or you can burnish the mandrel up and down over the dent, pushing on it at the same time.

If you are using round or oval dent balls then you can use the burnishing action. If it is a deep dent then use a very weak magnet to help position the ball under the dent, then push hard down on the body and get a colleague to hit the mandrel hard. There is some debate as to whether the mandrel should be hit downwards to cause impact on the rebound, to push the dent out, or to hit upwards directly on the dent. I have had success with both methods.

Fig. 10.37 Bouncing out a dent with a dent ball on a mandrel.

Fig. 10.38 Looking down a saxophone to assess the bend in the body.

Straightening a saxophone body

Straightening saxophones has become something I look forward to. It is fun to watch and usually works out very well. First, assess the damage to be sure it will respond to the technique. It works on instruments that have fallen over and landed in a way that creates a gentle bend in the whole main body of the instrument. You can see the bend by looking at the instrument from a distance or looking down the body's bore. I will also expect to find that the keywork is either very loose or will not move. You can sometimes see a bend in the length of the long keys.

It is best not to take any keywork off the instrument. Clamp the saxophone straightening tool into the socket where the neck typically sits (unless it is a baritone saxophone, where a special clamp tool is required to fit round the top collar of the body).

Fig. 10.39 After the support tool is fitted into the neck socket, hold the instrument as shown and swing the instrument down so that the bottom of the support tool strikes the bench.

The tool has to be aligned so that the main part of the tool is following the line of the curve. Find a solid bench or block that can be hit hard without worrying about any damage. The block needs to be quite a bit below elbow height, so the impact angle will be correct. Now bring the whole instrument up to a 45-degree angle with the tool pointing downwards and with one hand supporting the bow and the other holding it just below the point at which you think the main bend starts. I bring the whole instrument down with more force than gravity alone. The tool hits the block and usually springs the instrument body back to its original shape. It is not magic that lets this happen; it is because the metal likes to return to its most 'relaxed' state. In most cases, not only does it straighten the tube, but all the keywork returns to the condition it was in before the bend. (I always charge a lot for this repair as it requires skill and courage to do it – and when it goes wrong, it takes a long time to repair.)

Bent saxophone bell rim

Sometimes it is necessary to get the main bends out with simple tools. On school instruments it is sometimes appropriate to use brute force to make the repair quick and economical. The process pictured below achieved an acceptable repair for a school instrument, as can be seen in the finished bell.

If you have a rim tool and tapered roller you can remove bends in the bell rim.

Fig. 10.40 Bent saxophone bell rim.

Fig. 10.41 Pressing the bent rim out on my workbench.

Fig. 10.42 Using a rawhide mallet to knock out the worst of the bent bell rim.

Checking and Repairing Bodywork

Fig. 10.43 Finished bell.

Fig. 10.44 Rolling out a bent bell.

Saxophone neck joints

A good fit between the neck and the body on a saxophone is important for resonance, airtightness, and a feeling of security for the musician.

First check that the socket is round and parallel down its length. It is common for the clamping screw to have been over-tightened many times, distorting the profile of the socket. Start by checking to see if the slot in the socket is narrower at the top than the bottom and, if needed, use a lever to open the gap between the slot so that it looks parallel.

Now, using an internal spring calliper, measure how round and parallel the socket is. If the investigation shows the socket is very out of shape, then you have to decide if a repair is possible or if you have to do your best, through adjusting the tenon. My preferred design of tenon expansion tool is the trailing arm design. The design delivers even pressure across the roller and does not leave ridges on the tenon.

To stretch the tenon, make sure both the inside and outside of the tenon and the rollers are clean. Then using the neck expanding tool, apply gentle pressure on the roller, spin the tenon along its full length, remove and test in the socket and

Fig. 10.45 Very badly distorted neck socket – the socket is barrelled. It will be almost impossible to get the neck tenon to seal properly in the socket. The best solution will be to replace the socket.

repeat until the tenon slides smoothly into the socket. It should be tight enough to be airtight and the clamp screw should only need a little pressure to lock the neck in position. A little grease or oil can improve the action of the neck screw or lock screw on the thread and shoulder of the screw.

If you expand the tenon too far, use the neck shrinking tool. Using a collet that is a tight fit over the tenon, tighten the tool to close the die very slightly. Remove the neck from the tool and test in the socket. Keep adjusting until you get a smooth fit.

As a last resort, strap sand the tenon down with 3M 40-micron film and polish by hand or on a polishing wheel.

Removing a broken saxophone neck screw

If the neck screw is broken, use a screw removal tool. The very sharp teeth on the end of this tool snag the broken end of the screw, so that by applying a little pressure and rotating the tool, it will screw out.

Split saxophone neck

If a saxophone is dropped or badly handled, the neck can get folded and a split will appear along one or both sides of the neck tube. If a new neck is not available, then you will need the following tools and materials:

- Fine abrasive
- Soft solder flux
- Blowtorch
- 50/50 tin/lead or 94/6 tin/silver soft solder

Fig. 10.46 Using a special neck screw removal tool, press the sharp points of the tool into the broken end of the neck screw and rotate to unscrew the remains of the neck screw.

The two specifications of soft solder have a large plastic range, so you can bridge the gap across the split.

You can repair the instrument as follows: un-bend the neck to its original profile and use a fine abrasive to clean away the lacquer 1mm either side of the split. Apply soft solder flux to the split and using a very fine flame, heat the area of the split. Feed the soft solder over the split and, if needed, use a needle spring to puddle the metal to form a bead along it.

Un-soldered octave hole pip

There are two octave hole pips on a saxophone: one on the neck and the other at the top of the main body. The pips start to leak if they are not soldered in correctly in the first place, which is not uncommon. They can also leak when a cleaning cloth or brush hits the pip on the inside. Only a small part of the pip is visible on the outside of an instrument. It can be difficult to detect these un-soldered joints, especially if you don't go looking for the problem.

So as part of your repair process, give the pips a wobble. You should also be suspicious of the pips when you have an instrument that is, in every other respect, in perfect condition, but still the musician is experiencing intermittent problems.

The repair is to soft-solder the pip back in place. You may not want to focus the heat directly onto the pip and risk burning the lacquer, so use a heat transfer method, for example by heating a metal rod that is in contact with the pip.

Tenon corks

The objective of a tenon and socket joint is to create an airtight seal between the two joints whilst also being able to assemble and disassemble them easily. The cork has to keep the joints in the correct orientation and prevent any rocking motion from side to side. The tenon cork needs to be replaced if it is cracked, loose or chipped and thus causing any problems with the above.

Clarinet and oboe tenon corks

Supporting the instrument on the bench peg, scrape the old cork off the tenon with your scraper. I use a dedicated tool for this job, and I think it is worth the time to make one; the method can be found in Chapter 20.

Keep some of the cork you remove and measure its thickness; this will help you choose the right thickness of replacement cork.

Support the joint between the bench peg and your body and use a length of 180 grit workshop roll to remove the remaining glue residue from the tenon cork recess.

Mark the width of the groove at both ends of the sheet of cork with a cork knife. It is better to make the cork slightly too wide for the groove than too narrow. A 0.3mm oversize is a good margin to aim for. I find that marking with a knife is more accurate than a ballpoint pen, but a fine marker can also work.

Using a metal straight edge as a guide, lightly cut the top surface of the cork between the two marks using a sharp bench knife.

Once the top surface of the cork is cut, the strip will break cleanly when bent slightly.

Using a cork knife, cut a 45-degree chamfer on one end of the cork strip. If the angle is too close to 90 degrees, you risk creating a tunnel under the cork.

Using an old clarinet reed, spread a layer of contact adhesive over the bottom of the recess. I don't worry too much if the glue spreads over the edges of the groove; it can be removed later and it is better that there is glue in the corners of the groove than not enough.

Keep the two bonding surfaces apart until they are almost dry. I test the tackiness of the contact adhesive using my fingernail. You need to wait until the glue has just stopped feeling sticky.

As soon as the adhesive is dry to the touch, take the chamfered end of the cork and place it in the groove with the cut surface uppermost. With a light pulling motion, feed the cork into the groove. Pushing it down into position as you go, continue until the other end of the cork strip overlaps the chamfered end.

Using a very sharp cork knife, or a new razor blade, slice the excess cork strip away.

Using a rolling block (a piece of wood 75mm × 20mm × 75mm), firmly roll the cork joint back and forth on the edge of a flat work surface to crush the cork. This process improves the adhesion of the glue and, just as importantly, it softens the cork and makes it springy.

Whilst supporting the instrument between your body and bench peg, profile the outside of the tenon cork by strapping it with 240 grit workshop roll to produce the profile shown.

Continue adjusting so that it can be inserted into the socket two-thirds of the way. Be very careful not to sand away any of the wood or plastic tenon ring.

Using a strip of cloth, strap around the tenon cork to remove excess glue and clear away cork dust.

Apply cork grease and assemble the instrument. It should now slide in fully and firmly with minimal rocking motion. As a guideline, if the joint will go two-thirds of the way in without grease, it will be the correct fit when grease is added.

If I know the musician is a small child or frail adult, I will make the tenon cork slightly easier to assemble than normal. The downside of this is that the cork may become too loose with use and need replacing again after a year or so.

Fig. 10.47 Starting to remove an old tenon cork.

Fig. 10.48 Tenon cork removal tool, also used to remove neck corks. The curve on this tool can be altered to fit your hand size and position. (Instructions for making this tool are given in Chapter 20.)

Fig. 10.49 Contact adhesive (called contact cement in the USA). This type of glue is used to bond soft materials to harder ones, for example, cork or felt to wood or metal. It is very secure and does not slip with heat or over time. You cannot reposition this glue. Contact adhesive is spread on the two surfaces that you want to bond and then left separate for up to ten minutes for the two surfaces to become almost dry to the touch. I use the back of my fingernail to test it is dry. My current preferred choice is Evo-Stik Impact; it has a long 'open time' which gives me a long window of opportunity for completing the bonding process.

Fig. 10.50 Cork rolling block. This is used to soften the cork on tenon joints, neck corks and flute head corks.

Fig. 10.51 Aluminium oxide workshop roll (the UK/US name for a woven-backed abrasive) is used for strapping down tenon grooves, adjusting tenon corks and for tool making. It comes in 50m rolls and is 25mm wide. There is a choice of abrasive material and grit size; I find the 180 and 240 grit sizes most useful. If you can get 'J flex' specification, all the better – it is much more flexible than the standard workshop roll.

Fig. 10.52 Bench knife or cork knife. Repairers use a wide variety of bench knives, from scalpels to packing knives. I like using the design as the angle of the blade lets you cut onto a work surface with the blade parallel to the cutting surface, without the handle and your knuckles hitting the bench. Use a slicing motion (not a simple push) to make the cut. Made originally for the shoe industry, these are also called click knives and are made of good quality steel that can be kept sharp with a sharpening stone and strop.

Fig. 10.53 Pre-cut tenon corks for saxophone, bassoon and cor-anglais. These are quick and convenient, especially for bassoons and cors. It is easiest to use cork tubes when replacing bassoon bocal corks. If you specialize in saxophones and want to repair them in an authentic way, then you might want to invest in pre-bored saxophone neck corks.

Checking and Repairing Bodywork

Fig. 10.54 Measuring the thickness of tenon cork.

Fig. 10.55 Using workshop roll abrasive to clean the tenon groove on a clarinet.

Fig. 10.56 Marking the width of cork needed when replacing a tenon cork.

Fig. 10.57 Making a light cut along the top surface of the cork when cutting a tenon cork.

Fig. 10.58 Breaking the cork after a light cut has been made on the top surface.

Fig. 10.59 Making a 45-degree chamfer cut on the end of a tenon cork.

Fig. 10.60 Applying the glue to the bottom of the recess.

Fig. 10.61 Spreading the adhesive.

Fig. 10.62 Spreading contact adhesive on a tenon cork using an old reed.

Fig. 10.63 Applying contact adhesive to the chamfer of a tenon cork.

Fig. 10.64 Using my fingernail to test how dry the glue is.

Fig. 10.65 Starting to bond the tenon cork onto the tenon. Note the chamfered end is attached first and the chamfer is facing upwards.

Fig. 10.66 Using a thumbnail or spatula, press the edges of the tenon cork into the tenon recess.

Fig. 10.67 Trimming off the excess tenon cork on a clarinet tenon.

Fig. 10.68 Rolling the clarinet tenon cork after bonding to soften the cork and improve the bond.

Fig. 10.69 Supporting the joint on a bench peg makes it easy to strap-sand the tenon cork with a workshop roll abrasive.

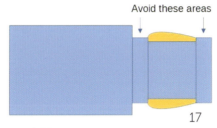

Fig. 10.70 Profile of cork tenon.

Fig. 10.71 This clarinet tenon cork has been profiled ready to fit into the socket.

Fig. 10.72 Ragging the tenon after sanding the tenon cork.

Saxophone neck corks

Saxophone neck corks require supple or flexible cork that will not crack when bending round the small-diameter pipe. Though you can also use pre-cut tubular corks, and install them in the way described in the bassoon section, I use sheet cork wrapped around the neck.

Use workshop roll to make a clean surface for a new saxophone neck cork. Do not scratch the lacquer that is not going to be covered by cork.

Cut the replacement cork of the correct thickness to the length of the original. Occasionally a neck will have a steep taper so I will adjust the shape of the cork to compensate for this.

The design of the cork/bench knife makes cutting long chamfers easier.

Apply contact adhesive to the neck and cork, keeping the two apart until both surfaces are dry enough to lose their tack. Use the back of your fingernail to test; it is ready when the fingernail does not stick.

Starting with the chamfered end of the cork facing upwards, stretch and roll the new cork onto the tenon, wrapping it over the chamfered end.

Use a razor blade or very sharp cork knife to trim off the excess cork.

After bonding a tenon cork I roll the tenon under pressure between a block of wood and my workbench. This improves the bond and softens the cork making a smoother, better fit. This ensures the adhesive makes good contact and softens the cork, making the fit smooth and firm.

It is important to know that the bore of a saxophone mouthpiece is parallel, so you must sand the cork in such a way to make it parallel too. That way the musician will be able to slide the mouthpiece on as far as they need and adjust it easily and smoothly (two-thirds to three-quarters of the length of cork).

Try to fit the neck cork to the actual mouthpiece the musician is using. The bore of mouthpieces varies. Remember to ask the musician to bring all the mouthpieces they use and fit it to the mouthpiece with the largest bore.

Checking and Repairing Bodywork **105**

Fig. 10.73 Removing the original cork.

Fig. 10.74 Measure thickness of existing cork.

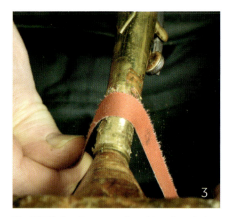
Fig. 10.75 Sanding away the old cork and glue.

Fig. 10.76 Cutting replacement cork.

Fig. 10.77 Cutting a chamfer.

Fig. 10.78 Applying glue to a saxophone neck.

Fig. 10.79 Wrapping the cork around the tenon.

Fig. 10.80 Trimming off the excess tenon cork on a saxophone neck.

Fig. 10.81 Rolling a tenon cork between a woodblock and a bench.

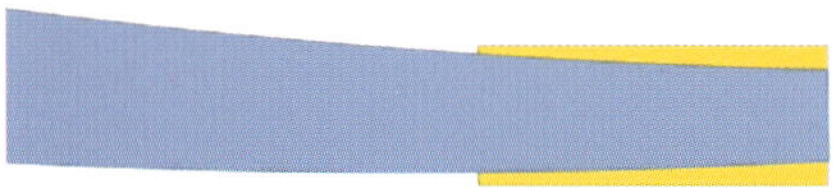

Fig. 10.82 Profile of a saxophone neck cork.

Flute head corks

The anatomy of the head joint and head cork assembly is described in the emergency repairs section of this book. When replacing a head cork you will need replacement corks and a tenon cork rolling block.

There are pictures and a description of the head joint cork assembly in Chapter 4. To replace the head cork, remove the assembly and then unscrew the retaining washer to remove the original cork. The quickest way to remove the cork is to cut down the length of the cork with a bench knife.

Choose a replacement head cork that is able to slide into the head joint on its own, so it can start to obscure the embouchure hole. If it goes so far in that the trailing edge is visible in the embouchure hole, then the cork might be too small (it should be around 17.5mm in diameter).

I like to use hot shellac to bond the head cork onto the reflector plate, but this is a personal choice. To do it with shellac, melt a little shellac on the back of the reflector plate and push the cork down the screwed spindle onto the melted shellac. This will then cool and stick the

Flute head joint tools

Fig. 10.83 Flute head joint adjustment tool. The middle ring is 17mm from the end. The other two rings are 5mm on either side.

Fig. 10.84 Pre-bored cylinders of cork specifically for flute head joints (Yamaha head cork on the left and a generic one on the right). They come in a variety of outside diameters, bore diameters and lengths. Except for those supplied by Yamaha, all head corks I have ever bought have been very dry, so I prefer to use original Yamaha head corks.

cork to the plate. Remove any excess shellac that might have been squeezed out. Screw on the clamp plate until it is tight on the cork.

Roll the cork between a cork rolling board and the bench to soften the cork. Melt a very small amount of candle wax (hard paraffin wax) around the cork at the end nearest the crown. Push the assembly into the larger end of the head joint and position the reflector plate in the correct position from the centre of the embouchure hole (usually 17mm). Use a cotton bud to remove any wax that has been deposited in the bore of the head joint or inside the embouchure hole.

Double reed crook corks (bassoon and cor anglais bocal corks)

These are tricky to replace using sheet cork and the wrap-around technique, so it is best to use the manufacturers' technique, which is to use pre-bored cork tube the right size for the instrument.

Fig. 10.85 Bassoon bocal corking collar.

When replacing a bassoon bocal cork using a ready-made cork sleeve, you melt shellac on the bare metal of the bocal and wait for it to go cold. Then you push the cork sleeve on.

Insert a close-fitting metal rod into the end of the bocal and slide a tight-fitting collar over the cork. The collar will prevent the cork from being burnt by the flame and also compresses the cork onto the bocal. Heat the metal rod until the shellac melts and sticks to the cork. Remove from the heat.

The profile of the cork should have a short leading-edge taper and then the rest of the tube should be a circular straight column. Gently roll the cork between a cork roller and the bench to soften the cork and to make it a smooth fit in the socket.

If you don't have a pre-prepared cork tube then you will need very supple or flexible cork. Use the same chamfer technique as normal tenon corks. You can gently crush the cork before bending it; this will improve its flexibility. Remember to compress the cork after gluing it by rolling it between a piece of wood and the bench, before sanding to the final fit.

Fig. 10.86 Applying shellac to a bassoon bocal.

Fig. 10.88 With the corking collar over the cork and a metal rod in the bore, heat the rod so the shellac will melt again and bond the cork to the collar.

Fig. 10.87 When cool, push the cork tenon tube onto the bassoon bocal.

Fig. 10.89 Support the bocal on a pin and sand the tenon cork to the correct diameter.

Bassoon tenons

Bassoon joints are often bound with thread. Don't replace threaded tenons with cork without first consulting the musician. There are often good reasons for using thread, such as stabilizing or strengthening the soft maple wood. The wood of bassoons is often treated with oils that prevent adhesives from sticking.

Corked bassoon tenons

To replace a cork tenon on a bassoon, use the same method as used for clarinets with the addition of the following step: degrease the bottom of the groove with a citrus oil-based degreaser. If you don't have a piece of cork long enough for the bell to long-joint tenon then you can use two pieces of cork. Put a chamfer at both ends of one of the pieces of cork and glue it in place. The second piece of cork does not need a chamfer and is used to link the two ends together.

Threaded bassoon tenons

If you don't need to remove all of the old thread, then don't. If you have gone back to bare wood, then anchor the first few turns of the cotton thread by applying a little contact adhesive or by melting some pure beeswax onto the wood first. Start winding the cotton around the tenon in an even and orderly fashion, adding a little cork grease on the thread every few turns as the layers build up. Finally, melt cork-grease into the thread with a hot spatula and add or remove a few winds to achieve a good fit in the socket.

After the thread is cut, I like to finish the end of the thread by scraping it into a taper with a cork knife on the bench. A 20mm taper will let the thread lie flat against the rest of the threads and become invisible. It also helps to prevent it from unravelling.

Tenons on historic instruments

I have spent years restoring historic instruments and making reproduction instruments, and for these I always use raw hemp thread for the tenons. I'm not too fond of cotton sewing thread or mercerized thread; the only good thing to say about cotton sewing thread is that it looks neat. Lightly twisted hemp thread has the following advantages: it does not absorb water and swell like cotton or linen; it lies flat when compressed; it self-amalgamates which means you don't have to tie it off at the end of the wrapping process; it absorbs cork grease; and you can add and remove thread easily as the wood swells and shrinks over time.

To replace a tenon thread on a historic instrument, start by melting a small quantity of pure beeswax on the cleaned tenon, then start winding the raw hemp thread around the instrument. After one turn, melt the wax again so the hemp is saturated with wax. This anchors the thread onto the tenon. (If you miss this step, you are storing up problems for later.) Continue winding randomly until it creates a tight fit into the socket. Apply some cork grease to the thread and refit it into the socket. If needed, add more thread to ensure it is a tight fit with the cork grease. Snap the thread; do not cut it with scissors. Breaking the thread teases the fibres apart and forms a tapered end which allows the thread to blend into the rest of the windings and not unravel. If you miss the step of anchoring the thread to the body, at some point in the future, old cork grease will stick the socket and outer thread together and all the tenon thread starts slipping on the tenon, making it impossible to separate the joints. If you ever have to solve this problem, start by warming the joint to try and soften the grease and rock the joint back and forth as if you are trying to snap the joint. Don't rotate the joint.

Discourage musicians from using PTFE plumber's tape to increase the diameter of the tenon cork or tenon thread. It causes a huge amount of extra stress on the socket and tenon.

CHAPTER 11

Checking and Repairing Keywork

Keys need to rotate smoothly and quickly with as little noise as possible. To do this, they need to have well-fitting pivots or axles.

Movement across the axle or axis of a key is unwanted as it seriously reduces the reliability of the pad to seal the tone hole. As this is a fundamental requirement of a good instrument, much of your time as a repairer should be spent understanding and fixing key mechanisms.

All keys rotate or are pivoted between the pillars in one of two ways:

1. A short pivot coming out of a pillar at each end of the key.
2. An axle in a hinge tube along the length of the key between the pillars.

A well-adjusted pivot does not allow the key to move across the axis of rotation and can only have a small amount of movement between the pillars (along the axis).

On many occasions, a key will be loose on its axle, and we call this wear, or 'play', in the mechanism. This is not the musical use of the word; we are using it to describe the unwanted movement. It is not always caused by true wear and tear and can also refer to excess movement left by the manufacturer. The process of checking the key mechanism is done one key at a time.

Unwanted movement in keywork

This is a very important part of the repair process as the success of the padding and overall regulation of the instrument depends on the smooth rotation of the keys without unwanted movement. You can work on the pivot keys and hinge keys to address these problems.

Improving pivot keys

Pivot keys are the most likely type of key to need attention; point screws, which are a sub-set of pivot screw, are the most likely to wear out.

If you have a headless screw that has become loose and you can't get a replacement, then it is possible to use a low shear strength threadlocking adhesive (Loctite 222 or equivalent). Only apply a very small amount at the end away from the point. The liquid is designed to flow into the thread. If it flows too far, then it can

Pivot key adjustment tools

Fig. 11.1 Close-up of two counter-bore cutting tips. They are slightly different in diameter and are attached onto two different types of shaft. The black shaft is a straight metal shaft; the white shaft is made from flexible nylon to get access to awkward saxophone pillars. These cutters are used to recess or counter-bore a pillar, which allows the point screw to screw further into the pillar and protrude further from the other side.

Fig. 11.2 Two designs of point screw reamers. These are used to make the cone deeper in a pivot rod.

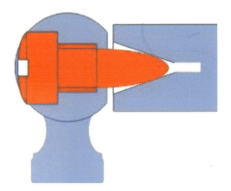

Fig. 11.3 A bullet-shaped point screw making good contact with the straight-sided cone in the pivot rod.

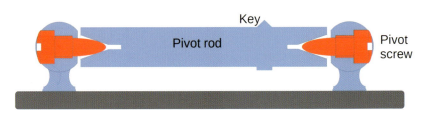

Fig. 11.4 A pivot key fitting correctly between point screws. The key rotates freely, and the point screws are tight.

get into the bearing surface of the point and the key. It takes twenty-four hours to firm up, so you might not notice the key is not moving until the next day.

A beautifully manufactured bullet-pointed screw is a joy to work with. In Fig. 11.3, you can see the point is in contact with the straight-sided cone. Now imagine if the angle of the cone is changed: the curved pivot screw will still be able to make good contact with the cone. Likewise, a different shaped curve of the pivot screw will still find a good contact point in the cone.

What you are aiming for is a perfectly adjusted key (Fig. 11.4). Here are the features that indicate that it is well-adjusted:

- The point screws are tight in the pillars and will not wobble or work loose.
- There is a small gap between each pillar and the ends of the pivot rod.
- The curved point of each screw is in contact with the cone of the pivot rod.

To confirm the key is set correctly, gently push the key towards a pillar to see if there is a gap, however small, between the key and the pillar. If there is, then push the key towards the other pillar; you should not see or feel any movement. There should also be a small gap between the key and the other pillar. Now confirm that there is no movement across the axis. In theory, no movement is possible, but it is not unknown for the cone in a key to become oval-shaped after hard use, so it is worth checking.

Checking straight-sided point screws

I am not a great fan of straight-sided point screws as they are slightly more difficult to get a good bearing surface between point and cone; however, they are extensively used on student-range instruments.

Figs 11.5 to 11.7 show that the best design of cone for a straight-sided point screw is a convex shape.

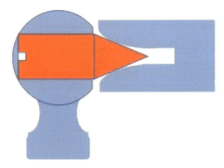

Fig. 11.5 Correct shape for the cone on a straight-sided point screw.

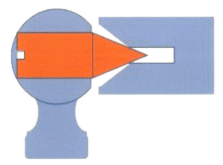

Fig. 11.6 The cone in this pivot rod is too straight and steep; the pivot can only touch near the point. This will wear quickly and will need regular adjustment.

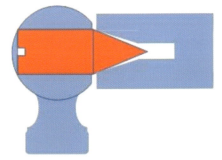

Fig. 11.7 The cone in the pivot rod is too straight and shallow. The screw is in danger of rubbing on the thread.

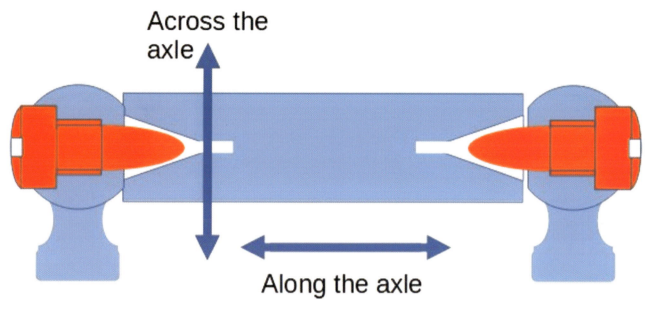

Fig. 11.8 Wear or 'play' in a key mechanism.

Methods of adjusting point screws

In Fig. 11.8 the screws are tight in the pillars, but the points are not touching the cones; this allows the key to move along the axis as well as across the axis. To fix this problem we can use a counter-bore cutter.

Counter-boring a pillar (Fig. 11.9)

To remove any unwanted movement in a key, we need to remove some metal from the pillar to make the counter-bore deeper. This will allow the points to extend further out of the pillar to make contact with the key. It only takes one rotation of the cutter to make a difference, so take it slowly, checking every rotation. You must choose the correct pillar to adjust and by how much.

Check in the following sequence:

1. Push the key towards one of the pillars.
2. Does that end of the key move across the axis?
3. If it does, then cut that pillar until the key stops moving across the axis and there is a tiny gap between the key and the pillar.
4. Now push the key towards the other pillar and repeat the process.

The result should be a perfectly fitting key.

> **Sequence for checking point screws**
>
> 1. Are the screws able to be locked in position?
> 2. Is there any movement across the axle?
> 3. Is there any movement along the axle?
> 4. Does the key rotate smoothly and quietly?

Fig. 11.9 Using a point screw counter-bore cutter.

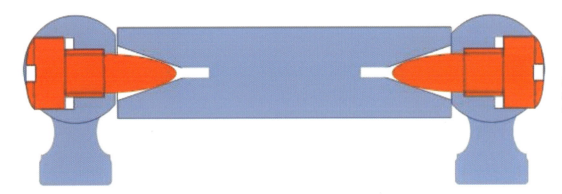

Fig. 11.10 Here is another poorly set key on point screws.

Keys that lock tight when the screws are tightened

In Fig. 11.10, we have the opposite problem to the previous example. If we look at the point screws in this diagram, we can see a white space between the shoulders of the point screws and the bottom of the counter-bores. These screws might wobble from side to side or work themselves loose. If we were to try to tighten the screws, the key would lock solid. This is adjusted by cutting the cones in the pivot rod deeper (Fig. 11.11).

Using a conical point screw reamer, you deepen the cone in the key at the end of the pivot rod. Start with one complete turn of the tool; there should be a minute shaving of metal that comes out.

Refit the key and tighten up the screw. Keep repeating the process until there is only a very small gap between the pivot rod and the pillar. Then work on the other end of the key until you have a perfectly set key.

The key is tight between the pillars when one or neither screw is tightened

There is yet another scenario that very occasionally happens, and that is when a key is tight between the pillars, even before screwing in the point screws, or when one of the point screws is set correctly. To solve this, you need to shorten the pivot rod or file off a pillar until it fits.

If you make a mistake and counter-bore too much, the key will lock up again when the screw is tight, and you will need to go back and open up the cone (the converse is also true).

Finishing touches to point screw adjustment

On best quality work, I perfect the operation by making one extra cut in the counter-bore so that when the screw is tightened, the key becomes sluggish. Then I will rest one pillar on an anvil and tap the other pillar sharply; this will bruise the metal inside the cone very slightly and release the key again. The advantage of this final step is that the bruised metal is now matching the shape of the point screw, so increasing the contact area. It also 'work hardens' the contact area, which in turn increases its working life.

When there is no excess movement, add the appropriate grade of oil to the pivot screws, hitch the spring, and check the key rotates smoothly.

Buffet point screw

In an attempt to save money, Buffet uses a technique borrowed from the glasses industry. Their headed point screws have a collar of polyurethane rubber around the neck of the screw, next to the shoulder. As the shoulder starts to reach the bottom of the counter-bore, rubber is forced outwards and starts to lock the screw; this gives the technician some latitude on where to position the screw. Although this seems to work when the instrument is new, I do not rely on this method and like to re-adjust the point screws to lock tight on the shoulder.

Fig. 11.11 Reaming a pivot rod.

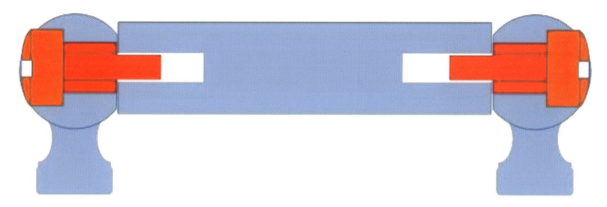

Fig. 11.12 A well set up barrel screw assembly.

Checking barrel screws

This form of pivot screw has straight, parallel sides. It requires a parallel hole in the key. When made well they are very good. As noted in Chapter 8, barrel pivot screws are the best design to use on plastic instruments, student flutes and some saxophones. I would go as far as to say they are the only good design to use on plastic instruments.

For a barrel screw to work well, the fit of the key or pivot rod between the pillars has to be good, and the pin needs to be a good fit into the hole (Fig. 11.12).

Methods of adjusting barrel screws

Barrel screws are the best design for plastic instruments because they allow for the expansion and contraction of the plastic body. As the plastic expands with heat, the body lengthens and the pillars move apart, and in the cold they move closer together. Metal keys do not expand or shrink as much as the plastic body.

It is important to leave some movement along the axis of the key when adjusting the instrument at room temperature – this is to keep the keys free in cold weather. Some people insist that there should never be any movement between the pillars; this is true for a point screw, but not for barrel screws. Movement along the axis of a barrel screw or hinge tube key does not change the movement across the axis, so the pad remains in the same plane relative to the tone hole. Therefore, if the pad is flat, it is unlikely to affect the sealing of the pad (assuming that there is not a deep bedding ring in the pad surface).

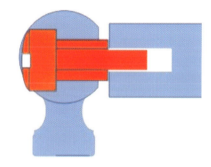

Fig. 11.13 This is a badly fitting barrel screw where the thread extends beyond the pillar.

Improving the workings of barrel screws

If we want to improve the fit of the pillars, we could swedge the key (even though there is no hinge screw). When the pin is a poor fit in the hole (*see* below), it can be quickly solved by opening out the entrance of the hole to accommodate the thread. If the hole is too large, then swedging could also be used.

The most common adjustment you might need to make with a barrel screw is to make sure the pin is straight and in line with the hole in the key. If you attach the key and there is any resistance to rotation, it usually indicates that one or both of the pivots are bent.

Barrel screws usually get bent when someone tries to remove the key without unscrewing the screw at one end. The key is pulled up and away from the pillar, bending the pin. To rectify this, put the key back and tap downwards, close to the pillar at each end of the key, with a hardwood mallet. This will force the pin back into its correct position without going too far the other way.

Fig. 11.14 Bent barrel screw.

Checking and Repairing Keywork

Fig. 11.15 Straightening a barrel screw.

Check if the pivot screw will stay in position

All pivot screws should be fixed in the correct position and not be able to move without the aid of a screwdriver. For headed pivot screws this means that the shoulder of the screw will be tight against the bottom of the counter-bore. This requires the counter-bore to be adjusted correctly to get the fit of the key correct.

When it comes to headless screws, another method is required to lock the screw. The most common way is to use the Nyloc method (Nyloc is a proprietary name that is synonymous with this method). This is a technique where a nylon is applied to a section of the screw thread. When the screw is inserted, the nylon makes a tight fit and locks the screw in position. Unfortunately, when the screw is removed and re-inserted, the effectiveness of the nylon is reduced. There is another problem with headless screws: the fit between the internal and external thread needs to be very good, or else the screw can rock in the pillar.

Buescher headless point screw

To prevent the Buescher headless point screw from going out of adjustment, the manufacturers drilled and threaded a small hole in the side of the pillar at 90 degrees to the pivot screw (Fig. 11.16). A very small screw locked down on the plain section of the pivot screw. Unfortunately, over the years the small lock screws get rusted in, or mangled by other repairers, and can be difficult to remove or reuse. It is worth spending the time restoring or replacing these screws.

New insert for a worn screw rod

When the point screw hole is very badly worn, usually oval in section, and it is already so large in diameter that you cannot make it any bigger, then you will need to renew the pivot hole.

- Choose a drill that is the same diameter as the point screw. Use this to drill out the existing hole to 3mm deep.
- Using a nickel silver rod, turn the outside to be a tight fit in the new hole and drill a <1mm small hole in the middle.
- Part off the insert at 3mm.
- File a small groove down the length of the insert and push it into the key.
- Use a viscous superglue, epoxy resin, or soft solder to fix the insert in place. The small groove helps the glue or solder to flow; don't worry if the small hole gets filled.
- When solid, re-drill the small hole and open the cone out to match the point screw.
- Adjust as normal.

Improving hinge keys

Keys can be attached to the body with a hinge screw running inside a hinge tube and supported each end by pillars. These work better than point screws when the distance between the pillars is short. If the manufacturer has designed and made the instrument well, then the hinge screws only go wrong when the keywork is bent, or the oil has become dry or sticky.

Fig. 11.16 Tiny lock screws for headless point screws on a Buescher saxophone.

Hinge key cleaning tools

Fig. 11.17 Use a pipe cleaner to clean old oil from a hinge tube. You might need to use a light oil or solvent to get stubborn oil out.

Fig. 11.18 This pipe cleaner has plastic filaments included in the soft cotton and is great for cleaning hinge tubes. Brass wire is sometime used in place of the plastic and is equally as good.

Checking hinge keys

- The hinge tube and hinge screws have to be straight.
- The fit of the hinge screw in the pillar and the hinge tube must be close.
- The hinge tube should fit between the pillars without a gap.
- The hinge screw needs to be a close fit inside the pillar.

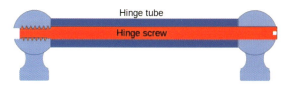

Fig. 11.19 Hinge key.

Fig. 11.20 Diagram of a hinge screw mounted across the body of a wooden instrument.

Fig. 11.21 These two keys are very well-fitting hinge keys on a Yamaha student oboe. The fit is so good that it is difficult to see where the keys meet.

Checking and Repairing Keywork

> **Sequence for checking hinge keys**
>
> 1. Check the key swings on the hinge screw.
> 2. Test for any movement across the axis.
> 3. Check the fit between the pillars.
> 4. Check that the hinge screw is a close fit in the pillar hole(s).

Fig. 11.22 The swing test. The key should be able to swing through 360 degrees without any hesitation.

Methods of adjusting hinge keys

Sometimes an instrument is not well designed, the manufacturing is not very good or the keywork has worn, so we need to check and adjust as necessary.

First, remove the hinge screw and clean the hinge tube using a pipe cleaner and solvent. There are special pipe cleaners with stiff wire or plastic braided into the cotton to clear old oil away. Run the hinge screw into the hinge tube and swing the key around (Fig. 11.22). It should be completely free to rotate. If there is any slowness, or a stiff spot, the key is bent in some way, so you need to work your way through the bent key section below.

As I have described previously, unwanted movement across the axis of the key needs to be identified and then improved. Put the key onto the instrument and tighten the hinge screw. Try to move the key. If there is movement across the axle, study the section on swedging.

The next test is to see if there is a close fit between the pillars. A small amount of movement (up to 0.1mm) is acceptable on most instruments.

The final test is often ignored and leads to frustration later on when regulating the instrument. Carefully check that the hole in the pillar is not too big for the hinge screw. It should be a tight fit so that the hinge screw can't move from side to side in the pillar. This extends to all the pillars supporting a stack of keys.

How to free off a bent hinge key

Dropping an instrument is a common cause for a key to bend, so look to see where it might have been impacted. The curve will be from the outside towards the body. Do not try to remove the key from the instrument until you have considered if unbending it on the instrument might be best. If it looks possible, slide a broad lever like duck-bill pliers under the key and gently bend it back to where it should be. Once it looks straight, remove the hinge screw. Clean the tube and try the swing test. If it passes that test, re-fit the key and tighten up the hinge screw. The key might still be a little bent, so it might exhibit a wobble or jerk when tightening up the screw. You might be lucky and it might be working; if not, you have to be patient and keep investigating.

It is useful to work out how the bend might have happened. Has the key been hit on one side or has the key been twisted in some way? Test to see if both the hinge tube and hinge screw are bent in the same way. Fig. 11.23 shows a key where both the tube and screw are bent together. The hinge screw will go in easily in one orientation and get stuck when inserted at 180 degrees. In the first instance, try straightening the key and hinge screw at the same time.

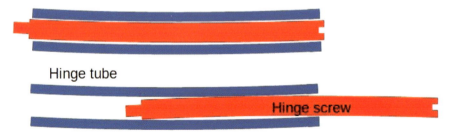

Fig. 11.23 Hinge keys bent whilst on the instrument – the tube and hinge screw bend together.

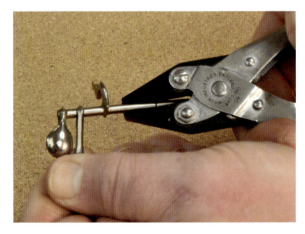

Fig. 11.24 Unbending a hinge screw.

Fig. 11.25 Looking at the end of a hinge key can sometimes show you which way the key is bent.

This method works for the majority of these repairs. You then have to solve the remaining problems by flexing the key between two fingers and a thumb while shuffling the hinge screw in the tube. There is always a sweet spot where the rod runs smoothly. Once I have found the sweet spot, push extra hard to over bend the key so that when it relaxes back it will be in the correct alignment. If bending with fingers is not firm enough, you can support the key between two fingers and tap down in between them with a wooden mallet. If that does not work, then use two parallel action pliers. Gently bend the suspect arm or tube and keep testing. If you resort to using pliers, you may end up crushing the hinge tube out of the round; this causes its own problems, so you need to use your swedging pliers to make the tube round again. Remember to do all these processes with the hinge screw in place (Fig. 11.25).

While working on the key, it might help to look at the end of the key; even without a magnifying glass, you can often see a gap that can be as little as 0.05mm. What you will notice is the different colour of the boundary between the hinge screw and hinge tube from one side to the other. Rotate the hinge screw to another position and look again to see if the boundary has moved. From these observations you can often work out which way to bend the hinge screw. To straighten it, use your fingers if it is a long hinge screw, or two parallel pliers if short. Be patient, as it occasionally takes an hour to straighten a key!

Hinge screw that has been nipped by a bent key arm, distorting the tube

A nipped hinge tube occurs when an arm, attached to the hinge tube, has been bent sideways. This causes a localized kink in the tube that binds onto the hinge screw. It is tempting to drill or ream this bump out, but this would be a mistake. Re-drilling should only be used as an absolute last resort. The better way is to use your parallel action pliers to hold the key arm and bend it back to where it should be and so straighten the tube. That way the arm will be able to do what it is supposed to be doing as well.

Fig. 11.26 Diagram of how a bend to a key arm can distort the hinge tube.

Checking and Repairing Keywork

Other types of hinge key bends

To straighten a hinge screw, the following method works surprisingly well. Drill a small hole (about 2.5mm diameter) in the handle of an engineer's hammer. (It appears that the weight of the hammer head helps to steady the process that follows.) With the steel showing approximately 40mm from the chuck, slide the hammer shaft on as far as the chuck. Start spinning the steel quite fast and at the same time angle the hammer so that it is trying to bend the spinning steel. Slide the hammer handle down the steel, going backwards and forwards until the steel becomes straight. I often practise this technique on a test rod of steel before working on a paying repair. Move the hinge screw out another 40mm and repeat. If the hinge screw is very long, make sure you steady the free ends so that it does not whip round and bend more or get tangled. I have seen this happen on a baritone saxophone right-hand stack hinge screw. It was quite dangerous, as well as upsetting.

In 2021 Music Medic introduced a special tool to do the same job. It is an adaptation of the tooling that commercial wire manufacturers use to straighten coils of wire. It is made from three grooved rollers that pinch together around the rotating rod steel.

Fig. 11.27 Diagram of three common hinge key bends.

Fig. 11.28 Straightening a hinge screw.

Correcting unwanted movement in hinge keys

Hinge key adjustment tools

Fig. 11.29 Swedging pliers, used to stretch and compress hinge tubing.

Fig. 11.30 Collet style swedging tool, used to shrink the diameter of hinge tubing. It must be used when the hinge screw is in the tube. It is only suitable for use on the ends of keys.

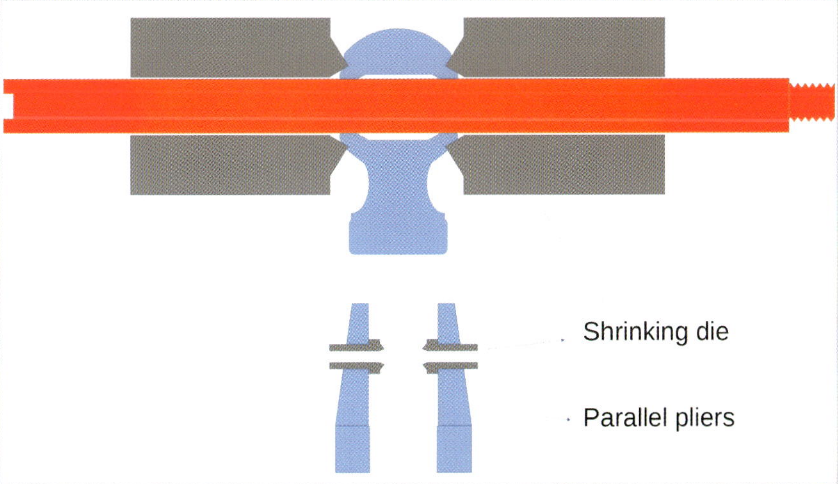

Shrinking die

Parallel pliers

Fig. 11.31 Tool to reduce the diameter of an oversized pillar hole. This tool is one you will need to make yourself. The central hole is the diameter of the hinge screw. There is an annular raised peaked ring about 0.5mm larger in diameter around the central hole. The sleeves do not have to be mounted in parallel pliers. I used a hammer to punch the cones into the pillar instead of using pliers.

Earlier I described the process of setting up a key mounted on pivot screws. Now we are looking at hinge screws. Once you have the key spinning smoothly on the hinge screw, mount the key onto the instrument and test to see how much movement there is between the pillars (along the axis). A small amount of movement, up to 0.1mm, is fine. Next see if you can wobble or move the key across the axis; movement in this direction will cause excess keywork noise, poor regulation, and poor pad seating. Removing lateral movement is important.

Movement across the axis indicates that the inside diameter of the key tube is too large for the hinge screw. (Do check that it is the right hinge screw for that key before going further.) Check to see if the key can be swedged down. The key has to have a clear section of hinge tube with no key arms or spring hitches to get in the way.

The idea of swedging is to reduce the diameter of the hinge tube until it is a close fit around the hinge screw, or to stretch the tube to make it longer. It works on the ability of the metal to flow, or move, under pressure.

The two tools I have for taking up wear are swedging pliers and a collet swedge.

Checking and Repairing Keywork **121**

Fig. 11.32 Two hinge screw keys: the key on the left can be swedged as there are sections of free hinge tube; the one on the right has no clear section of plain hinge tubing, so cannot be swedged. In this instance a replacement, oversized hinge screw has to be made and fitted. Replacing a hinge screw is quite an involved process, and sometimes you have to leave it as it is and find a working compromise with the regulation and padding.

Before using swedging tools:

1. Make sure they are highly polished on the inner surface.
2. Make sure they are a good fit around the hinge tube.
3. Have a rod inside the hinge tube before using the tool.

Fortunately, the hinge tube behaves in one of two ways:

1. When you crush the tube without rotating the key or tube, the metal reduces in diameter until it fits the hinge screw. You can then move the tool to another area of the hinge tube and crush it again. You may find the hinge screw is stiff in the hinge tube at the end of the process. This is due to uneven crushing that is nipping the rod in one or two places. Gently re-crush the tube at 90 degrees to the original crush and re-test. Repeat until it rotates smoothly. Do not be tempted to ream or drill out the hinge tube.
2. If you rotate the swedging tool while crushing the tube, the metal will flow sideways and lengthen the tube; this can be useful when you need to reduce the gap between the pillars.

Fig. 11.33a Swedging tool in action.

Fig. 11.33 Hinge tube swedging.

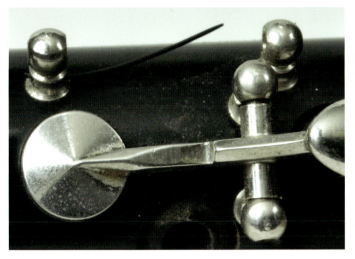

Fig. 11.34 This hinge tube is too short, so this A key will move from side to side, the pad will not seal consistently, and it will be noisy.

Fig. 11.35 After swedging the key is a good fit between the pillars.

For some keys, it is easier and better to use a collet style swedging tool. This serves the same purpose as swedging pliers but can only be used on the ends of keys (and is therefore particularly useful on side keys). Mount the collet in an engineer's vice and choose the collet that fits tightly over the hinge tube. Insert the steel in the tube with a little oil and gently tighten the collet to shrink the tube, or tighten and twist to both shrink and lengthen the tube.

Waisted hinge screws

For many years up to the late 1960s, Boosey & Hawkes in the UK used special long hinge screws on their top line clarinets. Making and keeping these long hinge tubes straight was difficult, however, and the viscosity of the oil in the long tubes slowed down the action. To solve this, they started reducing the diameter of the hinge screw in the middle of the rod. It did help, but ultimately it was dropped. If you try to swedge a key like this in the wrong place, you will create further problems; make sure you only swedge at the ends of the rod, where it is not waisted.

When the hinge screw is loose in a pillar

It is easy to overlook the fit of the hinge screw in the pillar. If the hole in the pillar is too big, the hinge screw will move around, which can cause the same pad seating and regulation problems as a worn key; unlike an oversized hinge tube, which is subject to constant movement, the oversized pillar hole is only subject to static pressure across the axis. We can therefore solve the problem by finding a way to reduce the diameter of the hole.

Fig. 11.36 A Boosey & Hawkes hinge tube.

Checking and Repairing Keywork

Hinge tube shortening tools

Fig. 11.37 This is the basic hinge tube cutter from Ferree's Tools in the US. They come in a variety of pin sizes. You need to buy or make the sizes you need for the instruments you work on.

Fig. 11.38 Here is a treasured set of hinge tube shortening tools. It consists of a cutting tool with a 2mm threaded hole down its middle. This cutter can be attached to a long or short driving handle. The pins in the box are specific diameters of hinge screw and have a 2mm thread. They screw into the cutter.

Fig. 11.39 The five-sided broach, sometimes called an English broach, is for opening out small holes. This long, slender tool is used to remove burrs inside small holes. They should not be used to open up hinge tubes as the holes they cut are tapered.

Fig. 11.40 Not an essential tool by any means, the burr removal tool takes the burr off the outside ends of the hinge tube.

Measuring wear on hinge tubing

If you get deeply involved in the repair process, you might want to quantify the amount of movement there is in keywork. I have found that measuring the inside diameters of very small holes is very tricky with the tools I have. Here is a way I have found to check the difference in diameter between the hinge screw and the hinge tube:

- Mount the instrument between centres on a lathe.
- Set up a dial test indicator to touch the outside of the hinge tube you are interested in.
- Gently move the key from side to side. The dial test indicator will record the amount of movement.

Fig. 11.41 Hinge screw loose in a pillar.

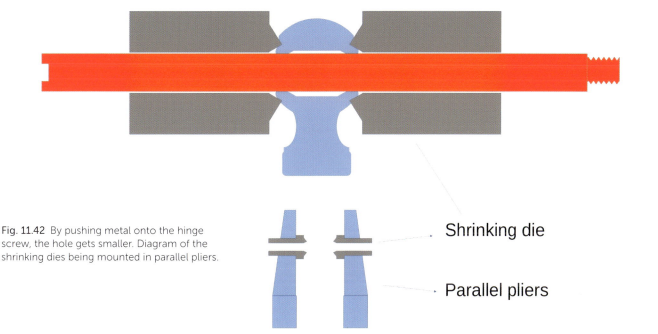

Fig. 11.42 By pushing metal onto the hinge screw, the hole gets smaller. Diagram of the shrinking dies being mounted in parallel pliers.

Shrinking die

Parallel pliers

Correcting a hinge tube that is too tight between the pillars

Shortening a hinge tube

There are occasions when you need to shorten hinge tubes. Running a file across the end of a tube is not good, as you can't keep the file square with the tube. The correct tool to use is what Ferree's calls a tubular hinge shortener. I own and have made various designs and my Kraus set is still my preference. To use one, find the size that fits smoothly in the tube and mount the tool in the bench motor. When the motor is spinning, push the tube onto the cutter. This will cut the end of the tube squarely and smoothly (Figs 11.43 and 11.44).

This cutting process can push up a burr at the end of a tube, both inside and outside. Remove these by scraping, filing, or using a specialist tool like the outside burr remover or a five-sided broach.

Fig. 11.43 Using a special tool to remove an external burr.

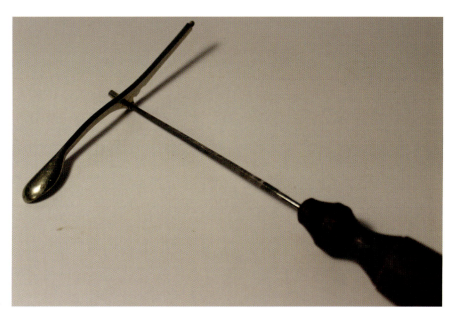

Fig. 11.44 Removing an internal burr.

Checking and Repairing Keywork

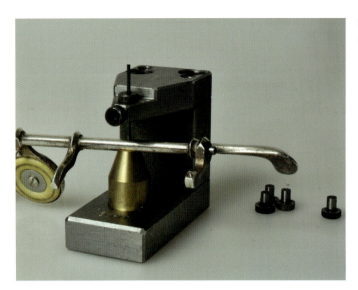

Fig. 11.45 Pin punch frame.

Improving pinned hinge rods

A pinned hinge rod sometimes needs to be disassembled. This might be in order to repair damage, take up wear, or to oil it, as part of an overhaul.

If the mechanism is screwed on, just unscrew it, but if it has a tapered pin, then it needs to be pushed or punched out. You need to push, or punch, from the small end of the pin. This will be the end closest to the body of the instrument. You will need to take the key off the instrument before you try and remove pins.

If there is a small piece of pin visibly sticking out, you can try using round-nosed pliers to squeeze it out; clamp one side of the pliers over the end of the pin and angle them so as not to block the wide end from coming out when you squeeze. If you can't see the small end, use Blu Tack to hold the relevant section of hinge tube upside-down over a block of lead. Use a tiny flat ended punch to knock the pin out, which will embed itself into the soft lead.

If you have a pin punch frame you can position the pin under the punch and knock the tapered pin out that way.

You should be able to reuse the old pins, but if you do need a replacement, I recommend Yamaha tapered pins, rather than the point of a needle spring. Do not push the pin in too hard, especially if the hole is not exactly central to the axis of the tube, as you can stretch the hinge rod on the weaker side and bend the whole hinge rod and hinge tube assembly.

Damaged key corks and felts

Key cork replacement tools and materials

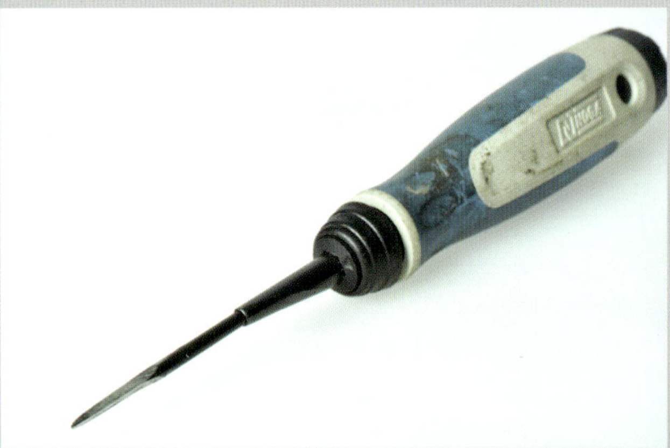

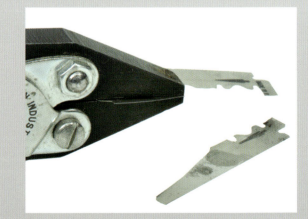

Fig. 11.46 Three-sided scraper. The Noga mini scraper with replaceable HSS or carbide blades works well for me. Blade width is 2.5mm.

Fig. 11.47 I use lots of razor blades to cut felt and cork around keywork. Domestic blades are made of soft stainless steel and don't work as well as the harder and more brittle industrial stainless steel blades. The industrial blades can be snapped to make long, narrow blades. Some technicians use scalpel blades to get into narrow spaces.

Fig. 11.48 Key cork removal.

Key cork and felt replacement

A heel cork is the piece of cork or felt used to act as a bumper between the keywork and the body of an instrument. It has two functions: to quieten and regulate the mechanism. The most sensible option for a repairer is to replace like with like. If cork has been used, then replace it with cork; if felt was used originally, use felt. That is not to say that I won't change it if I think it will improve the instrument's performance, for example by making it quieter or more precise.

Replacing key corks

The position and thickness of each of the key corks will vary from manufacturer to manufacturer, and careful observation of instruments in good condition will help you work out what is needed. In general, heel corks are between 1mm and 1.4mm thick, and adjusting corks are made using cork shavings, which are only 0.3mm thick.

Unless overhauling an instrument, only remove a key cork if it is of poor quality or badly damaged. It is sensible to take note of what thickness of cork is required for each key, or sort the keys into groups of similar cork thickness. This saves time later. Scrape the cork off with a three-sided scraper (Fig. 11.48).

Coat both the key and cork surface with contact adhesive and wait for the surface of the glue to become just dry to the touch. I test the surface with my fingernail and if it tries to stick, then it is not dry enough. Now press the two surfaces together. It should bond instantly, with no opportunity to re-position, so pay attention and get it right first time!

To shape the cork around the key, and remove excess cork, I use a new razor blade to slice it at an angle towards the metal edge of the key to make a clean straight cut following the shape of the key. Instruments look at their best when the corks and felts are cut at an angle to produce a tapered effect (Fig. 11.49).

Fig. 11.49 Shaping the cork.

Fig. 11.50 Key cork that has been trimmed.

Fig. 11.51 Key cork that has been trimmed in such a way as to minimize noise when it is operated.

In Fig. 11.51, the taper on the key cork is very pronounced. Changing the chamfer angle allows you to adjust the final contact area the cork has with the body; this affects how noisy the key will be when it hits the body and how stable the regulation will be over time.

A razor blade may only last for three or four heel corks before it starts to snag and stops cutting cleanly; this is the time to use another blade.

Link arm corks

Like key corks, link arm corks are pieces of cork or paper used to regulate the mechanism; they are key-to-key contact points. You will be using regular cork, wafer-thin cork, leather (from saxophone pads) or paper. For the most delicate adjustments use cigarette paper (using the sticky edge). This requires the most precise techniques. Small discs of paper or cork are put in place with fine-point tweezers. For emergency work, adhesive masking tape can be used. Be aware that the adhesive on these tapes tends to migrate or slip over time. Deciding what thickness these adjusting corks should be is determined by the interaction of the keys. They are nearly always used to adjust the time of arrival of two or more pads.

Fig. 11.52 Adjusting a link arm cork with abrasive. This is usually done with 600-grit wet and dry, or my preferred abrasive is 20-microm 3M film.

Replacing key felts

Unlike corks, the original felt can very often be re-glued rather than being replaced, unless you are carrying out a complete overhaul, in which case all felts would be replaced.

To make felt quieter, you can loosen up the fibres with a needle spring – this makes the felt less dense. This technique might only be effective for a limited period of time, however, since the felt will get re-compressed through spring pressure and handling.

There is a trade-off between quietness of action and precision of adjustment when using felt. In general, the softer the material, the less accurately you can make the adjustment.

Apply the contact adhesive to both surfaces, making sure the glue penetrates more than just the looser top fibres of the felt. Wait for it to dry and then push the key down hard onto the felt on a flat cutting surface. Using a new razor blade, slice firmly down from the edge of the key onto a cutting surface.

Fig. 11.53 Trimming off key felt.

Fig. 11.54 Bending a razor blade into a curved shape to cut a key felt. Unlike cork, felt needs to be supported when being cut.

Fig. 11.55 A finished bumper felt on a key.

Faulty springs

Two types of spring are used on woodwind instruments: needle springs and flat springs. Both are cantilever springs, fixed at one end, and are used to return the key to its 'at rest' position. Some musicians will ask you to adjust the 'weight' of the springs, but most of the time it is up to us as repairers to set the weight. In all cases the spring action, weight, or pressure needed to move the key should be constant throughout its travel.

If a key starts off feeling light and gets harder to move, it is most likely that the spring is too large (powerful) for the geometry of that key. You will not be able to adjust it correctly without changing the geometry or using a smaller diameter spring.

A simple test to check spring tension or weight is to use a fixed weight of Blu Tack on the key, or lever. I grade the weights very approximately as light (20g), medium (35g), and heavy (50g).

If a key has stopped springing into action, I want to know why. It could be that a key is rubbing on another key, the spring is loose in the pillar, the spring is about to break, the spring is the wrong size, the spring is not hitched on correctly, or that the spring is missing or broken. So carefully inspect the instrument. Once you are certain that a replacement spring is needed, it is always easiest to replace like with like.

Needle spring removal

Removing a needle spring is usually the most difficult part of the spring replacement process. I have a number of different tools and techniques.

When you want to remove a spring that is not broken and you want to keep it intact, then clamp the spring with a small toolmaker's clamp, close to the pillar, then using smooth-jawed pliers, apply pressure on the clamp and the far side of the pillar. If there is any broken spring showing, use

Spring work tools and materials

In addition to an anvil and hammer, you might also need the following tools.

Fig. 11.56 If you find working with very small screws difficult, then use a screwdriver with grabber called a 'starter screwdriver'. Mine are from Micro-Mark in the US.

Fig. 11.57 These two pairs of pliers have been modified to remove needle springs from pillars. The one on the left I made myself years ago and is designed to use replaceable needle springs for the push rod. It was not very successful and I do not use it much. I then bought a commercially produced version, which, as you might see, is not very worn either.

Fig. 11.58 Modified round-nosed pliers, with half of one jaw or blade ground away. This makes a great tool for pushing needle springs into position on a pillar.

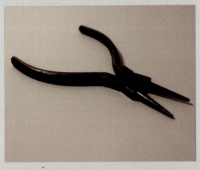

Fig. 11.59 Round-nosed pliers. These jeweller's pliers can be used as they are, or you can modify them for special purposes.

Fig. 11.60 Piano wire cutters by Maun.

Fig. 11.61 Needle springs come in sizes from No. 12 (0.35mm) through to size No. 000 (1.4mm) in 0.15mm increments. They are traditionally made in the same factory and with the same high carbon steel (silver-steel) as sewing machine needles. They have a point at one end and are tempered to the blue colour associated with springiness. I think that these are still the best design and material for oboes and older instruments. The most successful alternative spring is hard-drawn stainless steel wire (some top-end flutes use gold or silver wire springs). In the twentieth century, phosphor bronze was introduced for both wire and flat springs. Unfortunately, it is not easy to replace old phosphor bronze springs with any other material as they are large in diameter. Any replacement needle or stainless wire spring will be too powerful. So keep using phosphor bronze in these cases, or re-drill the spring hole (*see* Chapter 17).

modified round-nosed pliers to push it out as far as possible and then try to grip the fishtail with wire cutters to pull the spring the rest of the way out.

If there is no broken spring sticking out from the pillar, but there is some fishtail still showing on the other side, try pushing the spring further into the pillar and then push it back the other way and hope it comes out easily this time.

When no spring is protruding from the pillar you will have to punch the spring out. Use a needle spring with the point ground flat to punch the spring out. You will need to flatten the end of the broken spring by running a small needle file across the broken end of the spring to create a flat surface for the punch to sit on without slipping off. (Try not to damage the pillar, but sometimes there may be unavoidable collateral damage.)

In Fig. 11.64 the removed pillar is being held in place and supported on a lead block by Blu Tack (Fig. 11.64); the blunt needle spring is held by the toolmaker's clamp and the old spring knocked out into the lead.

On instruments where the pillar cannot be removed (saxophones or flutes), prepare a punch and the spring as above, and then support the pillar on the edge of the lead block to knock the spring out. If I can't support the instrument on my own, I ask a colleague to hold the instrument steady.

Removing a broken needle spring can prove difficult. I have mounted the instrument on the lathe, leaving both hands free to use the punch. By holding the punch in the toolmaker's clamp, I can keep it very steady and in line to make hitting easier.

Fig. 11.62 Needle spring removal.

Fig. 11.63 A punch made from a needle spring.

Fig. 11.64 Punching out a broken spring.

Fig. 11.65 Removing a broken needle spring.

Checking and Repairing Keywork **131**

Fitting new needle springs

Fig. 11.66 Working out how long the spring needs to be and marking the length.

After finding a replacement spring that is the same diameter and material as the original, offer the spring up to the instrument and key, to determine the overall length of spring required. You can bend the spring as it comes out of the pillar to mark where to cut.

Fig. 11.67 Cutting the needle spring to length.

You need to have high-quality piano wire cutters to cut through needle springs. I suggest you push the pointed end of the needle into the bench and hold the waste end when cutting a spring.

Fig. 11.68 Putting a fishtail flare on the end of the needle spring.

The blunt end of the spring is the end that will fix into the pillar, and this has to be hammered into a fishtail shape. Check the spring will fit tightly into the pillar and is the correct length. You have quite a lot of control on the shape of the fishtail and I use this to ensure the spring will be held firmly. Sometimes you will need to make it a long, narrow fishtail, and other times short and wide. (If your spring cracks when you hammer the fishtail, your springs might be a batch of springs that are not tempered enough and will be prone to breaking. By heating the blunt end of the spring over a flame for a few seconds, it will soften the metal slightly and it won't crack.)

Fig. 11.69 Pushing the spring into place.

Using round-nosed pliers or, better still, modified pliers, push the spring into place. The flat of the fishtail should be aligned horizontally across the pillar.

Now tension the spring by bending it in the direction you want the key to move. When you are tensioning a spring, you are bending the metal beyond its elastic limit and permanently deforming it. The exact shape of the bend you put in the spring is not the same for all keys and instruments. Some need a gentle curve throughout the length, whilst others need to have a fairly tight bend, close to the pillar, with the rest staying almost straight. Each shape has a reason. Sometimes a particular shape is needed to fit in a confined space between key parts. A very sharp bend should be avoided if possible, because it tends to weaken the metal at that point.

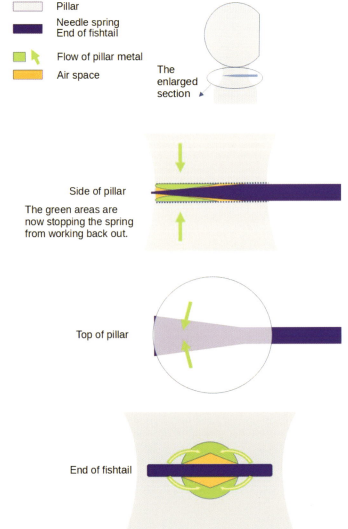

Fig. 11.70 Diagram of how needle springs fix into a pillar. The hard spring forces the softer pillar metal to flow in behind the fishtail top surface, locking the spring in place. The reason why a refitted needle spring is rarely as good as the initial fitting is because when you remove the spring, the displaced metal (in orange) is moved out of the way, but not back to its original place. The replacement spring has no metal to push back around it.

Oversized spring holes

Occasionally the spring hole has got bigger and bigger over the years and the replacement spring will be too large in diameter and too powerful for the key in question. Check to see why the spring might have broken or needed replacing so frequently. It usually indicates a design or manufacturing fault. If that is the case, re-design the spring mechanism. This usually requires a new spring hole to be drilled in a different location on the pillar (*see* Chapter 17).

Adjusting flat springs

Flat springs are used when a needle spring will not fit, or a needle spring would be too short. They are almost always used when the key pivots across the body of the instrument. Made from

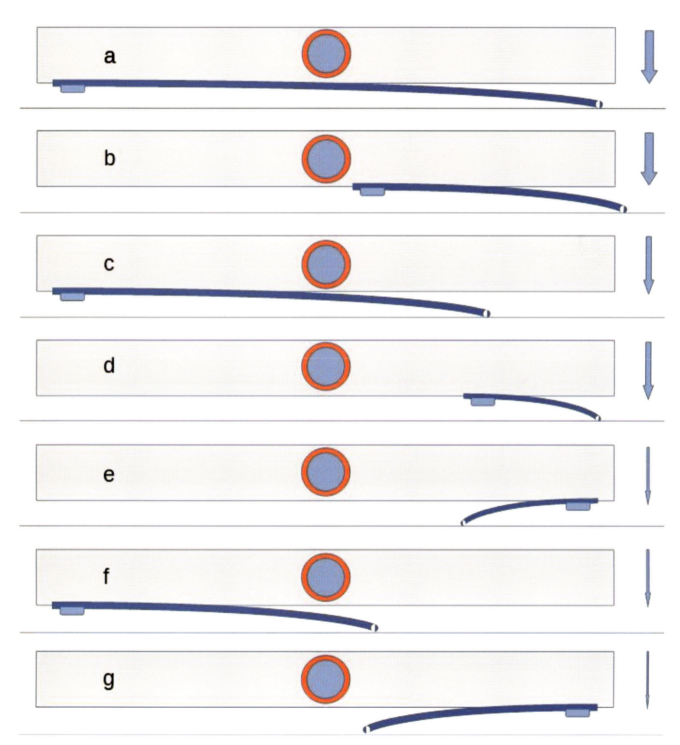

Fig. 11.71 Different key configurations, roughly ordered from best to worst, the criteria being how easy it is to shape the spring to prevent sliding at the tip, and how easy it is to exert a higher pressure. The diagram shows a key pivoted in the middle, and the springs all pushing the key down on the right-hand side. The arrows indicate how much pressure you have to exert to overcome the spring.

Checking and Repairing Keywork

sheet silver steel (blued spring steel), hard rolled stainless, or phosphor bronze, they are held onto the key with a small screw.

The manufacturer sets the material, thickness and shape of the spring. Pay attention to the way the curve is created on the spring. The aim is to shape the spring so that the tip of the spring does not slide. It can be tricky to achieve, and I sometimes have to change the shape of the key or the position where the tip of the spring touches. With patience it is always possible to prevent, or greatly reduce, the amount of sliding at the tip. By taking the time to do this, the key will operate smoothly and snappily for a long time.

Unsatisfactory solutions involve putting a short upward curve at the end of the spring or oiling and greasing the tip. These might work in the short term, but they are not the correct solution.

Each key presents its unique geometry, but there is a straightforward rule to make a flat spring work well: the tip of the spring should not slide back and forth when in use. How you achieve this is more of a problem.

When the key is on the instrument, operate the key and look to see if the spring tip is sliding. If the tip stays still and does not slide, you have a well set spring and it should be snappy and even (if not, there is a mechanical problem with the key itself). If the tip is sliding, then use a feeler gauge to locate the point where the spring stops making contact with the key. Remove the key and try and work out how to make the effective length of the spring longer. This can be done by reshaping the curve on the spring or, if needed, you can file away the bottom of the key under the spring. This is often required on clarinet A key (C5). The aim is to make the effective length of your spring as long as possible.

Other keywork checks

While inspecting the keywork, you should also be on the lookout for other defects and problems.

Bent keywork

Keep a look out for keys that are rubbing against each other or for keys bent under other keys. A good example of when this can happen is with the C10 on the clarinet. When the instrument gets dropped, this key often gets bent under C9. In this case use parallel acting pliers to unbend the key (Fig. 11.72).

Whatever tool you use to bend the keywork, think about where the weak point is on the key and decide if you want it to bend there, or if you want to avoid putting strain on that point. You then adjust how you pivot the

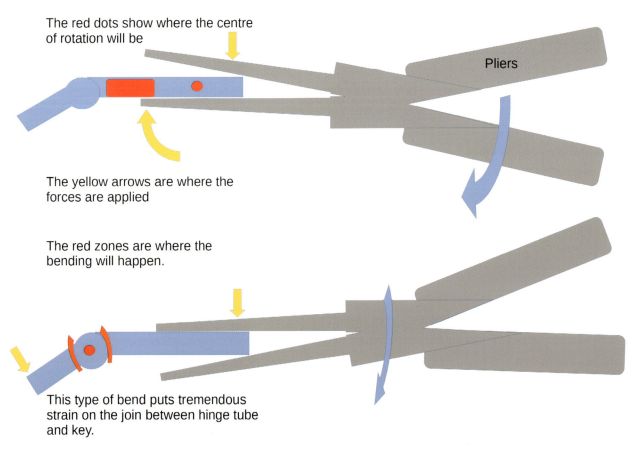

Fig. 11.72 How to use pliers to unbend a flute key.

134   Checking and Repairing Keywork

pliers and where you apply the counter pressure.

Cracks in keywork and solder faults

On older instruments it is worth looking for cracks in the keywork; they can cause major problems if they are missed. The metal used for the keywork is much poorer quality than modern metals and can crack apart if bent too often. You will have to re-solder or splice in a new piece of keywork to repair this.

Silver solder joints can also be weak areas in keys, so the tail of a key might start to break loose from the hinge tube. You will have to re-solder the key with silver solder. Soft solder will not work.

On some flutes, the threaded boss inside the pad cup is soft-soldered to the cup and the screw can push the boss off if screwed in too far or, if you heat the back of the pad too much, it can weaken the solder. Soft-solder the boss back on.

CHAPTER 12

Checking and Replacing Pads

You may have been thinking that putting a pad in was the most crucial part of woodwind repair, and it is, but it will only be really successful if you have first made sure that the mechanism is working correctly. I can't overstress the importance of testing and repairing the instrument for keywork operation and tone hole/body integrity before you start padding.

Tools for checking pads

Fig. 12.1 One of the essential tools in the toolbox. The feeler gauge is used to test if a pad is touching the bed plate or tone hole rim evenly around its circumference. The most sensitive and accurate feeler gauge is made from the thinnest cigarette paper (Rizla blue box) cut to a triangle shape. You can also use the 'lead in tape' from an audio cassette. (For those born after 1990 you might have to look up what a cassette tape is!) In each case, the end of the feeler gauge is tapered to the width appropriate for the instrument being worked on. (You can buy feeler gauge holders or make your own as in the picture above.) For clarinets and flutes, I use a tip width of 2.5mm to 3mm; for small oboe pads, 2mm. For saxophones, you can use the full width of the cassette tape.

Fig. 12.2 Cassette tape for feeler gauges. The lead-in tape is particularly nice to use.

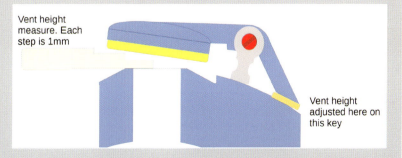

Fig. 12.3 Vent height gauge. This can be made from plastic, wood or cardboard. The surfaces have to be very smooth.

Checking pads

Unless you are undertaking an overhaul, you only need to change a pad if it is not doing what it should do. The primary purpose of a pad is to make a tone hole seal. Its secondary purpose is to act as a reflector of the sound vibrations trying to escape the hole.

Deciding whether to change a pad

You should by now be familiar with the pressure/vacuum testing process, visual inspection, and the use of a feeler gauge. However, these are such fundamental skills that I will repeat some of them here. It is crucial during the initial testing and the final testing (after the repair) not to fool yourself into thinking that the pads are airtight, when in fact they are not.

Fig. 12.4 The two black marks in the tone hole impression on this pad indicate pinholes that will leak air.

Even little black spots on the pad, where the tone hole impression is, can be a sign of a leak.

It is not uncommon for brand new pads to have pinholes in the membrane surface. This is why repairers often specify double skin pads (I am one of those people). The chances of both membranes having a pinhole is very small.

To test if there is a pinhole in a pad, very gently drag a sharp needle spring over the entire surface. The needle has to be almost vertical when you do this. The point will glide over the surface without damaging the membrane unless it finds a weak spot or a hole, then it will snag in the hole (Fig. 12.5).

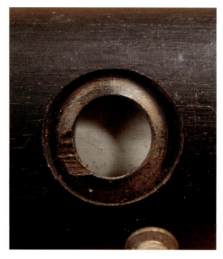

Fig. 12.5 Badly chipped tone hole.

Check the tone hole rim condition. It is always a good idea to carefully check the flatness and condition of the tone hole rim. Tiny blemishes caused by the grain of the wood, chips or an undulating bed plate can make seating a pad difficult.

How to use feeler gauges

Insert the tip of the feeler gauge into the middle of the tone hole and gently close the key, either using its own spring or gentle finger pressure. Now withdraw the feeler gauge. Using your sense of touch and possibly hearing, determine the level of drag on the feeler gauge and how tightly it grips the tape. Until you become experienced, you will not know if it is gripping too little or too much; the important thing, at first, is to establish a base level of grip. Next open the key and re-insert the feeler 45 degrees around the tone hole, close it again and pull it out again. Is the amount of grip similar to the first place you tested? Test again at another 45 degrees and so on all the way around the pad. Make a note at which position it drags more, less or the same. Repeat this test as many times as needed on the same pad until you can identify all the differences.

If the pad has the same drag characteristic all the way around the pad it is likely to be working well, so move on to the vacuum test and confirm your result. When you are satisfied you know whether or not it is even, move onto the next pad. Understanding what the feeler gauge is telling you is an important skill to develop as it is used when testing existing pads and installing a new pad.

How hard to push down on a pad key when testing

I am often asked how hard one should push on the pad when testing with a feeler gauge or doing a vacuum test. This is one of the trickiest skills to teach, and to learn, as the amount of pressure needed for top quality work is very small indeed. For the majority of instruments and players, the pads do not need to be adjusted to such sensitivity, but it is important to know how little pressure should be used when adjusting top quality instruments.

The reason that numbers are rarely (if ever) given for the amount of pressure needed to seat a pad, is that there are so many variables in the size and type of pad, quality and condition of mechanism and the opinion of each repairer. However, I think it is useful if I try and do it in this book and maybe it will start the process of refining the data and information for the future.

I conducted the following experiment using a Yamaha YCL650 clarinet, as it came out of the box. Although it is not a 'top-of-the-range' instrument, as usual I found the padding was good enough and it is a very playable instrument.

Here is how I measured the pressure I use when testing the pads with a feeler gauge. First, I unhooked the spring from the B key and made sure the side levers or C key were not attached. Then I rested the instrument on an instrument cradle so that the E/b (C15) pad cup was horizontal. Then I lifted the key up and put the feeler gauge tip into the centre of the tone hole and allowed the key to close. I did not feel any drag on the feeler gauge as I pulled it from under the pad, so I added some Blu Tack to the top of the pad cup and tried again. After adding even more Blu Tack I got to a point where it felt like I would expect, when testing a good pad. I then weighed the Blu Tack, which was 20g.

To confirm the results, I then put this 20g of Blu Tack on a number of different pads on the clarinet and tested them again at various points around the pad.

I was looking for some resistance or drag at all points I tested and the more even the grip around the pad, the better. I noticed that when the drag on the pad was similar all around the pad, it actually felt like it was gripping it harder at each point.

It is then necessary to re-test after the spring has been attached. Only push as hard as needed to get the same feel as you did with the 20g weight. If there is excessive movement in the mechanism (if a point screw is not set correctly), then the grip will not be the same, indeed it might be worse, so you will either have to improve the key mechanism, or compromise and re-seat the pad with the spring in place.

When I performed a similar test on other instruments, pad pressures seemed to be consistent across a range of instruments.

Testing saxophone pad seating

Using a leak light is a quick way to check the padding on a saxophone. It is not however, infallible. The leak light is inserted in the body of the instrument so you can inspect for light escaping between the rim of the tone hole and the pad surface when the key is closed. If light is visible anywhere around the tone hole rim, it proves there is a fault. Unfortunately, no light does not prove there is no fault. Using dim ambient lighting helps this process, or you can cup your hand around each key to darken that pad. Make a note of where the light is escaping and get an understanding as to how much extra pressure is needed to block the light or close the gap. To be entirely sure the pad is seating, use a feeler gauge to test the pad as well.

There are other places on a saxophone where leaks can occur. Some of these are difficult to detect but are also uncommon; I only go looking for them if all other tests fail. The fit of the neck to the body is, however, a common area of concern. If the neck is loose in the socket of the body, then refer to page 100. The speaker tube in the main body can also come un-soldered and loose.

Fig. 12.6 Using kitchen scales to weigh out 20g of Blu Tack.

Fig. 12.7 Testing the drag under the pad.

Checking and Replacing Pads 139

Replacing pads

The art of padding an instrument is probably the most frustrating part of instrument repair. Sometimes a pad will fit on the key and work very easily and quickly, but on many occasions it will require all the patience you have.

The installation process is fairly easy to describe, but it is difficult to tell you how to do it well, as it relies on your sense of feel, and gentleness of touch, both of which are difficult to quantify or put words to. To get good at it, you need to practise and know how well it is possible to get the pads to seal. Keep looking at, and checking, good instruments and aim to get your instrument as good as the best.

Tools for replacing pads

Fig. 12.8 The spirit lamp has been the standard method of heating keywork since instruments started being made. The fuel is a clean burning (non-smoking) alcohol, sold in the UK as methylated spirits (meths) and as denatured alcohol in the US. It is worth keeping the cap on the wick when not in use. This will stop excessive evaporation and also prevent the meths absorbing water from the atmosphere.

Fig. 12.9 Pad slicks (also known as pad irons). These thin flat metal paddles are used when installing pads. They are used flat against the pad surface and help manipulate the alignment of the pad when the adhesive behind the pad is liquid. They are also used to help align the pad cup to the tone hole rim. I made the darker examples in this photo out of gauge plate. Gauge plate is a precision ground sheet of high carbon steel.

Fig. 12.10 These small hand-held blowtorches are sold by jewellery workshop suppliers. The flame can be adjusted to be gentle (good for heating the backs of pad cups), as well as much hotter to undertake small silver soldering tasks.

Fig. 12.11 Hot air gun, used for melting shellac and hot melt adhesives when working on saxophones. This hot air gun is smaller than a hot air paint stripper. The one you choose might not look like the picture as there is a whole new range of temperature controlled hot air guns on the market, commonly used by the electronics industry. They are sold as hot air rework stations.

Fig. 12.12 Flat metal plate for tone hole checking and levelling. You can make these yourself.

Fig. 12.13 Rubber bung used for pressure testing. This example has a brass tube going right through it, but this is not necessary. A selection of sizes is useful.

Fig. 12.14 Pumice board. It is tricky to get hold of a suitable pumice block for this purpose. The best material I have found is a synthetic pumice. I had to buy it in a rectangular block (80 × 100mm) from France. I sliced it into 3mm thick sheets and flattened both sides of the stone on Abrafile emery paper, which gave me a very light, flat and self-cleaning abrasive for use on cork pads. It might be possible to get the correct material from nail bars or beauty parlours as they use it for exfoliation.

Fig. 12.15 This is a set of tone hole topping tools I made forty years ago. I have adjusted the sizes to suit the instruments I repair. I replace the abrasive pads quite frequently.

Fig. 12.16 Pad clamps, to keep a gentle pressure on a pad while the shellac or hot melt adhesive cools.

Fig. 12.17 These polished smooth-jawed duckbill pliers are very wide and spread the load over a large area. They are great for adjusting flute pad cups and saxophone work.

Fig. 12.18 Flute pad cup bending tool. This is one of several designs of specialist tool that is used to hold a flute pad cup while bending them to make them level with the tone hole. The screw moves the white nylon insert up and down the tool and will clamp the cup while you bend it.

Fig. 12.19 Flute pad cup L benders. These sit between the tone hole rim and the pad cup. You then push down on the opposite side of the pad cup to change the cup's position.

Fig. 12.20 These modified parallel pliers have circular nylon jaws to protect the delicate plating when you are pushing home the pad retaining grommets on open hole flutes.

Fig. 12.21 Specialist pliers that slide under the grommets of open hole flute pads so that you can lever the grommet out of the key tube. They are highly polished to avoid damaging the flute pad.

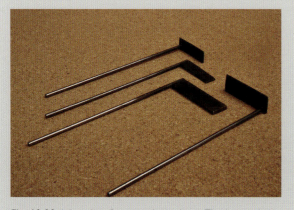

Fig. 12.22 L benders for saxophone keys. The brass plates of these tools sit between the tone hole and pad cup on saxophones. You can then manipulate the pad cups to align better.

Fig. 12.23 Saxophone leak light, LED design. Nowadays you can get flexible ones that are good for baritones. You can make your own light strips using caravan or under cupboard lighting kits; stick the strips back-to-back to give an all-round light.

Fig. 12.24 Saxophone key benders. These levers are hooked under the hinge tubes of saxophone keys so the pad cup can be manipulated.

Pad design and materials

There is a bewildering choice of pad design and materials available to choose from and it is not easy to test what is going to be best for your customers. Climate, cost and availability will all play their part in your choice. It will also be influenced by what the fashion is at the time.

Unless agreed with my customer before starting, I will use the same style of pad as is already on the instrument.

Look at all the pads on the instrument and get a feel for the look and style of padding. Some manufacturers like to have the edge of the pad showing. Some use traditional pads, others synthetic.

Here are a few important things to know about good pads:

- They have an airtight surface.
- They are compliant enough to conform to the contours of the tone hole.
- They are water-resistant, or, more specifically, are not damaged by water.
- They are wear- and abrasion-resistant.
- They are durable under repeated flexing and vibration.
- They are resistant to build-up of sticky layers.
- They are acoustically compatible; able to reflect vibrations.
- They are easy to install and replace.
- They are economical to manufacture in a variety of sizes.

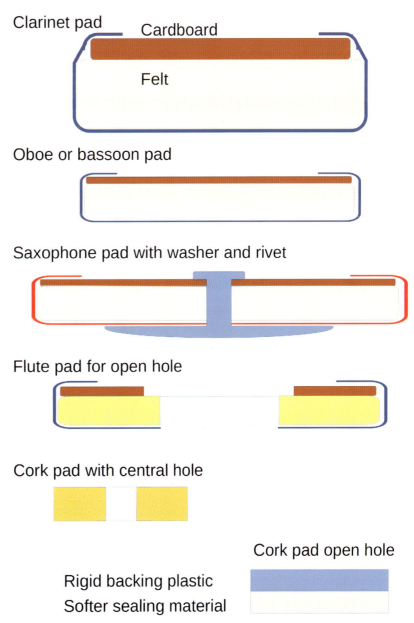

Fig. 12.25 Anatomy of a variety of pads. For most of the twentieth century the design and materials of choice were a cardboard disc with a felt disc on top of it, all wrapped in a natural membrane, either leather or goldbeater's skin.

Checking and Replacing Pads

There is an ongoing debate about what the exact specification of each of these components should be: the different thicknesses and stiffnesses of the cardboard; the type, thickness and fibre used in the felt; the choice of the membrane used. The membrane used to be thin leather, then a material called goldbeater's skin became more common. True goldbeater's skin is a cured animal intestine and was superseded in the 1970s by a thinner (and less satisfactory) membrane called fish bladder (derived from fish, as the name implies), or a synthetic membrane. Meanwhile, advocates of leather pads started experimenting with different tanning methods and a brilliant technician called Gordon Beeson added a disc of polythene between the felt and the leather to attain a superior leather pad, which, in my opinion, has not been surpassed. Beeson also spent many years perfecting the choice of leather and felt he used. It is worth keeping any examples of pads stamped GB (for Gordon Beeson) if you come across them. Buffet also developed a pad with a layer of Gortex over the top. As with all pad design, there is much debate as to the merits of each material.

Boosey & Hawkes tried using rubber pads in the 1960s; synthetic materials started to be used at the end of the twentieth century. Valentino was the first manufacturer to make a success of synthetic pads. It is remarkable that most manufacturers still use either leather or bladder pads almost thirty years after alternatives became available.

However, there seems to be a steady rise in the use of synthetic materials, and it is probably to the benefit of both manufacturers and musicians. I have worked with fine examples of composite pads made with different density foam and backings. These include Eddie Ashton's Superpads, which are neoprene with cork backing, Valentino Pro Pads and Ed Kraus's Omni Pads. As with older style pads, it takes a lot of practice to get good at installing them, but the principle of what we are trying to achieve remains the same.

My personal opinion is that the current movement towards ever harder and perfectly seating pads is a mistake, and we are losing a tonal complexity and smoothness of action. It has become too 'digital', too 'open or closed'. This is in complete contrast to the fashion of the early twentieth century, exemplified by Charles Morley in the UK, who used very soft stuffed pads that would cope with any number of faults in the tone hole. Once 'creased' or 'bedded' (which might take up to six months of use) these pads would then go on working perfectly for twenty or more years without an adjustment.

Synthetic pads

Synthetic pads are becoming much more common on new instruments and for after-market repairs. I believe they have a good future and may replace the traditional materials. Manufacturers are experimenting with different foam formulations and structures. Currently, one manufacturer, Valentino, offers self-adhesive pads that cannot be adjusted once the pad is installed. They work when the keywork is true and adjusted for that brand of pad and rely on the soft texture of the pad to cover the tone hole.

More sophisticated synthetic pads now incorporate a firm backing material of plastic or cork and you can adjust the position of the pad using the same sort of techniques as traditional pads. More care is needed in the choice of adhesive and temperature used, so follow the instructions that come from the manufacturer.

Ed Kraus's instructions for seating synthetic pads

Here are the instructions from Ed Kraus Music, who I consider the best of the current manufacturers. The pads will only seal properly if there is a small impression (seat) in the foam. 'Impression-less' padding is not possible. However, you only need the minimum impression necessary to be visible. It is important to note that if the pad hits the tone hole while it is still warm, the pad materials will compress and melt an impression into the pad. This may look right, but if the materials are melted together they become hardened, are no longer foam, and no longer capable of sealing properly. Start by making sure the pad can be made perfectly level to the tone hole, so dry mount the pad on the instrument and make sure the pad will naturally sit on the tone hole. Change the style or size of the pad if the first choice does not fit correctly. Now glue the pad into the key with hot melt glue and only when the key and adhesive have cooled down, are they are then seated with finger pressure. Don't rush. If you seat the pad while it is still warm, the ring will be too deep, or uneven. Please wait until the pad is at room temperature before putting a small impression into the foam. Press a little and hold, and if this did not make an impression, press a little harder and hold a little longer. The pads are made from special plastic foams. Most likely your feeler gauge is also plastic, so there is an attraction between the pad and the feeler gauge. This means that even where you might have a small area where the pad is light, the feeler gauge might still have some drag. It is important to make sure that you check that opposite sides of the pad have the same amount of drag. Only when opposites are the same (3 o'clock = 9 o'clock, 12 = 6) are you actually level. Just because the feeler touches all the way around doesn't mean the pad is level. Using a feeler gauge is not the only, or best, way to check the padding. You should also remove every key after final levelling and seating, and make a visual inspection of the pad seat with magnification to ensure that the pad seat is uniform in width and depth, all the way around the circumference. If there are any deep or wide spots, the pad will leak there, even though your feeler gauge says it is OK! You can also make your own vacuum or pressure test. Synthetic pads are heat sensitive. The process of heating the pad cup to melt the glue leaves the cup radiating enough heat to soften the foam layers slightly. Use only the flat face of a pad slick over the entire face of the pad to shift the pad while floating. If you touch only part of the foam of a warm pad with the edge of a pad slick, or try to put a needle into the foam of the pad, the foam layer of the pad will be ruined.

Adhesives for attaching pads

These are thermoplastic materials that become liquid when warmed and set again when cold. The process can be repeated as many times as needed. It is used for holding pads in place, where you want to re-position the pad during installation.

Shellac

The woodwind trade uses three forms of shellac: stick, flake and liquid. Stick and flake shellac is used to bond pads into pad cups. Stick shellac comes in two varieties: transparent or amber shellac; and white shellac, which is amber shellac filled with chalk powder. The chalk significantly affects the plastic properties of the shellac when melted. Both amber and white shellac can be softened or liquefied with heat (around 70 degrees) as many times as you like.

Amber shellac then remains pliable and manoeuvrable for a long time, making it perfect for seating most pads. However, on oboes and bassoons, you can use a padding technique that requires more practice – manipulating the pad surface to fit the tone hole – and the quicker setting properties of white shellac are useful for this. Stick shellac usually comes in 10mm square section sticks about 100mm long. I find these sticks too big to use, so soften the sticks over a soft flame and stretch them out into strings about 4mm in diameter. Many factories and repairers prefer to use flake shellac. These flakes are loaded into the upturned pad cup and heated over a flame; when melted, the pad is installed. Your choice of shellac or hot melt adhesive will sometimes be made by what is readily available to you.

Hot melt glues

These are the modern equivalent to shellac and are also thermoplastic materials. Usually used with a glue gun, you can use hot melt sticks on their own, like stick shellac. As with any new material or technique, it takes time to master. I have yet to convert entirely to hot melt adhesive but have found some formulations very good.

Glue pellets and specialist dispensers

These include some excellent glue pellets and specialist dispensers from Buffet, Ed Kraus, and Music Medic in the US that come as pellets and granules. My early frustration with hot melt glue was that it has a long 'plastic' phase where you think you have positioned it correctly, but over time it creeps back to an earlier position. The above suppliers are developing new formulations every year, so it is worth testing a variety of products to find one you like. The main advantage of hot melt glue is that it does not suffer from cold shock; this occasionally happens when an instrument has been cooled very quickly (put in the boot of a car after a concert) and a pad falls out, complete with all the shellac.

Fig. 12.26 Hot melt adhesives for attaching pads.

Washers

You will need to have many different thicknesses and diameters of washers for flute pads. They can be as thin as 0.2mm.

Cork pads

Oboes require cork pads. I buy these from a specialist supplier as they have to be premium quality cork. A good supplier will send pads made only from the finest, blemish-free cork, and they will have perfectly cut edges. We repair a wide range of oboes, and need a large combination of outside and inside hole diameters to cover all possibilities. Even with a wide range, we still have to re-cut some pads with a cork boring tool.

Fig. 12.27 A selection of flute pad washers.

Fig. 12.28 Oboe cork pads.

Goldbeater's skin

This is a sheet of ox intestine that has been used to hammer out gold to form gold leaf. It is very tough, flexible and can be moulded when wet. It is great for sealing oboe reed blades, as a cover for pin and socket linkages, and for making authentic style vintage pads.

Fig. 12.29 Goldbeater's skin.

Pad removal

If you are servicing an instrument, you will only be removing pads that are damaged. Damage might be a pin-prick hole in the surface of the pad, felt showing through the pad membrane, abraded edges, hard or brittle pads, or an uneven impression on the surface of the pad. Discoloration of a pad does not necessarily mean that it is defective.

Except for the flute, the removal method is to heat the pad cup enough to melt the adhesive. Both shellac and hot melt glues are used to hold pads on. In general, you cannot re-use old pads. I am in the habit of using a spirit lamp to warm keys on smaller instruments and a small blowtorch or heat gun for saxophones and larger pads. Heat the back of the pad cup in a way that deflects the flame away from the pad itself. Use a needle spring inserted in the side of the pad to prise the pad out of the cup (Fig. 12.30).

Flute pads (and a few other instruments) use a screw and washer to hold the pad in place. These have to be removed when the key is off the instrument. Flute pads can sometimes be re-installed, so it is essential to mark the flute pad and washers to tell you in which orientation the pad is fitted.

Fig. 12.30 A pad held in place with a screw and washer. Note the pen mark on the pad to show the orientation.

To remove a flute pad, I place the pad cup, with the pad facing up, on a soft surface. Using a screwdriver with a thin, wide blade that fits the small pad screw, I push down and turn anticlockwise. If the screw will not rotate, try tightening it gently and then unscrew. I make a note of the combined thickness of pad and pad washers when I remove a pad.

Installing bladder and leather pads

I will describe the process of installing bladder and leather pads first, as these are probably the type of pad that will need to be replaced most often. The majority of clarinets and some pads on all the other instruments use bladder or leather pads, which are installed using the following method. (Clarinet leather pads are treated in the same way as bladder pads but you don't need to puncture the side of the pad to let the air out.)

Starting with an empty pad cup, install the key on the instrument. Set the spring. Place a pad slick on the surface of the tone hole and close the pad cup onto the pad slick. Look to see how the rim of the pad cup sits on the pad slick. If there is a gap on one side then use your parallel acting pliers to bend the key arm, so that the cup is level.

Next, find a pad that fits in the cup; the thickness of the pad you choose is judged by the gap you observed between the pad slick and the depth of the pad cup.

Choosing the right size of pad

The advantage of using Original Equipment Manufacturer (OEM) pads is that they should be the right diameter and thickness. However, in many cases this might be impossible, so you have to learn how to choose the right pad yourself. The instrument looks good if the same amount of pad is showing all around the pad cup, but don't sacrifice the pad seating, just to get the pad looking good.

Figs 12.31 and 12.32 show a way to check that a pad cup is aligned with the tone hole correctly and what thickness of pad will be needed.

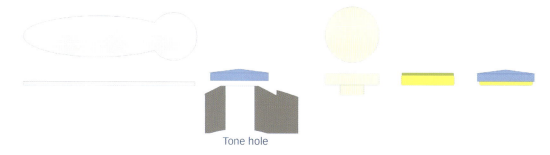

Fig. 12.31 Standard thickness pad slick for standard pads. From left to right: thin pad slick; how the pad cup sits over the tone hole; diagram of an optional dummy pad; style of pad that will work with this pad cup; how the pad will look when the pad is installed.

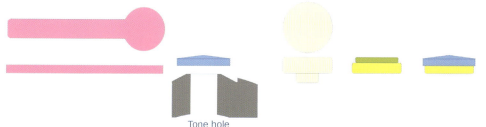

Fig. 12.32 Thicker pad slick for French step pads. From left to right: slightly thicker pad slick; the pad cup is sitting higher above the tone hole rim; the optional dummy pad; a French step pad; and how the pad will look when installed.

Checking and Replacing Pads

During this checking process, also look out for pad cups that are tilted from side to side as well as front to back. If the cup is not level from side to side, use parallel acting pliers on the arm to bring the pad cup level with the tone hole rim.

When a pad cup sits on the pad slick with a very large gap at the front, you may need to bend the key down at the front to make pad seating easier. If it is only a small gap then choose a slightly thinner pad than standard, otherwise when the pad is seated correctly it will have more pad showing at the front of the cup than the back.

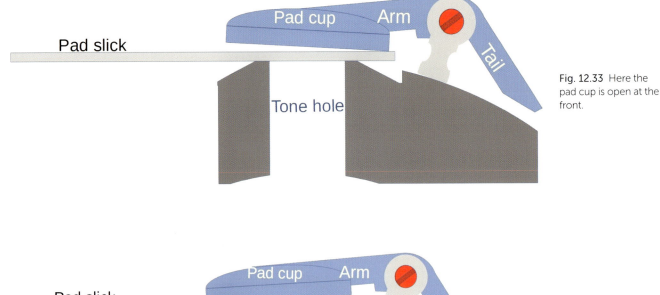

Fig. 12.33 Here the pad cup is open at the front.

Fig. 12.34 The pad cup is open at the back.

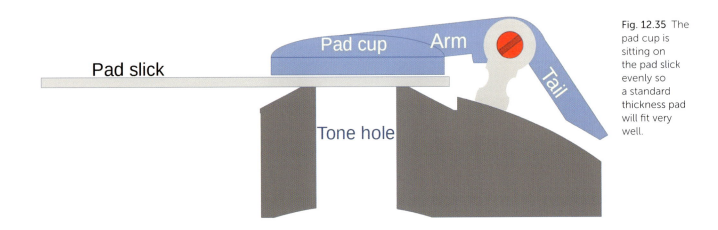

Fig. 12.35 The pad cup is sitting on the pad slick evenly so a standard thickness pad will fit very well.

If the pad cup has a gap at the back between the cup and pad slick, you will need to choose a thicker than standard pad or bend the key to make it more level. If you use a standard thickness pad, the pad will show more at the back than the front.

A standard pad is designed to seat when it has just over a pad slick thickness showing out of the cup. So in this situation a standard pad will be easy to seat.

Only bend a key if you can't find the correct thickness of pad. As you change the angle of the pad cup, it can bring the

148   Checking and Replacing Pads

whole pad cup forward or backwards over the tone hole rim. This will decentralize the pad on the rim and can cause problems.

When you have the alignment correct and have chosen the correct thickness of pad, remove the key from the instrument.

Seating the pad

This is the bit you might have been waiting for – it is what most people want to learn how to do. Seating a pad is a simple process to do and describe; however, getting good at it requires lots of practice and a rigorous testing routine.

This section deals with clarinet and similar pads, not flute pads, cork or synthetic pads.

Once you have chosen the pad that will fit, make a pinhole in the side of the pad using a sharp needle spring. This is to allow air to escape from the pad when it is warmed. If you miss this step then the pad will blow up like a balloon and will need to be replaced (Fig. 12.36). I also use the needle spring to roughen the cardboard backing of the pad, which helps the adhesive to stick better (Fig. 12.37).

Remove the key, remove the pad, and melt flake shellac or stick shellac into the bottom of the pad cup. When the shellac is molten, gently push and twist the pad into the cup and adjust it to look even in the cup. Judging the amount of shellac needs the benefit of experience. It is better to have slightly too much adhesive than too little, as the pad needs to 'float' on a layer of adhesive to enable final adjustments to the pad seating. You can always chip away excess shellac that squeezes out from around the pad cup, but if you have too little adhesive, you might not be able to seat the pad or the pad might fall out.

Put the key back onto the instrument and set the spring. Now, holding the instrument in a way that allows the heating flame to flow over the back of the pad cup, but away from any other

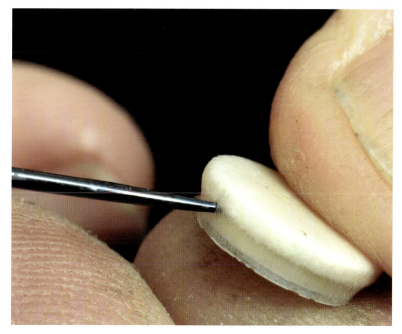

Fig. 12.36 Puncture the side of the pad to stop the pad from ballooning.

Fig. 12.37 Melting the shellac.

Checking and Replacing Pads

Fig. 12.38 Heating the pad cup to melt the shellac, and manipulating the pad with a pad slick to get it to seat evenly on the tone hole rim.

keys and the body of the instrument, keep heating the key to get the shellac to become mobile.

Once the shellac or hot melt is soft or liquid, open and shut the key a few times to let the pad settle. Now use your feeler gauge to test the grip of the pad all around the tone hole. If the feeler grips tighter in one area over another, re-heat the back of the pad as above and use a pad slick to manipulate the pad to improve the evenness of the grip.

The principle of using a pad slick is to keep the slick flat against the pad at all times. This keeps the pad surface flat.

Check and recheck

The most reliable way I have found to confirm my padding is to only have one key on the instrument at a time. Have all the other holes blocked with Blu Tack and then test the airtightness of the pad, one at a time. Only when the pad is airtight will I remove that key and put another key on. Do not rush this process. One of the most difficult parts of being a repairer is the discipline of vacuum testing for leaks. In its simplest form you block the holes of the instrument and draw a vacuum and see how quickly the vacuum drops.

Pad setting

To set or not to set the pad? There is much discussion amongst repairers as to the benefit, or not, of 'setting' the pad once you have seated the pad. Setting the pads is an attempt to permanently crease the surface of the pad onto the tone hole to improve the airtightness of the pad. It is a process the manufacturers frequently use, but in my experience, it only works if the pad has been adjusted to seat perfectly anyway, in which case there is no harm in setting the pad. If you wish to set the pad, then warm the back of the cup, but not enough to re-melt the adhesive. Then gently clamp the pad shut, using your fingers or a lightly sprung clamp, until cool. Do not attempt to try and disguise poor pad seating by using this technique; it will fail anyway.

An even more aggressive version of the pad setting described above (though I do not use this technique) is to steam plastic instruments and flute pads as a final step to make a strong impression on the pad. Use a steam generator to push steam into the bore of the instrument for a few seconds when all the pads are clamped closed. Then move the instrument to an oven set at 60 degrees and leave for a few minutes to dry. Leave the clamps on overnight. Make sure you re-test every pad carefully the next day and adjust again as needed. Note that this technique is out of favour on high-end instruments.

Installing saxophone pads

For many years I avoided working on saxophones as the equipment and materials were extensive and expensive. Knowing what I know now, I needn't have left it so long. If you want to stock up on pads, then I would choose ones with domed plastic rivets. A well-respected technician called Ralph Morgan carried out extensive tests for Selmer USA in the 1960s and concluded that low profile plastic domed pads were the best design regarding acoustics and durability. It is the design still favoured by Yamaha for a good reason.

It is essential to invest in a set of saxophone pad irons or pad slicks. They have a large hole in the middle that avoids the reflectors. Check that the metal they are made from is stiff and won't bend easily. You will also need a small gas torch or better still, a micro hot air gun.

Saxophone pad cup alignment

Before starting to pad a saxophone, follow all the recommended body and keywork checks, ensuring the keywork fits properly, and any dents are removed. It is particularly important to check and adjust the tone hole rims to make them flat.

We now need to make the pad cup sit parallel with the tone hole. It is a good idea to prepare the keywork on the body a day before padding, as this allows the metal to settle down to its natural position. Re-check the instrument and adjust as needed the next day.

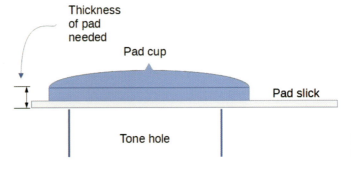

Fig. 12.39 Levelling a pad cup.

Fig. 12.40 Testing the pad cup alignment.

Fig. 12.41 Bending a pad cup to make it level with the tone hole using an L bender.

By laying a pad slick on the tone hole rim and shutting the key, you can usually see if the pad cup rim is sitting on the pad slick evenly all around. Use a large paper feeler gauge to test around the pad cup rim to find where it is not touching. Use the appropriate key bending tool in your tool kit to level the key with the tone hole rim.

It is worth knowing that pad cups do not always bend as a unit. If the pad cup has a spine running over the top it will be stiff to bend front and back, or one side of the cup might bend and the other side might not follow it. Change methods and tools until you find a way of moving the pad cup as one unit.

The tools you might use to bend the keys include L benders and saxophone bending levers. L benders sit on the rim of the tone hole in the area where the rim is too close, so by pushing down on the opposite side of the pad cup you can tilt the pad cup over.

The small semi-circular grooves in the end of the fork arms of the bending levers hook under the hinge tube or pivot rod. The base of the fork rests on the spine of the pad. With a pad slick resting on the tone hole you can apply pressure to the lever and bring the back of the pad cup closer to the tone hole.

Once the pad cup rim is parallel with the tone hole rim you can choose the pad that will fit best in the pad cup. The diameter of the pad should be a tight fit in the pad cup. The thickness of the pad and shellac is about 0.5mm thicker than the depth of the pad cup plus the thickness of your pad slick.

Fig. 12.42 Saxophone bending levers.

Checking and Replacing Pads

Using shellac or hot melt on saxophone pads

I am inclined to use hot melt glue rather than shellac for saxophone pads. It is less prone to thermal shock or cracking away from the pad cup. (Thermal shock is when the pad falls out of the pad cup, complete with all the shellac, and leaves a clean pad cup. It only happens very occasionally and only with pads stuck with shellac.) Experiment with a variety of hot melt glues to find one you like to work with.

You can choose to load the pad cup with glue, or add the glue to the back of the pad. I use both methods at different times. For consistent results, ensure there is enough adhesive to support the whole of the pad and allow the pad to float. If you use too little glue or it is unevenly distributed, you might not be able to manoeuvre the pad.

When the key is back on the instrument and the spring is hitched and set, see how it is sitting in the cup and how it rests on the tone hole rim. Testing with a leak light will reveal any major problems; you must also complete a feeler gauge to test for an even grip around the pad to check for further problems. If needed, heat the pad cup again to melt the adhesive. Make sure the hot air from the flame, or heat gun, is directed away from the pad and body of the instrument. Once the glue is soft again, manipulate the pad into position using a pad slick. Re-test and repeat as needed. Once happy, hold the pad gently closed until cool. The amount of pressure needed to test the pad seating is discussed on page 139. It is about 80g over the weight of the spring.

There is a good mechanical reason that on saxophone pads you can allow the pad to be very slightly tighter at the back of the pad (the side closest to the axle) than at the front. The reason is as follows: the distance the pad moves at any particular point on the pad surface is proportional to the distance it is away from the key hinge (axis), so when the pad near the hinge travels 1mm, on the far side the pad might travel 2mm. The pressure exerted near the hinge will also be higher than at the far side from the hinge. So if the pad touches the tone hole rim at the front of the pad first (point furthest away from the hinge), and there is a 0.5mm gap at the back of the pad (hinge side), then it would take a lot of force to close the 0.5mm gap. If, on the other hand, the pad touches the tone hole on the back of the pad and there is a 0.5mm gap at the front of the pad, then it would not take a lot of extra pressure to close the 0.5mm at the front, as it would only have to squash the pad 0.25mm at the back of the pad. Though the principle is the same for all pads, it is only true in practice on saxophones because they have such large diameter pads.

Checking for leaks

To help find significant leaks in the padding, use a leak light. The leak light is put inside the saxophone body, and when you close the pads, no light should escape around them. Just because a pad passes the leak light test does not necessarily mean the pad is seating well, however. A leak light only shows up serious leaks and can give false-positive results. A leak light will not detect all pad leaks because leather can be stretched over the edge of a tone hole rim without any support from the felt behind it. As soon as a vibration is set up within the instrument, the unsupported leather starts to flap around and create a leak. I suggest you always do a final check around the pad with a feeler gauge. At present there is no simple way to isolate each pad to test for airtightness, so careful feeler gauge work is essential.

Installing flute pads

The construction and fashion of flute pads has changed the most of all instruments in my career. In my opinion, very hard pads are not the best option for most instruments or musicians. They might be great for top professional musicians who have fine instruments and access to repairers on demand, but for most musicians, I am most interested in installing a pad that will stand up to the knocks and bangs of school life.

I will therefore confine myself to talking about installing regular 2.5mm thick felt and skin membrane pads. There are specialist courses for the installation of the new pads, such as those designed by David Straubinger. After removing the old pad, measure the thickness of the pad and any whole paper washers that might be hiding underneath. I like to use my digital callipers with a spring-loaded plunger to apply similar pressure to the pad each time I measure. The pad is compressible, so the same pressure has to be used to get a consistent result.

Aligning the flute pad cup

Put the key assembly on the instrument without any pads in the cups. Put a pad slick flat on the tone hole and close the

Fig. 12.43 Flute pad alignment tool.

Fig. 12.44 Flute pad L bending alignment tools.

152 Checking and Replacing Pads

Fig. 12.45 Flute pad alignment pliers.

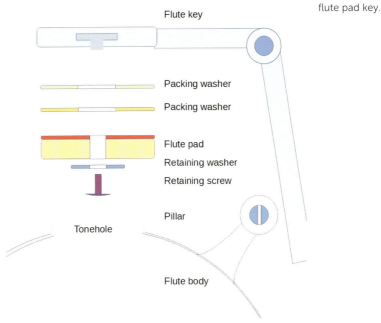

Fig. 12.46 Anatomy of a flute pad key.

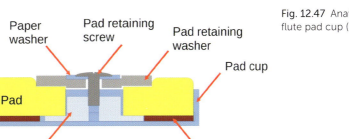

Fig. 12.47 Anatomy of a flute pad cup (inverted).

pad cup onto the slick. Use your eye and/or a feeler gauge to check that the pad cup is level with the tone hole rim. If it is not, then use your fingers or a pad levelling tool to manipulate the cup into the correct alignment. I describe a similar process in the clarinet section.

Depending on the design and materials used in the manufacture, the pad cup may not bend uniformly in all directions. There might be a spine on top of the cup or there might be a soft section of metal where the pad cup is soldered to the pad arm. You want to keep the pad cup flat and even at all times.

I have not found any one of the tools shown here better than another; it depends on the instrument. Whichever tool you use, it is essential that you make the changes in the area of the pad cup and do not end up bending the rest of the key mechanism simply to get the pad cup level. I have seen this happen on the right-hand stack of a flute, where, in an attempt to raise the back of the pad cup, the whole hinge screw is bent into a curve, causing the neighbouring pads to go out of alignment and spoil the entire action. Another alignment that you cannot always change is how central the pad cup is over the tone hole. The more central it is, the easier it will be to seat the pad.

Flute pads and washers

When you remove the original pad, I suggest you measure the combined thickness of the pad and any washers there were behind it. In this example, the combined thickness of pad and washers was 2.65mm.

Measure the inside diameter of the pad cup (for example, 18.5mm). If you measure the outside diameter of the original pad that you removed, you may find it is only 18.25mm or so. This is because the pad shrinks when being installed. The pad can be measured using callipers, but it is often quicker to use a pad measuring gauge.

The pad measuring gauge is quick to use because you don't have to worry about exact measurements; you can drop the original pad in and find a replacement that does not slide down quite as far.

Once you have chosen the correct diameter of pad, you measure the thickness of the pad. Let's say it is a standard 2.5mm. We now start adding thin paper pad washers (either the original ones and/or new washers from your stock of graded washers) to find a combination that also comes to 2.65mm in thickness.

Most flute cups require a base washer, either in paper or plastic. It is there to compensate for the profile of the pressed metal key and the step caused by the threaded boss. It makes the bottom of the pad cup level (a few manufacturers machine their pad cups and they are flat anyway).

When you have the right combination of washers to create the correct thickness, dampen the pad and install it into the pad cup. Mark a line with a pen at the point nearest the hinge (within the washer diameter if possible), then screw down the washer. Put the key back on the instrument, hitch and set the spring and see how it seats. If it looks like a good fit, flatten and dry out the pad at this point using a warm flute pad slick. Now test the

Checking and Replacing Pads

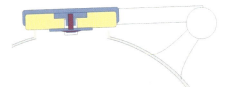

Fig. 12.48 This is how a flute pad should sit when it has the correct combination of paper washers behind the pad. It sits evenly over the whole tone hole.

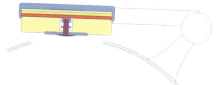

Fig. 12.51 If the pad and washer combination is too thick (too many washers) it will be tight at the back.

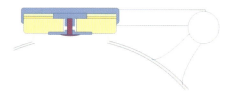

Fig. 12.52 Just the right number of washers.

When the pad is not gripping over a small section of the tone hole, you need to start using D sections or wedges of washer.

On top-end flutes, it is not unusual to have as many as twenty wedge-shaped paper washers under one flute pad. A washer as thin as tissue paper can make the difference. It requires a lot of patience for this level of work and the pad might have to come in and out of the pad cup many times. When padding high-quality flutes, you can use two feeler gauges simultaneously (one on each side) to get an accurate sense of where the pad is tight or loose.

grip on the feeler gauge around the pad at 30-degree intervals to see how even the grip is. Make a note as to where all the high and low spots are.

How to get the right thickness of flute pad and washers

If the pad is only touching the tone hole at the back, nearest the axle, then the pad and washer combination is too thick; if it is loose at the back, the pad and washer combination is too thin. Change the diameter and or thickness of pad and washer, and test again. Choose the pad that sits evenly on the tone hole and, if possible, looks parallel to the pad cup rim.

Fig. 12.49 A nice-looking flute pad.

If the pad is tight at the back and loose at the front, then remove whole washers from behind the pad, or use a thinner pad. Do not be tempted to use D washers or half washers to take up the gaps; only use whole washers.

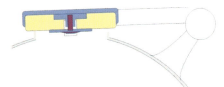

Fig. 12.50 If the pad and washer combination is too thin (too few washers) it will be loose at the back.

What to do when the pad does not seat on the sides, and other special cases

If the pad is tight on both sides of the tone hole only, then re-check how flat the tone hole is. If it is flat, then check for a curved pad cup and flatten if possible. If the pad is tight on one side and not the other, you might not have got the pad cup level with the tone hole earlier in the process, so go back and re-adjust as needed. (Some repairers object to this technique as they are concerned that the metal has some memory and can slowly creep back to its original position. This may be true, but I have found it can be accommodated for, with experience. Bending is, after all, how the manufacturers make the instruments in the first place.)

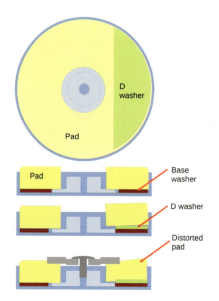

Fig. 12.53 D washer under a flute pad.

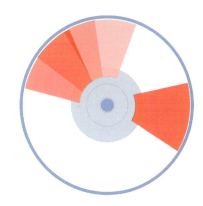

Fig. 12.54 How wedge-shaped washers can be used to build up a complex pad profile.

To finish seating the pad you can warm the back of the pad cup and gently close the key until it has cooled. This will leave a faint impression of the tone hole rim on the pad. Experience shows that attempting to get a pad to seat by warming the pad up and clamping it shut for twenty-four hours might only bring success for a few days. The pad will always change shape in a week or so and stop working as well.

Open hole flute pads

Replacing open hole flute pads takes the art of padding up another level. The principle is the same but the way the pad is held onto the pad cup is completely different.

Fig. 12.55 Open hole flute pads.

The open hole pad has a large hole punched out of the middle of the pad and this needs to be a good fit around the chimney of the pad cup. Once in place, a grommet is slipped over the middle and pushed onto the pad. Most manufacturers choose to put the grommet outside the chimney; others slide it within the chimney. In both cases they have to make them fit so well that the grommet will stay in place as well as being airtight. The amount you compress the grommet onto the pad makes a difference to the way the pad seats, so you need to find a way to be consistent, and limit how far the grommet is inserted. There are specialist tools for this. For most flutes, where the grommet sits inside the pad cup, then use a spacer washer (in green in the diagrams) that is a tight fit on the chimney. This will stop the grommet at the correct position each time.

Be careful when using open hole plugs on these instruments as you can easily push the grommet out by mistake.

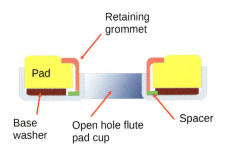

Fig. 12.56 Anatomy of an open hole flute pad cup with an external grommet.

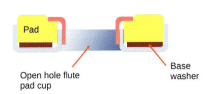

Fig. 12.57 Anatomy of an open hole flute pad cup with the less common internal grommet.

Working on open hole pads

Soon after starting flute repairs, I invested in a specialist pair of grommet pliers Fig 12.21. These make removing the grommet simple and prevent damage. I recommend you do the same. Not quite so necessary is a pair of grommet pressing pliers or pressing tool Fig 12.20. You can sometimes get away with using your thumb to push the grommets in place, or large parallel pliers, but you do need to limit how far you push them in. The final tool that you might find useful is a burnishing, or expanding, tool to tighten up the grommets if they begin to get loose.

Replacing an open hole flute pad requires even more patience than other pads. Remove the grommet with the special tool. Carefully extract the old pad and try to leave the packing washer in the original location. Now measure the old pad with digital callipers, at different places around the pad. If the pad is very even in thickness I might be lucky and find a matching pad of the same thickness and I can put it back together again with a good chance of an easy win. If any of the steps don't work out, I remove all the backing washers and assemble the pad and washers to get a starting thickness for the new pad combination.

With a new pad that is a tight fit in the pad cup, add whole washers until you have the same combined thickness that was originally removed. Put them in the pad cup, gently press the grommet home, and install the key on the instrument. Hitch the spring and test all the way around the pad. Make a note of the loose spots and follow the guidelines given earlier, as you would with an ordinary pad.

Dampen the pad with water and install for the final time. Use the pad slick to flatten the skin and I usually gently clamp the key overnight. Best quality flute repairs will use many segments of washer to build a micro profile for the pad. It will match the surface of the tone hole. This technique is not needed or economical for the majority of instruments.

Troubleshooting flute pads

Do not rely on the washer and screw, or the grommet to be airtight. If a flute is not airtight and you are pretty confident that the pad is seating well, then check the airtightness of each key when off the instrument. Do this with a soft-ended tube that is a little bigger than the washer. Try to draw a vacuum in the tube; if any air leaks, it will be from between the pad and the washer or between the screw and the washer. Seal these with a tiny paper washer and/or with wax. (I have seen repairers use nail varnish, which will also work.)

Pad and cup designs

There have been many designs used by manufacturers over the years to improve the speed of padding a flute and reliability of flute padding. Many involve the use of a flat metal or plastic washer that fits into the pad cup, under the washers, to make a level surface for the pad to sit on. In principle this is good, but only works if the tone hole is flat and the manufacturing is good in the first place.

Installing oboe pads

Installing skin pads on student oboes is the same process as for the clarinet. Some early models of oboe best suit very thin pads specified as oboe pads. If you come across an oboe with very shallow pad cups then you will have to buy the appropriate pads. You will often find these thin pads have white shellac behind them. This is no accident. The white shellac behaves differently and works better on flexible, thin pads. However, some keys have to have cork or synthetic pads to cope with the vent holes in the middle of the pad cup. You will need a selection of new 'ready-made' corks for the make of oboe being

Fig. 12.58 Ready-made oboe corks.

Fig. 12.59 Oboe cork with the top corners rounded off. This helps pad levelling.

repaired. They are the correct outer diameter and have holes pre-punched to suit the key design.

If you don't have access to pre-cut oboe pads then you will need to find a way to cut your own corks, using cork borers or thin-walled metal tubes.

As with other woodwind repair techniques you can use a variety of methods. I will describe the ways that I have used successfully.

Oboe cork pad fitting: floating method

With the key off the instrument, remove the original pad by heating the pad cup and using a needle spring to lever the pad out. If possible, measure the thickness of the original pad. Find a cork pad of the same diameter and the same thickness or thicker. If needed, trim the thickness of the pad down from the back of the pad, using a razor blade or file. Dome the back of the pad with a pumice block until it sits in the pad cup evenly. Gently crush the cork between two flat surfaces, to soften the pad. Melt shellac in the pad cup and insert the pad with a very gentle twisting motion. Try to leave the cork floating on a thin bed of shellac. Put the key back on the instrument and test for grip around the tone hole rim. If needed, warm the back of the key and float the pad around with a pad slick as needed. Finally tap the key shut a few times to slightly bruise the cork surface.

Oboe cork pad fitting: abrasive method

Roughly trim the thickness of the cork pad with a razor blade or abrasive until it is the correct thickness and slightly domed on the back. Shellac the pad in, as above. Finally, test the pad with a feeler gauge and see where it is tight and loose. If you find it difficult to keep track of the high spots, then you can cover a cigarette paper in graphite from a soft pencil, then put the paper under the pad, with the graphite side next to the cork pad, very gently close the pad and pull the paper under the pad for a few millimetres. This will transfer the graphite onto the cork pad, where it touches first (the high spots).

Remove the key and using a square sheet of pumice stone 40 × 40 × 3mm, stroke the pumice stone across the pad, keeping the pumice stone on one plane so it will remove the high areas of the pad. This process may need to be repeated several times to get the pad touching evenly across the whole tone hole. When it sits perfectly on the tone hole, tap the top of the cup to create the lightest of bed marks in the cork pad.

Troubleshooting oboe cork pads

Cork pads need to be kept at a constant humidity. If left unplayed for too long, or taken on a long-distance flight, they will dry out and shrink, causing a leak at the back of the pad. Cork pads can also be prone to sticking down, especially octave pads, and the two tiny pads (O6 and O8) between A and G pads on the top joint.

This can be due to moisture, or it can be that the impression of the tone hole on the pad surface is too deep. It can also happen if the profile of the tone hole itself is not sharp enough; a cork pad will stick to the rim if it is flat.

You may notice that the bed plates for some cork pads are much larger than the tone hole. This has two functions:

1. To allow the oboe maker to change the diameter of the tone hole during the tuning process, without having to change or re-seat the pad.
2. The larger diameter of the seating rim spreads the load on the cork pad surface, lessening the risk of deforming or cracking the pad's surface and causing a leak.

Installing bassoon pads

The process of fitting bassoon pads is the same as for the other instruments (except the flute), so please read those sections first. The pads are covered in fine leather. You may notice that on some older instruments the original pads can sometimes have a thread stitched in the middle of the pad, to hold the pad leather in place (similar to a saxophone rivet). I am not convinced that this is very effective, so I don't repeat the process myself.

The main challenge when working on bassoon pads is getting the pads on the boot joint to seal. The tone hole profile on most bassoons is challenging. I will often re-cut the tone holes (without changing the acoustics of the instrument) in a way that makes the rim of the tone holes level. This is not always necessary, however. The aim, as always, is to get the pad to seal each hole with minimum finger pressure.

White shellac is the easiest to use on the thin bassoon pads, as it becomes liquid more quickly and sets faster too. Thin paper-backed bassoon pads with

Fig. 12.60 This beautifully designed and manufactured tone hole on this Yamaha bassoon makes it much easier than usual to seat the pad. (The cartoon face it makes is rather amusing too.)

a white shellac can be sculpted and manipulated to conform to the contours of the domed double-holed tone holes at the bottom of the instrument. If possible, replace like with like; however, I do find myself tending to use thicker pads, as they are easier to install. I have not had any negative feedback over the years.

CHAPTER 13

Overhauls

An overhaul is a term we use to describe the renovation of an instrument. During an overhaul, every key is taken off and is cleaned and oiled, and the pads and corks are removed and replaced. In my opinion, the removal and replacement of springs is unnecessary. If a spring is not rusty and has no other sign of being defective, then it should continue working into the future. If you change a spring, there is a risk of changing the feel of the instrument, or of damaging the pillars or keywork. I only replace springs when the original one is not doing what it is supposed to do. It is something you might want to discuss with the owner or musician.

Before overhauling an instrument, agree with the owner or musician what is going to done. Decide how you are going to treat the body and keywork. Are you going to clean them? And/or are you going to polish them? Will you re-plate or lacquer any parts? These different options have big time and cost implications. Agree with the owner or musician on the choice of pad and any alterations they want made.

The process of overhauling an instrument is basically the same for all instruments but the steps take varying amounts of time depending on the instrument. To follow this checklist, you must have read and practised all the individual techniques and methods described earlier in this book.

> **Overhaul times**
>
> The estimated times to complete an overhaul, without polishing, are as follows:
> - Clarinet: 4 hours
> - Saxophone: 8–12 hours
> - Flute: 5–8 hours
> - Oboe: 8–12 hours
> - Bassoon: 8–12 hours

1. **Disassembly (15–45 minutes)**
   It might take several days to get back to re-assembling so use a storage tray to keep everything together.
2. **Pad removal (15 minutes)**
3. **Spring removal**
   Do not remove the needle springs unless they are defective. You don't need to remove the flat springs unless you are polishing the keywork.
4. **Cleaning (up to 60 minutes)**
5. **Polishing**
   This is a time-consuming process and I quote for it separately.
6. **Inspection (up to 30 minutes)**
   Looking for defects in the bodywork and keywork.
7. **Checking keywork mechanisms (30 minutes to 2 hours or more)**
   This section is one of the most important to get right. *See* Chapter 11 on keywork and follow the instructions carefully.
8. **Felts and corks (30 minutes)**
   As this is a complete overhaul, remove all the cork and felt pads. I usually sort the keys into piles that use the same thickness of cork. This makes gluing on the replacement corks and felts faster. Replace all the tenon corks.
9. **Re-padding**
   Clarinet: 1 hour
   Saxophone: up to 4 hours
   Flute: up to 4 hours
   Oboe: around 2 hours
   Bassoon: 2 hours
   Re-padding takes longer for professional instruments. Using the Original Equipment Manufacturer pads, or pads of the same make and design, makes the whole instrument look good, but if there is a good technical reason for changing the material or design of particular pads, then I think that is acceptable. It may be that the diameter of a bed plate is very close to the diameter of the pad cup and the seating ring is very close to the edge of the pad, so using a cork or synthetic pad is a good idea in these situations.

CHAPTER 14

Regulation

The regulation of an instrument is the adjustments you make to ensure that when two or more connected keys operate, they do so in perfect harmony. It also includes setting the vent heights.

Here are some of the terms I use:

1. Time of arrival: adjusting connected keys so the pads seal the tone holes at the same time. It is the most important part of regulation, affecting the ability of the instrument to play all the notes.
2. Time of departure: apart from some important exceptions, most connected keys should also start to move simultaneously. This is called the time of departure and this affects the feel of the instrument.
3. The vent height: the gap between the pad surface and the bed plate. This affects the tone colour and tuning. The subject of vent height is complex and is something to study and experiment with. Start on the basis that the vent height set by the good manufacturers is correct. It is not uncommon to build up a library of vent heights based on new instruments, or instruments you have been successful with yourself.
4. Spring weight or tension. This affects the feel of the instrument and the ability of some pads to seal the tone holes.

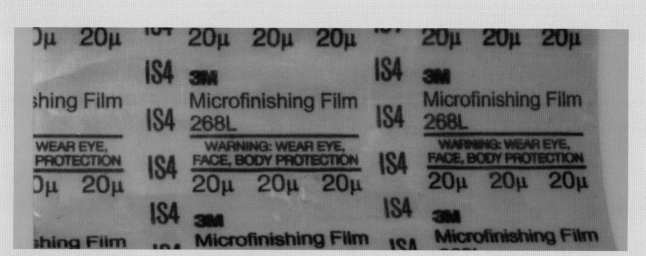

Fig. 14.1 Abrasive paper 3M micro-finishing film. This has a very smooth backing and uniform thickness. When cut with scissors into narrow strips it is excellent for thinning heel corks and adjustment corks. Available in many grit sizes, from 5 microns to 80 microns (I find 20 microns a useful grit size) and comes in 8 × 4-inch sheets and as rolls. I have found it a useful addition to my tool kit. It does not replace the original wet and dry paper for all purposes, as it is very springy and won't wrap around file boards or files.

Fig. 14.2 Large flat head screwdriver. This 'perfect handle' screwdriver was probably made around 1900. Used on the large adjusting screws that are to be found on a saxophone, for example, the long B and G# mechanism.

Fig. 14.3 Low shear strength thread lock. Sometimes it is necessary to stop an adjusting screw from moving. You can use nail varnish for this or a low shear strength screw lock. Anything stronger will make later repairs almost impossible. The threadlocking adhesive is quite runny and capillary action can take it to places you don't want it to go, so use very sparingly!

Sensitivity of adjusting screws

The sensitivity of adjusting screws varies from instrument to instrument and manufacturer to manufacturer. The most sensitive instruments are the oboe, followed by the flute. For this book I define the amount a regulating screw rotates in terms of minutes on a clock face. So 30 minutes will be 180 degrees, 15 minutes 90 degrees, etc. On flutes and oboes it is common to adjust down to +/− 3 minutes of rotation which is the equivalent of +/− 18 degrees, the amount shown in the diagram.

Fig. 14.4 Units of adjustment.

Time of arrival

Before moving on to this stage, you will have checked that the mechanism and the padding are satisfactory.

Example of setting the time of arrival on a clarinet

Here we are adjusting the link arm between the top and bottom joint of a Yamaha clarinet.

With all the keywork attached to the clarinet, assemble the instrument, making sure the two pillars are aligned with each other, as in Fig. 14.5.

Gently depress C17 and with your feeler gauge find out if C17 or C4 arrives first. If pad C17 is arriving first then you will need to add cork to the underside of key C4, until C4 arrives first.

With more cork added, gently depress C17 again and re-test C17 and C4. If pad C4 is now arriving first, sand the cork down until the two pads grip the feeler gauge evenly. Keep testing and adjusting until the two pads arrive at the same time and give the same grip as each other.

Fig. 14.5 Check that the link on C4 (2nd ring key) is going over the top of C17 (bottom ring key).

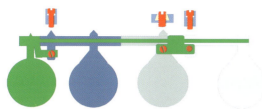

Fig. 14.6 Flute right-hand stack showing three adjusting screws.

Fig. 14.7 You can just see the regulation adjusting screw in the centre of the photo.

Fig. 14.8 Close-up of F5 to F4 adjusting screw and the felt for adjusting the vent height of F5.

Close F5; this should begin to bring F4 down. Using your eyes and then a feeler gauge, see which of these two pads arrives on the tone hole first. You normally find that F5 arrives first.

Using the adjusting screw that links F5 to F4, turn the screw one whole turn and test the time of arrival again. If F5 is still arriving first, repeat step 1 until F4 is first to arrive. With F4 arriving first, turn the screw anticlockwise half a turn (thirty minutes) and test again. If it is still arriving first, then unscrew a quarter of a turn (fifteen minutes) and test again. Keep repeating this process, halving the minutes of rotation until the two pads arrive at the same time (or, if you go too far, tighten the screw a few minutes of rotation again until perfect time of arrival is achieved).

Adjustments without screws

Many instruments do not have adjusting screws, so we use cork and paper shims to make the adjustments. With practice you will develop a sense of how much to add or take away in between testing.

When there is an adjusting cork, the sanding is done by inserting the abrasive strip between the two link arms and pulling the abrasive between them. The abrasive is a strip of 600 grit wet and dry paper or 40-micron abrasive film, about 5mm wide and 75mm long. If you are using paper to make the adjustments, it is best not to stack more than two high. If you need to go thicker, then replace the current spacer with a thicker one.

On good instruments this adjustment can be as small as one layer of thin cigarette paper, or if you are thinning cork, then you might need to draw the 40-micron abrasive film over just a few millimetres of the surface.

Time of departure

When the musician starts to push down a key, they like to feel a sense of solidity

Example of setting the time of arrival on a flute

For this section I am using the right-hand action of a Yamaha Boehm flute; this model has adjusting screws. The Yamaha flute is probably the most standardized instrument around the world. Once you have learnt how to adjust a flute like this, you can then use the same principles on other instruments even though the screws might be in different places or have different adjustment methods, such as paper or cork.

With just the right-hand action installed on the body of the flute, back off (unscrew slightly) all three adjusting screws. Check that each of the four pads has equal grip around the tone holes when pressed independently.

and security. This usually requires the key and connected keys to start moving at the same time. If there is a hesitation or delay between the first and subsequent keys starting to move, it is sometimes known as double action. Note that there are some keys where you must have some double action.

Example of setting time of departure on a flute

In this example I am using the right-hand action of a Yamaha flute.

Check and adjust the vent height of F5. This is the amount the pad opens from the tone hole, in this case 2mm. If you need to increase or decrease the vent height, then add or remove felt from under the tail of F5. I recommend felt rather than cork in this particular instance, as it is quieter.

> Gently depress key F5 on its own. Does key F4 start moving at the same time?
> Gently depress key F6 on its own. Does key F4 start moving at the same time?
> Gently depress key F7 on its own. Does key F4 start moving at the same time?

Create a list with the key numbers F5, F6 and F7. Under each key number write down if it moves with key F4, at the same time or not. You should end up with a list something like this:

> Key F5 = Yes
> Key F6 = Yes
> Key F7 = No

It is now possible to work out which key tails need adjusting to get them all to start moving F4 when pushed. In this scenario, key F5 and F6 are adjusted correctly, so the tail of key F7 needs a thicker cork or felt under its tail.

Here is another scenario:

> F5 = No
> F6 = Yes
> F7 = Yes

Since you adjusted the vent height of F5 correctly at the start, you do not make any changes to that key. In this situation you will make the tails thinner on both F6 and F7 until all three keys can start to move F4 without hesitation.

When you have a key where the tail needs a thicker cork or felt, you should check to see that the tail has not been bent out of line. If the cork or felt is similar to the keys either side, then I would bend the key back to look like the others and test again. You may find that you don't need to replace the felt or cork. If you decide to bend the key, do not damage the keywork, i.e. don't strain the joint between key and tube.

Special case regulation

There are a number of situations where there needs to be a gap between the keys that connect with each other. A gap will be needed when the swelling of one pad would cause the linked pad to be lifted off its tone hole (Fig. 14.9).

Saxophone bell keys, time of arrival

Saxophone bell keys. There are often large adjusting screws on the key guards on saxophones. The screws also have a large cylinder of felt attached to them. Using a pad slick as a screwdriver (did I really say that?), you can move these screws in and out to change the time of departure and the vent height of the key. On a service repair, it might be best not to adjust these.

Clarinet C5 and C6 (A to Ab)

Another of these exceptions is the C5 to C6 (A to Ab key) at the top of the Boehm clarinet. Here it is important to leave a tiny gap between the top of the Ab key and the adjusting screw on the A key. The reason for this gap is to ensure that if the Ab pad gets wet and swells, it will not lift the A key and cause it to leak.

Setting the vent height

Now we can check the vent height (the gap between the pad surface and the bed plate). After looking at a number of good instruments you will develop a sense of what looks like a good height. Before you get to that stage, you might want to use a pad gauge to measure and compare the height of each pad with similar models. For most instruments the vent height is only a problem if it is too low or close and causes the sound to become flat or muffled. If it is too high, then the instrument is not easy to play and the tuning is a bit wild.

If you work on professional-level instruments, you might want to keep a record of the vent heights you find work on particular models of instrument.

Fig. 14.9 There must be a gap between A♭ and A.

As a guide, the vent heights on a flute are 3mm, being slightly under 3mm at the top of the instrument and just above 3mm as you get to the bottom. Clarinets are 2.5mm on the top joint and 3mm on the bottom joint, progressing from smaller to larger as you go down the instrument.

Remember that the vent height of many of the pads will be set by a connecting key, so don't expect to have independent control over each pad.

Setting spring weights

The spring action, weight, or pressure needed to move a key should be constant throughout its travel.

I refer to the spring weights as light, medium and heavy; these loosely approximate to the following:

Light: 18g for flutes and oboes to 30g for saxophones
Medium: 22g for flutes and oboes to 40g for saxophones
Heavy: from 30g for flutes and oboes to 50g for saxophones

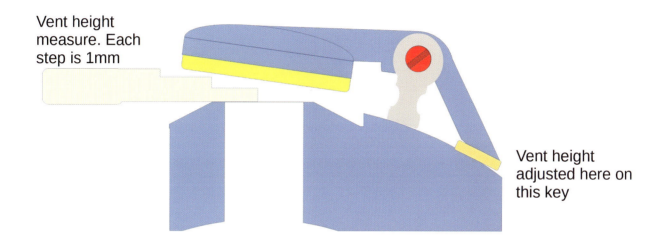

Fig. 14.10 A vent height gauge can be made from plastic, wood or cardboard. The surfaces have to be very smooth.

CHAPTER 15

Re-Assembly

We have nearly covered the basics of woodwind repair, but there is still one big topic still to cover: the final re-assembly and regulation of the instrument. I will go through the process for each instrument separately, and will list the following as required:

The keys you need to install
The spring tension(s) for each key
Any notes on the spring action
Any notes on regulation
Any notes on vent heights

There is a picture with an assembly order for each instrument, along with instructions on their regulation.

Once you have finished the regulation, I would recommend that you re-visit the instrument a day or more later and check the instrument again. This will give time for the corks and pads to settle. For some instruments you might want to play the instrument for a short time every day, for a week, re-adjusting each day.

Add a drop of oil to each key as you install it on the instrument and make sure you test the following for each key:

Smoothness of action
Pad seating and airtightness
Vent height of the pads
Spring tension
Time of arrival
Time of departure

If everything has gone well, then the final test should not show up any problems, but now is not the time to be complacent. I still put the instrument through a rigorous mechanical test and a final play test, remembering to use minimal finger pressure on the keys.

> **Legend**
>
> LH – left hand
> RH – right hand
>
> Capital letter note name indicates low register; lower case letter indicates upper register
>
> Sharp used in preference to flat except where common usage dictates otherwise
>
> 'Touch key' indicates where finger is in contact with a key
>
> 'Pad key' indicates a non-finger closure
>
> Pitch or letter name alone indicates a direct closure or hole

Clarinet

The instrument used is a wooden Yamaha YCL650. There are two distinct clarinet key configurations, with small variations on each type. In Germany and Austria they use a version of the Oehler system or German mechanism; the rest of the world (including the Yamaha Bb clarinet described here) uses the Boehm system.

Clarinet top joint

C1: LH Eb/bb
C2: C#/g#
C3: F#/b
C4: D/a
C5: Throat A
C6: Throat G#
C7: Alternate B/throat A–B trill
C8: Alternate Bb/c–d trill
C9: Alternate F#
C10: RH Eb/bb
C11: Thumb F/c
C12: Thumb Bb/register key

Assembly and regulation

Install C1, C2, C3 and C4

Medium spring

Vent height

C1: 2.5mm
C2: 2.5mm

Fig. 15.1 YCL650 top joint assembly order. The numbers are prefixed by C in the text.

Fig. 15.2 C1: LH E♭/b♭.

Fig. 15.3 C2: C#/g#.

Fig. 15.4 C3: F#/b.

Fig. 15.5 C4: D/a.

Install C5 and C6

Fig. 15.7 C6: Throat G♯.

Fig. 15.6 C5: Throat A.

Medium spring

It is a very good idea to check that the tip of the flat spring on C5 does not slide.

Regulation/vent height

C5: 2.2mm, then use the adjusting screw on C6 to create a gap between C5 and C6. It is one of the few situations where we want double action. The reason we need this gap is that C5 often gets waterlogged, swells up and then lifts C6 open. You want to adjust these two keys to open a similar amount so that when C5 is fully open, the heel of C6 is also coming to a stop. I often put a screw lock on this adjusting screw.

C6: just over 2mm

Install C7, C8, C9 and C10

Fig. 15.8 C7: Alternate B/throat A–B trill. C8: Alternate B♭/c–d trill.

Fig. 15.9 C9: Alternate F♯. C10: RH E♭/b♭.

Medium spring

These four keys need to be installed at the same time. It is best if you learn how to support the instrument between your body and the bench peg, to free up both hands. C7 and C8 are usually on a double hinge tube arrangement, so remember to oil between the inner tubes. Make sure the flat springs are in the correct location grooves in the body. I suggest starting with C10; then do C7, C8 and C9 at the same time.

Regulation/vent height

These keys often get bent, as there is a weak section where the arches of C7 and C8 go over C11. I suggest that if the vent height is too high or too low on these keys when the heel corks are what you think is the correct thickness, bend the keys to vent correctly. Check the touch pieces don't hit each other when opened. Set the touch pieces of C7 and C8 level with each other. All set to 2.3mm vent height. (The vent height of around 2.5mm for C10 will be set later in the process, but for the moment, make the touch pieces of C9 and C10 level with each other, or with C9 slightly higher if anything.)

Install C11

Fig. 15.10 C11: Thumb F/c.

I prefer to have the adjusting cork between C11 and C3 on the top of C11, not under the tail of C3.

Regulation/vent height

When C11 is level with the metal thumb hole, C3 needs to be shut. Vent height for

1st ring key C3 is set by the thumb ring and is around 2.0mm.

Install C12

Fig. 15.11 C12: Thumb B♭/register key.

Medium spring

It often helps if the cork speaker pad is chamfered to make a cone shape. It improves the tone of the throat note.

Regulation/vent height

The vent height should be as low as possible, consistent with a clear throat note. The height of the touch piece relative to the thumb ring can be important to some players. It might be that you will want to change the shape of this touch piece to make access easier for people with smaller fingers. The Yamaha specification is 1.8mm vent height. Using a pumice stone, a cork speaker key on a clarinet can be chamfered or made conical shaped to improve the way air escapes from the small speaker hole. This change can remove the buzzing sound that can occur if the pad is left flat.

Clarinet bottom joint

C13: LH F/c
C14: RH F#/c#
C15: RH E/b
C16: Alternate B/f#
C17: Bb/f, also ring keys alternate fingering Eb/bb
C18: RH F/c
C19: G#/d#
C20: LH F#/c#
C21: LH E/b

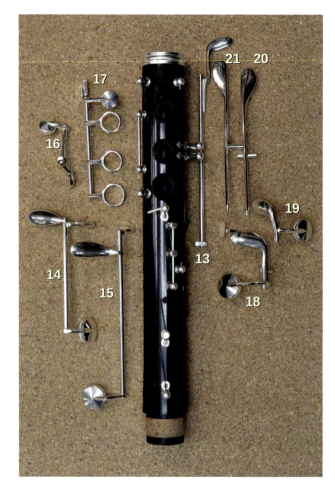

Fig. 15.12 YCL650 bottom joint assembly order.

Fig. 15.13 C13: LH F/c.

Assembly and regulation

Install C13

Light spring

My preference is to have this key spring working in the opposite direction to most other people: I like it to be sprung so that it pushes the link arm gently against C18. I also like to use cork or pad leather on the top side of this key, rather on the underside of C18. On plastic instruments, make sure that the key is a loose fit between pillars and between the pivot screws, to allow for the shortening of the plastic body in cold weather.

Regulation

The cork between C3 and C18 should be around 0.5mm thick. The heel cork under the key should not be so thick that it tries to close C18. (Buffet have recently added a regulating screw on the E arm, which is a good innovation.)

Install C14 and C15

Fig. 15.14 C14: RH F♯/c♯.

Fig. 15.15 C15: RH E/b.

Medium spring

This spring arrangement is different for each manufacturer. I will sometimes re-engineer the spring and spring hook on this key to give an even pressure throughout the travel of the key. Some clarinets in particular have a tendency for the key to get harder to open, the wider the opening. A good spring maintains an even load over its length of travel. On some high-end Buffet clarinets, the spring is attached to the key and fits in a slot in the body. I check to see the spring is not being constrained in the slot and alter the shape of the slot to improve it if necessary.

Regulation

No regulation is necessary at this point.

Install C16 and C17

Fig. 15.16 C16: Alternate B/f♯.

Fig. 15.17 C17: B♭/f, also ring keys alternate fingering E♭/b♭.

Medium spring
Regulation/vent height

C16: 2.5mm
C17: 2.5mm

Set the ring key height. I make them slightly above the finger hole rims when people with small fingers are playing the instrument.

Install C18 and C19

Fig. 15.18 C18: RH F/c.

Fig. 15.19 C19: G♯/d♯.

Medium spring

It is often easier to hook the spring on during the assembly rather than afterwards.

Regulation/vent height

C18 should have 1mm thick cork or felt on the T-shaped arm at the front (sometimes called the crow's foot in the UK). To set the time of arrival, push down

Re-Assembly

the touch piece of C15 and it will bring down C18. Bend the T arm up or down so that C18 and C15 arrive at the same time. Fine adjustments can be made by sanding the cork on the T arm.

At this stage it will be the touch piece of C14 that will be setting the vent height of C18. Make sure the vent height is high enough for C18 (about 3.5mm); if not, then bend the C14 touch piece upwards, making sure you do not change the C14 pad seating. As a simple rule, the bottom of the pad of C18 should be at least level with the outside of the body.

C19: check the vent height (about 3.5mm) and adjust it as required, either by bending the arm attached to the pillar, or changing the cork or felt thickness under the touch piece.

Install C20 and C21

These two levers will either have a pin and hole linkage with C14 and C15 or they will sit underneath these keys. If it is a pin and hole, then you need to put regulation cork on the heel of C15 (which is very small). On professional instruments I will offer to modify the instrument by drilling a 4mm-diameter, 2mm-deep counter-bore under the heel of C15, so that a piece of cork or felt can be fitted in the body to quieten the mechanism. This is a technique now used by a number of manufacturers. If the levers sit under the tails of C20 and C21 then you put the regulation cork on the bottom side of the keys near the link point.

Regulation

In both cases, regulate C20 so that C14 and C15 are both touching the T arm of C18 when at rest. This means that the time of departure of keys is now set.

Put the top and bottom joints together

Adjust the time of arrival between C4 and C17. This should be done when the two adjacent pillars (the ones closest to each other) are in alignment with each other. Use the feeler gauge in the normal way to check the time of arrival. Check the vent height of C10. The cork or felt under the touch piece of this key will stop on the bottom joint pillar. If the cork thickness is around 1.5mm and the vent height is wrong, then be prepared to bend the key up or down as required.

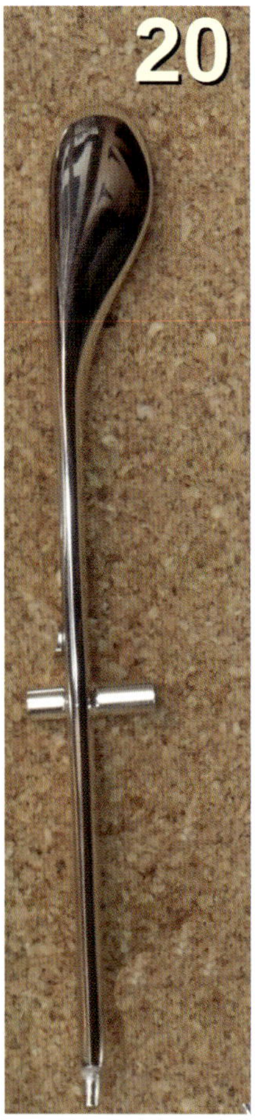

Fig. 15.20 C20: LH F#/c#.

Fig. 15.21 C21: LH E/b.

Fig. 15.22 The rings look too high.

Fig. 15.23 Lowering the bottom ring keys.

Fig. 15.24 Raising the bottom ring keys.

Fig. 15.25 Ring keys at the correct height.

Troubleshooting clarinet overhauls

Ring keys are the wrong height

To lower the rings, I put a pad slick or, in this case, a rule under the pad and push down on the rings Figs 15.22 to 15.25. This causes a torsional bend on the pivot rod.

If I bend it too far, then I can put the pad slick, or rule, under the ring keys and push down on the pad cup.

When the rings are at the correct height, they are just level with the tone hole inserts. For musicians with very slim fingers, I might make the rings slightly higher.

The first ring key does not open after you have lifted the thumb key

If C3 fails to rise when C11 has been lifted then you might have a dent in the cork under C11. Cut away the cork that is beyond the tip of the C3 tail. I put the regulation cork on the top of C11 to stop this happening.

The long B does not sound clearly (C17 to C4 regulation)

This can often be because there is movement across the axis of one or more of these two keys. Pay extra attention to the pivot screw at the bottom of C4 and the top of C17. These can sometimes be worn oval in shape, so check for movement in every orientation. If there is any unwanted movement, then re-fit that pivot screw.

Closing the very bottom key using C21 does not work

Often using the touch piece of C15 closes C15 and C16 perfectly but not if you only use C21. This is because there is lateral movement in either or both C15 and C16. The point screw at the top of C15 is under a lot of pressure and will often become oval, so that needs sorting. C16 also gets a lot of use and the hinge tube will be oversized. Unfortunately there is no opportunity to swedge out this wear on this key, so you either have to resort to fitting an oversized hinge screw, or in many cases the best you can do is find a compromise on a time of arrival adjustment that works.

Another key that often wears to an oval shape is the lower point screw on the second ring key.

Side lever keys (C21 or C20) have stopped working

Since around 2000, some manufacturers have been using plastic pins on the ends of these keys. If the levers are subjected to a sharp knock, then these pins can shear or break off. They can be replaced by drilling out the remainder of the plastic pin and replacing with a factory replacement plastic pin, or you can make your own metal replacement pin. A metal replacement needs to be smaller in size than the original plastic one, and then capped in a piece of old pad bladder to keep the mechanism quiet.

Bass clarinets

There are some problems that are unique to the bass clarinet. For example, the middle socket of some bass clarinets can become difficult to put together and take apart, yet still be insecure when pushed home; this is because the socket is not parallel or round. This is more common on those bass clarinets that have an adjustable tenon ring around the middle tenon socket. The adjusting screw is designed to keep the ring and pillars in place even when the wood swells and contracts. Unfortunately, it usually has the effect of making the opening of the socket contract. If the tenon is tight going into the socket, do not reduce the diameter of the tenon until you have checked and have satisfied yourself that a constricted socket is not the problem. If the socket has constricted, then you have to make a special reamer to open out the socket. This special reamer is a large version of the vintage socket reamers shown on page 226 (Fig .17.102).

Regulation compromises

There is so much axial and torsional flex in the long pivot rods on the low notes of a bass clarinet that regulation can be very, very tricky. A good bass clarinet design is one that has cradles at intervals along the long pivot rods to stop the flex. Even with these cradles you might need to spend time with the musician to find a compromise on the regulation. They might want one particular fingering of a note to work, rather than another. So don't assume that the compromise that suits you will work for the musician who will be performing on the instrument.

Flute

Part of the overhaul of a flute must include the replacement of the head cork. Some of this has been covered in the emergency flute repair section. The model used here is a Yamaha YFL312.

Flute head cork replacement

Remove the head cork assembly following the instructions in the emergency repair section. Choose a new head cork that becomes tight in the head joint as it reaches the embouchure hole. Test this by dropping the cork into the head joint and see where it stops. Use a Yamaha head cork if possible; they are the nicest. Slide the chosen head cork onto the cleaned spindle. If the cork has a tapered end, this must go at the clamp plate end. Screw on the clamp plate and tighten.

Roll the head cork assembly between the bench and the cork roller to make the cork springy.

This is a very important step, especially with solid silver head joints. If the cork is too large in diameter or not soft enough, you can stretch the diameter of the head joint which will affect the tuning of the instrument. Some manufacturers and repairers will put a very small amount of candle wax onto the cork, to aid insertion. I sometimes do this, but you then have to remove all traces of the wax from the bore and from inside the embouchure hole.

Using the repairer's tuning rod, push the head cork back up the inside of the head joint until the 17mm line is central in the embouchure hole.

Non-standard head joints

The majority of flutes have a head cork; a few use O rings. If, when you have removed the crown, it does not look like there is a cork, then you will probably see the clamp plate is far down the screwed spindle and there will be a nut as well. Before doing anything else, check that the reflector plate is in the correct position and that it is airtight. If everything is in order, put the crown on and do not do anything else. If it is leaking or in the wrong position, loosen the nut and push the assembly out. Reassemble in the correct position and make it airtight.

Fig. 15.26 Head cork assembly.

Fig. 15.27 Soften the head cork.

Fig. 15.28 Flute head cork assembly shown out of the instrument.

Flute key layout

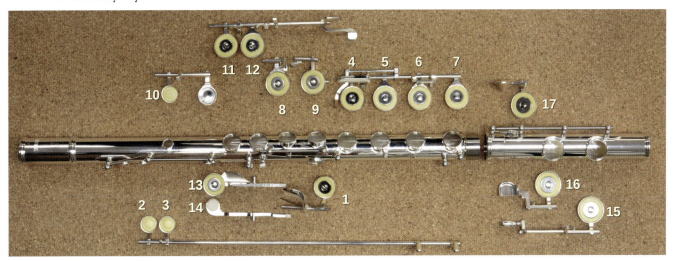

Fig. 15.29 YFL312 assembly order. The numbers are prefixed by F in the text.

F1: G#
F2: C–D trill middle register
F3: c–d trill upper register
F4: Correspondence F#
F5: F/alternate Bb
F6: E
F7: F# touch key
F8: G
F9: Correspondence (split) G
F10: C
F11: A
F12: Correspondence A and alternate Bb pad key
F13: Thumb B
F14: Thumb Bb
F15: Low C
F16: Low C#
F17: D#

Install F1 (G#)

Fig. 15.30 F1: G#.

Medium to heavy spring
Regulation/vent height

Set the vent height at approximately 3.5mm. Re-check the height once F2 is on, as you don't want the top of the F1 arm to hit the hinge tube of F2.

Install F2 and F3 (trill keys)

Fig. 15.31 F2: C–D trill middle register. F3: c–d trill upper register.

Medium spring

If the spring on either of the trill keys is too heavy or strong it can cause both trill keys to be slow to respond. The trill key pads have to be seating very well indeed for the springs to be the correct weight. Make sure you get the trill touch pieces under the correct bottom stack springs when installing.

Vent height

Set the vent height to about 2.5mm or just under.

Install F4, F5, F6 and F7 (right-hand stack)

I have shown these keys as a pre assembled group. During an overhaul the group should be completely dismantled, cleaned, and oiled with light oil. Make sure that the hinge screw down the middle of this stack is absolutely straight.

Fig. 15.32 F4, F5, F6 and F7.

Fig. 15.34 F5: F/alternate B♭.

Fig. 15.36 F7: F# touch key.

Fig. 15.33 F4: Correspondence F#.

Fig. 15.35 F6: E.

Re-Assembly 175

Medium spring
Regulation/vent height

Fig. 15.37 Typical American student flute.

Fig. 15.38 Jupiter flute.

Fig. 15.39 1980s Yamaha flute.

You will find that the adjusting screws for this stack can be found in a number of different locations. Some flutes do not have adjustment screws, but rely on using paper between the keys. Adjust the time of arrival for F5, F6 and F7 with F4. The adjusting screws on flutes are quite often loose and need a very small application of threadlocking adhesive to stabilize them. Now set the vent height of F5 using felt or cork under its tail. The vent height should be just over 3mm. Press down F5: does it immediately start to move F4? If it does, then the regulation of F4 is correct. If not, it is said to have double action and the tail of F6 and/or F7 is holding F4 down too much. Find out which one is holding it down and bend up the tail, or thin the cork or felt under the tail.

Now push down F6: does it immediately start to move F4? If it does, then the regulation of this key is correct. If it doesn't, then it has double action and the tail of F7 is holding F4 down too much. Bend the tail upwards, or thin the cork or felt on the bottom of the tail of F7.

Install F8 and F9

Fig. 15.40 F8: G.   Fig. 15.41 F9: Correspondence (split) G.

Medium spring
Regulation/vent height

Adjust the vent height using the heel cork under F8 after the regulation of the E link, *see* the images for F8 and F9 below. If these two keys are separated, then set the time of arrival using the adjusting screw between the two keys. (Note that on some instruments the metal tab that the adjusting screw works on has a weak section and will often bend down very easily – so much so that the screw does not work. You can use a screwdriver blade or similar lever to bend the tab back up again to make the adjusting screw work.) Check the time of arrival between F6 with F9. This adjustment is done with the cork under the E link arm that goes over the pin on the lower side of F9. Now you can set the time of departure of F8 so that there is no double action with F9.

If there is no split E mechanism on the instrument, then these two pad cups are joined together, and you have to adjust the time of arrival by generating a torsional twist in the hinge tube between the pad arms. Put a pad slick under the pad that is arriving first and push down on the other key, the base side closest to the hinge. Keep adjusting until they arrive together. It is important to only apply pressure at the base of the key pad cup, not at the end of the key, as you don't want to undo all the work you have put in making the pads seat well in the first place. Some repairers think this is the wrong way to make the adjustment and they would rather do it by adjusting the pad thickness with washers and half washers until it is balanced.

Vent height

3mm to 3.2mm.

Install F10

Fig. 15.42 F10: C.

Medium spring
Vent height

Set the vent height to about 2mm or a fraction over.

Install F11 and F12 (left-hand stack)

Fig. 15.43 F11: A.

Fig. 15.44 F12: Correspondence A & alternate B♭ pad key.

Medium spring
Regulation

Set the time of arrival between F11 and F12 using the adjusting screw. Test and set the time of arrival between F5 and F11. The adjustment is made by either bending up or down the link arm located at the far bottom end of F11, or by increasing or decreasing the cork at that point. Re-check the time of arrival of F5 and F4 again at this point. There is sometimes a compromise to be achieved balancing this stack of keys. Check and adjust the time of departure of F12 with F11 and F5 with F11. These are both controlled by the single cork under the tail of F12.

Vent height

Vent height is set by the F5 but will be approximately 3mm.

Install F13 and F14

F14 is the final key of the main joint, also sometimes called the Briccialdi key. Check that there is a thin cork under the F12 link arm where it goes over the tail of F14. Then adjust the heel cork under the tail of F14 so that there is small gap between the F12 link arm and F14. This is an important gap to have.

Fig. 15.45 F13: Thumb B.

Fig. 15.46 F14: Thumb B♭.

Medium flat spring under F13
Regulation

Using a feeler gauge, check the time of arrival between F13 and F11. If it needs adjusting, either adjust the thickness of the cork or felt under the F14 touch piece where it touches the pad cup of F13, or use smooth jaw duckbill pliers to bend the F14 lever up or down as required. On top-end flutes you need to ensure that F13 and F14 touch pieces are level with each other, or set to the requirements of the musician. Some musicians are quite sensitive to the feel of these keys.

Vent height

Approximately 2.75mm.

Install F15, F16 and F17

Fig. 15.47 F15: Low C.

Fig. 15.48 F16: Low C♯.

Fig. 15.49 F17: D♯.

F15 and F16: medium spring
F17: strong spring
Regulation

Adjust the time of arrival between F15 and F16. This is usually done by bending the touch piece of F16 up or down without disturbing the seating of the pad. There is a cork under the touch piece that can be used to make this adjustment if needed.

Vent height

Set the vent height of F17 while at the same time trying to make the touch pieces of these three keys level with each other. Vent height approximately 3.3mm.

Troubleshooting flute overhauls

If you are having particular trouble seating a flute pad, check that is sitting centrally over the tone hole. Look at the bedding ring and see that it is not too close to the edge of the pad cup or the depression caused by the retaining washer. Check the pad is not leaking from between the retaining washer and the pad. Sometimes the retaining screw and washer can tighten up on the threaded boss, before it gets tight on the pad.

Troubleshooting piccolos

If you are getting inconsistent regulation or pad seating on wooden or plastic piccolos, check that the screws that hold the pillar strap onto the body are all tight. You might need to take out some springs to get good access to some of the screws.

I have come across a number of wooden and plastic piccolos where the tenon that goes into the head joint is made of metal and the bond between it and the body has become loose or is able to twist. The first problem is usually separating the metal component from the body. On plastic instruments you might try gently heating the metal to soften the adhesive; on wooden piccolos look carefully to see if there are one or more rivets holding the two parts together. If you see the head of a rivet, carefully drill it out and the two parts will separate. Once apart, you can clean the two parts and epoxy them together again.

On wooden piccolos I also install a solid silver rivet. This is done by drilling a 1mm hole through the metal tenon and through the wood beneath. Make a very small countersink in the hole on the outside. Next, square off the end of a 1mm piece of solid silver wire and hold it in a chuck so that you can use a round end hammer to make a very small flare (this is called 'upsetting' the end). Cut the wire to about 8mm long and taper the cut end to make it easy to feed into the 1mm hole. Using tweezers, feed the wire from inside the instrument out through the hole. Insert a mandrel into the bore of the piccolo to finally push the flared rivet head against the wood of the body. With the mandrel in a vice and holding the rivet tight against the inside of the bore, cut and file the outside portion of wire until there is about 0.5mm protruding. Square off the end of the wire and using a ball-ended hammer, tap the wire until it forges itself into the countersink and tightens up the rivet. Carefully file and polish the head of the rivet flush with the outside of the tenon. The inside head of the rivet will bury itself into the wood and become almost invisible.

Saxophone

There have been many different key configurations designed for saxophones over the years, especially when it comes to the speaker key mechanism. There are too many to cover them all in this book so I will be explaining the process needed for a Yamaha YAS480 alto sax; this is a good design that can be found around the world.

Saxophone holder

This genius design, by John Cook in the UK, can hold a wide variety of saxophones safely while you work on them. You can rotate the instrument in all but the vertical axis.

Fig. 15.50 Saxophone holder.

Fig. 15.51 YAS480 assembly order. The numbers are prefixed by S in the text.

Saxophone key layout

S1: Correspondence F#
S2: F
S3: E
S4: D
S5: Low C# pad key
S6: Low C# touch key
S7: Low B
S8: Low Bb
S9: G# pad key
S10: G# touch key
S11: Side Bb
S12: Chromatic/fork F#
S13: Side C
S14: F# pad key
S15: Bis Bb (also known as 1 & 1 Bb linkage)
S16: Side C pad key
S17: Side Bb pad key

S18: Correspondence C pad key
S19: B
S20: A
S21: e
S22: f# pad key
S23: Automatic octave key mechanism
S24: f# pad key
S25: Eb/D#
S26: Low C
S27: Palm d
S28: Palm f
S29: Palm eb
S30: Thumb octave pad key
S31: Front/fork F (E)
S32: Crook octave pad key

Install S1, S2, S3 and S4

Fig. 15.53 S2: F.

Fig. 15.54 S3: E.

Fig. 15.55 S4: D.

Fig. 15.52 S1: Correspondence F#

Fig. 15.56 How the vent height and time of departure is set.

Medium spring
Regulation

If possible, remove the key guard that protects the tails of these keys to make regulation easier.

S2, S3 and S4 all have their tails underneath a bridge key (regulation bar) which is part of S1 (the long bar going downwards in the photograph). Press down on the pearl of S2; this should close S1. Adjust the time of arrival of S2 with S1 by changing the thickness of the cork between the top of the S2 tail and the underside of the bridge key of S1. On this Yamaha they have helpfully provided regulation screws. Next, press down the pearl on S3 and adjust the time of arrival with the S1 pad, using the cork between S3 and S1. Regulate S4 and S1 in the same way.

Vent height

Check the vent height of the S1 pad and decide if it is correct (it should be around 3–4mm). It is the heel corks of S2, S3 and S4 that set the vent height of S1; it might be that only one of the heel corks is setting this height at first. In the example shown, it is the heel cork of S2 that is touching both the body and the regulation bar, therefore determining the vent height. When you have got the vent height correct on S1, adjust the other two heel corks until they touch both the body and the regulation bar. In summary: adjust the time of arrival corks first, then leave them alone. Adjust the time of departure corks until the vent heights are correct and all the keys can depart with S1 simultaneously.

Re-Assembly 179

Install S5 and S6

Fig. 15.57 S5: Low C♯ pad key.

Fig. 15.58 S6: Low C♯ touch key.

S5: medium to light spring to open the key.

S6: there are quite a few variations on how this key works. Some manufacturers have a flat spring that clips around the link pin on S5. This clip design is to help release the S5 pad from the tone hole if it has not been used for some time and has become stuck.

Regulation/vent height

The bumper under the key guard sets the vent height of this key. There is no time of arrival to be adjusted.

Install S7 and S8

Fig. 15.59 S7: Low B.

Fig. 15.60 S8: Low B♭.

Medium to strong spring
Regulation

Adjust the time of arrival between S7 and S5. There is often an adjusting screw. If not, you will have to use a cork or bend the key to adjust it. To check the time of arrival, push S6 down, which will open S5; next, push S7 closed and this should bring down S5. Adjust the time of arrival of S5 so that it only just closes with S7. It is better that S5 should be lighter on the feeler gauge than S7. S8: allow S6 to close S5 and push down S8. There is a small tab of metal under the S8 touch piece that brings down S7. You can decide to bend the metal or adjust the cork at this point, to get the time of arrival between S7 and S8 correct.

Vent height

The only vent height adjustments you have to make with this group of keys are that of S7 and S8. These are adjusted by the bumper felts under the key guards. You might be lucky and have large screws for doing this; if not, you have to add or remove the bumper felt to get the correct vent height. Do not assume that a big opening is the best setting. An experienced performer may ask you to adjust this height to improve the balance or stability of the saxophone.

Install S9

Fig. 15.61 S9: G♯ pad key.

Light spring
Regulation

To set this regulation, press down S2, which brings the link arm of S1 down on the top of the S9 pad. To set the time of arrival of S1 and S9 use the topmost adjusting screw on the S1 link arm. Use a screwdriver blade that fits the slot nicely. Check that the tip of the adjusting screw is domed and smooth. The easiest way to check the time of arrival on these keys it to use your feeler gauge between the tip of the adjusting screw and the top of the pad. Once that is gripping gently, you can then check the pads themselves; you might need to turn the screw another four minutes tighter to take account of the thickness of the feeler gauge. Because this area of the mechanism is never very robust, you also need to re-check the time of arrival between S2 and S1. It will often have worsened since you first adjusted it as the added back pressure of the S9 on the S1 link arm stops the S1 pad from seating as well as it did when first adjusted with S2. Therefore, you need to decide if you want to back off the adjustment between S1 and S9 or increase the thickness of the cork that sets the time of arrival between S2 and S1. Finding a compromise for the time of arrival between these three keys is very important, as failing to get it right can stop the bottom three notes from sounding.

Install S10

Fig. 15.62 S10: G♯ touch key.

Strong spring
Regulation/vent height

On many instruments the link arm can be easily bent in such a way as to stop it from doing its job. To find out if it might be bent: with the spring in place, find the two regulation tabs on the touch piece of S10 and see if there is a gap been the tabs and keys S6 and S7. Now check that the link arm on S10 is touching the link arm on S9. If the answer to both of these questions is yes, then the instrument will work; if not, then the key is bent. You can unbend it while it is still on the instrument by pressing down the link arm and the touch piece. Keep bending until there is a small gap (lost motion) under S6 and S7. (The bending on most instruments is a torsional bend in the hinge tube.) To refine this regulation, you can adjust how the link arm of S10 acts on S9.

On S9 there is sometimes a movable link bar; the position of this can be changed by loosening a screw at its end (as on the YAS480), moving it and tightening it again. The position of this bar has three actions: it alters the vent height of S9, the amount of pressure S10 applies to the S9 pad, and the amount of double action with the table keys. The further the bar is away from the S9 axle, the less the key will open, but the more pressure S10 will then apply to the S9 pad.

First, see how it sits when you add the keys. Check to see if there is 0.5mm of double action between the table keys and S10. Next check the vent height of S9. If it is too narrow, you can loosen the link bar; move the bar towards the key hinge, lock it up, and test again. Make sure there is still double action between S10 and the table keys. Keep adjusting the key until a good balance is found. As a general rule though, it is best to have the link bar as far from the hinge of the key as possible to maximize the pressure S10 applies to the S9 pad.

Install S11, S12, S13, S14, S15, S16 and S17

Fig. 15.63 S11: Side B♭.
Fig. 15.64 S12: Chromatic/fork F♯.
Fig. 15.65 S13: Side C.

Fig. 15.66 S14: F♯ pad key.
Fig. 15.67 S15: Bis B♭ (also called 1 & 1 B♭ linkage).

Fig. 15.68 S16: Side C pad key.
Fig. 15.69 S17: Side B♭ pad key.

Medium spring
Regulation/vent height

Check and adjust the vent height of S14, S16 and S17 with cork under the heels. Using the lower of the two large adjusting screws on the S1 arm, set the time of arrival between S1 and S15. Check the gap between the tails of S16 with S11 and S17 with S13.

If the two side keys or rocker keys, S16 and S17, are unsprung, you will have to make sure the touch keys S11 and S13 have strong springs on them to keep the side keys shut. They will always have a captive pin mechanism as the key has to shut the keys and force them to open. It can be a tough adjustment to make if you want a positive action and for it to be quiet. You have to adjust the angle and size of the pin mechanism to minimize the gaps, and therefore the noise, without compromising the free movement of the key. You might try adding plastic tubing or cork. It is easy to make an adjustment that stops the keys from closing completely, so always re-check the pads with a feeler gauge after fitting the keys. When S16 and S17 each have a flat spring to keep them shut, the touch piece S11 and S13 only have to push down on the tails to open the key.

Install S18, S19 and S20 (left-hand stack)

Fig. 15.70 S18: Correspondence C pad key.

Fig. 15.71 S19: B.

Fig. 15.72 S20: A.

Medium spring
Regulation

Use the adjusting screw or the cork on the regulation bar (bridge key) on the back of S18, to set the time of arrival between S19 and S20 with S18. Adjusting the vent height and time of departure of this left-hand stack is similar to the process used on the right-hand stack. You use the corks under the tails of S19 and S20. Adjust the time of arrival between S20 and S15. There is usually a felt under the touch piece of S20 to make this adjustment.

Install S21 and S22

Fig. 15.73 S21: e.

Fig. 15.74 S22: f♯ pad key.

Strong spring
Regulation

Set the vent heights.

Install S23 (speaker key mechanism)

Fig. 15.75 S23: Automatic octave key mechanism.

The speaker mechanism keys might take many different shapes and forms. The function of this group of keys does not become apparent until more of the instrument is assembled. The speaker key mechanism enables the switch between the opening of the S23 pad and the S32 pad. When S30 is pushed down, it will open S32 unless S24 is also pushed down; this is when the switch over should take place and S32 shuts and the pad key on S23 will open (more of this later). At this point, it is essential to check that each of the keys rotates smoothly and with as little noise as possible. It is fairly common for the hole in the top pillar of this group to be oversized, which causes problems in the regulation of the keys. Use the hole shrinking tool to make the hinge screw a good fit in this pillar.

Install S24

Fig. 15.76 S24: f♯ pad key.

Medium spring

Install S25 and S26

Fig. 15.77 S25: E♭ / D♯.

Fig. 15.78 S26: Low C.

Medium spring
Regulation/vent height

Adjust the bumper keys attached to the underside of the key guards to get the vent height correct. The vent height of S26 is quite sensitive and should be kept as low as possible, consistent with good tone quality. If the note is prone to bubbling, then try lowering the vent height.

Install S27, S28 and S29 (palm keys)

Fig. 15.79 S27: Palm d.

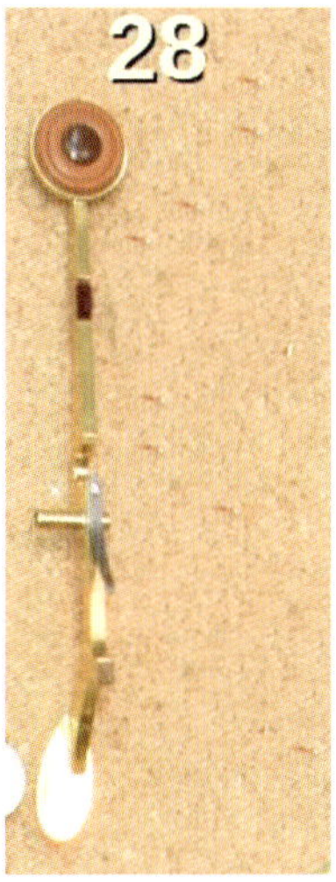

Fig. 15.80 S28: Palm f.

Fig. 15.81 S29: Palm e♭.

Strong flat springs

It is worth taking the time to adjust these springs so the tips of the springs do not slide when opening and shutting. It will make for a long-lasting action and give them a lovely feel to use.

Install S30

Fig. 15.82 S30: Thumb octave pad key.

Strong spring
Regulation

You can now begin to see how the speaker key mechanism works. By now, you should have checked that the keys are not bent or out of alignment. However, it is common for the touch piece of the speaker key to be bent down relative to its link arm or tail. This bend is a torsional bend of the hinge tube and is challenging to identify. Experience will tell you if that has happened. (In simple terms, if the thumb speaker touch piece feels low, then you might have a problem.)

The speaker key mechanism shown is typical of the modern design. You can use a 1.4mm cork on the bottom of the key arm that holds the neck key pin; make sure the pin looks straight, and parallel to the body when the cork is touching the neck receiver. The rocker arm should also be parallel with the hinge tube, and the second speaker key should also be in its closed position. The bottom rocker arm should also be in the same orientation as the top pin arm. If you now push down on the bottom arm and hold the second speaker shut, it should bring up the pin arm. Keeping the bottom arm down, if you now release the second speaker key and push down on the pin arm, the second speaker will open.

Add S30. Now is the point at which you can tell if the speaker touch key is bent. The lever arm of S30 should engage with the rocker arm of S23. The top of the speaker touch piece should be level with, or just above, the height of the thumb landing pad. If the key is bent, the touch piece will be lower than the pad. If so, you need to bend it up by holding the connecting arm against the body and lifting the touch piece until it is in the correct place. By doing it in this way, it will naturally try to unbend in the weakest area and will therefore be the natural place for it to have bent from in the first place. You can put a cylinder of cork under the speaker touch piece to act as a stop and prevent it from bending in the future.

Install S31

Fig. 15.83 S31: Front/fork F (E).

Regulation

S31 is the rocker key that fits under, and lifts, S28. This touch piece mustn't open the F key (S28) very much, only 1 or 2mm. Only playing the instrument will confirm what the correct opening is.

On some better instruments, there is a sliding sidearm that helps you set the opening and at the same time helps get the time of departure feeling good too.

Install S32

Fig. 15.84 S32: Crook octave pad key.

The next check is to put the neck key on the neck and the neck onto the instrument. I will now see if there is a gap of at least 0.5mm between the pin and the neck key (at least the thickness of paper). If there is not, I bend the speaker key away from the body to create the gap. When S30 (speaker key) is pushed down, the pin should now lift and open the neck key. With the speaker touch depressed, close S24; this will allow the neck key to close and the second-octave vent hole to open. Keeping both S30 and S24 closed, the final important check is to make sure there is now a gap between the pin and the neck key. If not, then the most likely problem is that the speaker touch is travelling too far, in which case you have to put a cork stop under the touch or the connecting arm.

Troubleshooting saxophone overhauls

The octave mechanism on saxophones can be tricky to get working, even though you have followed the regulation instructions correctly. This is because they can be subject to frequent damage by the musician, so by the time you get to see the instrument, you can't be sure that the octave keys have not been bent a long way away from the original manufacturer's alignment. If you are having a problem with the octave mechanism, see if you can have a good look at a similar model of instrument and look for differences. (*See also* Chapter 4 for troubleshooting ideas.)

Other members of the saxophone family

All saxophones work on the same key system and principles. It is even possible to get flexible LED lighting to feed around the bends of a baritone saxophone.

Oboe

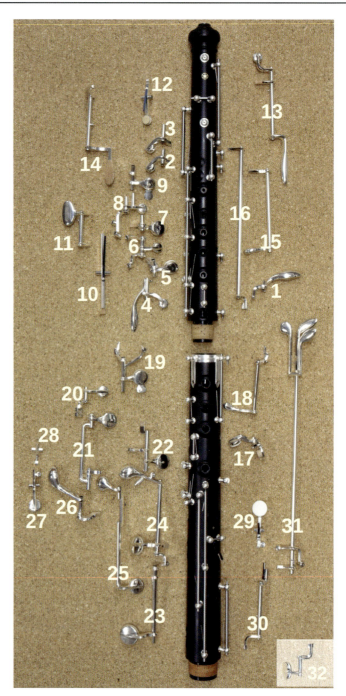

Fig. 15.85 YOB241 assembly order. The numbers are prefixed by O in the text.

The oboe I am using in this example is a mid-range Yamaha YOB241 oboe. It is a covered hole oboe with the following extra keywork over and above a student-range instrument:

- Semi-automatic octave mechanism, this arrangement makes moving from one octave key to the other easier: keys O12, O13 and O14.
- Two trill keys on the top joint, O2 and O3.
- Conservatoire bar (or link arm), O10 used to operate O5 and O7.
- This instrument has an English thumb plate also used to operate O5 and O7.
- Double articulated F vent on the bottom joint, O11 and O12.

Make sure every key is oiled with a medium or light oil.

184 Re-Assembly

Oboe key layout

O1: G#
O2: B–C# trill vent
O3: C–D trill vent
O4: RH G#
O5: G
O6: Correspondence Bb
O7: A
O8: Correspondence B
O9: C
O10: Conservatoire bar/link arm
O11: Thumb-plate/B
O12: Lower octave key vent
O13: Side/upper octave key
O14: Lower octave (also known as 'back octave') touch piece
O15: LH B–C# trill touch key
O16: C–D trill linkage arm
O17: RH F
O18: C–D trill touch key
O19: F#/conservatoire Bb & C touch key
O20: Correspondence E & Fork F
O21: E
O22: D
O23: Low B
O24: Low C
O25: C#
O26: D#/Eb
O27: Fork F vent
O28: Fork F vent rocker arm
O29: D# vent key
O30: Low Bb linkage
O31: Feather keys, includes LH D#/Eb, low B touch key, low Bb touch key
O32: Low Bb pad key

Fig. 15.86 O32: the bell key.

Install O1

Fig. 15.87 O1: G# touch piece.

Strong spring

Pay particular attention to the spring on this key. It is always very short, and it needs all the help it can get to work well. The diameter of the spring also affects the way the spring feels. Occasionally I have found that someone has attempted to increase the spring pressure by putting in a larger diameter needle spring. A larger spring rarely helps, so I end up having to put back a smaller spring and at the same time change the position of the spring hitch or the geometry of the key.

Install trill keys O2 and O3

Fig. 15.88 O2: B–C# trill.

Fig. 15.89 O3: C–D trill.

The trill keys go on early as the rod screw needs to be inserted from the lower pillar upwards. If you leave it until later, the O8 gets in the way. On this instrument, the hinge screw has a point that will act as the pivot screw for the second octave key. Re-check for cracks between holes.

Medium spring
Vent height

The heel corks need to give a vent height of about 0.5mm.

Install left-hand stack: O4, O5, O6, O7, O8, and O9

Fig. 15.90 O4: G#.

Fig. 15.91 O5: G.

Fig. 15.92 O6: Correspondence B♭.

Fig. 15.93 O7: A.

Fig. 15.94 O8: Correspondence B.

Fig. 15.95 O9: C.

Re-Assembly

Light and medium springs

O4: moderately light spring keeping the pad open.

O5: medium spring.

O6: light spring keeping it closed on this model of oboe. (I explain the alternatives later.)

O7: medium spring.

O8: light spring keeping it closed on this model of oboe.

O9: medium spring.

Regulation/vent height

O4 (first key on this stack): the spring on the O4 has to be light enough to be over-powered by the spring of the O1 (G# touch piece), though not so weak that it will stay closed if the pad gets slightly wet or sticky. When assembling, push down the O1 touch piece, so the link arm of O4 goes under the O1 link arm. Check and adjust the heel cork on the O1 touch piece tail, or the regulation cork under the touch piece, so that the vent height of O4 is 1mm. Pay particular attention to the point where the O1 touch arm cork makes contact with the O4 link arm. You want to use the principle of levers to apply maximum closing pressure on the O4 pad, i.e. the point of contact should be closer to the O1 hinge than the O4 hinge.

O5 (second key on the stack): don't worry too much about vent height on this key at this stage. On some instruments you can only adjust them when more keys are added.

O6 (third on the stack): this is the key that is closed when playing A and opens to sound Bb. On this instrument, which has a conservatoire bar, the key should have a light spring holding the pad open. Adjust the time of arrival between O5 and O6. Adjust the cork or adjusting screw on the link key, which on this instrument is on the lower arm of O6. An instrument with well-fitting hinges will need to be adjusted to within +/– 3 minutes of rotation.

O7 (fourth on the stack): don't worry too much about vent height at this stage. On some instruments it can only be adjusted when more keys are fitted.

O8 (fifth on the stack): this is normally closed and sounds a B and C when open. On this instrument, which has a conservatoire bar, the spring is a light spring holding the pad open.

Adjust the time of arrival between O6 and O8, using the screw or adjusting cork found at the end of the link arm of O8. Adjust the time of arrival between O7 and O8. This adjusting screw is the other screw on the O8 link arm. If the instrument has well-fitting hinges, it should be adjusted to within +/– 3 minutes of rotation.

O9 (sixth on the stack): this key should only open by the thickness of a piece of paper in the first instance. There is an adjusting screw on the tail of this key. The musician or teacher might want this adjusted when collecting the instrument as it can be set to suit different styles of oboe fingering.

Install O10 and O11

Fig. 15.96 O10: Conservatoire bar (also known as a link arm).

Fig. 15.97 O11: Thumb-plate B.

Strong spring
Regulation

O10 is called the conservatoire bar (also known as a link arm) and is used to control O6 and O8. It is only on some English instruments that this key is missing and replaced by a thumb plate only mechanism. This Yamaha oboe is dual system. The powerful spring on the conservatoire bar needs to be strong enough to overcome the two medium springs on O6 and O8 and keep the two pads shut. O11 has to have an even more powerful spring to overcome the conservatoire bar spring to keep pushing the bar down. Check that both O6 and O8 are closed when just O10 is installed. If necessary, adjust the screw on the tail of O6 to make sure that the bottom end of the conservatoire bar is not touching the body of the instrument. Check that O11 overpowers O10 and most importantly, when O11 is pressed down, it travels far enough to leave a gap between the underside of its link arm and the top of O10.

I have just described an instrument with a thumb-plate and conservatoire style of keywork; if the instrument has only got a thumb plate, then it is usual for the tail of the thumb plate to have a very powerful, pre-tensioned spring protruding from it. Boosey & Hawkes use a needle spring, whereas other manufacturers use a flat spring; the principle is the same. Before fitting the spring, you put a curve on it. The key is designed such that this spring will come under tension as you install the spring, so the free end of the spring will be very difficult, but not impossible, to move.

Install the octave keys (O12, O13 and O14)

Fig. 15.98 O12: Lower octave key.

Fig. 15.99 O13: Upper octave key.

Fig. 15.100 O14: Lower octave (also known as 'back octave') touch piece.

Light and medium springs

O12: light flat spring.

O13 and O14: medium springs.

Regulation

This instrument has the most popular type of octave mechanism called the semi-automatic system. Rather than having two independent keys for the first and second register octave holes, the first-octave hole, O12, is a rocker key that is opened by O14 and then closed by O13 when it opens the second-octave hole.

Vent height

The vent height of these keys has more to do with how the instrument feels to the musician than any acoustic effect. In general, musicians do not want these keys to travel very much, so keep the vent height small.

Install O15 and O16

Fig. 15.101 O15: B–C♯ trill touch key.

Fig. 15.102 O16: C–D trill linkage arm.

Regulation

It is crucial to make sure that there is a gap (lost motion or double action) at the link arms between these keys and O3 and O4. If you don't have this, then there is a risk that these trill keys will remain open, and the instrument won't play.

Fig. 15.103 O17: RH F.

Fig. 15.104 O18: C–D trill touch key.

Install O17 and O18

Medium spring
Regulation/vent height

Set the vent height on O17. O18 will get regulated when the two joints are put together.

Install right-hand stack: O19, O20, O21 and O22

Fig. 15.105 O19: F♯/conservatoire B♭ and C touch key.

Fig. 15.106 O20: Correspondence E and fork F.

Re-Assembly

Fig. 15.107 O21: E.

Fig. 15.108 O22: D.

Light and medium springs

O19: medium spring.
O20: light spring.
O21: medium spring.
O22: medium spring.

Regulation

O19 has a link arm that goes over the join, to press O4 on the top joint. I suggest you wait until you have completed the assembly of the top and bottom joints before you regulate this key. You can set the vent height at this stage.

O20 and O21: using the higher of the two adjusting screws on the tail of O20, set the time of arrival between O21 and O20.

O22 (fourth key on stack): using the lower of the two adjusting screws on O20, set the time of arrival of O22 and O20.

Fig. 15.109 O23: Low B.

Fig. 15.110 O24: Low C.

Install O23 and O24

There are two ways that these keys get mounted: either both are hinge keys, or O23 is a hinge key and O24 is a pivot key. Yamaha has very helpfully mounted O23, O24, O25 and O26 as hinge keys, making assembly and repair much more straightforward than on most other oboes. Before fitting O24, look to see how O25 is mounted. If it is on a pivot screw, make sure that the top pivot screw is tight in the pillar before fitting O24 as it will obscure the head of the point screw.

This Yamaha oboe also has what is known as a low B link. This is a link arm between O23 and O24. It needs to be adjusted so that O23 and O24 arrive simultaneously. The link arm on this particular instrument works well because the link arm extends quite a long way from the hinge screw. This improves the mechanical advantage on the lever and puts less strain on the mechanism. This regulation is difficult to do on less well-designed instruments unless there is no wear in the mechanism.

Medium spring
Regulation

Set the time of arrival between O23 and O24 using the adjusting screw at the bottom end of O24 (if there is one). The adjusting screw at the top of O24 is linked with O21 and should not close O21 completely when O24 is shut. The final adjustment of this screw is done when play-testing the instrument and is used to help play in the third-octave register.

Fig. 15.111 O25: C♯.

Fig. 15.112 O26: D♯/E♭.

Install O25 and O26

Yamaha have helpfully mounted these keys on one hinge screw with a bridge key on this oboe.

Medium spring
Regulation/vent height

The only regulation to be done here is to set the vent height of O24 using the link arm on O24 which sits under the touch piece of O25.

Fig. 15.113 O27: Fork F vent.

Fig. 15.114 O28: rocker key.

Install O27 and O28 (F vent mechanism)

Light spring
Regulation

This Yamaha oboe has a double rocker F mechanism as opposed to most oboes, which have only O27. The dual rocker improves the tuning and stability of the instrument and is designed to keep O27 closed except when the forked F fingering is played (which is when O21 is open and O22 is closed). To adjust a single rocker mechanism, close O21 and turn the adjusting screw on O27 until it closes at the same time as O21. On a double rocker mechanism, still set the time of arrival between O21 and O27, and rotate the adjusting screw on the tail of O22 so that O27 shuts when O22 is open.

Install O29

Fig. 15.115 O29: D♯ vent key.

Light spring

This key has a double spring mechanism. It needs a light spring that is enough to open the key. The second spring is screwed to the instrument's body and is bent upwards so that it pushes on the heel of O29 to force it shut. This spring has to be stronger than the opening spring. The tail of the second spring should be bent in such a way as to make it parallel to the body.

Regulation

There are several different regulations to be done on this key: there must be a gap (lost motion) between O29 and O24; and between O29 and O26. The arrows illustrate where the gaps should be. Push down O24 (RH little finger), then using the tip of a screwdriver, or fingernail, depress the free end of the long spring (in red) that closes the O29 rocker key. Use the adjusting screw (a1) to set the time of arrival between O24 and O29 (test the time of arrival with a feeler gauge under each pad in turn). Support the body of the oboe between you and the bench peg to facilitate this test. Failure to get this adjustment right will result in the musician not being able to move from Eb to any of the lower notes.

Install O30, O31 and O32

Fig. 15.117 O30: Low B♭ linkage.

Fig. 15.118 O32: Low B♭ pad key.

Fig. 15.119 O31: Feather keys.

Fig. 15.120 shows O31; it is a combination of a hinge key (shown in green) and a pivot key (shown in blue). The three touch pieces at the top of O31 are called the feather keys.

The low Eb and low Bb (in green) are attached to each other and the hinge tube. When the Eb touch piece is pressed down it will depress the spring under O29 (in Fig. 15.116 it is shown in red), which will allow the Eb pad O29 to open. The middle touch piece (in blue) is attached to the hinge rod (also in blue), that goes right to the bottom of the key and is connected to the small lever that lifts the link arm of O23, so shutting O23. When low Bb is pressed down (the right-hand touch piece) it moves the link arm down and connects with O30 at the adjustment a4, then on to key O32 via the link a5, to close the pad on the bell.

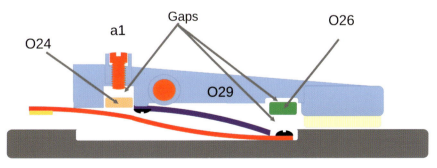

Fig. 15.116 O29 at rest with the tone hole sealed.

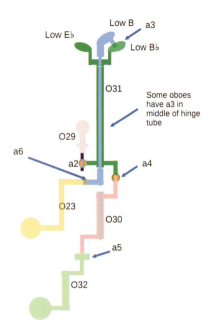

Fig. 15.120 Diagram of the feather key mechanism.

Medium spring Regulation

This is the sequence for regulating the feather keys:

1. Unscrew adjusting screws a2 and a4 and check there is a thin cork at a3. On professional instruments, the link arm a3 is not present – instead there is a small bridge key in the middle section of the hinge tube and there will be an adjusting screw.
2. Set the vent height of O23 using cork at a6 (the cork under the low B tail in blue).
3. Test that there is a gap (lost motion) at a2 and a3. If there is no gap at a3 then the two outer feather keys may have been bent towards the body of the instrument. Investigate further: you may need to bend these two keys together, away from the body, until there is a gap. The aim is to make sure that the low B lever is not pushing up the low Bb lever and accidentally opening O29 (the Eb key).
4. With the bell attached, allow the feather keys to sit at their resting positions and adjust a4 so that O23 and O30 depart at the same time when the Bb feather key is depressed.
5. Adjust a5 to set the time of arrival between O23 and O32.

The feather keys are very easily bent up or down, so be prepared to unbend them if they look wrong. The link key between the bell and bottom joint also gets bent easily, so be prepared to unbend that key too.

There are up to three links between the top and bottom joint. Assemble the top and bottom joints and align the stack key pillars (this is the most reliable reference point).

All oboes have an arm that comes from O19 over the top of the pad cup of O4. Close O19 and adjust the gap between the arm and the top of the pad cup so that the O4 and O19 pads arrive at the same time. I do this using my feeler gauge between the arm and top of the pad cup and then add five minutes of rotation to the screw. Make a final test with the feeler on the two pads.

Some instruments have a conservatoire bar, O10. There has to be a small gap between the link arm on O19 and O10.

The last link that an oboe can have is O2, the second trill key. This is operated by O18 on the bottom joint. There has to be a gap (lost motion) between the two keys.

Troubleshooting oboe overhauls

There are many different key systems used on professional oboes – and they could each take a chapter to describe – but the principles for pad seating and regulation are the same. Here I will try to highlight some of the common features that might need extra explanation. (For the design and operation of octave bushes, please *see* Chapter 4: Emergency Fixes.)

Articulated C#

Many mid-range and all professional oboes have an articulated C# near the bottom of the bottom joint. The C# pad is usually attached to O25, but on some instruments this pad can be on a separate rocker key; it is then called an articulated C#. O25 will still open and shut the key, but O23 will also be able to shut the pad. You will need to regulate the time of arrival between O25 and O23 using the adjusting screw on the C# rocker key.

Double ring key on Gillet system

On Gillet key system oboes, the key operated by the third finger on the right hand is an open hole key with two ring keys around the same hole, one on top of the other. The sequence for setting this key is as follows:

1. Seat the cork pad of the inner ring key.
2. Then check that the top of the second ring sits level with the inner ring. Use wafer thin cork on top of, and around, the inner ring.
3. Now you can set about regulating both these keys with other keys on the bottom stack.

Where the Bb to B link is not on the feather keys

On some instruments the link arm that links the B feather key to the Bb feather key is missing. This is because the manufacturer has located this regulation link to a point half-way down the O31 hinge tube. To regulate the B to Bb pads, use the adjusting screw found here. The part of the key that this adjusting screw is attached to is nearly always associated with an extra link arm that closes one half of the double ring key when the Eb feather touch piece is operated.

Bassoon

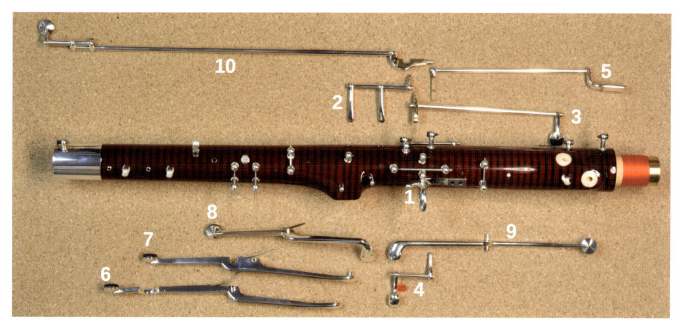

Fig. 15.121 YFG812 wing joint assembly order. The numbers are prefixed by B in the text.

The bassoon used in this section is a top-level Yamaha custom bassoon YFG812.

Wing joint back

B1: Crook key lock
B2: Link keys from c touch key and c# touch key, both to LH third finger ring
B3: Vent key for c
B4: Crook touch key/F touch key
B5: Crook key/F touch key
B6: d touch key/flick key
B7: c touch key/flick key
B8: a touch key/flick key
B9: C# key
B10: Crook key/linkage key

Install B1

Fig. 15.122 B1: Crook key lock.

Strong spring

This may need some grease on it to make it work smoothly.

Install B2 and B3

Fig. 15.123 B2: Link keys from c touch key and c# touch key, both to LH third finger ring.

Fig. 15.124 B3: Vent key for c.

Spring

The spring on B2 has to overcome the spring on B3 to keep B3 shut.

Vent height

Adjust the felt under B2 to regulate the vent height of B3.

Install B4 and B5

Fig. 15.125 B4: Crook touch key/F touch key.

Fig. 15.126 B5: Crook key/F touch key.

Re-Assembly 191

Medium spring
Install B6, B7, B8 and B9
Strong spring
Regulation

Make sure there is a 1mm gap between the cork or felt under the touch pieces of B7 and B9, and the top of B2.

Vent height

Set the vent height of B6 and B8 to 2mm.

Install B10
Light spring

There is a spring on the link arm of B10 that connects with B2 and B5. It is there to make it easier to set the time of arrival between the 'pancake' key (B29) and the crook pad. The crook pad will work with a vent height of 0.5mm upwards. If you find that the spring will not stay in position, you may need to find a way to lock the spring using one of the techniques described in the flat spring section of this book.

Regulation

This will be done when the rest of the instrument is complete.

Wing joint front

B11: E–F# trill/eb
B12: D–Eb trill
B13: C ring touch key/third finger ring

Install B11 and B12
Medium spring
Regulation

Make sure there is a small gap under the adjusting screw between B11 and B12.

Vent height

Set the vent height to 2mm.

Fig. 15.127 B6: d touch key/flick key.

Fig. 15.128 B7: c touch key/flick key.

Fig. 15.129 B8: a touch key/flick key.

Fig. 15.130 B9: C# pad key.

Fig. 15.131 B10: Crook key linkage key.

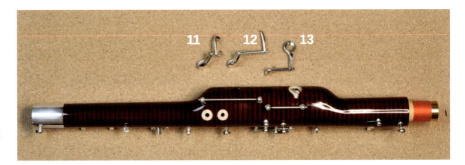
Fig. 15.132 YFG812 wing joint front assembly order.

Fig. 15.133 B11: E–F# trill/eb.

Fig. 15.134 B12: D–Eb trill.

192 Re-Assembly

Install B13

Fig. 15.135 B13: C ring touch key/third finger ring.

Light spring
Regulation

When pushed down, this ring key has to end up level with the metal finger hole (tone hole), so that the finger can seal the tone hole and also keep pressure on the ring key. When pressed down, the key also needs to shut B3 when B2 is pressed down at the same time. To describe this another way: press down B2 and it will open B3. Now press down B13 and it should close B3.

Boot joint front

B14: Low F touch key/g vent touch key
B15: F#
B16: G#
B17: RH alternate (front) Bb
B18: G touch key
B19: A ring/g vent
B20: Low F pad key
B21: C–C# trill

Install B14

Fig. 15.137 B14: Low F touch key/g vent touch key.

Light spring

Fig. 15.138 B15: F#

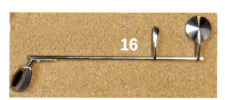

Fig. 15.139 B16: G#

Install B15 and B16
Medium spring

Fig. 15.140 B17: RH alternate (front) B♭.

Fig. 15.141 B18: G touch key.

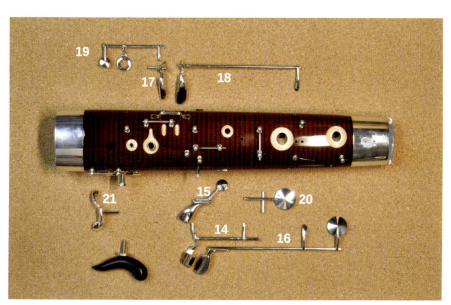

Fig. 15.136 YFG812 boot joint front assembly order.

Re-Assembly 193

Install B17 and B18

Light spring

Fig. 15.142 B19: A ring/g vent.

Install B19

Light spring

Regulation

Check that the pad is closed when the ring key is level with the metal tone hole insert. The finger has to comfortably seal the tone hole and also shut the pad. Also check that B14 shuts the B19 pad. The link arms on B14 and B19 do get bent quite often so be prepared to unbend the keys as needed.

Fig. 15.143 B20: Low F pad key.

Install B20

Medium spring

Regulation

Make sure that B14 can close B20 (there is regulation cork under the tail of B20).

Install B21

Medium spring

B21a will be installed later.

Fig. 15.144 B21: C–C# trill.

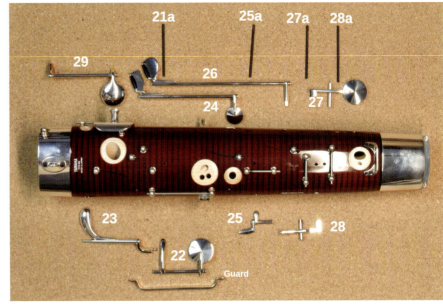

Fig. 15.145 YFG812 boot joint back assembly order.

Boot joint back

B21a: Alternate (front) Bb key connecting pin
B22: Bb key
B23: Bb touch key
B24: Thumb F# touch key
B25: F# linkage key rocker arm to close low F key
B25a: Thumb F# connecting pin to hold F key
B26: G# touch key
B27: G pad key
B27a: G touch key connecting pin to close G key
B28: G# key rocker arm to open G# pad key
B28a: G key connecting pin
B29: 'Pancake' low E

Install B21a

The push rods are all different lengths so if they get muddled up then you will have to experiment to find the correct order.

Install B22

Fig. 15.146 B22: B♭ pad key.

Strong spring

Regulation

Make sure that B17 is able to open B22 at least 2mm. Put the key guard back in place with the two wood screws.

Fig. 15.147 B23: B♭ touch key.

Install B23

Light spring

Regulation

Make sure there is a gap between the tail of B23 and the underside of B22, and that B23 can lift B22 at least 2mm.

Install B24

Fig. 15.148 B24: Thumb F# touch key.

Strong spring

Install B25a

Push rod.

Install B25

This key operates as follows: when B24 is opened, it lifts the point arm of B25 and this pushes the rod through the instrument and closes B20.

Regulation

There needs to be a very small gap (paper thickness) between the end of the push rod and B25.

Fig. 15.149 B25: F# linkage key rocker arm to close low F pad key.

Install B26
Medium spring
Install B27a

Push rod.

Fig. 15.150 B26: G# touch key.

Install B27
Medium spring
Regulation/vent height

The vent height is set near the touch piece of B18. Make sure that the pin is long enough for B18 to shut B27. Do not be tempted to put thicker cork where the push rods go, as the cork will simply get punctured.

Fig. 15.151 B27: G pad key.

Install B28
Regulation

Ensure that B28 is not keeping B16 open and also that B26 is able to open B16 3mm.

Fig. 15.152 B28: G# key rocker arm to open G# pad key.

Install B29
Medium spring
Regulation/vent height

Set the vent height using the felt under the tail of B29.

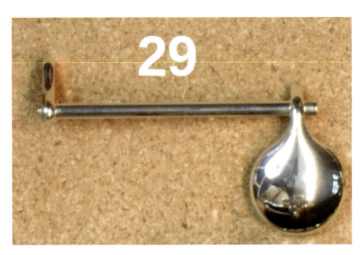

Fig. 15.153 B29: 'Pancake' low E.

Long joint

B30: Low C key
B31: Low D touch key

B32: Low D key
B33: Low C# touch key
B34: Low Eb
B35: Low C# key

B36: Low B touch key
B37: Low Bb touch key
B38: Low B key

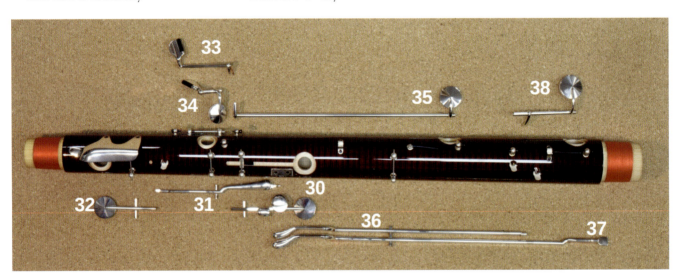

Fig. 15.154 YFG812 long joint assembly order. The numbers are prefixed by B in the text.

Install B30

Fig. 15.155 B30: Low C key.

Strong spring

Install B31

Fig. 15.156 B31: Low D touch key.

Install B32

Fig. 15.157 B32: Low D pad key.
Light spring
Regulation

Set the time of arrival between B30 and B31 using the link arm at the end of B31 that goes under B30.

Install B33
Light spring

Fig. 15.158 B33: Low C♯ touch key.

Install B34
Heavy spring
Regulation

Some bassoons require a very thick cork, so I use a wine cork.

Fig. 15.159 B34: Low E♭.

Install B35
Heavy spring
Regulation

You only need to make sure that B33 is not holding B35 open.

Fig. 15.160 B35: Low C♯ pad key.

Install B36 and B37
Medium spring

These are double hinge keys, so remember to oil both axles.

Fig. 15.161 B36: Low B touch key.
B37: Low B♭ touch key.

Install B38
Medium spring
Regulation

There is quite a lot of flex in the long keys, so the time of arrival of B38 and B30 needs to be adjusted under the touch piece of B36 so that B38 arrives before B30. The musician will tell you if you have this balance right for them.

Fig. 15.162 B38: Low B pad key.

Re-Assembly

Bell

B39: Low Bb key

Install B39
Medium spring
Regulation

Adjust the touch piece height to be level, or just above, B37, and make sure the key is not noisy when it opens.

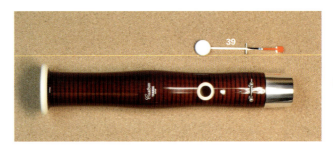

Fig. 15.163 YFG812 bell.

Fig. 15.164 B39: Low B♭ key.

U-bend fitting

The U-bend on the bottom of the boot joint connects the two bores of the instrument. You need to have an airtight seal, which is achieved with a cork or rubber gasket. When checking or overhauling the bassoon, check this seal. You can use a feeler gauge around the cork joints, as you would with a pad.

To replace the cork, clean both surfaces. Using a good piece of cork of the same thickness as the original, mark where the two bore holes need to be cut. This can be done by making an impression on the cork or by careful measurement. Using thin-walled metal tubing or a cork boring tool, cut out the circles in the cork.

Coat the U-bend and one side of the cork in contact adhesive and when tacky, bond them together, making sure the holes align. Trim the cork around the U-bend.

Carefully flatten the cork on a sheet of abrasive that is on a flat surface. Install the U-bend on the bottom of the bassoon, puncturing the hole for the index pin as needed. Using a feeler gauge, test the cork seal and adjust as needed.

Before final assembly and tightening down the lock screws, lightly grease the cork.

Troubleshooting

Occasionally, after a full overhaul, an instrument can still lack power or resonance. Check the sockets are round, especially the boot joint to long joint, and the wing joint. The wood is very thin around the socket and can be distorted by the wood warping or the metal band being bent slightly. Use digital callipers or internal spring callipers to make the measurements. If needed, make a reamer to re-shape the hole. You will need to re-cork or increase the threaded binding of the tenon to make it fit. On the dozen or so times I have made this adjustment it has been successful.

Threaded tenons are notorious for leaking if the musician does not get into the habit of adjusting the amount of thread needed as the weather conditions change.

PART FOUR

Specialist Repairs

CHAPTER 16

Specialist Repair Tools and Materials

This section is concerned with less common repairs that you might want to undertake and includes the tools and materials you may find useful for them. I have deliberately not tried to smarten up the tools that I make and use in my workshop as I want readers to have the confidence to go ahead and undertake repairs without feeling that they have to buy everything or spend more time making the tools than doing the repairs. You have to get all the important dimensions and angles correct, but it makes no difference to the performance of the tool if a clearance channel is not straight, or if you use scrap material rather than new material to make it.

To undertake specialist repairs you will need some engineering skills and practice. If you do not have these, then finding a night school or a specialist engineer to work with you will be time well spent. It is also worth keeping some scrap instruments around, as you can scavenge material and parts from them.

Most of the procedures we need to undertake can be accomplished with an engineering lathe, drill press and maybe a milling machine. I have successfully used my lathe as a milling machine in the past. You can use your ingenuity to find a way.

Lathes

Choosing a lathe

Always buy the best lathe you can afford. It is better to buy a small lathe of better quality than a larger, poor quality, machine. A used or second-hand lathe is often a good choice. To give you an idea of the type of lathe you need, I use a Myford Super 7 long bed for all my repair work. The long bed is 780mm between centres and is generous to use. The standard 475mm will handle everything except bassoons. I recommend finding something with a gap of 475mm or over between centres. Similar lathes are the South Bend and Boxford lathes. I only use my bigger lathe (Harrison M350) for instrument making and tool making. You can get a very usable machine if you choose well. I do not recommend any

Fig. 16.1 If you are going to undertake extensive repairs and toolmaking, a lathe is essential. The new generation of mini lathes are good, but I, along with many other technicians, like the Myford Super 7 lathe, pictured here.

particular brand in this book, since the makes and models are changing so fast. Find a reputable engineer and use trusted reviews to find the best available in your location.

If you do buy a second-hand machine, check the bed for wear. Be prepared to replace the chuck on a second-hand lathe, as they wear out surprisingly quickly.

Digital readout

I would very strongly recommend that you choose, or fit, your lathe with a digital readout (DRO). Measuring the distance along the bed is almost impossible without a DRO and this is one of the most useful measurements we need to make. I recommend you use magnetic spars, not optical ones. All the magnetic systems I have seen have a very satisfactory accuracy of 5 micron. The benefit is that the magnetic spars and their reading heads are much smaller and less delicate than the optical systems. In 2019 it became possible to hide the magnetic strip under the cross slide, which is brilliant, and this is when I added the second axis DRO to my Myford.

Lathe tooling

The simplest form of lathe tool is one you grind yourself out of high-speed steel (HSS). They work well and are very adaptable. I sometimes still make them,

Fig. 16.2 Interchangeable tool holder.

but it is a skill to do this well and many of us choose to use tools with replaceable inserts. They come in a huge variety of shapes and materials.

An interchangeable tool holder allows you to set the correct tool height of each lathe tool in its own holder or carrier. When you want to change tool, you release the current carrier and replace it with the tool you want to use next. It makes changing tools very quick and accurate.

Fig. 16.3 Standard lathe tool in quick change holder.

Fig. 16.4 Boring bar in quick change holder.

I recommend only buying a premium quality boring bar with a solid carbide shank and interchangeable cutting inserts. They are very stiff and prevent chatter. I bought mine second-hand; I

Fig. 16.5 Close-up of a boring bar cutter, for boring holes.

have Sandvik, Sumitomo and Korloy brands.

Fig. 16.5 shows my favourite boring bar tool, for boring holes. The design of these boring bars allows you to start boring a hole without drilling a pilot hole first. The interchangeable carbide tip has three possible cutting edges, so when one gets blunt, you move it around.

Fig. 16.6 Parting tool.

Parting is the process of turning a groove across your work piece. It can be left as a groove or you can turn completely across the work and part the two pieces. The parting tool itself has interchangeable carbide tips. There is a cutting rake on the front, and two sides of the tool, so it can be used as a parting tool and also be used to make shallow cuts from side to side.

Fig. 16.7 Circular cutting insert on lathe tool.

My favourite lathe tool for outside turning of wood and plastic is this circular cutting tool. It has a high rake angle 8mm diameter cutting tip. This gives a

Fig. 16.8 Magnetic tool holder.

super-smooth finish and if the tool gets blunt you just rotate it a few degrees to present a new sharp edge.

I store my heavy lathe tools on a magnetic strip set horizontally. This keeps them secure and clean and does not take up valuable bench space.

Milling machines

Fig. 16.9 Milling machine.

Myford VM milling machine. This was my third biggest investment in machinery, after the lathe and a digital readout for the lathe. It has been invaluable for instrument making, repairs and tool making. I have fitted a digital scale on the front of the table and on the quill.

The Proxxon drill is a sensible design of good quality. The spindle and quill are well adjusted. It is great for drilling small holes accurately. I have made a foot plate that allows me to mount it on the cross slide of my lathe.

Fig. 16.10 Micro drill press.

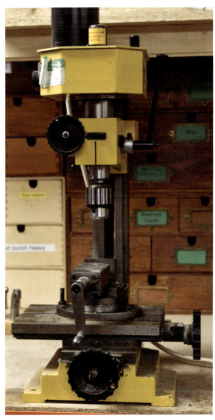

Fig. 16.11 Small milling machine.

The small milling machine shown in Fig. 16.11 can cope with most requirements of the woodwind repair workshop. I also made a baseplate for it from 8mm steel plate. This allows me to bolt this milling machine to the cross slide of a Myford lathe, or other suitable lathe.

Measuring tools

Fig. 16.13 Internal spring callipers.

A pair of simple spring callipers is great for measuring to the bottom of sockets and down bore holes. Each turn of the screw only changes the tips by around 0.01mm so they are accurate enough for our needs and are great for making simple comparisons between one object and another. They have two significant advantages over digital or dial callipers: they have very long jaws, and they let you measure the inside of an object even when the entrance is constricted. By way of example, you can check if the entrance to a clarinet barrel is constricted, and by how much, by setting the spring calliper at the bottom of the socket and then squeezing the arms together to extract the tips from the socket; let the arms spring back to the original position and use your digital callipers to get the measurement. Then measure the entrance to the socket for comparison.

To quickly measure the diameter of pads you can use the tool shown in Fig. 16.14. It is made from two strips of wood or plastic attached to a back-board

Fig. 16.12 The cutting ends of two types of milling cutter. Left: an end mill that only cuts on the side; right: a slot mill that can cut on the end and the side.

Specialist Repair Tools and Materials 203

Fig. 16.14 Pad measure.

Fig. 16.16 Belt linisher.

independently, which means you can hold round and irregularly shaped items.

To know how well your work piece is centred, use a dial test indicator. The independent jaws also allow you to have your piece off centre; I have used this feature to create a tone hole insert with an off-centre tone hole (this was because I failed to centre the cutting tool on the tone hole and cut an eccentric counter-bore.)

If you want to hold the outside of a delicate item and don't want the chuck jaws to mark the surface, you can bore out a piece of hardwood that will fit over the work. You then make a slit along the length of the collar, put the collar over the item and grip them both together in the chuck.

In Chapter 17, I describe making a simple tool for holding an instrument when replacing a tone hole. Fig. 17.28 shows a drive dog being used to fix the instrument in position. The same drive dog can be used in combination with a catch plate on a lathe to rotate the instrument.

to form a tapered channel. The measurements are marked after you have made the tool.

Fig. 16.15 Digital callipers with spring loader.

Digital callipers are useful for measuring pads. I have fitted a spring-loaded pressure device to provide consistent pressure when measuring soft materials like flute pads. Dial callipers and Vernier callipers are also very good and they don't need new batteries every few months.

There is an air leak testing machine made for woodwind repairs that is based on the Dwyer Magnehelic differential pressure gauge. It is a machine that you can make yourself, with a bit of ingenuity. I also designed a leak testing machine, based on a bubble film flow meter.

A belt linisher or band sander is a very useful workshop tool – great for tool making and key making.

Tools for holding instruments

Often the most difficult part of machining an item is working out how to hold it. The three-jaw self-centring chuck only became universal in the early twentieth century and is now accepted as the go-to method for holding material on a lathe. However, the original techniques of turning, between centres, using mandrels, collets and four-jaw independent chucks, are still very useful ways to hold your work.

Self-centring chucks are useful, but they do have the following disadvantages:

- They are not, on the whole, very accurate.
- They can leave marks on your work.
- They don't hold anything other than parallel parts.

Precision engineers use the four-jaw independent chuck when they require a high degree of accuracy. Each of the four jaws can be moved in and out

Fig. 16.17 Pin chuck.

A pin chuck is useful for holding very small drills and wires in a lathe or bench motor.

Polymorph

Just occasionally I want to create a tough plastic tool, and the perfect material is often a plastic called Polymorph. It comes in small granules that melt when you put them in boiling water. Once the opaque pellets become clear you pull them out of the hot water and squeeze them together into a putty that can be shaped however you need. Once it has cooled completely, it becomes an extremely tough, nylon-type plastic. It can be hammered, pulled or crushed without breaking.

Once soft, you can manipulate it with your fingers to mould around metal work pieces. When it cools it sets to a very strong resilient plastic, like nylon. I have used this to hold complex metal components both in a vice and in my lathe chuck. When you have finished machining, you heat it up in boiling water to soften it again and remove the plastic.

Sometimes a pillar on a saxophone gets pushed in, forming a dent in the body. I have used Polymorph to pull the dent back out again. I did this by moulding Polymorph around the pillar to grip it. I left enough plastic above the pillar to form a loop which I could then hook a dent hammer on and pull on the pillar to remove the dent.

Fig. 16.18 Leather-lined clamp for holding a mouthpiece if you want to work on a baffle.

Fig. 16.19 Undercutting and overcutting tools.

I have also used it to make a form to burnish a bell against. There are endless uses for this cheap and versatile plastic.

Specialist undercutting and overcutting tools are needed if you are replacing tone holes or tuning instruments.

Fig. 16.20 Slide hammer.

The slide hammer is a tool for removing dents; you can use it to provide a sudden pulling action. Attach the item to the hook on the left and slide the red weight sharply to the right.

Fig. 16.21 I inherited this tool from Derek Winterbourn; it is an engineer's tap with the same thread as is used on thumb rest screws.

Rather than having to look through a pile of similar-looking tools, you can put unique handles on them.

Fig. 16.22 Adjustable reamer.

An adjustable reamer is designed to ream out, or enlarge, holes. By adjusting special nuts at each end of the tool, six cutting blades are moved slowly outwards or inwards to change the diameter of the hole it will cut. Each blade has a very slight taper at the front end of the reamer to allow it to enter the hole. Each reamer will adjust over a 1.5mm range so for clarinet work, you would choose one with the range 14.5 to 16mm.

Specialist repair materials

Fig. 16.23 Silver steel rods.

Silver steel rods, also known as high carbon steel, of various diameters, are used for tool making. Nickel silver rod and sheet can be used to make new keywork. You can sometimes re-use keys from scrap instruments.

Fig. 16.24 Blackwood.

I always have spare blackwood around the workshop. I use it for making some tools, replacement barrels, sanding down to create blackwood dust, and occasionally for repairs. The species is not endangered and there are new plantations in Tanzania, so it is readily available from specialist suppliers.

Fig. 16.25 From left: blackwood, ebonite and Delrin.

Specialist Repair Tools and Materials

Fig. 16.25 shows blackwood, ebonite, and Delrin. It can be challenging to see the grain on some blackwood, but you can usually tell it is wood by looking at the end grain. Ebonite is vulcanized rubber. Experience has shown that it is the best plastic to use when bonding to African blackwood. It can easily be machined, and hand worked, to a very high tolerance and finish. Its mechanical strength is good, and it bonds very well with epoxy resins. It is impervious to water, and its co-efficient of thermal expansion is small. It does, however, smell of hydrogen sulphide (rotten eggs) when machined. Ebonite is used for the manufacture of replacement tone holes and tenon joints. Depending on which instruments you work on, you will need rod that is around 40mm in diameter and 20mm in diameter.

Delrin is the brand name of a nylon that is not as nice to machine as ebonite and will not bond well with any adhesive. I only use it for tool making.

Fig. 16.26 Blackwood dust.

I took time out to make lots of blackwood dust for filling cracks. I cleaned my lathe down, so as not to contaminate the wood dust, and put a sheet of cardboard over the lathe bed. Then, spinning some blackwood at high speed, I tried

Fig. 16.27 Bassoon push rods.

out several abrasives, until I found one that gave the right size dust, then just kept sanding!

I have found that the best material to make the push rods that go through the boot joint of a bassoon is bamboo satay sticks! I buy them from the Chinese supermarket. They must be made from bamboo and not any other wood, so look for the sticks with a hard, shiny surface. Try to find the small diameter variety; if you can't, you will need to hammer the sticks through a steel plate of the right diameter to fit the bassoon.

Fig. 16.28 Pinning rod.

I get asked to pin cracks quite often and have, until now, used threaded stainless steel wire. I have recently been testing carbon-fibre rods to replace the wire and it seems to be a good alternative.

Adhesives

I have introduced superglues and thermoplastic glues earlier in the book; the other useful group of adhesives are the thermoset group exemplified by epoxy resins.

Fig. 16.29 Epoxy resin.

Araldite is the original epoxy resin glue. Standard retail packs of epoxy have additives that make them non-drip. This is useful for many applications, but you will also need to find a source of less viscous or liquid epoxy resin, such as the brand West System.

These are thermoset plastics that you cannot reuse. Thermoset plastics are used for permanently bonding rigid or solid surfaces, such as replacement tenon joints or tone holes. Epoxy resins should not be used for attaching cork or pads.

To improve the effectiveness of epoxy resin it is a good idea to create some mechanical keying (small scratches) on the bonding surface, and to clean or degrease the surface before applying the glue. Epoxy resins are commonly classified by their curing time. My experience is that the quick-cure formulations are not as strong as the long cure formulas. Where strength is not the most important attribute, then five-minute or even quicker formulations are very convenient. Make sure you mix the two components very well before using them. Epoxy resins work better if warmed during the mixing or application stage. It improves the chemical reaction and de-gasses the liquid. You can also speed up the curing time of the 24-hour, or long-cure, formulations by applying gentle continuous heat from an incandescent light bulb or another gentle heat source. (Be careful not to damage or dry out any wooden instrument body with too much heat.)

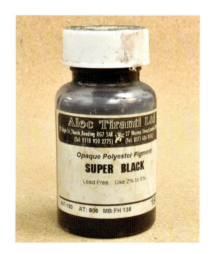

Fig. 16.30 Resin dye. This black resin colouring is labelled as opaque polyester pigment; it is, however, suitable for epoxy resins too.

Abrasives and cleaning materials

Fig. 16.31 Emery sticks.

Every so often I make a quantity of emery sticks by gluing wet and dry paper onto wooden sticks using contact adhesive. Other repairers simply wrap the paper around an old file. To hold the paper in place, when not in use, make yourself a holding bar.

Fig. 16.32 This wire bar that sits under your workbench will hold the emery paper in place when you are not using it.

Fig. 16.33 Very fine wet and dry abrasive pads.

3M abrasive papers are like very fine Scotch-Brite pads. Each colour denotes a different grit size. The finest gives a polished finish – excellent for key making and for polishing the rims of saxophone tone holes.

A rubberized abrasive block is also great for key making; these blocks have abrasive mixed into them.

3M Scotch-Brite and 3M micron polishing paper is the modern equivalent to wire wool. I use this more than wire wool these days as it is more pleasant to use and does not leave iron dust around. The 100mm × 75mm pads come in fine and ultra-fine grit and are fantastic for re-finishing crack repairs on wooden instruments.

Wire wool comes in different grades from 0000 to 4. I only have 0000 and 000 grades, to use for finishing wood surfaces.

Fig. 16.34 Rubberized abrasive block.

CHAPTER 17

Specialist Repairs

Spring work

When a key does not open or close with a smooth and positive action, it is usually because the hinge or pivot is faulty, but it can sometimes be because the wrong spring has been used or the design of the spring is not good.

Why spring hitch design matters on needle springs

A spring hitch is the piece of metal on the key that a needle spring pushes on. Its shape and position are critical to the smooth functioning of the key. A good design for a spring hitch is where the point of contact between the spring and the key is tiny, and it needs to behave like a fulcrum. It also wants to encourage the spring not to wander from side to side; this is why a round spring hitch with a semi-circular groove in it is most commonly used. For convenience and simplicity of manufacture, the spring hitch is sometimes cut into the key arm.

Fig. 17.1 shows a view from under the G# key of an oboe (O4); as the key is depressed, the spring hitch slot moves to the left (arrow). The point of spring contact moves from point A to point B, almost halving the spring length (red lines). This makes the key feel terrible. To improve this, remove metal from the zone around B so that the spring keeps contact only at point A. So now, the distance between the pillar and hitch is constant when operated.

The key on the right of the diagram shows a round spring hitch that is sited slightly further away from the spring pillar. The key will feel good, as the spring stays the same length at all times.

Why the spring length, diameter and distance from the axle matters

The diameter of a needle spring of any one length will define how far, and how much force will be needed, to bend the spring to a point where it will still spring back to its original position. This is called its elastic range. The elastic range of a short spring with a large diameter will be much smaller than that of a long spring with a smaller diameter. A large diameter spring will exert more force for the same deflection as a smaller diameter spring.

Another relationship highlighted in Fig. 17.2 is the distance from the centre of the axle to where the spring is touching the spring hitch. In the diagram, the small diameter spring is furthest away from the axle and the large diameter, nearest.

Torque is the amount of force required to cause an object to rotate around its axis. The further away from the axle the force is applied, more energy is being used to rotate the object than is being used to move the axle sideways (which is wasted energy). To make the point, imagine the spring was pushing on the key just behind the axle; all the force would be trying to push the key to the left.

In summary, there is a balance between length of the spring hitch, the distance the spring has to travel and the diameter of the spring. In general,

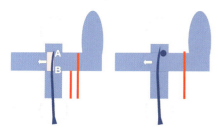

Fig. 17.1 Diagram showing how the spring hitch slot design can affect how a spring behaves.

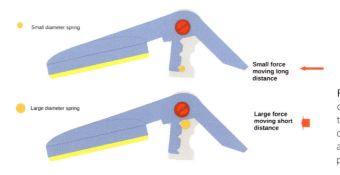

Fig. 17.2 A side view diagram of a key with two examples of the diameter and location a spring could be positioned.

the longer the spring hitch and spring length, the better.

Drilling new needle spring holes

Drilling needle spring holes is a difficult process and rarely works as well as one would like. It helps to practise the process lots of times to get good at it. I usually have to make a new extended drill, as the last one is either mislaid or broken. I buy the drills for springs in packets of ten; they go down to 0.5mm in diameter and are very fragile.

To make the extended drill, spinning the lathe at high speed (2,500 rpm) and very carefully, use the selected drill to make a 4mm deep hole in a 200mm length of silver steel/nickel silver, or brass, rod that is between 2 and 3mm in diameter. Once the hole is made, turn the drill around and superglue the shank of the drill into the rod. You now have an extended drill that will enable you to approach the pillar at the correct angle to drill the new hole for the spring.

Using a centre punch, make a dot where you want the hole to be. Drop some liquid paraffin or another fine lubricant on the pillar and the drill. With the extended drill in a bench motor, drill the hole by pushing and withdrawing the drill repeatedly until it is through the pillar.

It is possible to make a jig, or drill guide, to help position the spring hole. I have seen several designs. The problem with guides is that they are great for manufacturers, where they know what size and where every spring should be, but as repairers, every repair is different, so practising doing it freehand is often best.

A one-off guide can be made by using the drill to make a hole into a small piece of wood and sculpting the wood to sit against the pillar with the hole in the desired position. Hold the wooden jig in place and drill the spring hole, using the hole in the wood as a guide.

Filling an oversized needle spring hole

Fig. 17.3 An oversized needle spring.

Occasionally you can make a customer very happy by sorting out a spring problem that no other repairer has been able to solve for them. In this example of a bass clarinet spring that keeps the C#/G# hole closed, the spring used is too big in diameter. The result is that whilst not much pressure is being applied to the pad and as you try to open the key, the key gets harder to push down.

Fig. 17.4 Enlarging the spring hole.

Start by opening up the existing hole, using an extended drill; open the hole to 1.3mm in diameter.

Fig. 17.5 Drilling a spring hole in the insert.

With a piece of brass or nickel silver rod, no smaller than 5mm in diameter, in the lathe, use a tiny centre, or spotting, drill to spot the end of the rod. This will make sure the drill will be centred. Next drill a small hole down its centre. In this case, I want to use a 0.7mm diameter spring, so I have drilled a 0.7mm diameter hole, 4mm deep.

Fig. 17.6 Making the insert the final outside diameter.

Now, using a sharp lathe tool, turn down the outside diameter to 1.3mm in the following way: start by accurately calibrating the cross slide so that you can make a precise final cut. The final cut should be at least 1.5mm deep (so you will be reducing the diameter by 3mm in one cut). By making a large final cut, the metal ahead of the lathe tool will not flex away from the tool. Using this technique you can turn a 1.3mm diameter rod up to 4mm long without much difficulty, and it will be parallel.

Slide a smooth needle spring (one size smaller than the final spring) down the centre of the insert and break the new insert off. Press the insert into the hole in the pillar. Remove the small spring. Select the final size of spring and cut it to the correct spring length, put a fishtail on the end and install it in the pillar. The spring will expand the insert and keep it in place, and the fishtail will stop it from rotating.

Fig. 17.7 The correctly sized spring.

Sometimes the process above is not possible or appropriate, in which case you have to hope that the pillar can be removed from the instrument; you can then clean the old spring hole and fill it with silver solder, then re-drill it.

Flat spring locking

Flat springs need some way to stop the tip from wandering away from its optimal position. This is done in three ways:

1. Through using two spring screws. You usually see this method on bassoons, especially the whisper key (B10). The two screws are positioned along the length of the spring about 2mm apart from each other.
2. With a channel for the tip to fit into. This is the most common method of keeping the tip in position. If the spring is not bent in the correct way and the tip is allowed to slide up and down, then the channel has to be very smooth and made from a hard material. A well set up flat spring will not slide, and the material of the channel is not so important.
3. With a flat-ended spring which is butted up against a ledge.

Fig. 17.8 Flat-ended spring butted against a ledge.

Here the manufacturer has filed away the bottom of a key to create a ledge that a square-ended spring can butt up against to stop it from rotating.

Improving the action of keys

There are ways of improving the performance of a key mechanism. By understanding how key geometry affects the way a key works, you can then make small changes to improve the instrument. Most mass manufacturers have already optimized their instrument design so the following section mainly applies to older instruments. Having said that, I still come across new instruments with simple flaws in their design; for instance, the link arms on the thumb-ring and the first ring key on a Bb clarinet (C11 and C3), or the G# touch piece to pad key on an oboe (O4 and O1).

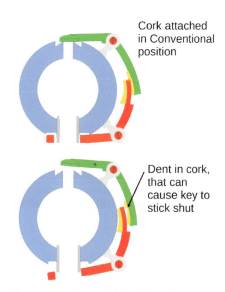

Fig. 17.9 Clarinet C11 (thumb key in red) and C3 (first ring key in pink) with cork stuck to underside of C3 link arm.

For the mechanism in Fig. 17.9, the regulation cork has been stuck to the underside of C3 (this is the conventional place to attach the cork). The cork's position and thickness control the pad vent height and the pressure that is applied to the C3 pad with any given thumb pressure. In the lower image, you will see that the C11 link arm has forced a dent in the regulation cork. This may stop the key from opening as it tries to slide past the ridge.

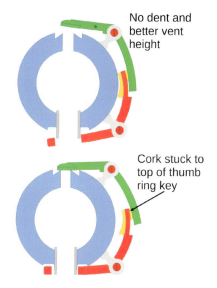

Fig. 17.10 Clarinet C11 (thumb key in red) and C3 (first ring key in pink) with cork stuck to top of thumb ring link arm.

Fig. 17.10 is my preferred set-up, which is to attach a short length of cork to the top of C11 (red). This method removes the risk of the key getting stuck in a dent and also improves the venting of C3 and slightly reduces the travel of C11.

In Fig. 17.11 can see another version of the leverage principle, only here I have flattened out the keywork. Pay attention to where the regulation corks are between the two link arms. Also note the dark pink blocks on the left which represent how far the key has to travel.

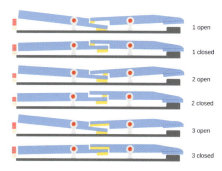

Fig. 17.11 The vent opening is the same in each pair, the travel the lever on the left has to move is different.

On the top pair (1), where the regulation cork is on the left of the right link arm, the end of the lever on the left

Specialist Repairs 211

travels three units and will exert a high pressure on the pad.

On the second pair (2), where the regulation cork is on the right of the right link arm, the end of the lever is travelling only two units. The pressure on the pad will be slightly less than example 1.

On the bottom pair (3), with a long cork across the right link arm, the lever on the left travels three units and the pressure on the pad will be the same as for example 2.

In summary, the worst choice is option 3; the lever has to move a long way and the pressure on the pad is less than it could be. Option 2 is best if you want a short, snappy action and the pad is relatively small so the amount of pressure on it can be small. Option 1 is best if you have a big pad and want to add extra pressure to keep it closed.

Removing a stuck hinge screw

Try not to damage the head of the screw. If a screw does not undo with normal pressure, apply a few drops of penetrating oil (Balistol is my first choice) to all the joins and screw heads. I then warm the key and pillars up with a hot air gun or spirit lamp, adding more oil if needed. Then I leave the oil to do its work for at least ten minutes or days if possible.

A screw can refuse to rotate if there is corrosion in the pillar and thread, the key is bent, or the oil has dried in the hinge tube. It is the last situation that can sometimes be the most difficult to resolve.

When it is well lubricated, use a screwdriver that is a good fit in the slot and supports the instrument well. I apply lots of pressure to the screwdriver with the palm of my hand and try not to let the screwdriver slip. I keep my other hand out of the way in case it does! First, try tightening the screw. This might sound odd, but it sometimes breaks the corrosion and frees off the screw without any more problems. It has the advantage that if the screwdriver does slip out it only damages the head in the tightening direction and not the loosening direction. You, therefore, have two chances of breaking the corrosion. Next, try loosening the screw, then tighten, then loosen again. Keep doing this, adding more heat and more oil as you do so. If that process fails, and as a last resort, you will have to cut the key off. In most cases, it is a hinge key that is stuck.

Cut it at the join furthest from the screwed end. Use an extremely thin jeweller's saw blade (size 5/0, 6/0 or 8/0); if you are very lucky, you might find some special 4mm deep blades that are only 0.2mm thick. (Though I have never tried it, you could use a 0.2mm wide cut-off saw blade in a high-speed Dremel or jeweller's flexible shaft drill.) Try not to remove metal from the pillar. Once you have cut through the hinge screw, rotate the whole key anticlockwise, in the direction that will unscrew the pillar. You only need to rotate it enough to work the key off the hinge screw, or unscrew the whole unit from the pillar.

If you can't rotate the pillar, lever the key upwards and try to work the key off the hinge screw; the risk with this approach is that you break the screw off in the pillar and spend time trying to remove it.

Tools needed to make a hinge screw

Fig. 17.13 Selection of tools needed to make a new hinge screw. These are the tools you use to cut threads on the inside and outside of metal. I would recommend getting High Speed Steel (HSS) tools with a split die design. You could start by getting a metric set for general tool making; you will almost certainly then need specific taps and dies for instrument repair, which you buy as required.

Fig. 17.14 The photo is of a die in its holder; the three screws allow you to adjust the exact diameter of the thread you are cutting. Start by leaving the two side screws undone and tighten the central screw – this opens up the die and cuts an oversized thread. If the thread does not fit, then close the die up slightly and re-cut the thread. Keep adjusting until it is the fit you require.

Fig. 17.15 This file is less than 1mm thick and has cutting teeth on the edges and the sides. It can be used to open up the screwdriver slot on pivot screws and hinge screws.

Fig. 17.12 Micro saw blade. It is only 0.2mm thick but 6mm deep. It is perfect for sawing between a hinge tube and pillar when removing stuck hinge screws.

Fig. 17.16 If you get involved in extensive key improvements on older instruments you might want to invest in a machine that cuts a neat screwdriver slot in the end of hinge rods. This tool could be improved by changing the diameter of the metal disc that clamps the blade. If the diameter was 1mm smaller than the outside diameter of the blade, then it would limit the depth of cut to 1mm, which is suitable for a screwdriver slot.

Making a replacement hinge screw

You may need to make a replacement hinge screw if a replacement is not available from the manufacturer, or you need to make an oversized one to make up for wear.

Fig. 17.17 Use a file to reduce the end of the rod to the major diameter of the thread.

Put the rod of the correct diameter in the bench motor, leaving 4mm exposed. Using a no. 4 cut file, reduce 3mm of the exposed rod down to the outside diameter of the thread required.

Fig. 17.18 Use a micrometer to measure the outside diameter.

A micrometer is used to measure the outside diameter of the new hinge screw. On the left of the Fig. 17.13 are the engineer's tables that give the diameter needed. In this case it is for the most common thread in the UK, which is 9BA – an outside diameter (OD) of 1.95mm.

Fig. 17.19 Filing a taper on the end of the metal rod.

When the rod is at the correct diameter for the thread, file a short taper on the end of the metal to help get the cutting started square to the axis.

Fig. 17.20 Applying cutting lubricant to a tapping die ready to cut the thread on a new hinge screw.

Next, set the die in the die holder and open the split die up which will produce a large diameter thread.

Fig. 17.21 Cutting thread on hinge screw.

The bench motor is rotated by hand using the hand wheel under my left hand. Whilst the die is held square to the rod, rotate it three turns clockwise to cut the thread, followed by 1/3 turn anticlockwise to break the cutting chips. Repeat until the thread is complete. When the threading is finished, file off any burrs left behind by the die and test the rod in the pillar. If the thread is too tight, close up the split die and re-cut the thread. Repeat until the thread runs smoothly in the pillar.

Next mark the overall length of the rod, plus 0.5mm and cut to length.

Fig. 17.22 Cutting a slot in the end of the hinge screw.

If you don't have a special tool to make the slot then you can use a modified hacksaw.

Fig. 17.23 Close-up of modified hacksaw blade.

Fig. 17.23 shows how I have ground away the wavy shape along the blade that creates a kerf or clearance channel; this is

Fig. 17.24 Tool for cutting a screwdriver slot in a hinge screw.

Specialist Repairs   **213**

called the 'set' of the blade. By removing the set, I can cut a much narrower slot that will be more suitable for the head of a hinge screw or pivot screw.

Fig. 17.24 shows the specialist tool that cuts the slot in the end of hinge screws. If you want to use this tool to cut the slot on a pivot screw, then you have to make a special holder.

Fig. 17.25 Detail of finished screwdriver slot.

To add extra sparkle to the instrument I like to continue the tradition of good makers who dome and polish the slot end of the hinge screw.

Fig. 17.26 Finished hinge screw.

Tone hole replacement

A tone hole might need to be replaced because it is chipped or because there is a crack running through it.

Tone hole replacement tools and materials

Fig. 17.27 This setting-out jig took about an hour to make, and I was comfortable replacing a tone hole on a clarinet using it.

Fig. 17.28 shows the instrument body held in place with a tool called a drive

Fig. 17.28 The nut used for the bolt is a type that is designed to be a captive nut in wood; it sits flush with the surface. .

dog; it comes as basic tooling with many lathes. You could make a drive dog yourself out of wood or metal, it only needs to clamp onto the tenon and stop the joint from rotating. You could even make the drive dog in a way that allows you to measure and fix the rotation of the joint by specific amounts.

Fig. 17.29 Mounting the instrument on a milling machine. (I am lucky enough to have a large milling machine and a dividing head.)

Fig. 17.30 Wobble stick. This is an engineer's tool to find the edges of components. We use it to find the centre of tone holes.

Set the centre of the chuck on the axis of the instrument. Insert the wobble stick in the hole and start the machine spinning at 800rpm or more. Move the instrument up and down its axis to find the longitudinal centre of the hole. Lock the axis and turn your attention to the sides of the hole. With the wobble stick still spinning, rotate the dividing head to find one side of the hole. Take a reading of the angle (or make a mark on the

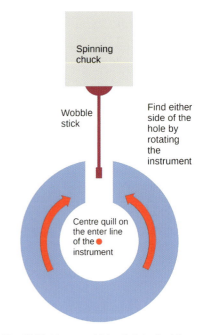

Fig. 17.31 Use a wobble stick to find the rotational centre of a tone hole.

machine) for that side of the hole. Rotate the instrument to find the other side of the hole. Take the angle (or make another mark). Calculate the angle between the two edges and divide by two. That will be your centre.

Fig. 17.32 Undercutting tool and overcutting tool, used to shape the inside of a tone hole.

Fig. 17.33 Micro boring head. This is a very useful tool if you have a milling machine.

You need to choose and set up the cutting tool to be flat across the bottom cutting surface. For woodwind repair you can use this tool to make the counter-bore when replacing a tone hole. The micro adjustment controls the diameter of the cut you make.

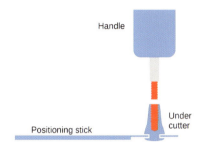

Fig. 17.34 Diagram of undercutting.

Fig. 17.34 shows how the cutter can be kept captive on a stick, to make insertion and extraction easier.

Replacing a tone hole

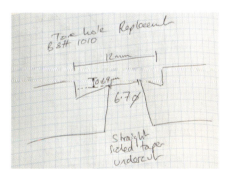

Fig. 17.35 Log book with initial measurements.

Make a note of the initial measurements needed before replacing a tone

Fig. 17.36 Getting ready to measure the top of the bed plate to the outside of the body.

hole. The two measurements that are difficult to reverse-engineer later are the distance between the tone hole rim and the outside diameter of the instrument. The other is the shape of the undercut.

Use the depth bar on digital callipers to measure the top of the tone hole bed plate and the outside of the instrument.

Fig. 17.37 Mounting the instrument on a milling machine.

Fig. 17.38 Centring the hole.

Find the centre of the hole using a wobble stick. You can do it by eye and with drills and pointed rods. I wish I had learnt the wobble stick method many years ago.

Fig. 17.39 Preparing to cut the counter-bore.

After centring the tool, you can use the micro boring head to machine away the damaged tone hole bed plate and create a counter-bore for the replacement tone hole.

Fig. 17.40 Drill out the old bed plate.

Using the micro boring head, drill/counter-bore the wood to about half the thickness of the instrument body wall thickness. The exact depth is not critical, but needs to be between 1.5mm and 3mm below the bottom of the bed plate cone.

Fig. 17.41 Time for some more measurements.

You need to know the depth of the counter-bore, then subtract the tone

Fig. 17.42 Preparing to hand turn the top of the new tone hole insert.

Specialist Repairs **215**

rim depth. This will give you the overall length of the replacement insert.

To make the tone hole insert, turn down the ebonite to 0.1mm smaller than the counter-bore diameter. Drill a hole in the centre that is the diameter of the tone hole at its smallest part.

As you can see, I have moved the ebonite out quite a long way out of the lathe chuck, more than is considered good practice. I have it this far out because in the next step I will be hand turning the end and do not want to have my hands close to the chuck.

Fig. 17.43 Hand turning the tone hole bed plate.

I am using the boring bar as a tool rest and an old piece of silver steel, ground to a curve, to hand turn the top of the tone hole.

Fig. 17.44 Polishing the tone hole insert.

When you are happy with the shape of the new tone hole (which should match

Fig. 17.45 Zero the DRO.

the others on the instrument), you can use wet and dry paper or Scotch-Brite to polish the bed plate.

Touch the left-hand side of the parting tool against the finished end of the tone hole, and set the DRO to zero.

Fig. 17.46 Set the correct length and part off.

From your earlier measurements you can work out how long the new insert needs to be. Subtract the measurement from the outside of the body to the top of the original tone hole, from the depth of the counter-bore, and this is the length of the insert. In the previous step you set the parting tool to zero; now the parting tool has been moved by the length of the insert plus the thickness of the parting tool (2mm for my parting tool). Part the insert off.

Fig. 17.47 The new bedplate insert.

Before bonding the insert to the tone hole, scratch the bottom and sides of the insert and the counter-bore. This will give the epoxy resin a mechanical key that will strengthen the join.

Spread warm epoxy on the glued surfaces and push into place. Remove excess glue with a cotton bud and methylated spirits. When the epoxy has set hard, ream out the new tone hole with a drill and/or use an overcutter tool to match the original specification. Use a knife or undercutting tool to replace undercuts.

Fig. 17.48 Finished tone hole.

Tone hole replacement: recorder thumb hole

You may be asked to repair the thumb hole of a recorder, where the player's thumbnail has worn a groove across the thumb hole. When this groove gets too deep, the player can't play second octave notes very well. Filling the groove with a filler is not successful, so using a variation of the tone hole replacement is needed. The process is much the same, only you might use an artificial ivory in place of the ebonite and use a file to smooth the top of the insert to blend with the body of the instrument.

Repairing cracks

It is not uncommon for wooden clarinets and oboes to develop cracks, mainly in the top joints of the instruments. The forces involved in the cracking process are considerable and very complex. Since you can't get wood to crack 'on demand' there is no way of testing what is going on or what treatment will improve the situation.

Though usually a traumatic experience for the musician, once repaired, the instrument can go on to perform well for many more years.

There are two schools of thought on how best to repair the crack. One is that you should try and close the gap by drying the instrument, usually in the fridge, for a week or more, then to glue the instrument. However, this will bring the instrument back to its original dimensions and put the wood under stress again when it gets saturated with water. An alternative approach is to leave the wood in a stress-relieved state and to fill the gap with superglue while it is still open. This is the way I choose to do it. Whichever way you choose, it is necessary to replace any bed plate when the crack goes into a tone hole.

Use the least viscous superglue you can get, start feeding the glue in at the ends of the crack first. This allows the glue to run into the very finest gap before hardening. As the ends fill, move your applicator towards the middle. Keep adding glue in one continuous stream until the gap is full. File and polish away any excess glue when it is hard.

Pinning a crack

With the advent of water thin superglues, pinning is only done when gluing the crack has failed on more than two occasions. Pinning a crack should be a last resort, as it is difficult to do nicely, and it will leave evidence of being repaired and devalue the instrument.

Before pinning a customer's instrument, I suggest you practise drilling and inserting pins on a discarded instrument by drawing an imaginary crack down the instrument, then following the steps below.

You will see that I describe two materials that you can use for the pinning: carbon fibre and a more traditional screwed stainless steel pinning wire.

Mark an entry and exit point either side of the crack. This should be at least 8mm on either side of the crack line.

Using a 1.8mm diameter twist drill, touch the drill on the entry mark and angle the drill at 90 degrees to the body, as if to drill directly through the instrument. Start drilling and when the hole starts to form, bring the angle of the instrument around so that the drill bit is aiming for where you want the exit hole to be on the other side of the instrument. Practise this until you get the entrance and exit holes just as you marked them. Practise this technique with different distances from the crack and see if you can get the drill to break through to the

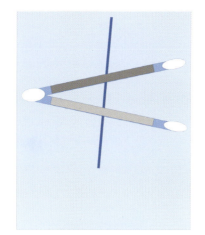

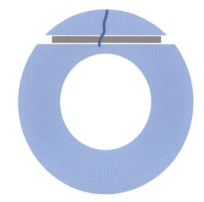

Fig. 17.49 Diagram of a crack and where the pins will be placed.

Fig. 17.50 Drilling a hole.

Fig. 17.51 Breaking through on the other side, hopefully where you marked the exit to be.

bore. By practising this process ten or more times you will get the confidence to work on a client's instrument.

Pinning with carbon fibre

Fig. 17.52 Getting ready to mark the length of carbon fibre rod needed.

Once you have drilled your dovetail holes using a 1.8mm drill, roughen up the surface of the 1.3mm diameter carbon rods with 240 grit abrasive. Cut the carbon rod to a length that will be hidden inside the hole.

Fig. 17.53 Only a tiny amount of black dye is needed when mixing with low viscosity epoxy resin.

Now insert the pin and work back and forth in the hole to spread the glue.

Fig. 17.54 Working the resin and rod into the hole.

Specialist Repairs 217

Pack the end of each hole with a mixture of blackwood dust and epoxy resin. Leave to harden.

Pinning with a threaded metal rod

Drill a tapping size hole in the dovetail configuration as above. If your threaded wire is 2mm then use a 1.8mm diameter tapping drill. (This is the largest diameter I would use.) When using metal pins, try to start one end of the hole in a hidden place. This could be inside a pillar hole, or under a key. This hides the hole and filler.

Fig. 17.55 File a 30-degree taper on the end of the pinning rod.

Sharpen the end of the threaded rod to a 30-degree angle; this creates a form of thread cutting tap.

Fig. 17.56 Using the pinning wire to cut its own thread in the wood.

Using a bench motor, run the thread through the hole. Now unscrew the pin and mark the pin at a point where it is shorter than the hole it is going into. Use a triangular file to cut halfway through the metal rod. Wet the rod in epoxy resin (mix with black pigment) and put some in the hole.

Fig. 17.57 Screwing the pinning wire into place. You can just about see where the wire is filed in half: it is the bright spot on the wire in the centre of the picture.

Screw the rod back into the hole and judge when the rod will not show at the far end, and the filed notch will have entered the hole at the near end. Bend the rod back and forth until the rod breaks inside the instrument's body.

The final process is to force blackwood dust into the holes at either end with more black epoxy resin. Leave to harden fully.

Fig. 17.58 Filing the blackwood dust and resin filler down so it is smooth and flush with the body.

Use a wide mill cut file to smooth away the excess resin and blackwood filler.

Fig. 17.59 Second stage finishing with Scotch-Brite pad.

Finish with ultra-fine 3M Scotch-Brite. I sometimes fail to judge the length of the pin correctly and the bright metal pin is still visible. When this happens use a small grinding burr, or better still a 2mm diameter slot mill in the milling machine, to 'drill out' the metal and create a new cavity to pack with blackwood dust and resin and re-finish it.

Fig. 17.60 Loading a strip of cloth with Vonax polish.

To finish the crack repair, rub Vonax polish onto a strip of cloth. Then strap the body. If you see a glassy patch where the crack is then you might have excess glue still sitting above the wood surface; if so file this off and re-finish.

Fig. 17.61 Strap polishing the repaired body.

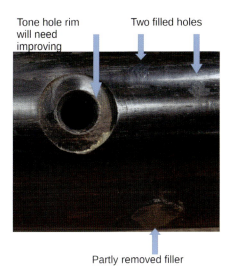

Fig. 17.62 The finished repair.

Modified stainless steel pin method

During the writing of this book, I explored new ways of pinning in discussion with instrument repairer and designer Jan Provazník. We noticed that the rod was pulling out of the resin sleeve during the experiments with carbon fibre pins; hence, we now roughen the rod first. Using a rough surface prompted the idea of using a threaded stainless-steel rod embedded in epoxy resin, rather than screwed into the wood. I drilled a clearance hole in the wood and coated the inside with resin and also wetted a pre-cut length of screwed rod (I also successfully used roughened steel rod). I inserted the rod into the hole and packed both ends with blackwood dust and resin. This method was also successful and was easy to undertake.

In summary, it appears that all three methods work well, so you can choose the method that works best for you. I suggest you fill the crack with water thin superglue after pinning.

Mending broken keys and joints

Soldering tools

Fig. 17.64 Third hand for soldering. Normally sold to engineers for holding dial test indicators, I have adapted this movable arm for use when soldering. The jeweller's tweezers are clamped at the end.

Fig. 17.65 Here are two methods of holding components when soldering. The jeweller's tweezers at the bottom are the most used tool. The device at the top of the photo is also worth having. The silver steel wire has a brass stabilizing foot at one end and a brass weight near the other end. The tip that holds the item in place can either be a point or it can be a brass cup that will sit over the top of a pillar to hold the pillar in place.

Broken keys and hard soldering

Fig. 17.66 To use silver solder you need a flux, a chemical that removes the oxides on the metal you are bonding. Most of the time I use Easy-flo flux mixed to a creamy consistency. This needs to be mixed fresh each time you want to solder. Some people prefer to grind fresh borax as a flux; you can see the cone and mortar on the right of the photo.

Fig. 17.63 Brazing hearth. In our trade we don't need a big soldering bench or hearth. Compressed mica or vermiculite board is very good, as it reflects heat back onto the workpiece. If you can't find that material, then you can use firebricks from a building supplier.

In the foreground of Fig. 17.66 is a length of easy flow-silver solder wire that is held in a piece of hinge tubing; this makes it easier to position the tip of the wire in the flame when you are ready to apply the solder. The white rod is a length of pre-fluxed easy-flow silver solder, great for tool making. The wooden handle in the picture has a Tungsten needle attached to it, for manipulating the molten solder.

Silver solder is also called hard solder. It melts around 700°C. With the sort of forces that instruments are subject to, the silver solder joints on instruments rarely fail. Silver solder is used to assemble keywork, in keywork repairs, and to attach pillars to straps used on flutes and saxophones. Silver solder comes in different diameters and thicknesses and as various alloys. We usually use easy-flow grade, which is slightly yellow in colour and is not of silver hallmark quality.

When a key cracks or breaks it will need to be hard soldered together. This technique requires a very hot, concentrated flame, hard solder, and hard solder flux. Hard solders are all variations of silver solder, an alloy containing silver. Jewellers use solder with a very high proportion of silver, and they melt it at higher temperatures than the engineering-grade silver solder that our trade uses. You can use a cadmium-free silver solder to reduce long-term health damage from fumes.

Using a blowtorch

To hard solder you need to get the metal hot enough. For most keywork, you can use a small jeweller's butane blowtorch or chef's blowtorch. For larger keys and tool making you might need to use a plumber's blowtorch or a gas air commercial blowtorch.

When you start using an unfamiliar blowtorch, spend some time getting to know its characteristics. In the photographs opposite you can see that if you bring the torch too close to your workpiece you will have a cold spot exactly over the bit you want to be hot. Find the hot and cold zones on a fire brick as shown in Figs 17.67 and 17.68.

Fig. 17.67 Nice orange circle showing the optimum heating zone.

Fig. 17.68 The cold zone is the dark circle in surrounded by orange hot zone.

When working on silver or silver-plated keys, try and keep the flame very slightly orange if you can. If you have too much oxygen and a very blue flame it is called an oxidizing flame and will tarnish the silver.

How to hard solder

Clean both surfaces with a file or emery cloth, and ensure they mate together in the correct alignment. I give some suggestions on how to hold the joints together in the tools section of the book. Some good joint designs are shown in Fig. 17.69.

I prefer to use powdered flux that I mix with water to a creamy consistency, rather than borax flux favoured by jewellers. Apply flux to both surfaces with a small brush. Holding the two

Fig. 17.69 Solder joints designs. The bottom design is the only one that can be used to join two existing parts back together. The others will shorten the key.

components close together, heat the area gently until the flux is dry. Then place a small pallion of solder on the sticky flux. Heat again until the material is red hot and the solder will suddenly flash along the joint. Cool down, brush, and wash away the remaining flux in water or a 'safe pickling' bath.

Mending broken soft-solder joints

Soft solder melts at around 200°C. It is used to join metal parts together, such as the pillar strap onto a flute or saxophone. It is sometimes used to attach the threaded boss used on flute pad retaining screws.

Fig. 17.70 Soft iron binding wire, used to hold components together when soldering. Available in a number of diameters, this one is 0.65mm (22 wire gauge).

Fixing a socket, pillar or pillar strap that has come away from an instrument

Woodwind instruments have a few joins that are made with soft solder. There are two types of soft solder used in our industry: traditional lead solder (an alloy of lead and tin) and modern lead-free soft solder, which has a low melting point and is an alloy of tin and a small amount of silver. Lead-free solder is becoming more popular with manufacturers as it is safer to use. Yamaha and other leading manufacturers use lead-free solder. However, as repairers only use soft solder very infrequently, lead-based solder is safe to use. You can mix the two types of solder, so repairing one with the other is not a problem.

Do not try to substitute soft solder for hard solder; it will not be strong enough, and it will make it almost impossible to hard solder the join later. You might think that you have removed all the old soft solder, but you haven't! There will still be a layer of base metal that is contaminated with the lead and tin as an alloy.

There are various grades of soft solder, each with different characteristics. The lead solders all melt at the same temperature, but the flow temperatures are different. Similarly, both the tin/silver alloys melt at the same temperature. However, both the 63/37 tin/lead and 96/4 tin/silver will also flash flow into the join at the melting temperature, whereas the others give you a mushy paste-like puddle that can be manoeuvred around with a metal rod before flowing. Both characteristics are useful. Being able to puddle the solder is good for emergency repairs to splits and to fill large gaps. The flash solders are best for well-fitting joints.

I recommend using the tin/silver alloys on silver and silver-plated instruments to minimize the darkening effect of oxidation on the solder.

Fig. 17.71 Using an old table leg wrapped in a towel to support a saxophone ready for a pillar to be soldered back on.

Support the instrument or components securely. Remove any keywork

> ### Soft solder melting temperatures
>
> All the tin/lead solders melt at the same temperature (361°F/182°C) but they flow at different temperatures.
>   63/37 tin/lead flows at 361°F/182°C flash flow
>   50/50 tin/lead flows at 421°F/216°C mushy stage
>
> Both the tin/silver solders melt at 430°F/221°C.
>   96/4 tin/silver flows at 430°F/221°C flash flow
>   94/6 tin/silver flows at 535°F/279°C mushy stage

that is close to the soldering area. Scrape clean the two solder surfaces and apply soft solder flux to both surfaces.

Supporting the pillar in the correct place, hold it there with soft iron binding wire or a clamp. Then choose how to add the solder. You could use a soft solder holder, a 50mm-long metal tube (hinge tube is good) that is large enough to allow your soft solder to be fed down the middle. Thread the soft solder down the tube with about 10mm of solder showing at the end of the tube. An alternative is to cut and hammer a small piece of solder into a shape that sits close to the solder joint. Using a large flame that is not too fierce, warm up the area slowly until it reaches the solder melting temperature. You can learn this by practising on some scrap instruments. When it is the right temperature, feed in the soft solder at a place that will not be too conspicuous. (Practise getting the correct amount of solder to feed in without getting a drip.) Wipe away any flux that has spread over the lacquer as soon as possible. With modern lacquers, you should not have any burning, but with older cellulose lacquers, burning is almost impossible to avoid.

Another technique that can be used when it is difficult to balance or hold the pillar in the correct place, is called the 'sweating' method. Clean both surfaces as above. With the pillar off the instrument, melt solder onto the base of the pillar. Let it cool and add more flux. Now hold the pillar in place on the instrument using pliers or spring clamps and warm the joint up with a large gentle flame. When the solder melts, the pillar will suddenly move and get close to the body. With a steady hand, adjust the pillar to the correct place. Remove the flame and let cool. Clean away any flux as soon as possible.

If you need to remove excess solder, then scrape with a scraper, then polish. I will sometimes touch up bare metal with a thin layer of water-based acrylic varnish on modern instruments.

Separating stuck tenon joints on wooden instruments

The blackwood used on woodwind instruments is a very stable wood, but it does still expand and contract depending on how much water it is exposed to. The instrument manufacturer therefore has to accommodate these changes in the design and manufacture of their instruments. The instrument works best if the tenon is a tight fit, but if it is too tight and water is left in the joint for too long, it swells and gets stuck.

We therefore advise customers that if the tenons start to feel tight and difficult to put together and take apart they should be adjusted. This can be done on a lathe. It is quick and you sometimes don't have to remove any keywork.

Some manufacturers, like Buffet, leave the fit of their tenon joints tight. This is good as it allows the retailer/repairer to adjust the final fit once the musician has started using the instrument. We always explain this process to the customer when they buy a new instrument. Sometimes, however, the customer waits too long before bringing it to us and the joints are already stuck together.

To separate them, you can wait a few days for the wood to shrink, or you can start rocking the joints back and forth, as you would if you were trying to break the instrument in half. Don't try and rotate the joint; it does not help. In most cases this rocking action separates the two parts. If that fails then find, or create, a gap, however small, in the join between the two joints.

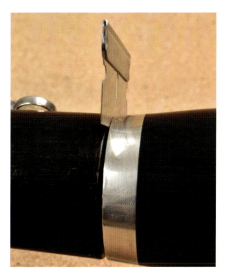

Fig. 17.72 Wedging open a stuck tenon joint.

Slip a razor blade in this gap and rock the joints back and forth again; this creates a crack on the other side to the razor blade so you can then slip one or two blades into the new gap on the other side and slowly jack the joint open, putting in thicker fillets each time.

Lining a socket

This is required when you have a broken socket, a crack in a tenon, or when the tenon is too loose. The simplest to repair or line is a clarinet barrel. If your lathe chuck is large enough to clamp the barrel's largest diameter, hold it in the chuck with a cardboard cuff to prevent denting the barrel. Before securing the chuck tight, true up the socket by gently pushing a rotating centre into the socket.

Fig. 17.73 A three point steady modified to become a rotating steady.

A modified three-point steady is shown in Fig. 17.73. Rather than having three bearing points I have replaced them with a ball bearing race that is exactly on the axis of the lathe. The instrument is supported by the bearing using a conical 'spectacle' plate.

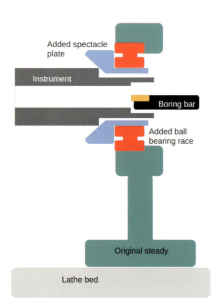

Fig. 17.74 Cross-section diagram of the rotating steady design. The spectacle plate, coloured blue, is a push fit in the bearing, so different sizes can be used. Instructions on how to make a version of this tool are given in Chapter 20.

Fig. 17.75 A broken socket on an Amati clarinet in C. The metal ring, bottom right, has the remains of the broken socket still inside.

Fig. 17.76 Support the ring between the vice jaws and knock out the remains of the clarinet body.

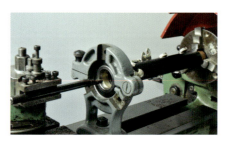

Fig. 17.77 Lathe set up to create the counter-bore. The boring bar is in a tool holder on the left and the chuck is on the right. The roller steady is supporting the end of the instrument.

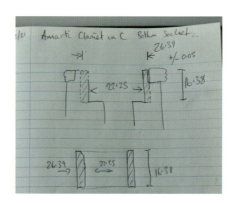

Fig. 17.78 Record the repair measurements in a log book.

Fig. 17.79 Counter-boring the clarinet. The clarinet is now held in the lathe jaws on the left and supported on the right by the spectacle plate mounted in the roller steady.

Fig. 17.80 The finished counter-bore. To make the process simple, I usually make the counter-bore diameter the same as the inside diameter of the ring.

Fig. 17.81 Boring the new socket insert.

Fig. 17.82 Measuring the internal diameter of the replacement socket to make sure it will match the top joint tenon.

Fig. 17.83 Machining the replacement socket insert in ebonite. The outside diameter needs to be a good, but not tight, fit into the counter-bore.

Fig. 17.84 Using a parting tool to cut the ebonite to the final length. No particular precautions need to be taken when using a parting tool in ebonite, but if you are parting metal then lock the saddle and reduce the spindle speed right down. Then use lots of cutting fluid over the blade.

Fig. 17.85 Checking the replacement liner not only fits into the counter-bore, but also that the ring fits and the length is correct.

Fig. 17.86 Assembling the new socket and ring using epoxy resin. I will warm the resin and the components with my hot air gun. This will make the resin fluid and get the chemical reactions off to a good start.

Fig. 17.87 Creating a chamfer on the inside of the new socket using a three-sided scraper.

Replacing a broken tenon

The number of tenon joints I am being asked to replace has slowly declined over the years. However, it is a useful repair to know how to do, especially in regions of the world where instruments are difficult to source.

If you were to simply glue the two broken parts together, the joint would not be strong enough, so we have to find a way to strengthen the join whilst still retaining the original dimensions. We do this by creating a new socket (called a counter-bore) in the body of the broken joint. You then make an insert that will be glued into this counter-bore. The insert extends beyond the body to create the new tenon.

In this example we are replacing the broken middle tenon of an oboe.

The steps for the procedure are as follows:

- All pillars in the area of the counter-bore are removed.
- A counter-bore is cut in the body of the instrument.
- An insert is made in ebonite (occasionally blackwood).
- The insert will need holes drilled to accommodate the threaded part of the pillars (blind holes).
- The tone hole will need to be re-drilled.

There are two methods I use to cut a counter-bore in the body of an instrument. For the oboe re-tenon I describe here, I am using a method that guides a rotating cutter along a shaft that is concentric with the bore of the instrument. Elsewhere, I describe the repair of a clarinet socket using a method that rotates the instrument and keeps the tool stationary. Both methods achieve the same goal; you simply choose the best method for the repair in hand.

Taking good measurements before you start is essential. For this oboe repair you need the following measurements:

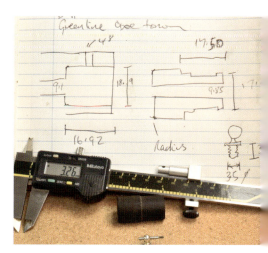

Fig. 17.89 Use a log book to record useful information.

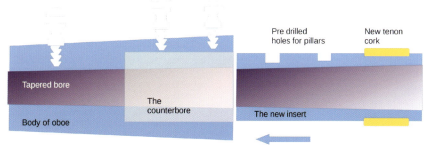

Fig. 17.88 Sectional diagram of the body and insert. (The angles of the bore are exaggerated and the proportions not quite right.)

Specialist Repairs 223

1. A series of bore measurements in the area of the break. You need enough measurements to be able to re-create the taper, or profile, of the bore of the instrument. It is sometimes helpful to plot these out on a graph to see what it looks like as you will have to re-produce this shape later when you make a reamer, or bore out the insert. (For how to measure internal bore diameters, *see* below.) The diameter of the bore is very sensitive on top quality instruments, so you really need to measure to a tolerance of +/− 0.03mm. In practice, this means you should aim to machine parts to 0.1mm. These measurements are very difficult to make, and replicate, especially on tapered instruments like the oboe, so you have to keep measuring and adjusting to get it correct. On occasions I have had to make a second insert to get it right. To give an idea as to why the bore measurement is so sensitive, a bore diameter of a typical oboe, at the middle tenon, is 9mm. The tuning of the instrument is affected by the surface area/volume of the bore along its length. If the diameter at the tenon is increased by 0.1mm then it increases the surface area at that point by 3 per cent, which can change the character or tuning of the instrument. (A typical clarinet is 14.75mm; if the diameter is increased by 0.1mm then it increases the surface area at that point by 2 per cent.) Don't let this put you off, as there are plenty of instruments needing new tenons that are not that sensitive.
2. The outside diameter of the tenon nearest the shoulder.
3. The outside diameter at the other end of the tenon.
4. The distance from the tenon shoulder to the far side of the closest tone hole. This is the depth the counter-bore will be. For stability and strength it is good practice to make the depth of the counter-bore at least the same as its diameter.
5. The length of the existing tenon. If you don't have the broken piece of tenon, you might have to measure another instrument of the same make. It is not safe to measure the depth of the corresponding socket (especially on the top tenon of a clarinet). Some manufacturers find that the tonal quality and tuning of the instrument is improved if there is a gap left between the joints.
6. The diameter and width of the tenon cork groove.
7. The diameter of any tone holes that will be affected. Include any undercut information. To see an undercut more clearly, roll some white paper and insert it in the bore and under the hole in question. This will show up the undercut more clearly. If needed, make a putty mould of the undercut.
8. The diameter and length of any pillars or screws that you removed earlier.

Measuring tapered bores

Oboes, bassoons and saxophones have conical bores. The clarinet family have a nominally cylindrical bore, but in practice they have many tapered sections along the bore. The modern flute has a cylindrical body and a tapered head joint.

If you have to undertake any work that might affect the bore of the instrument it is advisable to measure the bore before, during, and after the work.

You will need:

- Hardwood, to make sticks of about 200mm long
- Wood or metal, to make a movable plate.
- Cocktail sticks or round toothpicks (about 2mm in diameter)
- Measuring callipers
- File
- Drills
- Measuring stick

The moveable plate can be made from a hardwood (like blackwood), brass, or a combination of both. The thread for the lock screw can be made in wood, it does not have to be strong. None of the sizes are critical, as long as it ends up fitting in the bore.

Cut, file, or sandpaper both ends of the cocktail stick so that they are rounded and will go about 3mm into the bore. Slide the moveable plate until it touches the end of the joint and locks in place. Remove it from the instrument.

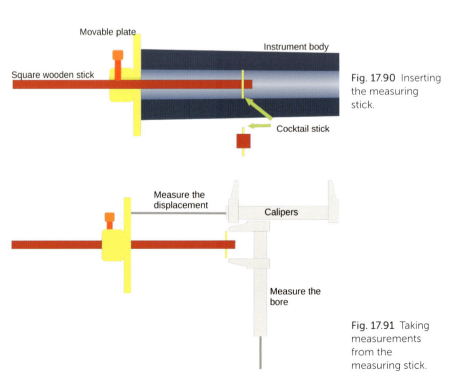

Fig. 17.90 Inserting the measuring stick.

Fig. 17.91 Taking measurements from the measuring stick.

Take a displacement measurement from the far side of the cocktail stick to the movable plate.

Measure the diameter of the cocktail stick, divide by 2 and take this number away from the displacement. This will give you the displacement from the end of the joint to the middle of the cocktail stick. Record this measurement. Now measure and record the length of the cocktail stick. Next, shorten the cocktail stick by about 0.5mm or less with a file or sandpaper, keeping the ends rounded.

Re-insert in the bore and repeat the process of measuring as many times as necessary to get a profile of the area you are interested in. You will eventually have enough data to make a reamer (or create a table and a graph that shows you what taper you have).

The beauty of this technique is that you don't have to make anything to a precise measurement before you use it. If you break the stick, just use another one.

Making a tapered reamer

To work on the bores of instruments, you need to be familiar with reamers. On parallel-bored instruments you can often use an adjustable reamer, but tapered bore instruments need tapered reamers.

The accuracy of the taper and quality of cut needs to be related to the quality of instrument you are working on. So don't expect to be able to work on professional quality instruments until you are sure you can take accurate measurements and have the right tools.

The following is a method for making a short, tapered reamer which, if made well, can be used to make a number of replacement oboe tenons.

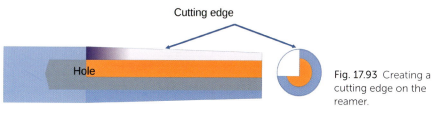

Fig. 17.93 Creating a cutting edge on the reamer.

Start with silver steel rod that is larger than the maximum diameter of the bore and about 40mm longer than the length of the reamer you want to make. Using the exact measurements you recorded when you measured the original bore, turn down a series of steps along the steel that match the measurements. A digital readout on the lathe is almost essential for this task. It does not matter if the diameters or displacements are irregular.

With the lathe spinning at around 300rpm, file down the ridges until it is smooth, but you can still see a faint line of the steps you made. Change from a file to workshop roll or wet and dry paper and smooth it down to the final shape without going below the steps.

Keeping the workpiece in the lathe, drill a hole down the length of the reamer; it does not have to go right through to the end, only the length of the cutting edge.

Before working on the reamer any more, do your best to confirm that the taper is correct. You might be able to fit it into the existing instrument, or on another instrument of the same make and model. Make any adjustments needed for it to be an exact fit.

Using a milling machine (or if you don't have one, a hacksaw, grinder or hand file), cut away between a quarter and just under half of the diameter of the tapered tube you have made. Take your time to make the front face of the cutting edge very smooth and sharp. For cutting

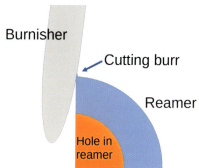

Fig. 17.94 Burnishing a burr on the cutting edge.

or reaming one or two instruments, there is no need to harden and temper the steel.

You create a cutting burr by rubbing a polished steel burnisher along the cutting edge. This will push a ridge of metal up and over the outside diameter of the reamer, and this will create the cutting edge.

Test the reamer and adjust it until it cuts well. Check the dimensions of the taper it cuts using the same technique as you used when measuring the original. Once you are satisfied it does a good job, then continue with the tenon replacement.

Fig. 17.95 Finished reamer similar to the drawing.

Rotating tool method of cutting a counter-bore

Fig. 17.92 The orange blocks represent the turning tool cutting the silver steel; you can see the steps on the top side of the diagram.

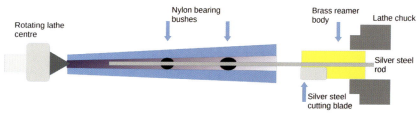

Fig. 17.96 Configuration for an oboe re-tenon.

Specialist Repairs 225

Fig. 17.96 shows a counterbore reamer held in the chuck; the instrument is guided by a shaft that is held central to the bore of the instrument. The shaft needs to be supported in the bore of the instrument. My solution is to make two oval nylon bushes of different diameters. These become guide bushes that are a smooth fit on the shaft and when pushed up the bore the two bushes get tight. You don't need to make them specific diameters as they will keep sliding up the bore until they get tight. You want the two bushes to be about 40mm apart and about 40mm from the broken end of the instrument.

Fig. 17.97 Making the guide bushes for the oboe counter-bore tool.

Fig. 17.98 Two nylon bushes on the guide shaft ready to be inserted in the oboe.

If you are re-tenoning a parallel-bored instrument, like a clarinet, you can either use an integral shaft like the Boosey &

Fig. 17.99 Here is the cutter body machined to its outside diameter.

Hawkes cutter shown in Fig. 17.102, or make the nylon bushes a tight fit in the bore.

The counterbore cutting tool is made or adjusted to fit the instrument you are working on at the time. For this book, I made a new tool, using ideas I have picked up over the years, and simplified it to make it as easy as I could for a technician with limited resources.

The easiest and cheapest material to make the bodies of cutting tools out of is brass, or even hardwood. (For years I struggled making tools completely from steel.) The yellow area in Fig. 17.96 is the body of the tool. The counter-bore diameter should be around 0.5mm larger in diameter than the tenon you are replacing. Making the counter-bore smaller in diameter can be necessary on occasions but it makes manufacture and fitting of the replacement insert much more difficult and the resulting tenon weaker. If you go much larger in diameter you will weaken the body of the instrument. Machine the brass body of the cutter 0.3mm smaller than the counter-bore diameter.

Fig. 17.100 Preparing the platform to mount the cutting blade.

Having turned the outside diameter of the counterbore, saw in half lengthways. (I could have done this on a milling machine, but it would have taken four times longer).

Fig. 17.101 Part finished counter-bore cutter. Please note that there is no significance to the groove on the left of the cutting body. It already existed in the piece of brass I chose.

To finish the counter-bore cutter, I take off all the burrs, screw on a silver steel cutting blade (1mm thick). Grind the side and end of the blade to size. I put a small radius on the profile of the cutter (top right-hand corner in the photograph) so that the counter-bore does not have a sharp angle at the bottom (curves are stronger than sharp angles).

The reed socket end of the oboe joint is supported on a centre in the tail stock (Fig. 17.104). Whilst feeding the joint towards the chuck using the tail stock hand wheel, I am also pushing the joint hard to the right, towards the tail stock. In this way I am reducing the risk of the cutting tool snatching the instrument and breaking the whole joint.

Fig. 17.102 These early twentieth-century clarinet socket cutters used by Boosey & Hawkes inspired me to use brass for the body of my own socket cutters. Note the adjusting screws located behind the cutting blade that can used to precisely adjust the diameter of the socket.

Fig. 17.103 The broken oboe body with the guide shaft, guide bushes and cutter in their relative positions.

Fig. 17.104 The nerve-wracking part: using the lathe and counter-bore cutter on an oboe.

I wrap the body of the instrument in a cloth to make holding it more comfortable and to give me more control. Make sure you perform a risk assessment first, thinking about what your fingers, clothes, etc. might snag on.

Fig. 17.105 Part way though cutting.

Fig. 17.106 The complete counter-bore; you can just see the pillar holes now showing in the walls of the body.

The next step is to create a drawing of the new tenon insert and record all the dimensions needed to make the insert.

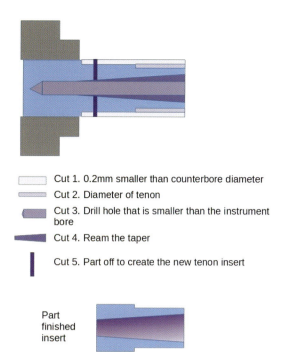

Cut 1. 0.2mm smaller than counterbore diameter
Cut 2. Diameter of tenon
Cut 3. Drill hole that is smaller than the instrument bore
Cut 4. Ream the taper
Cut 5. Part off to create the new tenon insert

Part finished insert

Fig. 17.108 Stages of making the insert.

If the instrument is plastic, make the replacement tenon in ebonite. If it is a wooden instrument, use ebonite or blackwood. The replacement insert needs to be a good fit in the counter-bore and the bore must match the bore of the instrument.

Start with a piece of your chosen material, in this case ebonite, at least 20mm longer than the final insert, and with a bigger diameter than the counter-bore diameter.

Turn the outside of the ebonite 0.2mm smaller in diameter than the counter-bore, using a standard turning tool.

Face off the end of the ebonite to square it off. This becomes my first zero point.

Now turn the rod to the finished counterbore diameter. (Do not assume the tenon length is exactly the depth of the socket: some manufacturers leave a gap at the bottom of a socket for tuning purposes; this is especially true for clarinet top joints).

Drill a pilot hole down the ebonite that is about 0.5mm smaller than the smallest bore diameter on your drawing of the insert.

Change tools to a small boring bar or reamer and increase the diameter of the bore until it is 0.2mm smaller in diameter where it joins the original bore.

Use a reamer or boring bar to make the bore of the insert exactly as the original taper and profile.

Using a parting tool, move the left-hand corner of the parting tool to the end of the turned rod. Zero the DRO and move the tool left to the length of the

Fig. 17.107 Diagram of counter-bore and new insert.

Fig. 17.109 Here I have put the insert back in the lathe and I am hand filing a radius on the end of the tenon that will be glued into the counter-bore. This will match the radius I put in the bottom of the counter-bore for strength purposes.

Specialist Repairs 227

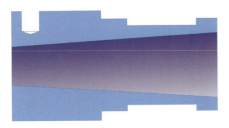

Fig. 17.110 The insert.

tenon plus the depth of the counter-bore *plus* the thickness of the parting tool. Part the new insert off.

Usually there will be one or more pillars screwed into the body in the region of the broken tenon. The bottoms of these pillars will extend into the area the counter-bore is being cut. This is why we remove the pillars during the preparation stage. After cutting the counter-bore and making the replacement tenon, install the insert and mark the position of the pillars on the replacement tenon with a sharp point.

Remove the insert and drill a shallow hole where the pillar marks are. The hole has to be deep enough to accept the protruding pillar and the diameter of the hole needs to be larger than the outside diameter of the pillar thread.

Before gluing, put all the parts together to make sure they all fit and all the measurements are correct. File some rough grooves on the insert to allow the glue to escape; the grooves should intersect the pillar holes as you need the epoxy resin to escape as the pillar is screwed in.

Mix the epoxy resin and warm it up slightly to de-gas it and make it more liquid. Push the insert in and screw in the pillars, making sure the screws are coated in resin.

Align the pillars carefully, using the hinge screws as needed, and wipe away excess resin from inside and outside.

I like to hold the instrument in the lathe overnight while it cures, applying pressure along the body to push the insert tight in and keep the axis straight. When fully cured, carefully drill out any tone holes that are now obstructed. On a clarinet this will be the C#/G# hole and the third finger hole. On this oboe it is the G# hole.

Fig. 17.111 Drilling the holes for the pillars in the insert. The drill press is on the cross slide of the lathe. (The Proxxon drill is a great machine, but a little fast for drilling large diameter holes; I suggest you find a mini milling machine to adapt to fit on your lathe cross slide.) The insert is held in the lathe chuck and the chuck is locked in position by engaging the back-gear.

Fig. 17.112 The insert ready for gluing.

Fig. 17.113 Drilling out the obscured holes.

The last task is to make a final ream and polish of the bore using a reamer and polishing stick.

The oboe used in this sequence is a professional oboe that had undercut tone holes. So the final part of the process was to replace the undercut. I had to find an undercut tool that had the same shape as the original. In Fig. 17.114 you can see me inserting the undercut fraise (the strawberry-shaped end) into the bore, where I will position it under the G# hole.

Fig. 17.114 Inserting an undercutter.

Fig. 17.115 The T bar is screwed into the undercutting tool shown in the last picture and pulled up into the tone hole and the tool rotated to cut a taper on the inside of the tone hole, called the undercut.

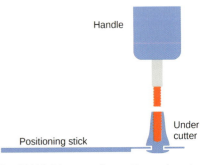

Fig. 17.116 Diagram of a captive undercut tool. The handle can be wood or metal as in the image above.

Fig. 17.117 It now looks just like it used to.

The bore can now be reamed and polished to its final size, the tenon cork put on and, in this case, the metal tenon cap reinstalled.

Bassoon repairs

You may be asked to improve a bassoon with poor resonance. They will be older instruments, made before the 1990s, after which manufacturers started to cast the bore linings in resin rather than inserting an ebonite liner with glue.

Fig. 17.118 Cross section of bassoon finger holes.

Fig. 17.118 shows the cross-section of a 1960s bassoon with an ebonite lining that has become detached from the bore. This can cause a loss of resonance. The picture also shows the beginnings of the wood rotting at the base of the finder holes, where it meets the bore, and demonstrates how thin the wood is around the area of the ring key groove on the third finger hole (tone hole on the right). Air can escape through the short grain of the maple; this can be sealed with superglue.

Fig. 17.119 Longitudinal cross section of a bassoon boot joint showing potential problems.

Apart from the bore lining, there are other problems that can occur. In Fig. 17.119 you can see a gap between the brass base plate and the wood of the boot joint (black line). The base plate can be removed and re-sealed with silicone sealant. The photo also shows how close the push rod hole can be to the bore lining. I have come across bassoons where there is a leak between the push rod hole and the bore of the instrument. This can be sealed by lining the push rod hole with thin tubing and epoxy resin.

If the damage is not too severe, then oiling the body can cure all three of the problems above.

Oil impregnation

One way to deal with all the problems above in one go is to impregnate the whole instrument in oil. Oiling is quite a scary procedure as it is not reversible. Unlike oiling blackwood and boxwood instruments, the purpose of oiling a bassoon is not to prevent cracking, but to improve the airtightness of the wood.

Linseed oil

Chip Owen of Fox Bassoons suggests you use raw linseed oil (never boiled linseed oil). I have used it to oil a couple of bassoons. It is cheap and readily available and does work.

In all cases, remove all the keywork and pushrods. I also remove the U bend and the U bend base if possible. If you feel bold, you can follow my method to build a tank from soil waste pipe, used in underground plumbing. Then fill the tank with oil and submerge the bassoon. I then attach a vacuum pump to the tank and watch all the air being sucked out of the wood. It can take up to ten minutes or so. Then I stop the vacuum pump and allow the pressure to rise back to atmospheric pressure. This forces the oil deep into the bassoon after thirty minutes or more, remove the instrument and let it drip dry it for a few hours. Finally, I wipe all the un-absorbed oil from the whole instrument. This takes a long time, and I repeat it every day until there is no liquid oil left inside or outside the instrument. Now leave it for the oil to become hard. If you fail to remove the surface oil, you will be leaving a varnish of oil that will alter the instrument's tuning, so be careful.

This process will increase the weight of the instrument and make it very airtight and resonant.

If you prefer to be less bold, it is possible to improve a bassoon by applying the oil with swabs over time. I would always remove the keywork and then apply the oil mixtures to the bore and tone holes using a felt swab attached to a stick and saturated in your choice of oil. Repeat this until no more oil is being absorbed. Wait for it to harden and remove any excess oil as needed.

Bassoon bocal dent balls

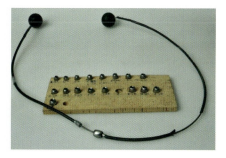

Fig. 17.120 Bassoon bocal dent balls.

To remove dents from bassoon bocals, unsolder the octave tube (pip) from the side of the bocal (it is sometimes easier to melt the soft solder that holds the pip in place if you scrape the plating away from the join first). Starting with the smallest dent ball, trap the ball in the middle section of the wire strop and pull it into the bocal and past the dent. Pull back the dent ball and replace it with the next larger dent ball. Repeat this process until the dent is removed.

Bassoon finger hole replacement

There are two places where rotting can cause major damage to older bassoons: the wing joint finger holes E, C and D, and the low Ab key hole on the boot joint. The finger holes can rot away even when the holes appear to be lined. Use a silver steel rod with an L shape on the end to probe the bottom of the finger hole where it meets the bore.

Fig. 17.121 Longitudinal cross section of a bassoon wing joint.

First, make very careful measurements and drawings of the existing hole. This includes the taper of the finger holes and the angle the holes are drilled at. Drill ebonite rod to re-create the same size and taper of hole as is being replaced. You can then easily check the diameter and length of the hole between the original and the replacement. Leave the outside diameter of the rod at least 4mm larger than the bore.

Wing joint finger holes

Use a countersink cutter to open the entrance of the tone hole you are working on. This helps prevent unwanted splintering around the hole. Using twist drills of increasing diameters, slowly drill out the finger hole 0.2mm at a time until the hole is about 4mm larger in diameter. I suggest using the slow speed of a cordless DIY drill. These have high torque and are very controllable. It is vital to maintain the original angle at all times.

When this is done, turn down the outside of the replacement tube so that it fits the enlarged hole. Check it will fit before cutting it down to a length at least 10mm longer than the depth of the hole in the instrument.

Shape the inside end of the new tone hole liner so that 1mm protrudes into the bore, and angle the end so that it looks even all the way around. Once it is fitting well, apply epoxy resin adhesive on the inside of the hole and the liner and glue it in place, checking the depth and orientation down the bore. When the resin is set, file the outside of the liner until it is flush with the outside of the bassoon. Finally, check the tuning of the instrument.

Replacing the low Ab

The Ab hole gets rotten because it is a hole that is kept closed and all the condensation collects there when the instrument is put in the case after playing. Make detailed measurements of the original hole, including the bed plate (you can take photos as well). Use a lathe to recreate the diameter and depth of the tone hole out of ebonite. In this way you can keep checking the diameters and tapers with the original. The outside of the ebonite is left for the moment.

Then, either using a milling machine or a hand grinding tool like a Dremmel or Proxxon, remove the rotten wood. Don't make the hole too big since any rot left will be saturated in resin and hidden when the repair is finished.

The aim is to remove wood in such a way as to make it easy to turn and file the ebonite to fit into the enlarged hole. Avoid making the new hole bigger than the ebonite rod. When satisfied that the new liner will fit the hole, bed it in with epoxy resin and wait for it to cure. Using tone hole cutting tools and hand files, shape the tone hole bed plate to match the original (using the photo as a guide). If you have bigger and more complex machinery you can use the milling machine to cut out the old wood.

Alterations

Tool for marking new hole positions for a thumb-rest

Fig. 17.122 A quick and reliable way to mark the new position of thumb-rest screw holes on a clarinet is to have a small length of L-shaped aluminium extrusion, approx. 10mm × 10mm and 30mm long. I have filed notches in the aluminium to act as spacing guides. The extrusion will naturally sit parallel to the body, so lining up the new holes exactly. This device will not work on oboes or other tapered instruments.

Moving the thumb rest position

Changing the position or changing the type of thumb-rest is a common request, so getting good at it is useful. To find out where to move it to, remove the existing thumb-rest and ask the musician to play the instrument. Look to see where they put their thumb and pencil a line at that position.

Fig. 17.123 Here is an example of a key alteration that made life much easier for a musician.

Using the guide, draw two parallel lines along the body that intersect with the original screw holes. Offer up the thumb-rest, so the rest's bottom is just above the pencil line for the new thumb position. Mark the new hole positions.

Centre punch on the spot for the new holes and then drill a 1.5mm-diameter hole 4mm deep for each screw. Using a larger drill or a countersink bit, open the top of the hole about four turns, 0.8mm deep. This provides space for any wood that gets lifted when you insert the screw. Using an appropriate thread tap, make a screw thread into the new holes. You might not have a tap with the exact thread the screw has, but it will be near enough and better than not using a tap at all.

If you are going to fill the original holes, do that now; otherwise, fit the new rest. It is easiest to fill the original holes before screwing the thumb-rest into position. Depending on the customer's requirements or if you think they might want to move the rest back again, you can use black wax to fill the holes (reversible filling), or glue and blackwood dust. I have used many different ways of filling old holes; my current method is to force blackwood dust in the hole using a metal rod, then put a few drops of thin superglue on the dust. It sets immediately and can be filed down and finished off with ultra-fine 3M Scotch-Brite (buff if needed).

Fit the thumb-rest and tighten it down well. (If it is not a standard size wood screw, or I don't have a suitable tap to hand, I taper the entrance of the hole so as to encourage the screw into place. With the screw partially inserted, I heat a 5mm diameter rod of metal almost to red heat and rest it on the top of the screw; when the screw is hot, screw it into place. The heat will soften the blackwood resin and soften the wood, making the screw go in easily.)

Adjusting the bore of a saxophone mouthpiece

When a musician uses a number of different mouthpieces it is very helpful if the bores of the mouthpieces are all the same. If one mouthpiece compresses the cork more than another, the larger bore mouthpiece will be loose. It is very difficult to make a bore smaller; slightly easier to make it larger. This is not a repair to do without practising lots of times first on a scrap mouthpiece, to get a feel for what to expect.

The bore of a saxophone mouthpiece is parallel with a domed end, where it blends into the baffle of the mouthpiece. Make a reamer with the final diameter you need. Then grip the reamer in a lathe chuck. With the lathe running at around 80rpm, hold the mouthpiece very firmly and as true to the axis of the machine then feed the mouthpiece onto the reamer. It will often chatter and grab as you start cutting, but will eventually settle down and allow you to complete the reaming. Check the diameter; if necessary, adjust the reamer to make a bigger cut and repeat.

Adjusting keywork to suit the musician

Fig. 17.123 shows the thumb keys for a 1980s Selmer bass clarinet. The new piece of keywork is the plate that is silver soldered to the end of the left-hand touch piece and extends under the tips of the other two touch pieces. Not only does the new plate double up the function of the link arms that you can still see between the touch-pieces (covered in cork); it also makes it easier for the musician to move from one key to another securely. I worked closely with the musician to sculpt the metal to exactly the shape hey found most useful.

This type of alteration should be within the scope of an enthusiastic and competent repairer and requires nickel silver (or brass), a hacksaw, a few files, a smooth jaw engineer's vice and silver soldering equipment.

PART FIVE

Materials and Tool Building

Materials Used for the Body and Keywork of Woodwind Instruments

Metals

Nickel silver or German silver

The majority of keywork, pillars and some instrument bodies are made from nickel silver, also called German silver. It is an alloy of copper, zinc and nickel. It is strong, easy to work, and easy to join together with solder. Nickel silver was originally chosen for its silver-like shine when silver plating was not commonplace. Now that silver plating is now more accessible and cheaper, manufacturers are moving away from nickel silver keywork and using bronze, which can also be silver plated. Bronze is an alloy of copper and tin with traces of phosphor or silicon to improve its properties. Bronze is cheaper and easier to cast to a high-quality finish than nickel silver.

Brass

An alloy of copper and zinc, brass is used to make metal-bodied instruments and some keywork. It tarnishes over a few years, so is usually lacquered or electroplated.

Silver

Silver is used on more expensive instruments. In the UK, you used not to describe an item as solid silver unless it had an official stamp called a hallmark. Before 2007 when the law changed, manufacturer's catalogues were often unclear as to what metal was used. We can now call any alloy over 92.5 per cent silver content solid silver. You might find a number stamped on the metal like 925: this designates that 925 parts in 1,000 are silver. Silver can be shaped to high precision and enables the craftsman to make a better and more sonorous instrument. Silver is heavier than nickel silver and bronze and has a slightly dull ring to it when flicked sharply with a fingernail (this test works best on a head joint).

Silver plating

Silver plating is a way of covering a metal (base material) in solid silver. It is an electroplating process that uses a solution of cyanide and silver. The resulting layer is very thin, only 10–25 microns thick. Like all silver, it will tarnish, especially if in contact with sulphurous compounds like coal smoke or some hand creams. Some manufacturers cover the silver plate in a very thin lacquer to prevent tarnish or, on high-class instruments, they rhodium plate the surface. Rhodium plating is even thinner than silver plating so you shouldn't use silver polish on these instruments, only the microfibre cleaning cloth supplied.

Nickel plating

Nickel plating is another electroplating method that covers the base metal in nickel. It has a slightly grey tint and often has surface pits when old. It is much tougher than silver plating and can be polished aggressively before the plating wears through. Nickel plating is being phased out because of concerns about skin sensitivity and allergic reactions. With experience, you will find that you can differentiate between nickel plate and silver plate.

Mazac

Some instruments made in the 1960s used a magnesium aluminium alloy called zamak for keywork, which will break when bent more than twice and cannot be soldered or repaired. These alloy keys can be identified by raised casting numbers visible on the underside of the key. Wooden Boosey & Hawkes Regent model clarinets are the most common zamak-keyed instruments in the UK.

> ### What metal is it?
>
> When you want to know what metal has been used, it is sometimes simplest to find the model number engraved on the instrument and look up the specifications online. For example, the YFL212 is silver plated, and the YFL312 has a solid silver head joint.
>
> If this is not possible, then (using the flute as an example) look at the area where the head joint slides into the body. On a plated head joint I would expect that section to look a dull silver colour compared to the rest of the instrument which will be brighter.

Plastics

Different types of plastic have been used for making woodwind instruments; ABS is currently the preferred plastic. Previously manufacturers used Sonorite (also called Resonite) which is a Bakelite type of plastic, and before that, ebonite, a vulcanized rubber. Ebonite is still used

> ### Is it plastic or wood?
>
> There are some plastic instruments that are designed to look like wood. The easiest way to check is by looking at the end of a joint: plastic will be shiny, and wood will be dull; you might even see the ends of the wood fibres.

for premium mouthpieces. Plastic is readily available, quick and cheap to manufacture and therefore associated with student instruments. However, many ebonite instruments were made as premium quality instruments. Old ebonite may look grey-green in colour rather than the original black.

Woods

African blackwood

The bodies of the majority of wooden woodwind instruments are made from African blackwood (*Dalbergia melanoxylon*). It is very dense and does not absorb water or oil readily. It is very stable and can be machined to a very high accuracy and quality.

Maple

Maple is a white-coloured wood that by tradition is stained red/brown by the manufacturer. It is used to make the most common bassoon called a Heckel bassoon. It is a very porous wood and the bores of the first two sections have to be lined with ebonite or resin. After staining, the maple is lacquered to seal the wood. The better bassoon manufacturers soak the new instrument in an oil to improve stability, airtightness and resonance.

Rarely used woods

Other woods that have been used are rosewood or palisander for its beauty. Boxwood was used up until the 1890s and starts out a cream colour but over time becomes a dark brown.

Composites

These were first tried after the Second World War by Conn in the USA. They used the same wood, resins and laminate structures used to make wooden aeroplane propellers, hence the nickname 'propeller clarinets'. Buffet introduced an African blackwood and resin composite in the 1990s. It is heavier than natural blackwood. Though it won't crack in the conventional way, it can break at the tenons if dropped. These instruments found favour with military bands for working outside and in extreme climates. Clarinets, oboes and bass clarinets have been made from this composite.

Plating

Silver plating

In recent years, a new silver plating solution has become available on the market that does not use cyanide. This is great news for instrument repairers, as it allows us to plate keywork ourselves.

You can either buy a ready-made plating kit, or make up the equipment yourself. You will, however, need to buy the correct solution and pure silver anodes.

The equipment needed is:

- Constant voltage power supply – 1 to 12 volt.
- A water heater. I used a 'slow cooker' from a cookery shop.
- Glass or ceramic beakers or bowls larger than the component to be plated.
- Cables to connect the circuit together.
- An anode cage, usually made from titanium. A cage is the simplest way to get the silver anodes into the solution without contamination.

The solutions needed are:

- Cleaning solution: this can either be a caustic solution or an electro cleaning solution.
- Very pure water. This is sometimes referred to as distilled or de-ionized water. The most suitable water, however, can be obtained from a three-stage domestic water filter system. Aquarium supply shops use these filters for their fish tanks, and you may be able to buy filtered water from them. The filter system has three stages: a) 5 micron sediment filter, which removes sediments; b) KDF/GAC filter, which reduces high levels of chlorine and reduces levels of heavy metals in the water, as well as balancing the pH of the water; c) carbon block filter, which reduces high levels of chlorine and volatile organic contaminants.
- Silver plating solution, with brightener.
- Brightening top up solutions.
- 99 per cent pure silver anodes.

Nickel plating

The same equipment can be used to nickel plate components. You just need to replace the silver solution and silver anode with nickel solution and nickel anodes.

I have been successful with both processes.

CHAPTER 19

Cleaning and Polishing Tools and Materials

Polishing

Polishing machine

Your polishing motor should be big enough to take an 8-inch mop. You will need a few polishing wheels or mops to use with the different polishing soaps or abrasives. Practise polishing on scrap instruments before working on a customer's instrument.

Keywork can catch easily on the mop and be flung out of your hands, hit the workbench, and bend. It is unlikely to seriously damage you, but it could hurt. Always hold the piece as shown in the photo, with the item just below the centre line of the mop.

Don't push hard against the mop, especially when polishing plated keywork, as it will rip its way through the plating in seconds.

Use a separate mop for different polishing compounds.

Good lighting is essential. I now use low voltage LED light bars as they are excellent and safe. For many years I have used a cardboard box around the back of the wheel to catch the fluff and dirt. It also provided a soft landing for keys that got caught on the mop and snatched out of my fingers.

If you want to even up or refresh your polishing mop, then 'dress' the wheel by pushing the toothed edge of a hacksaw blade against the spinning mop.

Polishing finger

Made from leather, these simple little finger pockets protect your fingers from the heat of polishing and keep your fingers clean.

Fig. 19.1 Polishing machine.

Fig. 19.2 Polishing finger.

Cleaning and Polishing Tools and Materials 239

Fig. 19.3 Ultrasonic cleaning bath.

Fig. 19.5 Tins of traditional British metal polishes.

Fig. 19.6 The strapping cloth is being held at one end on a screw or nail.

Ultrasonic cleaning bath

This is a great tool for deep cleaning keywork. It can be used with plain water or a solvent.

Barrel polisher for keywork

If you undertake lots of overhauls you should consider investing in a barrel tumbler or magnetic polisher. These machines contain metal or ceramic medium and a soapy liquid containing a very fine abrasive. The keywork is put into the machine and it rolls around for an hour or so. You then extract the keys and rinse them before a final dry, and a rub with a finishing cloth.

Tins of traditional British metal polishes

For keywork I like to use Brasso, Silvo, a dry silver polish cloth, and 25mm-wide strips of polycotton material (an old bed sheet). Brasso and Silvo are UK proprietary wadding-based polishes but there are many other alternatives that will work well. Many countries use polishing creams that come in tubes. Use what is easy to get hold of near you. I find that attaching one end of the cloth strip to the bench helps to strap keys.

Polishing mops

I have a variety of mops to go on the polishing machine. These have a fibre washer on one side of the mop and a leather washer on the other. Put the leather washer side on first. As you start the machine, it will tighten itself on the spindle. Since we are polishing complex curved surfaces, I have found a soft G mop specification perfect. The mops are held in place with a tapered, threaded nose. The common speed of rotation is 3,000rpm.

Fig. 19.4 Barrel polisher for keywork.

240 Cleaning and Polishing Tools and Materials

Polishing soaps

I use the following polishing compounds, or 'soaps' as they are known in the UK:

- Rouge, Luxi or Menzerna for silver plate finishing
- Hyfin for all other metals
- Vonax for plastic and wood

Wet and dry abrasive paper

For finer work on keywork and bodies you can use a selection of wet and dry paper with grit sizes 400, 600, 800 and 1200. I choose the best quality I can from long established brands – it is more expensive but worth the extra. It is designed to be used in water, on metal or wood.

Fig. 19.7 Polishing mops.

Fig. 19.8 Polishing soaps.

Fig. 19.9 Wet and dry abrasive paper.

Cleaning and Polishing Tools and Materials

CHAPTER 20

Making Tools

Making a tenon scraper

This simple tool makes the removal of cork from tenon joints so much easier. It is also a good introduction to tool making.

You will need

- Length of silver steel about 8mm in diameter and around 200mm long
- Blow torch
- Large hammer
- Steel block, anvil, or block of steel about 50mm in diameter, held in an engineer's vice
- Grinder of some sort
- Bucket of cold water
- Emery paper
- Sharpening stone
- Wooden handle

Forge the end

Heat a 15mm length at the end of the steel to red hot. While hot, hammer this area onto the steel block so that you create a fishtail shape (like a needle spring) at the end of the steel, re-heating as needed. If possible, form a curve in the end. Allow the metal to air-cool; do not quench in water.

File or grind the cutting edge

When cool, use a file, grinding machine, or grinding disc to make a straight edge along the end of the fishtail. Then grind the convex side of the fishtail to create a thin edge, like a chisel. No need to try and sharpen the tool at this stage.

Harden and temper the tool

Heat the end of the tool up to red hot, then plunge into a pot of cold water. Clean the black oxide off the blade. Very carefully and slowly warm the shaft of the tool with the blow torch and watch for bright metal to start changing colour (a light straw colour to start with and then getting darker). Stop warming the shaft once it starts to change colour and then waft the flame towards the cutting edge and chase the colour towards the blade. Get ready to plunge the blade into the water again when the last 4mm of the blade reaches straw yellow.

Sharpening and fitting the handle

Without getting the tool warm (as that would lose the temper you have just created), grind the blade on a hand sharpening stone, or grind wheel, to a sharp edge. Cut the shaft to about 75mm from the blade end and file or grind the handle end to a square taper, to form a tang.

Make a hole in the handle about 1mm smaller in diameter than the steel you used, and as deep as you want the tang to go. Heat the tip of the tang to red hot, trying not to heat up the rest of the shaft. Push the hot end into the handle and burn the shaft into position. Quench the whole tool in cold water. The tool is now ready to use.

Making a rolling steady

A revolving or rolling steady is something I developed over thirty years ago when I first started making clarinets. The idea of supporting the end of the wood on a steady is not a new idea; the important detail that I added was to make the support rotate. I am sure I am not the first, or only, person to have thought of it, as it is common practice in high volume manufacturing nowadays. Fig. 20.1 shows the original steady I converted to a revolving steady.

To help those repairers who don't have access to lots of machinery I had a go at making a rolling steady from easily available materials and tools. I started with a ball bearing race with an internal diameter of about 40mm. While gripping the internal bore of the bearing in

Fig. 20.1 Myford fixed steady modified to use a roller bearing rather than three fixed points.

Fig. 20.2 Roller steady made from scratch.

Fig. 20.3 Some of the materials needed.

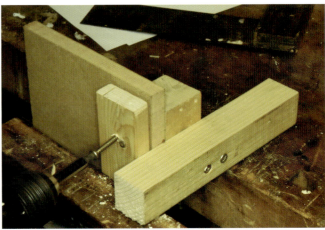

Fig. 20.4 Screwing the parts together.

the chuck, I positioned and glued, with epoxy resin, some blocks around outside of the bearing.

None of the wood is anything special, and I used an easily available roller bearing that had an internal bore of about 40mm (make sure the bearing has dust covers).

In the end I had to change the design several times during the construction, as new problems came to light – this is why it looks very crude!

To get the alignment correct, I held the roller bearing in the lathe chuck and used epoxy resin to bond four wooden blocks around it to keep the bearing in place.

I then cut a hole in line with the middle of the bearing.

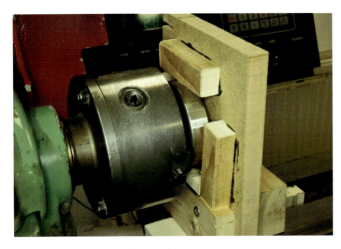

Fig. 20.5 Aligning the roller steady.

Fig. 20.6 The bearing is now fixed in position.

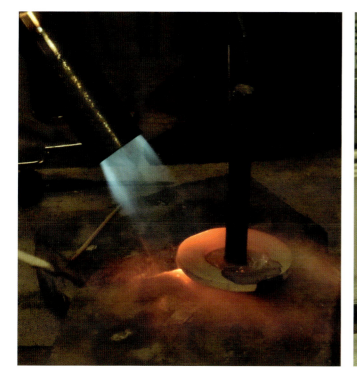

Fig. 20.7 Building the clamp mechanism.

Fig. 20.8 The clamp now in place.

Fig. 20.9 The spectacle plate in place. This insert, with a tapered cone in the middle, will allow a variety of different diameter instruments to be supported.

Fig. 20.10 The steady being used.

A collection of washers and a bolt were brazed together to create the clamp.

The rolling steady was now ready for the spectacle plate to be made. The spectacle plate fits inside the bearing and has a tapered entrance that fits the repair in hand.

Different spectacle plates can be made for different-sized instruments. This one is made from a material called Tufnol, but plastic, wood, or metal can be used.

Shortly after making this revolving steady, I used it on an instrument that would not have fitted in my original steady, and it worked just fine.

Making a sacrificial mandrel

A very safe and accurate way to mount instrument joints onto a lathe is to create a 'single use' mandrel. It relies on friction between the mandrel and bore of the instrument. This method ensures the bore is always concentric. You make a new mandrel every time; this ensures it is perfectly centred on the lathe. The mandrel needs to be made of a hard wood and turned down to make a firm but not tight fit into the bore of the instrument. If you leave a shoulder on the mandrel, then you can get extra friction by pushing the joint up against the shoulder.

Making Tools   **245**

Drive mandrel to hold a barrel

A good example of when a drive mandrel is useful is when you are working on barrels; if you are dealing with a student barrel then you can risk clamping the barrel directly in the chuck, but for anything more precious you can hold it in this way.

Using a medium-density hardwood, like oak or sapele (not beech or boxwood), hold the wood in the three-jaw chuck extending 40mm. Turn down a 35mm length until it is a tight fit in the socket of the barrel that you are working on. Turn down a 10mm length to be a tight fit to the bore of the barrel. This will create a stepped mandrel that will support the barrel in the socket and the bore.

Do not be tempted to take the mandrel out of the chuck until you have finished the entire repair, as it will never be able to be put back in the chuck accurately. You can now push the barrel on the mandrel and machine the exposed socket as required.

This technique can be adapted for many other circumstances.

Threads of screws on woodwind instruments

Where possible, buy in, or scavenge, the correct replacement adjusting screw or pivot screw. If you can't find the exact replacement, it is useful to know what other makes and model of instrument are likely to have the same thread, so you can find a substitute. The list below helps with this process and also gives you the specification of tap and die you might need to get if you are going to make your own replacement.

American instruments

In general, America still uses imperial measurements. American threads are specified using the ANSI codes. Using the example of the 2-56 thread, the first number is the ANSI diameter #2 (0.0860in), and the number of teeth per inch is 56.

Listed below are some examples of pivot screw threads and which instruments use them.

2-56

Armstrong flutes
Gemeinhardt flutes
Selmer US flutes
Conn clarinets
King clarinets
Vito clarinets

1-72

Artley flutes
Selmer US bass clarinets
Bundy bass clarinets
Bundy piccolo

2-64

Bundy flute (Signet uses a different thread)
    Artley clarinet

3-48

Bundy saxophone
Signet saxophone
Beucher saxophones
King saxophones

4-48

Conn (some saxophones)

5-40

Armstrong saxophones
Vito US saxophones
Conn bassoons

6-32

Fox bassoon

Metric screws

These are measured in millimetres. The first number is the nominal outside diameter of the thread; the second number is the pitch in millimetres.

2.0 × 0.40

Buffet flute
Yamaha flute
Yamaha piccolo
Vito clarinet
Selmer Paris clarinets
Yamaha (some clarinets)

2.1 × 0.35

Buffet clarinet

2.1 × 0.40

Selmer oboe
Bundy oboe

2.25 × 0.40

Yamaha (some clarinets)

2.5 × 0.45

Leblanc Noblet
Selmer Paris harmony clarinets

2.5 × 0.50

Noblet saxophones
Vito (some saxophones)

2.85 × 0.60

Selmer US bassoon
Bundy bassoon

3.0 × 0.50

Selmer Paris saxophones
Schreiber bassoon

3.0 × 0.60

Yamaha saxophones

4.0 × 0.75

Heckel bassoon

List of Suppliers

Ed Kraus Music (materials and tools. Wholesale only. Minimum quantity numbers apply):
www.krausmusic.com

Music Medic (materials and tools):
www.musicmedic.com

Ferrees Inc. (materials and tools):
www.ferreestoolsinc.com

Boehm Tools (specialist tools):
www.boehmtools.com

Luciano Pisoni (pads and materials):
www.musiccenter.it

Prestini pads:
www.prestiniusa.com

J L Smith (specialist tools):
www.jlsmithco.com

Dwyer Magnehelic:
www.dwyer-inst.com

Maun Industries (tools):
www.maunindustries.com

Yamaha Music (components and instruments):
www.yamaha.com

Cambridge Woodwind Makers (information):
www.cambridgewoodwindmakers.org

Acknowledgements

My thanks to Yamaha Music UK.

Without the help of Rosemary Bangham, my daughter, who patiently sorted out my spelling and grammar, I don't think this book would have been completed. Thank you, Rosemary. I was very lucky to have the help of Humphry Gleave, who patiently oversaw the photography over many weeks, and Susannah Bangham, who also helped me with photography. I am very grateful to have been able to discuss specific issues with Thomas Dryer-Beers and Eddie Ashton.

I would also like to thank all the people who have shared information and skills with me over the years. Though not an exhaustive list, the following had a particular influence on my career: Peter Hudson, Geoff Else, Ted Planas, and Jon Steward.

Authors of other books on the subject are: Erick Brand, Ronald Saska, NAPBIRT journals, Reg Thorpe, Stephen Howard.

Index

bassoon
    adjustment 191
    assembly 27, 191, 206
    bent keywork 134
    bocal 103, 107, 229
    bocal cork 49
    crook 103, 107, 229
    emergency repairs 49
    key names 27
    keywork 37, 89
    oiling 17, 229
    order of assembly 27
    pads and padding 75, 145, 156, 159
    rot 229
    tenons 16, 109
    testing airtightness 20
    tone hole 157
    tools 12

clarinet
    assembly 23, 168
    bent keywork 134
    crack repair 87
    emergency repairs 37, 48, 173
    finger bush 88
    key names 168
    keywork
    Leak testing 20
    moving thumbrest 230
    oiling bore 52
    oiling keywork 17
    order of assembly 168
    pads and padding 75, 137, 159
    regulation 162, 168, 211
    Screwdrivers 12
    socket repair
    socket repair 221
    socket repair 221
    springs 130, 165, 210

    sticking thumb ring 211
    tenon replacement 223
    tenons 102
    tone hole replacement
    tone hole replacement 214
    tone holes 62
    undercutting 224
    water problems 47, 51
cleaning
    brushing 18
    drying 51
    polishing 15, 19, 117, 135, 159, 237, 239
    pull through 52
    swab 52
cork
    cork pad 62, 75, 190, 141, 146, 156
    cork tenon 102
    crook cork 102
    cutting cork 127, 128
    key cork 127
    neck cork 102
    softening cork 46, 102, **174**

flute
    assembly 24, 68
    bent keywork 134, 152
    dents 32, 90
    emergency repairs 37, 42, 155, 177
    headcork 37, 43, 106, 174
    headjoint 92
    key names 24
    leak testing 20
    open hole 142, 155
    Order of assembly 24, 175
    Pads and padding 75, 137, 146, 159
    regulation 34, 67, 162, 175
    Screwdrivers 12
    springs 76, 130, 165, 211
    sticky pads 38, 52

stuck foot joint 93
washers 146, 154
wear in keywork 111

Keywork
  bent
  cup alignment 150
  fitting 111
  making 213
  polishing 159, 205, 239
  spring hitch 18, 68, 209
  stuck 17, 212

material
  adhesives, glues, resins 144, 162, 176, 206
  body 57, 253
  key making 204, 231
  keywork 57, 235
  nickel plating 237
  silver plating 237
  springs 76 130

oboe
  adjusting screws 68, 162, 184
  bent keywork 118, 190
  bent keywork 134
  cork 16, 155
  crack repair 87
  Eb key 190
  emergency repairs 39, 48, 156, 190
  Feather keys 190
  key names 184
  keywork 65
  Leak testing 20
  moving thumbrest 230
  Octave bush 48
  oiling bore 52
  oiling keywork 17
  order of assembly 26, 184
  pads and padding 52, 75, 137, 159
  regulation 16, 162, 184, 190
  screwdrivers 12
  socket repair 221
  springs 130, 165, 210
  tenon replacement 223
  tenons 102
  tone hole 62
  tone hole replacement 214
  twisting pillar 89
  undercutting 224
  water problems 47, 51

oiling
  how to oil 80, 117, 229
  type of oil 17, 51, 114, 212, 229
  when to oil 21, 38, 51, 87, 114, 123, 167, 229

Padding and regulation
  adhesives 144, 162, 176
  ballooning pad 149
  double action 164
  emergency padding 37
  feeler gauge 137
  fitting 137, 145
  pad slick 140
  regulation 21, 34, 40, 161, 168
  regulation 161
  seating 34, 75, 139, 144, **149**
  time of arrival 162
  time of departure 162

pads
  Bladder 75, 144, 147
  construction 31, 75, 143
  cork 62, 75, 190, 141, 146, 156
  emergency repair 39
  inspection 20, 32, 34, 138
  leather 20, 75, 84, 143, 144, 147
  seating 147
  size 153, 156, 204
  sticky 38, 45, 52, 156
  storage 80
  synthetic 144

saxophone
  adjusting screws 68
  adjustment 12, 151
  assembly 17, 25, 178
  bent keywork 134
  broken neck screw 101
  crook *46, 61, 90, 100*
  crook cork 103, 105
  dents and bends 81, 93, 98, 205
  emergency repair 37, 45, 52, 184, 207
  key names
  keywork 12, 65, 111, 151
  keywork wear 111
  leak testing 20
  leaklight 20, 33
  low notes bubbling 46
  Mouthpiece fit 231
  neck *46, 61, 90, 100*
  oiling
  Oiling keywork 17
  pads and padding 52, 75, 137, 151, 159, 178, 207
  Point screw threads 246
  regulation 12, 76, 162, 164, 178
  Soldering 219
  springs 130, 165, 210
  sticking pad 207
  testing airtightness 20, 33, 61
  tone hole 207
  tools 127, 128, 162

screws
- adjustment 111
- barrel screws 70
- bent screws 118, 134, 115
- butress thread 63
- headless 70
- hinge screws 71, 121, 213
- locking screw 89, 138
- neck or crook screws 93, 101
- pivot screws 70
- point screw 70
- stuck screw 118
- thread size 246
- tipped screws 67

Springs
- adjusting 14, 129, 165, 209
- blue steel 134
- broken and faulty 45, 129, 210
- fishtail 132
- fitting 132, 159
- flat springs 76, 133, 211
- gold 134
- loose 130, 210
- needle springs 76
- Oboe Eb 189
- phophor bronze 134
- removing 130
- setting 21, 42
- silver steel 134
- stainless steel 134
- stuck 130
- tension setting 129, 133, 165, 209
- twisting 89
- unhooking 18

tone holes
- chipped 89, 138
- distorted 93
- flattening or topping 94, 141
- repairing 90
- replacement 214
- unsoldered 93

First published in 2022 by
The Crowood Press Ltd
Ramsbury, Marlborough
Wiltshire SN8 2HR

enquiries@crowood.com
www.crowood.com

© Daniel Bangham

All rights reserved. No part of this publication may be reproduced or transmitted in any form or by any means, electronic or mechanical, including photocopy, recording, or any information storage and retrieval system, without permission in writing from the publishers.

British Library Cataloguing-in-Publication Data
A catalogue record for this book is available from the British Library.

ISBN 978 0 7198 4029 6

Cover design: Sergey Tsvetkov

Typeset by Simon and Sons
Printed and bound in India by Parksons Graphics

Related Titles from Crowood

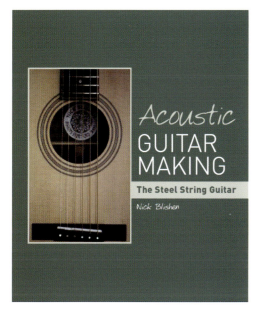

ISBN: 978 1 84797 374 0

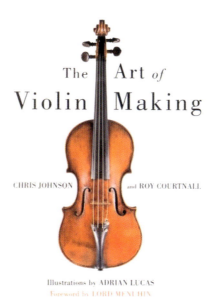

ISBN: 978 0 70905 876 2

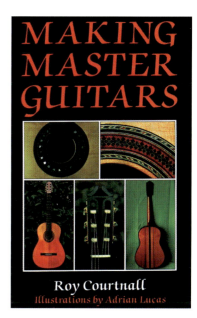

ISBN: 978 0 70904 809 1

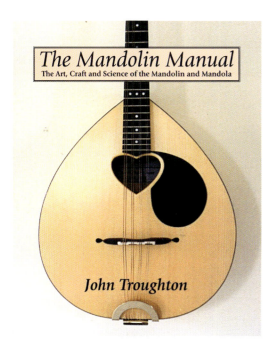

ISBN: 978 1 86126 496 1

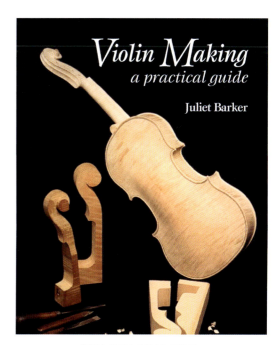

ISBN: 978 1 86126 436 7